Love in an Unexpected Place

A Novel by Colin Macanulty

PublishAmerica
Baltimore

© 2008 by Colin Macanulty.
All rights reserved. No part of this book may be reproduced, stored in a retrieval system or transmitted in any form or by any means without the prior written permission of the publishers, except by a reviewer who may quote brief passages in a review to be printed in a newspaper, magazine or journal.

First printing

This is a work of fiction. Names, characters, places, and incidents either are the product of the author's imagination or are used fictitiously. Any resemblance to actual persons, living or dead, events, or locales is entirely coincidental.

PublishAmerica has allowed this work to remain exactly as the author intended, verbatim, without editorial input.

ISBN: 1-60703-707-6
PUBLISHED BY PUBLISHAMERICA, LLLP
www.publishamerica.com
Baltimore

Printed in the United States of America

Chapter 1

When her father died, Sofi and her twin sister Sara migrated to opposite ends of the house. The sound of Sofi playing her father's piano could not be suffered by her sister. It seems they were both so heartbroken they found it was impossible to share the pain of a loss that had come just a year after the death of Maria, their mother.

On her own, Sofi was diverted from her grief. She had the piano in her workroom and her father's bookcase. A large sofa split the work space in two. A sizable window provided so much light that sometimes the curtains had to be drawn early in the day. It was a large house and there were many other rooms but this was where Sofi's creative work took place. She read her father's books to fill the empty stages between music and poetry. The piano recalled many personal memories. The poems she tried to put to music; not always successfully; she discovered they had a voice of their own.

In this environment the young woman who inhabited it had a solitary trace. She ventured forth only for exercise and music lessons. Her only desire was to compose her own music and write poetry. The piano looked out across a rose garden her father had left as a legacy. Never a day passed that she did not remember him and the inspiration he had given her before he died from an inherited disease he could not avoid. His tall frame red hair and intellect had dominated her life.

Now she channeled her feelings into the music. Those aspirations had been supported by her father. When Sofi turned eighteen she was far along in knowing where her future life would lead and fully grounded in the creative process. Her music teacher knew he couldn't do much more to advance her talent. If she was to go on to a musical career playing or composing she would have to be placed in other hands. That meant leaving home for at least a month at a time. Her sister Sara who also had musical ambitions as a singer seemed content to attend a musical conservatory in the city, Vienna.

So a new regime for Sofi was arranged by her guardian Aunt Marianne, her father's sister. Sofi was put to advance in composing skills by the fortyish, handsome Gustav. He had been vetted by Marianne and she had her misgivings but depended on her sister in law Charlotte to chaperon Sofi, who would be staying in her house for the year.

Sofi traveled to piano lessons by train but in her mind she really was swept along the coastal road sitting beside the driver of gig pulled by two horses to whom she fed her lunch at the end of the journey. The lunch carefully prepared by her aunt who said she was too thin. She would never be fat. Thoroughbreds never got fat her mother had told her.

Charlotte was soon nudged aside by a much stronger will and personality than she could handle. In a month Sofi was in the middle of her first passionate love affair. That she was barely over the age of consent was no barrier to her first freedom and exposure to what she supposed was love but that she recognized later was really a substitute for the lost attention of her father.

When she had been formally introduced to Gustav in the company of Marianne and Charlotte he had seen a young girl. When she appeared for her first lesson she strode in with the books he had recommended in a soft lilac dress that clung to her body as if magnetized and with shoes to match. She deliberately did not take off her shoes but crackled her arrival across his lovely, carefully polished oak floor. He soon lost his musical composure. While he sat at the piano she put her feet on the stool and took off the shoes then put on satin slippers and advised him that she was now ready.

Sofi was fine tuned for action and she hit every chord in Gustav's keyboard. She found him very willing and in that month lost temporarily at least, some of her interest in music. When Gustav returned from a short holiday he found that Charlotte had discovered his love notes to Sofi and being horrified had exposed his extra marital lessons to his wife. The lovely pupil was despatched back home where she found once and for all, her mate.

Karl came from a fairly prosperous family who considered the boy too quiet for any other career but to follow his father behind a desk in a bank or a business office and he duly delivered their low esteem. However, and there is always an however, although Karl was as shy as he was gentle there was strength in his gentleness. He was six feet tall not quite handsome and never did seem to attract girls much less young women of substance. His mother, who had some classical concert experience was found to replace Gustav.

At Sofi's first visit Karl was studying outside the open window. She sat down at the piano and showed an effortless ease of style to Karl's mother who was dazzled by the performance. When Sofi saw Karl standing tall to see her through a small window she repeated her adagio piece. He listened and looked then went back to his studies. When the lesson was over Sofi managed to let him see her with the light advancing behind her. She was disappointed at first with his apparent lack of reaction. Then her keen eye saw the slight smile of sexual recognition cross his face. It took her four visits to get him to the end of the piano but once she got him there she threw her heavy lidded sexually loaded slow smile at him and he sat down on a chair normally occupied by his mother. As he did so her left hand tinkled the base keys. How was he to know it was the wedding march?

Sofi discovered there was no lust in him. His personality might look flat but his feeling for the spoken word and his literate vocabulary were sharp enough to allow Sofi to jump into his mind and she liked it. In addition he had a strong tenor voice and she loved to sing soprano, high. Eventually, though he was an accountant his lack of calculation determined her to break down his reserve.

When Sofi met Karl her desire for a musical career was again put on hold. He was not musical or artistic. He was an accountant and an apprentice bank manager. Considering her known high spirits and his quietness both sets of relatives wondered what had attracted Sofi. Karl wondered too but never had the courage to ask her. The first time they were parted she wrote him passionate poems.

> 'Where have yesterdays feelings gone?
> I did not feel them go.
> Today I am full of newer dreams
> and in the heyday of my happiness.'

Karl then realized what everybody else had missed; she loved him. Sofi, the beautiful boisterous intelligent passionate artist no more than nineteen now, with the experience of only one love affair behind her had learned enough from it to know that an honest and true man should have delivery of all her passion raw though it was. Into his calm waters she sailed and was never tempted by the distant shore. The love was mutual.

As Karl dreamed about Sofi and wondered how he could manage to handle this dramatic change in his life an inner voice began to speak… *'Oh to shake out the life we lose in dreams and all those proxy moments beyond our discretion where the will is lost and all the sirens we failed to wake disappear into the void yet those we do remember may never have occurred or we could not avoid. When the wind stops and you look out at the silver birch that enjoy only the wet ground around the river then you wonder why you came back to find that beyond all the years there is nothing left but the image of a girl as she walked beside the water. Her white dress contained her virtue at least in your eyes but later you were to find that there was no end to it and you wonder why it mattered so much then. As you looked at her you knew there would be no other ever in your stars. She searched your face as she washed your feet in the water letting loose her red hair and waiting for you to make a move in any direction. You crossed the shallows that seemed so deep but for once you were brave for you knew your life depended upon it if you were to leave even the slightest evidence of your existence and for that we are bound to gather up our courage so that the light of love should touch whichever shadow we are under.'*

With the inner voice to boost him Karl picked up his courage. "I've been offered a job in the north." Karl informed her.

Sofi was surprised. "In the north! Why would you think of going there?"

"It's the only place where I can have early promotion to be a manager." Karl became hesitant but she didn't think that was unusual until he blurted out the rest of his news. "That's the only way I can support both of us."

Sofi looked up. "Both of us!" Her tone gave him courage.

His voice grew stronger. "Yes. I want to marry you as soon as possible."

Sofi took his hands. "But I'm only nineteen. Do you really think I'm ready to be a wife? I'm just a child."

Karl gave her a wry smile. "I thought you were older than that."

Sofi sighed like a southern belle. "Really. How clever of me."

He grew serious again. "Will you marry me?"

She led him on a little. "Of course I'll think about it."

He couldn't contain his impatience. "How long will you think about it?"

Sofi complained about his lack of romance. "You haven't loved me. You don't tell me every day you love me. You are a slow coach you know."

His face had a pained look of doubt. "I do love you. You know that very well. I suppose I've had too much respect for you to seduce you with attention and words to get you to sleep with me."

Sofi had a surprising question. "Are you a virgin?"

"Isn't it obvious? I thought the man was supposed to worry about the virginity of the woman." Karl bit his lip. "That music teacher?"

There was a tinge of sadness wrapped up in her answer. "How did you know about him?"

"I heard it talked about, rumors fly between women."

Sofi tried to reassure him. "He was a father substitute. I realized that fairly quickly. I don't think it did me any harm. It got rid of my inhibitions at least."

Karl regained his composure. "I didn't know you had any."

Sofi held on to him. "Then I suppose I'd better say yes. Though I don't know what my Aunt will say. Perhaps I should get pregnant. Can we elope?"

Karl was elated and ready to agree to anything. "If you like."

"Really. You mean it?"

He went backwards. "Was Gustav a good lover?"

"Even if I knew I wouldn't tell you."

Karl liked the answer. "You could try me."

Sofi covered the projected move and the sexual offer.

"Is it very cold in the north?"

"Sometimes. But they have nice summers and there's a beach."

Sofi got excited again. "Maybe I could paint there!"

"My mother says you've lost interest in the concert career. Is that true?"

Sofi grew quiet. "No, I don't want to abandon a creative life. I can still play and write no matter where I am. But it doesn't matter so much now at least not at the moment."

"Why is that?" Karl wondered, innocently.

She turned over his hands kissed the palms and said a word he couldn't understand. "I found something better to do. Someone to love." This line later became one of her poems...

'There will always be
someone to love.
One with a kind heart
and a gentle hand.
Even if it's the only
faith you have then believe...
there will always be
someone to love.'

Karl was still curious. "What was that word you said? Was it for me?"

"I'm afraid so. You are stuck with me now."

He couldn't hide his excitement. "Then you've decided. Will you tell me the word?"

"Of course I've decided. There's nobody else I would think of marrying but you."

"The word." Karl insisted. "What was it?"

"Macushlah. It's an Irish word...*my love*."

He wanted to know everything. "When did you decide that?"

She had lost her coyness. "When you sat at the end of the piano and I wanted to touch you instead of the keys."

He grew eager. "Shall we wait until we get the ring on your finger?"

Sofi was more confident. "Let's love each other before we go to the frozen north and before anyone tries to stop us."

Karl relaxed a little with a smile. "I should have mentioned the bank offer earlier."

Sofi disagreed. "I think it's soon enough. I'll be twenty in a few weeks. That's quite a respectable age. You can come to my place. I've got silk sheets in the drawer waiting and two blue silk dressing gowns one of which ties at the waist with a bow." Sofi picked a flower from the vase on the table and put it to her lips then offered it to Karl.

Karl was still tentative. "Should I use a condom?"

Sofi howled. "Not if you want me pregnant!"

He changed the subject. "I'm glad we have a glass door. You looked lovely when you came here that first time and stood out there ringing the bell and the rain was on the glass. I saw you were wearing the red coat. You looked like Monet's wife. I love the red coat."

"It goes with the lipstick." she cracked, and then quoted a line of poetry… *'Parted crystals just coagulate again over a heart traced on a frosted pane.'*

"What do you get from me?" Karl asked, still full of wonder.

She looked him in the eye. "Relief from myself."

He was still a little doubtful. "Did you ever think that I didn't love you enough?"

"Oh no!" she cried. "You have to believe you will be loved."

Karl still needed reassurance. "How did you know then if I'm as slow as you say?"

"Do you think a girl doesn't know a lover when she feels him against her?" Sofi took a deep breath. "And you whispered it to me."

Karl took both her hands. "Are you sure it was my voice you heard?"

She pressed his hands. "The words you didn't speak were all I needed to hear."

"Why does the world have to be so mysterious?" Karl wondered when faced by this enigma.

She reassured him. "I'll show you why and then it won't be a mystery."

Karl smiled in anticipation. "How will you do it?"

"I'll find a way," Sofi said, "and all you will have to do is understand. You have such a quiet grace about you and you are so shy but I'll help you and then it won't be difficult."

"I've broken my solitary habits for you." Karl still held the bloom she had given him. "I've found a girl who is full of romance though she knows I cannot dance."

"Now you're talking like a lover!" Sofi rose up and embraced him. "I don't want to live here anymore. There are too many memories. I know I have to make my own life with you."

Karl again rose to the occasion. "Why don't you go up north and look for a place for us?"

Sofi was surprised by his sudden decisiveness. "Really! I could do that?"

Karl went on with confidence. "It will have to be furnished of course. But we can make it our own as time goes on."

Sofi glowed. "My father left me some money. I get it when I'm twenty one."

"I will have a little too. Anyway," Karl advised, "through the bank we can get a very low interest mortgage when we get the chance to buy later. Yes you should go up there and scout out the place and see if you like it. I have to go away for a week or ten days to get some instruction on how to run a country store."

Sofi came back to basics. "When will we get married?"

Karl was now full of assurance. "You go and rent the house and then with that in hand we will just do it."

Sofi hugged him. "I never realized you were so decisive. I'll tell everybody you overpowered me."

Karl laughed. "The devil in you knows better."

"He's scratching me right now. Watch out!" She paraded around the room. "I know I look good in silk."

***

After both families were told of their decision to get married Karl went off to his seminar in another city. Sofi sat down at her father's desk and wrote a letter so full of passion she felt she would have to destroy it but did not. She ran all through the house with flowers from the little garden in her hand. She called out into every room. She called out goodbye. Finally in the room where she was born she beat a mad tattoo on the window and scared off the birds. She took down all her father's books and put them in boxes. She stripped naked and one by one she wore her every dress and walked around in every shoe. She danced and flounced around in each skirt as high as it would go. She wore long stockings. Sofi lay on her bed and opened her long legs as wide as she could. All the while she played Elgar, her father's favorite. At the peak of Nimrod her orgasm came. She could not contain it and felt the pleasure and the pain of it right through dinner with her aunt sitting opposite her and now and then holding her hand and asking her if she was doing the right thing. For the first time she felt no guilt. The man who had brought all this on she loved. She rose from the table and put on her light Paisley cape. Sofi walked for some time on the strand where the canal made it smooth enough. Someone had left a green apple there but she did not pick it up, just noted it for further use. When the wind picked up she let loose a scream into it and took the string from her hair then ran as far as she could go into the future. She came to a place where they had made concrete emplacements during a war. She remembered trying to imagine that she was in the middle of the pyramids when she painted the scene. "*Where is the new world?*" she called out to the water. She had dreamed once that messages of love came from the water. She went down on her knees. Anyone seeing her might have thought it was a prayer and indeed it was, but to Aphrodite, for her temper was Attic. As the little white waves of the ebbing time came in lighting the world she felt those secret vibrations that the lap of the sea marks in time with the pull of the moon on the blood. She was in ecstasy. The coolness of the evening could not affect her drawing heat from the sun through the sand. In her dream the message had not been clear but now all its indications became suggestive enough for her to know she stood on the edge of the world. On one side her self knowledge and on the other all the mysteries. She was quite determined to face and was ready for what would come. While in this mood she finally decided to send her passion letter to Karl. Her confession of love with the hope he would understand her complexities and the underlying faith she had in love. She suddenly stood up and laughed out loud from wondering whether or not he would take her advice if he ever kissed her again. She dug her heels into the soft sand and then passed some of it through her hands as she had done a hundred times before. Now it struck her how manifest the change in her would come out every time she repeated the rituals of a lifetime. Would they all be different now though they came from the same source. She threw the green apple into the water but not before she took a bite from it. She was pleased with its sweetness. Sofi went home and took the letter from her secret place reading it aloud not changing a word of it yet placing it in her memory before throwing it into the fire.

***

Once in the north Sofi walked into the little town from the train station and from one end to the other it was empty like a ghost town she had read about in western stories; all that was missing was the tumbleweed blowing down the street. Michelle, the young woman she had arranged to meet to help find a place to stay and work turned out to be one of the owners of the local hotel and she explained the lack of people.

"It's too early for visitors but when the better weather comes then this place fills up. Right now it has the pulse of a tortoise."

Sofi had done her homework and she knew something of the artistic heritage of the town and of the artists who had lived here at the turn of the century.

Michelle looked at her list. "You said you wanted a studio with a south western view."

Sofi was enthusiastic. "Yes. I need lots of light but not too early in the morning."

Michelle encouraged her. "There is the other shore and we have a place to show you. It has a history that may interest you. The woman who built it was and perhaps still is a famous actress. She fell in love with an opera singer of hardly any renown, almost famous you might say and built this hideaway as a love nest to lure him here. He didn't come; she preferred Paris; so now she has a substantial summer residence that she leases out on a yearly basis."

"How far away is it?" Sofi looked across the bay.

"From there just around that crescent beach. Ten minutes by car if the heavy rain last night hasn't washed out the road."

"Sounds interesting and expensive," Sofi said, "but let's try it first."

The house was at the level of the sea right in the lap of the shore. The light here was so chaste you felt you could be in the mountains and closer to the sun but there were no mountains and precious little sun. The sand curved away smoothly and into the shape of a scimitar. A short breeze was blowing though the water seemed calm. Sofi later found that not far away where the two seas met you could not risk your foot in the water. There were no eddies in the tidal portions but in the dunes the conflicting breezes blew the sand into peculiar shapes.

Near the middle and towards the handle of the sword the red house stood just above some rocks that supported it. Michelle said there were hares further along that were once hunted for sport but since there were now no crops to save they lived peacefully on the grasses in competition with no other animal but small boys with traps. The only flowers were wild bog roses and the occasional bluebell that signaled water deeper down. The ozone had the heavy smell quite usual when the water offshore is not very deep. The prevailing wind moved the clouds so fast they had no shape. When you stood near the rim there was only one habitation to be seen. All else was hidden on the other side of the places where the sudden influx of sand had forced evacuation years ago. Only this house built right on the beach had risked another sandstorm such as the one that had covered the spire of a nearby church.

In the days when ships cleaved under canvas this shore might awaken to the sight of a dozen or more vessels worth no more than salvage as they pitched helplessly in the shallows and the hidden rocks. From the rear the house was not imposing but when Sofi went round to the front and stood on the beach to look at it she knew it was right.

"Is there any furniture in it?"

Yes." Michelle advised. "The couple who were last to rent it died of the Spanish influenza after they left here to find their relatives when the war finished. Their children will just sell off the personal furniture that didn't come with the house. They live quite far away in another country altogether.

"Is the actress asking very much for it?" Sofi wondered.

"You're the first to show any interest." Michelle said. "This place is a bit out of the way. I think you will find her easy to deal with and if you like the additions you can put in a reasonable bid for the furniture and whatever else you fancy."

"We will be dealing through the bank." Sofi said. "My fiancee is going to be the new manager sometime soon.

"He will have a quiet time," Michelle advised, "though they are trying to put it on the map. There were some famous artists here thirty odd years ago. We have a new fishing harbor of course and a train line

"I know about the artists." Sofi said with enthusiasm. "I've been exploring them. I had heard of one of them but not the others. There was a sad story here."

"Really." Michelle said. "I didn't know that. I hope if you take it we can become friends. The locals are mostly fishermen and it's a pretty close society."

Sofi felt good. "Just what we want. We have lots to do."

"Do you paint?" Michelle wondered, obviously quite taken with the likelihood of a friendship with Sofi

"Yes I do but the piano is my main interest and of course I write. So this is just dandy. I won't disturb anybody with my practicing."

When they entered the house there was a musty smell about it and Michelle tried to explain. "That's a combination of not being lived in and the ozone. A fresh set of people and that will all go away. We have tried to keep it clean. There should be no cobwebs to put you off."

As they walked through the house Sofi was taken with some of the furniture. "They had good taste. Looks like arts and crafts. I can live with this for a while if not forever."

"So you're interested?" Michelle asked.

Sofi's imagination was running wild as she contemplated her life in this house with Karl. "Oh yes! Can I stay here by myself for a few hours just to make sure?"

"Of course. It's just early afternoon. I'll come back for you in a couple of hours and perhaps my sister and *I* could have you for dinner. You can stay the night too if you want to take more time."

Sofi was so excited she embraced Michelle. "Thank you. You've been kind. It's more than I ever expected."

When Michelle had gone Sofi went out into the garden and picked some of the wild flowers. Back inside the house she wandered around and finally stopped at a little side table that held a copy of Joyce's Ulysses. She picked it up and opened it at the first page. There were a few loose pages not connected with the novel. They were handwritten and hard to decipher.

"*A dedicated woman I need.*"

"*Oh, if I was Irish I'd say, bejesus… I'm not, so I won't! But then who does? Surely now you'd hardly expect a woman to read the stuff you write?*"

"*Why, I'd hold every door open for such a woman. I'd even sing her a song every night before she dragged me to bed.*"

"*To shut you up?*"

"*Oh, even you have to admit I've a fair tenor voice.*"

"*My friend, some songs we thought immortal have been struck down by your tonsils never to rise again.*"

"*You're surely a good friend to me. I'm highly strung you know,*"

"*Violin or guitar? I'm just glad I'm queer.*"

"*Hush. Why is that?*"

"*Because then I don't have to hug you coming or going. I can still hear the violins crying in your wake.*"

"*Bloody amateurs! That beautiful girl liked me.*"

"*I didn't think she was that beautiful.*"

"*Perhaps she didn't show you all of it.*"

"*And what is there to know about such a woman?*"

"Only that you can never expect to have all of her. Don't expect to have all her heart forever. What have I lost my dear fellow? It seems like yesterday that day I went up the stairs to cry with the telegram in my hand all crumpled to pieces before the day was over.'

"Have you got over her now?"

"If I could throw stones at her window I'd stand in the snow like the Holy Roman Emperor did with the Pope of Rome once upon a time and promise to worship her forever if she'd press her lips against the glass."

"Ah, love. Even pity cannot bring us to our senses."

"What else but love is in our senses?"

Sofi was charmed by the conversation. Two anonymous men. It was so natural. Falling from the book into her hands and into her mind set. Someone who had lived here might have written this down and she imagined it was part of a larger piece, probably a novel. The mystery of it intrigued her. It was quite warm in the afternoon sun. Sofi took out a deck chair and sat down to read the opening chapter of Ulysses but all the excitement had made her more tired than she realized. She dozed off and fell into a dream.

She was sitting at a table with four chairs and looking down a wide passage way to a tall french window. At first she didn't realize that she was on a ship so calm was the ocean. She rose from her chair when a large dog appeared pawing at the glass door for entry. When she got to the door she realized she was at sea. It was blue and smooth. She tried to let the dog inside but found the door locked and keyless. There was a sound behind her but when she turned there was just the hum of a fan and two little duck like feathers blowing around the floor. She stooped to collect them but they seemed designed to avoid her and when she looked around it was to a small saloon with padded benches around the walls and tables set for a meal. She tried every door but all were locked against her. There was a companion way at one end and she ran towards it but tripped on a carpet rung and fell her length. As she sat there soft music she did not recognize came over the speakers and the room grew darker. She struggled to the stairs again and was able to see a shadow looming above her blocking out the light. Sofi turned and went back to the table and sat down to wait out developments.

Michelle's voice woke her up.

Sofi apologised. "I'm sorry. I was dreaming. I was trapped on a ship for some reason."

Michelle sat down beside her. "I've a feeling you're a very sensitive young woman and you seem to have identified with this place if you are having dreams already."

Sofi looked around her. "Do you know any thing at all about the recent renters?"

"I don't know much." Michelle admitted.

Sofi continued. "Were they writers?"

"I think the man was trying to write something; but they were here such a short time I really didn't get time to know them. If you are still coming to dinner with us tonight I know a lady who will know more about them. She has lived here all her life. She's an artist. This place was once full of them as you know but I think fame left her behind. I've seen some of her work and it is quite wonderful."

Sofi was thrilled. "Can we have her along tonight?"

Michelle was pleased with her reaction. "That's what I was thinking."

Sofi kept wandering around. "I'm sure we will be taking this house. I have no way of contacting my fiancee but he has your number. I would like you to hold it for us. I'll call you in a few days and both of us will come up to conclude the offer."

Michelle smiled in wonder at the young woman. "You haven't asked how much they want for rent or the lease details."

Sofi sat down. "Oh no! I forgot about that part. Write it down. I don't want to know. My Karl will deal with it no matter how much they want."

Michelle laughed. "You are in love with this place. I can tell you that it's a bargain. Let's get you down to the hotel and invite the Lady Anne."

"The Lady Anne?" Sofi was again intrigued.

"Yes" Michelle said. "That's what they call her. Oh I suppose she has another name but that's what they call her around here. I've been trying to get her to let me write her biography but she has put me off so far."

Sofi continued to be happy.

"I can't wait. I'd better put this manuscript back where I found it. The family should have it."

Even the early evening light had to be shaded especially from the old lady's eyes the woman Michelle called Lady Anne. When she came into the house so gracefully Sofi rose to meet her and realized at once that Michelle's judgement of her as a woman of substance was justified. She was brown skinned from a lifetime of exposure to painting in the open air.

"Apart from a trip to Paris and one to Barcelona I've never moved from this beach." she told Sofi in the manner of older women declaring themselves to the younger.

"There's not a wrinkle on your face." Sofi assured her.

Anne touched her cheek. "The wind blew them away."

"Does the light bother you?" Michelle asked, while standing ready to pull down the shade.

Anne shrugged her shoulders. "It has made my existence here worthwhile. It inspired a whole generation of us."

"The light appears blue white to me." Sofi said.

"Then you have a rare eye for color my dear. Do you paint?"

"In the most amateurish way. " Sofi replied. "The piano seems to be my forte."

Anne wrinkled her copious nose. "Your language is good too. I have a feeling you have wit."

"Perhaps my father's influence." Sofi assured her.

Anne showed her interest. "He was a writer then?"

"No." Sofi said. "He was a doctor but actually preferred his brother's printing business."

"Ah" Anne responded. "An anarchist too I bet. From what I know of Barcelona that hotbed of anarchism the printers were the first to take it up."

Sofi changed the subject. "I didn't know him long enough to discover his politics. I know you're an artist but I haven't seen any of your work I'm afraid."

Anne put up her hand in a faint gesture.

"I would be shocked if you had heard of me. Other stronger voices blocked me out a long time ago."

Michelle spoke up. "That may have been true then but you are becoming quite famous now. I have some copies to show you Sofi."

"Did you always know what you were meant to do?" Sofi wondered.

Anne didn't hesitate. "I think so. The colors always seemed clear to me. But I was among men with genius and not expected to be an artist. In those circumstances one must work away quietly and steadily."

"It's different now since the war." Sofi said. "Much easier for a woman."

Anne was not so sure. "Not any easier to produce art."

Michelle's sister Susannah came in.

"It's such a lovely night. Perhaps we could sit out in the garden. I've set up the white table and chairs."

"We will need cushions." Michelle said. "Wait until I can get them unpacked."

Later when Sofi saw portraits and photographs of Anne she could see that the woman had always had her present elegance. The string of pearls around her neck was visible all through her life of art and a multitude of photographs that Michelle had acquired.

"The pearls are so beautiful." Sofi said. "I'd like to touch them for good luck."

Showing her pleasure Anne encouraged her.

"Yes. Why don't you? My husband got them for me the first month we met. How he ever afforded them he never told me because in those days he had just come north without any money. It took him a week to get here by pony and trap. My mother knew he couldn't pay the rent at first but when he said he was a painter she trusted him as much as I did from the first day I saw him get out of the trap with that old easel. You must come over and see it sometime."

"I'd love to do that." Sofi said.

Michelle came in again and spoke to Anne.

"You haven't changed your hairstyle since the early portraits I've seen of you."

"No. It was long when I was a girl but I suppose being among all those men and being ambitious to be as good as they were I mean as an artist,

I subconsciously decided to get it cut short and I've always kept it that way."

"There's not a grey hair in it." Susannah said as she passed by with the cushions. "How do you do it?"

"My mother said to wash it in tea leaves."

Anne laughed when she saw the look on Sofi's face.

"That would keep it dark, she said."

"Did you do it?" Sofi wondered.

Anne touched her hair. "Just the once."

Sofi complimented her. "It has lasted a long time then. Perhaps your mother was right."

"I'm not so vain as I once was. But if it changes I'll try it again." Anne suddenly noticed the large vase of clematis at the side window as they walked out to the garden. "Oh I'd love to paint those flowers!"

"You can have them." Michelle assured her. "I'm flattered you like my arrangement."

Anne cautioned her. "You shouldn't be. I might change it. Artistic licence you know. When you paint for the love of it then it has to be quite personal."

"I understand." Michelle said, and she guided Anne to the end of the white table. "You can still have them. I'll have Bill bring them over to you when he walks you home."

Anne looked at Sofi. "I was thinking the young woman might do that."

Sofi was flattered and showed it. "That would be nice. I've hardly seen the town."

As the food was being transferred outside Susannah was anxious to make sure everything was perfect for her guests.

"Do we need a table cloth?"

"Not at all." Anne said. "This table is lovely and reflects the light very well." She turned to Sofi to resume their conversation. "Michelle says you are thinking of the actress house."

Sofi sat opposite to Anne. "Yes. I love it. I hope my fiancee likes it too when he comes up."

"And you will be married soon?" Anne enquired.

"Hopefully before we move up here." Sofi said.

Anne gave her some advice.

"You should do it here you know. It would make a big difference to your connection with the locals. They are a tight group. It would help your husband too. The new bank manager I believe."

Sofi's face lit up. "What a good idea."

Anne was pleased with her reaction. "Michelle says you have been pursuing a musical career. I hope getting married will not stop you. You know when I married my husband everybody thought I would never paint again but I did and still do. All through his lifetime he supported me."

"I know we're young," Sofi said, "but we just want to get on with our life together. Whether I'll continue my music seriously or not will depend on how things turn out for my husband. I want children while I'm young. I was a late baby. I don't want that for my children." Sofi then changed the subject. "Michelle thought you might know some of the history of the house."

"Oh yes." Anne said, now aware that Sofi knew where she was going and meant to get there, would listen to advice but keep her own counsel. "I watched them build it and knew the lady who had it put up."

Sofi picked at a piece of cheese. "She was an actress I believe."

"Yes." Anne said. "Quite famous in her day but who would know her now. You need a film career to be known today. No, she was a stage actress of some renown."

Sofi was full of interest. "How did you meet her?"

"She wanted my husband to paint her portrait. It was to be a gift for her lover."

Susannah was passing… "Her lover?"

"Oh yes she lived quite a scandalous life for those days."

"And how did it end up?" Sofi wondered, full of interest too.

"The man never came up this distance and she didn't live in the house any longer than the month she waited for him." Anne suddenly lost interest in the actress. "How old are you?

"Just through twenty."

"You're quite beautiful and you don't need tea leaves."

"Not yet." Sofi took the compliment with grace but was still interested in the house. "Who rented the house after the actress left?"

Anne picked at a gherkin. "That was a success story to begin with but then it turned tragic. But I won't tell you about them at least not tonight, it's too sad. They were friends of mine. And of course the latest people lost their lives. I hardly knew them. Just passing in the street. They minded their own business. He had been a newspaper man I believe and wrote novels that nobody would publish."

Susannah came out of the house with fruit drinks and the news that there was a call for Sofi. "I think it's your fiancee. Is his name Karl?"

Sofi began the conversation with enthusiasm. "I've found a house. I love it! You must come up right away. It's just for rent at the moment but I want you to buy it for us."

Karl picked up her excitement. "Good! I have two days off before I go away again. I'll borrow the car and be there tomorrow afternoon sometime. Where are you staying?"

"With Michelle and Susannah. They own the local hotel and do real estate on the side. I'm sure I can stay overnight with them. I love the house and this place. It's not the frozen north Karl it's Eden."

Karl tried to calm her down. "Hold on Eve, Adam has only had one bite of the apple."

"Did you enjoy it?" Sofi quipped.

"Yes. But how did I end up wearing the dressing gown with the bow?"

Sofi laughed then put her hand to her mouth suddenly wondering if they had been overheard. "Perhaps you had more to hide."

"I'll see you soon," Karl assured her. "Keep your excitement until then."

Sofi would not let him go. "I've only got one pair of knickers with me. Could you love a girl who wears them two days running?"

Karl reached back into history. "Well, as Napoleon said to Josephine. 'I'll be home soon. Don't wash'!"

Sofi still kept him. "I've opened up Pandora's box haven't I?"

"You have. " Karl said. "If I was a Dutchman I'd be flying."

When Sofi came back to the garden she was full of questions.

"How long have you been here Michelle?"

Michelle poured the coffee. "We took over this place two years ago. It belonged to my Uncle and we were his only relatives.

Anne cut in. "They have livened up the place. A salon in the country. If we get such young people as we had a generation ago this little town will get back some of it former class."

Susanne spoke up. "I don't think it ever lost it at least not all of it."

Anne smiled in appreciation. "We had one or two fine poets and half a dozen of the best painters this country has ever seen but nobody musical. I hope you stay young lady. But we're not looking for a club. We need some culture."

Sofi was still full of questions for Anne. "Did you and your husband have an equal partnership?"

"Oh yes. I think that was because neither of us could ever make our mind up about anything but art and so we were never troubled by minor things like not having enough money or how clean the house was every day. We had no need for tolerance or compromise. We just did our work and then fell in love again when it was over for the day."

"We haven't had an argument yet." Sofi admitted.

"And I predict you never will." Anne assured her. "Strong women don't need to argue. What an array of food Susannah. I'd be interested to know how you cooked the fish and the lobster."

Susannah beamed. "I hope you both like white wine, it's all we have at the moment."

Anne touched Michelle's arm. "It won't loosen my tongue my dear." She seemed completely unaware of how much she had already let out to Sofi.

When the meal was over Anne and Sofi began their walk arm in arm to Anne's house.

"I'll help you meet the local people Sofi. They have a hard life sometimes."

They walked slowly past the cemetery that lay on the side of a slight grade. "It's not very full." Sofi commented, and then wondered if she had said the right thing. She had forgotten that Anne's husband was in there.

But Anne was not upset. "No. They either take their time dying here or do it in the sea."

Sofi was now at ease with her and asked, facetiously. "What does the undertaker do to pass the time?"

Anne laughed but it seemed Sofi had touched on a local worthy. "When I was a girl he went to the beach every morning to see how many boats had perished during the night or how many were still in the ocean between the peril and his boxes. Nowadays he cleans shop windows every morning and watches the women strain to pick up the milk from the doorsteps." She giggled again. "You can bet he'll be there when they keel over. His motto could be… 'in our end is his beginning.' she changed the subject abruptly. "Michelle said you had a dream in the house. Do you day dream a lot?"

"It seems to be a habit." Sofi admitted.

"I suppose that is part of what art is too." Anne thought. "Dreaming while awake. Do you remember the dream?"

"I do."

"The ones you don't remember may be the ones that make you creative."

Sofi pondered this for a moment or two.

"Where is your house?" she wondered.

"It's all the way through here. Some morning you can come to visit me and see the sparkle of the sun coming through the crown of the beech trees and wonder at the pebbles shining like jewels. It may inspire you. Now look at those trees stretching for the light. I should cut some of them down. The older ones especially but I haven't the heart. I've grown so sentimental since my husband died. Everything should live out its time. Don't you think? My father made this pathway crooked. He said he didn't want to see around the corner. Here we are."

Anne's house stood foursquare across the end of the gravel road and made it a dead end.

"It's lovely." Sofi exclaimed.

Anne was proud and delighted.

"That's our atelier to the right of the house. It's built on the end of an older place made by a German man who had a workshop long before our time. There's a big garden behind the house. I'm hoping you and your fiancee will spend some time with me out there. I'll try not to bore you with all my stories from the past." She laughed at herself. " Perhaps it's ironic that is all I've got left to look forward to."

Sofi encouraged her. "I'm just an amateur painter but I would like to study with you."

Anne expressed doubt. "I'm not sure I can teach the art. It's so personal and local with me. I suppose I could help you a little with words but you will have to learn the technique by yourself like I did."

When they entered the house the first thing Sofi saw was a guitar propped up in the hallway.

"What a lovely instrument." Sofi touched the strings but did not play them.

"Yes. My husband played it. Apparently he learned it in Cuba one time when he was marooned there in his youth among all those lusty Cuban women. His only flattery was that instrument." She turned coy. "I don't suppose there were too many notches in it."

"Anyway," Anne put her hand up to her mouth with shyness "they didn't do me any harm. Could you play it?"

"I could try. But I really only play the piano."

"Tell me about your fiancee. You haven't said much about him."

Sofi face shone. "I suppose one must be quiet about a quiet man a gentle man."

Anne pursued Karl's character. "Has he wit? That's important in the dark nights up here. A man who comes to bed just for sex and sleep is no fun. He should laugh with you sometimes too. But it's early yet. My husband once came to bed wearing a red cock feather hat and I laughed for a week. See I'm still laughing. Oh, he was a wit. His sister was funny too but unconscious of it of course. She was a vegetarian but he told me she ate clams in secret." Anne lay back and howled. "Didn't shut her up of course. And at the sight of a veggie she was rooted to the spot."

Sofi went around the room looking at the paintings.

Anne noticed her attention but did not explain anything.

"Sit down and play something for me. The piano has been asleep for a long time. I don't know how it will respond to being awakened. Try not to traumatize it. What will you play?"

"You already have some music on the top. Shall I play that for you?" Sofi suggested.

"Go ahead." Anne agreed." I always keep that music close by and sing it sometimes to myself. That world has gone under.

One has to grow old with all these memories. But let me rest my weary legs first. Thank God for this chaise longue. If I fall asleep just slip out."

As Sofi played Anne started to remember the words. Her broken voice getting softer and more intimate.

"*Girls, were made,*
to love and kiss,
and who am I,
to interfere with this?"

Anne's voice wandered and Sofi played her softly to sleep.

***

The next morning waiting impatiently for Karl to arrive Sofi saw that there were no hills to be painted blue. No rushing streams to show the vigor of the country. She turned and turned to look back at the red house not able to separate herself from it. It was the only mysterious thing in a land that so far for her, held none. The clouds looked ripe for rain. As a light smirr of it came on her face she wondered what harvest it would bring from this sand worn barren place. She would learn that almost everything came from the sea and formed the attitude of the people to life. A day to day in tune with the weather existence. With all the privileges of youth Sofi hadn't seen much further than her own gratification until she met Lady Anne. Who now and over time she thought would give her a different perspective. She had found the reality of an isolated community living within itself importing everything else.

Sofi avoided the long snake like seaweed wrestling with the foam. The geese were on their way to heaven. The horizon sucked down the sun and every shape under the firmament rumpled together spinning. Here a bird and there a star. The light curdling the throat of the earth as the pulse of summer throbbed away. The image of her father faded and from the direction she knew Karl would come a shaft of love to warm her mind. When she had left Anne and gone back to the hotel she had written a note to Karl.

LOVE IN AN UNEXPECTED PLACE

Dear Karl,

I'm sure you've listened to every echo of love before but this call is not a call from a mountain fastness. Oh no! It's from a girl now suddenly a woman stretching out for her power in the world. Is there a secret jewel casket for my voice and my message? I have written one for you.

'My memories of you are of such short acquaintance that they should not leave me much to regret. And yet as I step on this shore I still turn my head to look for you once more. I cannot shed this great desire to have you return to me. I have loved you. I can feel your spirit working on me still. Even at this distance my will is lost.'

My darling, I thought that whatever event would make me a woman would take time and perhaps come upon a gentle wind. It came like a hurricane does, this love. All my preconceived notions of it lost in the vortex and with hardly any effort on your part. Perhaps if we all knew what a stranger would bring we could avoid them or guide ourselves to one of the compass points to the north of us where some of the passion could cool down. But I have to tell you that my emotions have gone south to the sunflowers; they will not slow down. All my hormones are pointed in your direction and if I could look at their pattern I suspect they are swinging like the rings of Saturn. No need to go there; I am here waiting for you. The wheat grass beaten down in the night has risen again by noon. The clouds were like rocks this morning. The Lady Anne says that we will see some green gooseberries by early May. The wind so far has no ripening in it. I couldn't sleep and discovered that the owls in the night mostly hoot in B flat. There is a weak sun this morning but even that is welcome as your strength is still inside me and it won't go away. What happened to my body? How did it finally come together? How did all my blood suddenly find a way to conjugate the world? I looked at my face in the mirror and I liked it for the first time. I am fully aware yet not nervous not anxious to please having given and received such pleasure. My emotions are not extreme but soft and contented for I suspect now that there may be a lifetime of these days ahead of me. But I want you to know that just one morning like this would be worth a life. All my love, Sofi.

P.s. Hurry. I can only stay unwashed for one day!

It was Michelle who had to break the news to her that Karl had died on the way up.

"It was a collision with a truck the police said. He died instantly."

Sofi did not cry. She turned and ran up the scimitered beach past the red house the grey lighthouse and out to where the two seas meet, for no settled place could contain her grief.

Chapter 2

As Terence traveled through the country he could see that like many another where they had once been plentiful it was devoid of oak beech and birch. There were no orchards. The only flowers he saw were bog roses crowding out every rival which might have suited his grandfather who had become interested in latin flower names just as his memory began to fade. There were no perfumes in the air that might have recalled memories. Apart from some manuscripts in various forms of completion Terence came empty handed to this new world which was as strange to him as the supposed East Indies were to Columbus. At least Terence had a map and knew he was on a peninsula between two stormy seas. For all the lack of ambience this was a quiet and seemingly welcoming world. Even the hum of the ancient car he drove did nothing to remind him of the chaos of the trenches where he had spent two years of purgatory and had been further tested or perhaps punished by a shell that killed all around him leaving Terence with a shattered leg now held together with an ugly brace.

In the field hospital he had been attracted to a nurse, Frances. In time they made love in a far flung gazebo. They first came together when the pain in Terence's leg became unbearable. Frances came in frequently and gave him illegal pain injections. When the pain went away depression took over as he tried and failed to walk. Alcohol was forbidden. Frances supplied it in mineral water bottles with the liquid suitably mixed with the original water. Soon he asked her to leave out the water and every night he went to sleep inebriated. In a colony of hundreds of war wounded they escaped detection. She became his personal nurse. Every day as she pushed him around the grounds she tried to soothe his depression with a mixture of sex and alcohol not always in that order. As time went on they fell in love and his pain eased considerably. Frances gradually weaned Terence from the need for chemical help. She had with all the sympathy of her calling shown that his wounds had not totally disabled him.

When she came one night fresh from confession he had posed a question.

"What's the point of love if your priest says there's something greater?"

She took his hand and when Terence glanced down at her she gave him such an innocent look he realized that for them there was nothing more.

"How can I live without you?" These were her last words to him spoken on the telephone. Words that stayed in his head every time he thought of her or saw her in his imagination or dreams. He remembered that when they were alone she never undressed in front of him such was her delicacy. She just appeared like Venus fresh from the bath naked and lovely ; a woman of sensual depths. Once, when he was attending a service at a funeral home he saw her pass the window. She wore a spring skirt and red shoes. Whenever he could he hobbled out after her and down every street to find her but she had gone and there was the feeling now of sudden loss. Where could he find her? Find her like again? Would all that was to follow be bloodless?

They had left the hospital together with renewed confidence only to be informed that the Spanish Influenza was killing millions around them and two weeks later it killed Frances too. It was now his hope that he could in this jalopy outrun the disease. He was well aware that he could not run away from the sorrow.

Terence went to stay for an extended time in the house of his Aunt Elizabeth an actress of yesteryear who had come up from a lower class of society than his father, her cousin. Yet everybody said that she had the beauty the will and the taste of the famous Archduchess Elizabeth late of Savoy. Although her stage star was waning now she never had any trouble finding guests for her celebrated parties ; so many people wanted to see her at home ; in the smartest part of Paris of course.

When he met her again to discuss the play he had written in the infirmary he soon saw as their day together went on that her wounds were deeper than his for which there might still be a cure. She said she was pleased that he had come out of hell still with hope in his heart and perhaps a clear mind. Elizabeth had visited the troops nearer to the trenches than the Generals who ran the war would go themselves and had seen the desperation in the faces of the men. As she sang to them and showed them her legs she reminded them of a previous world by little forays into the sentimentality of the music hall. Elizabeth had joined them in their misery; couldn't escape it. She cried in public against all the rules of conduct; that she was there to offer hope and diversion and not to share their misery.

The grand Elizabeth had lost her husband in a previous war but had not gone into mourning for long. Her love life in Paris was renowned and some said distinguished though she had never remarried. Terence decided to go and see her to ask her help to get the play he had written on to the stage. In Paris it was raining. Skin was out and long pants with a Paisley type patterned skirt over them to the knee was in and not just for the rainy season. Fashion like the weather dictated the sophisticated and others in Paris. The lack of skin did not seem to detract from the imagination and the streets were still full of young men and old ; the warm and the cold looking to extend their passion or to find it again.

Elizabeth was aging but could still stroll with sophistication and recall her memories for those she said distinguished her as a woman. Tall and still slim, Terence thought that some of the men who still looked at Elizabeth's beauty however faded as it was now would in times gone past have thrown down their capes and their fortunes for her attention and the sound of her perfectly literate speech and beautiful voice.

She was involved at this moment of time with a shirt manufacturer who, in his mansion she said, had some lovely works of art. He was a patron of the arts. He had a box at the Opera and various other musical establishments. Yet the closest his workers ever got to art was to load it into moving vans or to dust the frames twice day.

"I envy you Paris." Terence said.

"There's more than one." she informed him.

As they looked at the lunch menu Terence was not sure how to begin. His mind fluttered like the tricolor outside the door. She may have suffered the loss of some of her other assets yet Elizabeth still had a good mind. It had been said of her by one of her literary lovers that her intelligence gave the woman more beauty than nature ever could.

She was well aware of his recent loss. "Have you been looking around here at the women and feeling guilty?" she began.

"It's only been two months since Frances died."

"I didn't wait that long. Henri had been such a good lover and I needed to take another before I forgot the joy of it and got old before my time.'

Terence smiled indulgently. "Did you shock people?"

"Oh yes." She laughed out loud. "The men!"

"I don't have your shock appeal." he admitted.

"Why don't you try? A woman must be able to tell that you're attracted to her. You shouldn't need lessons. I didn't. I thought the world was becoming more sexually honest these days but it looks as though it has left you behind. If you've been without a woman for a length of time let's hope you find one who will be a little more careful with you in the beginning not to overwhelm you darling. Men are as fragile as eggs when they might be cracking. She will have to patch you up if she thinks you are worth it! It has stopped raining. This city dries out quickly. Look at the women! They are out there already sans coats. A wet coat has no style. All the rain does here is serve as an excuse to go indoors where all the real pleasure lies. At my age it only affects my bones. Yet the hormones are never still. What can you do about them? I tell myself the rouge is just a subterfuge. In my conversations I tell myself that I'm still that young woman over there who is sitting up very straight adjusting her hair and hoping that the rich young man she is with has some energy left from making money for extensive travel through his earthly estates."

"How can you guess all that?" Terence wondered.

"Don't you know that's what this place is all about?" she advised him.

The waiter arrived. "What will you order today Madame?"

"M'selle if you please and I will have the oysters."

"How will you have them?"

Elizabeth gave him a look. "Raw, of course."

Terence ordered a salad and brought a frown to Elizabeth's face. "What's the matter? You are either inhibited or very sure of yourself."

"I haven't reached the oyster stage yet." he admitted.

Elizabeth had the answer to that. "When you do you must let the shell open up Terence. It's the only way to have them or a woman."

Elizabeth seemed to be talking to someone who wasn't there. "The only symptom of youth is that my hair is not grey. Oh how terrible that must be. One must hold the curtains open as long as possible my dear. Ah, but you came here for advice and here am I gabbing on about my life."

She daunted and then raised his hopes at once.

"You have written a very bad play. But there is some good dialogue in it and I suggest you try a novel with what you can salvage. I know you're disappointed but I intend to make up for my criticism. A proposed rental of my house in the north has not gone through because a tragedy of some kind has taken place and so I offer you the free use of my house to get yourself in order and as a place where you can write in peace."

She had taken him by surprise. "How can I thank you." Terence blurted out. "I didn't know you had such a house."

Elizabeth sighed. "No need to discuss that fiasco. I was lucky at the beginning of my career and so far as I know you are my only living relative. Do you have any money?"

Terence spread his arms. "A disability pension. I can probably manage on that."

She gave him further encouragement. "Just in case you shall have some starter money too. Now, as you become a successful novelist I don't want to hear that you've been climbing trees and taking all your clothes off."

Terence looked at her doubtfully.

"And what writer does that?"

"I read it somewhere that D.H.L. is prone to it."

Terence moved his sore leg.

"Send me a postcard if you need me

Elizabeth showed mock shock.

"Postcards are so vulgar! I'll send you a telegram if I have any money left. Why I hardly know where my next bottle of champagne is coming from! Actually all I have to worry about is the class of funeral I will have. I'm hoping for *un enterrement de premier classe*. Would you see to that?"

"Of course." He had no idea what he was agreeing to but she soon put him right.

"Oh, and I'd like four black horses with plumes." Turning to the waiter. "I don't suppose you have a cucumber sandwich?

The waiter skipped away. "You may be right."

Elizabeth knitted her eyebrows.

"Even the hired help have an act these days."

Terence surprised Elizabeth by asking a personal question.

"What happened between the Duc de Rus and you?"

She stretched one eye into a slant.

"He didn't care for my first wrinkle."

"Was that the only difficulty?"

" No." She replied, smiling roguishly. "He collected beds that Napoleon had slept in and we all know his wife was not clean."

"I see that Anatole died last week."

"Yes, poor fellow. He died as no true artist should."

Terence could not resist. "And how was that?"

"Famous of course! Such is ignominy! I'm surprised you've written anything of substance at all. I just remember before the war all those precious little shallow essays you used to write for equally mortifying magazines."

"Those magazines! They might not have been so fashionable in your circles but they paid hard cash."

"Well at least now I know it wasn't self deception on your part and you've always been so considerate. I remember once when you were a small boy you said my hat was lovely when it was so obviously, at least your mother thought so, a disaster. You have charm my boy and that alone will take you a long way especially with women. You've had lots of experiences now so why don't you just go and recollect them. Write them down and don't listen to those people who say you should write about what you know. It's what you don't know that sparks the true imagination and never make the mistake of imagining that whatever you create is a substitute for life. The thing I like about you my dear is that although your face has changed I don't believe for a moment that your character has. Change is in the air. Go and see what you can do with it."

As he pocketed her check Terence could not help wondering with the arrogance of youth what life held for his aunt. "What are you looking for now for yourself?" Terence asked her.

She shocked him with a mythical metaphor. "For a serpent with its tail in its mouth."

Terence was shocked. "How awful!"

"Yes." she sighed. "Such is eternity my dear. When you find another woman I must advise you that you may never recover from Frances. She might have been like the first pyramid, solving all your problems while all the rest are just pale imitations fiddling around."

"I have other dreams." Terence advised her.

A woman walked in with two little dogs that she fussed over.

"Beware of a woman who is obsessive with dogs." Elizabeth warned. "Like them she might have a short memory."

They went to her house and to his dismay she asked him to loosen the bottom latch of her corset whereupon she lay down on the chaise like a toy that a child had put together in the wrong order, totally contradicting the glamorous photographs of herself where she lay in a similar position like Cleopatra scantily dressed waiting for Caesar to visit her on her barge on the Nile. The jaded smile she gave him just before he left her came back to him now as he came closer to his destination. Her last words were that in a year free of care he might write a good first novel and find love everlasting. Touched, he ventured to kiss her cheek but could not quite make the journey across her bosom.

Chapter 3

Terence stood on a rock and looked through the spitting sea mist at the red house. He knew that Elizabeth had built it in the hope that she could lure a lover here to live with her far away from other female temptations. Her lover had other ideas and with the popularity of the operetta in Vienna moved there to begin a singing career far from these hinterlands. Elizabeth stayed one late summer but with the onset of autumn became doubly depressed with lack of a lover and the regularity of gale force winds. So she had abandoned the house to the elements and other people who rented it and she only paid attention to it when Terence came back from the trenches with a shattered leg and literary ambitions she had bruised.

Terence moved into a house that had been well preserved by local caretakers. He fell in love with the studio that looked out over the sea. Every window blind in that room was hand painted in gold with operatic scenes and various handwritten love poems from the arias. When he looked around the house there was no reaction in his mind. There was nothing to change or rearrange. Terence knew nothing of the Persian carpets except that he liked them and the artist in him had a dim realization that whoever had made them had meant the patterns to represent lakes and gardens and rivers. Little did he know that living fingers had squeezed out the colors from wild plants and blended them together. How long this process had taken he could not realize yet he was in awe of the artist. As he looked out to sea and listened to the rumbling wind life suddenly became simple again. He would search for the fundamentals and try to put them in place. As he watched the birds of passage he smiled. Perhaps further flight was not for him.

As Terence walked through the little town he realized that he had arrived in a place without mystery and wondered if his imagination would prosper in it. Later, he stood on the balcony behind the top of the house and looked through his field glasses at the half buried church steeple. Many years ago it had been the victim of a great sand storm and was now abandoned to nature. As he looked at it in detail he imagined that like humanity it had settled into the way things were. Some changes are permanent. He felt a new surge of life run through him. He was ready to start again. Like the church the world had not quite buried him.

"You have the beginning of a good novel." His Aunt had said. Finally her voice sounded genuine and loud and clear and full of inspiration. It was true she had built this house in vain. But at least she had tried to conjure up love until she knew that it didn't exist. All the images he had seen on the long journey up north suddenly became clearer and he knew they added up conclusively to a new set of circumstances. Now he found he was eager to explore them. He retreated inside the house as a web of rain wound its way across the dunes peppering the sand with little spit balls.

It was almost Spring according to the soltice but the wind still blew and he stayed home filling his first few days listening to recordings of

Elizabeth's bel canto lover. It was a voice full of tricks to hide its problems. A blemished voice getting softer and more intimate. Nevertheless the choice of romantic music sustained Terence for a few days. Then at the end of the second week the postman Erik suggested he pay a visit to the town hall where local artists were holding an exhibition.

From curiosity boredom and not knowing where to start his novel Terence attended on the final night though he still suffered pain from his leg wound. Most of the artists were older than Terence but as usual the women they attracted were young and for the show were mostly dressed in long turn of the century dresses. He soon discovered Albert the local art teacher who was curator of the exhibition and another fugitive from the war though not an active participant. He introduced him to one of the artists, Susannah. Despite her good looks Terence looked around for the young woman he had come across on his second day as she walked past the house and on one other occasion as he sat on the promenade.

As Terence looked at the art mostly derivatives of earlier masters he noticed Michelle come in. As she stood ahead of paintings in the center of the room he thought she had the focus of a barmaid with a full house ; she would have no time for small talk. She did not smile at all as she moved across the large room looking at the other paintings finally stopping at the portrait of a young girl standing fully dressed on a beach watching young boys of her own age running naked into and out of the light blue water. Perhaps imagining herself as the subject as no doubt many other young women had done comparing her restriction with their own.

Terence was not always confident with women but his motives were never base and that seemed to leak through. He was handsome if not ruggedly so. The room had become quite busy but elbows were not flying yet. Terence was waiting for his new acquaintance Albert to come back to him. While he waited he looked at six water colors all landscape views of the sea. He especially admired one that flew into the distance and exerted an influence on him. Five of these paintings were the work of Susannah. The one he admired was by her sister Michelle and had been placed in the most difficult position next to copies of the well known masters of yesteryear. Michelle was well aware of him in the gallery and noticed his attention to her work. When he turned around to look at her the tilt of her head and her slow uninhibited smile charmed him. Before they could speak Albert appeared and stood between them.

"Who painted these?" Terence asked, quite unaware that he was standing fairly close to the artist who had painted the one he liked so much. The tall young woman with creamy hair held back as if by invisible hands stepped aside sensing a turn of events in her life unexpected yet expectant. The notice she craved perhaps now close and rare.

"These are all nice!" Terence declared to Albert before he could introduce him to Michelle. "But this one this distant view is quite marvelous." Michelle stood radiant in his praise but speechless. At that cogent moment Michelle was called away by one of the sponsors and her place was taken by Susannah.

"Here is your artist." Albert said, bringing forward Susannah as he drifted away with Michelle. Terence had noticed the difference in the quality of paintings but still misunderstood in believing that Susannah was the artist of the complete set.

He was full of praise. "There is a sure lightness for color. Nothing too dark. Your red in this one at the end has a Scandinavian look and yet your blues are of the Mediterranean."

Susannah was so pleased with the praise that she hesitated to enlighten him that it was the work of her sister.

"I've never been to the south," she said, "studied the art of course."

"Then you must travel." Terence said. "Although there seems little need to do so. There's enough here to last for some time I think."

As Terence insisted on discussing only one painting Susannah became embarrassed made her excuses and wandered away.

Albert returned and apologized for leaving so abruptly.

Terence smiled. "I will have to get back down to work. I'd like to meet the young artist again."

"That's good, she and her sister Michelle have been called away but they'd like you to come and have lunch with them at their hotel tomorrow. By the way," and Terence heard the pride in his voice, "Susannah's sister Michelle painted the watercolor you like so much. She's was a student of mine"

Terence wondered at Susannah's mild deception but didn't mention it to Albert. "A lunch with two lovely women will be a nice change for me."

"The show is over almost everything is sold." Albert said. "I'm hungry now let's eat."

After dinner Terence and Albert decided that they would take a tour of the beach.

Terence was excited. "Look at those shapes! The water has fissures like the bark of a tree."

"Another trick of the light." Albert said. He was dressed for the show like a turn of the century artist. The dilettante type who never painted anything of distinction but looked the part right down to a flamboyant hat. Upon the hill above them a yellow house kept guard with its tall green roof and green shutters on its many windows. Terence sported a bog rose in his lapel. He had picked it from a hedgerow that bordered a bowling green. It was too early in the year for players and the lawn was covered in leaves. Earlier he had passed a tramp who was fast asleep on a bench. Quite in character Terence placed some coins in the man's rigid hand. The dog sitting at his feet did not object.

"I wonder" Terence asked, "what inspired those earlier people who made this place famous apart from the light and the cheap living. Perhaps like me their body was in the north but their soul somewhere else in the less stringent but not so simple south."

"I think," said Albert, "that they had lived among the great artists of the day in Paris Berlin and Vienna, and as far south as Rome. They knew what the art world was all about and they just wanted a return to some sort of romantic life in their own country. There wasn't much influence from here. They had to create it."

Terence agreed. "They did well but that tone of spiritual isolation is over. We are not to hide from the world."

"Are you political?" Albert asked.

"I am but I haven't come out yet?" Terence replied. "I'm one of the post war unstable ones changeable like the weather." He pulled his coat tighter. "Does this wind ever stop?"

Albert sympathized. "It never does until well past midsummer when the heat diverts it. I have a woolen cape at home you can borrow while you're here. Even the women who lie naked on the beach have an easy time. If they're hardy enough nobody bothers them anymore.

"What else should I know?" Terence asked, smiling.

"They don't recognize fame here." Albert informed him.

As the evening sun finally appeared and he could loosen his collar, Terence continued. "What about infamy?"

"They see little of that." Albert advised.

"What do they see then?"

Albert thought for a moment. "The older people see a heritage disappearing. The young would like to follow it wherever it went."

"I don't see any sailing ships to take them away." Terence said. "Do they still close everything up on Sunday?"

Albert gave a mixed answer. "Mostly they do but in the tourist season greed overcomes spirituality and they might open again after the service."

Terence nodded knowingly. "It was ever so."

"Some of them are still devout." Albert said. Just then the hour rang on the church bell.

"How many churches?" Terence wondered.

"Only two now." Albert said. "One of them with a broken bell and no money to fix it."

Terence kicked the loose sand. "Do you know the pastors?"

Albert smiled. "I must introduce you to the young broken bell. Very modern in his outlook. Would play the guitar in church if they would let him."

"And the young girls," Terence wondered, "are they still as virtuous?"

Albert laughed. "I wouldn't know. I teach look over their shoulders but I'm not allowed to touch."

Terence was curious. "No revolts. No revolutions. No disturbances. No protest marches."

"All quiet on the western front." Albert reported.

Terence stopped and looked at Albert. "What will change it?" Albert did not reply as they walked on. As they reached the red house they saw the two sisters farther down the beach in earnest conversation and still in their costumes, both sporting parasols.

"It's cold." Terence shivered.

Albert smiled. "You'll know its really cold when the milk freezes in the pantry and the frost comes in the door."

"I hope I last that long."

"I hope so too." As Albert said goodnight and continued up the beach he called back. "It gets lonely up here. Stay awhile."

A creeping mist quickly took him out of view.

Chapter 4

The next noon Terence came around to the hotel and entered the lovely garden. There was a tree that stood just taller than a man and was already full of large white buds but no flowers. Beyond it and closer to the back of the hotel Michelle sat on a lawn chair. She had a dog at her feet and was seemingly focused on a heavy book. She wore a long white dress the fashion of a former time which may have reminded her or rekindled her memories when all was well because she didn't look too happy. From the distance of the garden fence about twenty feet, Terence could see that his estimation of her beauty from the previous sights of her was confirmed. Approaching her he saw she wore bangles on both wrists. Her hair was blond and drawn back from her forehead to the back of her head. Hearing his step she put down the book to her lap and sat up straight; a difficult feat in a lawn chair with a sloping back. On her feet he saw she had black lace up shoes with silver buckles.

The previous evening he had been introduced to her sister Susannah but not Michelle. Later that night in the moon glow of the northern spring he had seen them walking on the beach deep in conversation. There had been a hint of rain earlier and they carried parasols as if they had come from a fancy dress ball. Next to her there was an empty chair probably for

Susannah. When she turned her head his eyes found her flushed lips. For the present the rest of her came into focus and he set up a little dream time before saying hello to her. It was of finding her out in the garden apparently so he thought unprepared to meet anyone, especially a man. A stranger who had the advantage of having had the time to see her first and transfer as much of the spirit he found in her into his own. He realized at that moment that he had come upon her when she was most vulnerable; that is off guard. He did not notice Susannah who was on the telephone in the shadows of the hotel verandah.

When he had come to stay in the red house he had been received by the caretaker since Michelle and Susannah had been advised by the agents of Aunt Elizabeth that she didn't need them to look for a renter. The caretaker discovered that Terence had come north to write and soon the sisters and the whole township were aware of it. Some days ago Michelle had found him sitting on a white wrought iron art nouveau type bench looking out to sea. Both sisters were intrigued by the appearance of a writer so far north. As she came towards him the wind suddenly gusted and his hair partly shrouded the profile that had captured her attention. Although Terence was unaware of her interest it just seemed so natural to Michelle to be fascinated with him. Terence was one of those men who look as though they have a nice tan when actually it is the color of their skin though they are Caucasian. As Michelle came closer she expected him to turn and look at her. She scuffed her feet but there was no reaction. Michelle could have walked behind the seat instead she wet her feet on the grass a few yards in front of him and then stepped over to the seafront wall held on to the rail and slowly removed one shoe after the other and shook off the dampness. She wore a green suit with a hemline just below the knee so that when she lifted each foot a good piece of her leg appeared. When she was finished cleaning the shoes she had to straighten up her stockings above her ankles with her hands. Michelle restrained her urge to look at him but when she finally did he was openly admiring her in a quite satisfactory manner at least as far as she was concerned. Now she knew he must speak first and he did but merely wished her good morning. That was so short she wondered if her effort could be worth the trouble. He should rise physically if not to her bait at least with good manners. He did not get up. He seemed glued to the seat. It was then that she noticed the brace bulging out from the bottom of his left leg and felt a twinge of guilt but at the same time she found him more attractive. She instinctively wanted to embrace him, not physically but with attention. Yet her inborn discretion forced her to move on without introducing herself. Later, Albert told her all he knew of Terence including his war service and leg wound.

She at first seemed to him to be a rare form of butterfly and yet he had not found any desire to throw his net over her. She had a pearl at her ear and wore a pink shirt ruffed at the neck and her eyes were blue. When Michelle saw Terence come toward her she wondered at once how he had found the audacity to wear the white suit that he sported complete with an ugly rose in the lapel for those were all the flowers that were available at this time. But she was distracted at once by his beautiful voice that flew out at her like a hoarse lark and indeed for a moment she felt slightly out of her depth. But only for a moment that wonderful moment when she knew he admired her more than the painting that had found him so enthusiastic.

LOVE IN AN UNEXPECTED PLACE

Now she sat in her garden on a beach chair close to a rose tree. Her view was limited by the tree on one side and the hotel on the other. She was reading a book but it did not take away her boredom ; the ennui of a dying winter refusing to die. She shivered a little in the noon coolness. It was too early to be sitting out in the garden but she hated the inn. At least out here she could watch things grow ; not quite in any profusion yet but in time. The hotel was a place of labor a place full of books mostly chosen for other people that she had read over and over again. Outside, nature did not offer much change. It grew it retreated it grew again. When she slept with a man that happened too. She thought she knew everything yet did not feel wise. The man coming towards her through the gate seemed to have been more attracted to her younger sister. He introduced himself. She had never heard of him. It didn't matter.

Michelle put down the book to her lap.
"What's your book about?" he asked.
"It's a book of hymns."she replied quite self consciously.
He was curious. "Are you so religious?"
She thought that was a bad start. "Not really. But I do play the organ in church on Sunday when the regular player is away."
He stood with his hands in his pockets.
"Away? What does he do?"
"He fishes." she said, pertly.
"Not for men." he supposed.
"No," she angled her head, "nor for bread alone."
There was the empty chair but he didn't sit down.
"I believe I was invited for lunch with you and your sister."

Michelle stood up. "Of course. My sister is on the telephone, let's go inside."

When they entered the hotel Susannah was standing with the telephone in her hand and was obviously having an emotional conversation. She seemed to cut it short since she was so upset, yet she put the phone back carefully in the cradle and greeted them with a smile.

"I see you've met my sister."

He turned to Michelle. "I haven't found her name yet. I'm Terence."

Susannah was obviously in a hurry and spoke for her sister.

"This is Michelle and I am Susannah." they nodded and smiled at each other. "I've just been called to the house of the Norwegian painters. There are seven of them and they seem to have a problem with the house we rented." She turned to her sister. "Could you entertain Terence for lunch? Would that be alright with you Terence? Michelle made the soup today and that is her speciality so you are sure to like it." As she spoke Susannah drifted away and in a surprising move Michelle took his arm and led him through the dining room to a terrace filled with tables.

"I'm not putting you out I hope." Terence asked. "Your sister seems quite worried about the painters."

Michelle surprised him again. "I think she's in love with one of them. But you will need some food. Why don't you sit down and I will serve you personally. There's a menu in front of you. Would you like some wine?"

"I think I prefer beer today if you have any."

"No problem." she said. "Look on the back of the wine list."

"I'll have the Belgian." he said, without looking up at her.

"Good choice! You make your mind up quickly."

He made a wry face. "I suppose modest ones have that tendency."

"I'll presume that was meant for wit and not humility."

"That's another choice" Terence said. "I'll have the soup of course and I'd like to try the fish."

Michelle took the menu. "Should go well with beer. Baked or fried?"

"I'll try it fried if you please. I must tell you that my stomach is not used to rich food. What do you suggest?"

She came closer to him. "Why not try the baked halibut in blue cheese with some of those little spring potatoes. After the soup of course."

He showed some doubt. "Will the Belgian beer go with that?"

She smiled at him. "The German is lighter but I don't suppose you could stomach that."

"The war is over." he replied, softly.

Michelle gave a wry smile. "Is it?"

Terence reflected a little. "I had a poor memory before the war and I wonder how much worse it will be now."

Michelle proffered advice. "Better to have a little loss at this time otherwise you may never forget all you've been through."

Terence wondered how she knew so much about him and changed the subject. "Do you cook all this yourself."

She crinkled her brow. "Why? Can't you imagine me getting my hands dirty?"

He complimented her. "You look awfully smart to be a cook."

Michelle was equal to that. "I'm well paid to be a cook sometimes and smart all the time."

He tried again. "I suppose in that case they call you the chef."

"Well," she said with more confidence "now that we've got me tagged what are you up to in that big house?"

"If I could cook I might not be here." he said.

"What would you be doing?" she wondered.

"Asking you over for dinner."

She was surprised but had a quick answer.

"Breakfast might be a better idea. I only eat buttered toast and coffee for that."

Terence was pleased. "So you'll come."

She could hardly restrain her pleasure.

"Of course! I don't often get asked for breakfast. If you can make coffee and toast."

He teased her. "You sound as if you already had it in your mind."

"You can solve that mystery yourself. I am not handing out clues. So how do you decide who to ask for breakfast?" she wondered.

"I consider the question; would my mother like them? If they came to her house would she offer them tea and her home made fairy cakes?"

She blew out some air. "Fairy cakes!"

He pretended to be flustered. "If you don't feed the fairies they can get angry. Like not crossing a gipsy's palm with silver. Albert says you paint."

"Not for money thank goodness. I like to go on the beach and try my luck in all kinds of light."

"It's good you paint out of doors." he thought.

"Why is that?" she inquired.

"Well it's more likely to be an immediate sensation. No brooding gigantic canvases."

"They don't sell." she advised. "What do you think of my sister's work?"

"Well it's full of peasant scenes but no idea of how they live and their working conditions."

Michelle frowned.

"Has she any other problems?"

Terence was brutally honest. "Here she is in this wonderful light and she hasn't got control of the color the mood or the form. She's painting this place in the dark!"

Michelle was a little daunted. "You're quite a critic. What have you got that we can critique?"

"When the stuff I have in this notebook is done perhaps you can ease your knife into me but maybe you could feed me first."

"Of course! Coming up!" she disappeared into the hotel.

In his pocket Terence held the beginning of a chapter.

'Mr Sacha took a drink now and again. His habit was frowned upon by his wife and he had to hide his supply of liquor in the hothouse at the bottom of the walled garden. Mr Brown the gardener who did all the work around the estate had a habit too. He regarded Mr Sacha as a parasite and felt no remorse over sampling the hidden bottle when convenient. He substituted his sips with a little rainwater. Gradually neither of them could tell the difference between the ancient rainwater and the malt whisky. Since they were savoring forbidden fruit neither of them had the opportunity to compare their snifter with other more potent spirits. So eventually as the years rolled on they both became almost teetotal and happy in their secret addiction. Since there was no lack of rainwater and Mr Sacha was very rich they could both afford their habit. Mrs Sacha and Mrs Brown both ardent Rechabites who forbade alcohol had these two problem drinkers in common and were both under the illusion that their faith had worked wonders as promised in Jeremiah chapter xxxv, verses 6 and 7. They were fond of reading verse seven to their husbands.

'Neither shall ye build house nor sow seed nor plant vineyard nor have wine.'

Since Mr Brown had built the hot house and planted the seeds and Mr Sacha had provided the spirit the women never knew how ironic this was to both men each guilty in his own way.

In the other pocket Terence had his small notebook and a pencil. He wrote everything in pencil as if like the rest of his life whatever he wrote down could never be permanent.

Michelle came back with a tray of food.

"Coming up. Careful with the soup. It's hot and some of the older men say it's an aphrodisiac."

"I'll tell you when I need it." Terence quipped.

"I'll be glad to tell you too! But then you're coming from the war. You were hurt."

"Yes. But nothing permanent." he assured her.

"You smile." she complimented. "Others are bitter."

"I was too until the memory came back to me of the bodies around me in the mud and of all the men not whole anymore."

Michelle sat down with him.

"How did you survive the pain of it?"

"Apart from the drugs I just continued to write the play I had planned before the war. Of course it turned out badly. My mind had lost all feeling and I wrote like a sergeant major barking orders on parade or so my Aunt informs me. She's in the acting business you know and I suppose I should pay attention to what she has to say."

"But will you?" Michelle wondered.

He blew on the soup. "I think you get more stubborn when you've got nothing to lose."

Michelle was sympathetic. "But wasn't that your lifeline?"

"I thought so. But she was right. You either fly with art when it's good or drop anchor when it's bad."

"Mixed metaphor!" she advised him.

"Yes." he admitted. "I'm full of them. A long way to go."

"But you're stubborn."

"Not really." he said. "I've still got one leg to stand on and I can sit down to work. So I suppose in that way, yes."

Her curiosity showed now. "What work will you do?"

"I'm writing a novel." he ventured, a little self consciously.

She surprised him with her reaction.

"What on earth gave you the idea you could write a novel? Do you expect to improve on all the roman a clefs in the library?"

"Depth and perspective I hope." he said, defensively.

"Not real life then?" she insisted.

Her voice had grown softer so he took the question with some grace.

"Hardly. My aunt suggested it and I just thought it was time to stop reading the fiction of other people and make up some myself. Since the world seems to be in the process of destroying itself I supposed a little creation however small could be my contribution to try to put it back together again."

She smiled at him. "A noble thought."

"You mock me." he answered.

She surprised him. "There may be some of that but I think it's mixed with something else. I might be hiding something I'm a little afraid of at the moment."

He confronted her. "If you're going to be frank then let it all come out of you. Probably do us both some good. What's really on your mind?"

Michelle tried. "Like everybody else I'm caught in two minds. One is the reflex to hide the truth or part of it and the other is to blurt it out.

"There may be another." he suggested. "Which is to find the right words to make the truth palatable. Have a preface to soften it if need be."

"Is that your way?" she questioned.

"No not always but I'm aiming for it. I'm writing it down. Trying to civilize myself after losing so much of my veneer. I'm down to the raw nerves."

"Life is always long for those who get the hang of it early enough." she said. "When you feel old enough it's time for you be embalmed."

He smiled broadly at her. "Actually I prefer ashes."

"All the quicker to return perhaps." she retorted.

Terence sipped the soup then tried to change the subject.

"Your trees are in bud now."

"Yes but I miss the tulip tree that died last summer in the hot weather." She looked out to sea. "It was so young."

Michelle disappeared to get the entree. When she brought out the tray Terence was sitting opposite a large high backed chair with his good leg perched on top of it. He looked peculiar in that position but also very fine now she thought all in white and a small blue cravat at his neck. His hair was very black as was his moustache. She thought he looked handsome but had to disapprove of his brown high top boots.

She called out. "Here comes the fish."

He countered. "Stay well out of the way in case the old men are right about the soup."

"I have heard that the blue cheese is the antidote." she advised.

As he looked at the meal Terence reflected on their first meeting. "I wouldn't know. I saw a woman in green take off her shoes the other day. I don't think there's any cure for what went through my mind."

She teased him. "You must speak up when a woman gives you a signal."

"The trouble was I could hardly stand up."

Michelle sat down and beamed. "You did look set in your ways."

This seemed to get under his skin. "And what did you do in the war?"

"I suppose you mean while you kept our civilization free? My dear I am that civilization. I kept the home fires burning."

He started to eat. "I bet you did. I bet you did."

"Was I worth preserving?" she wondered.

"Time will tell." he said, without looking at her.

"Did the soup raise any hopes?" she quipped.

He buttered the bread. "Take off your shoes again and I'll find out."

She laughed at him. "You had your chance. No more signals."

Terence shuffled his feet. "Where is the green?"

"Hurry through amber before it turns red." she opened the silver dish. "Ah, here's the fish!"

"That's a big plaice." he gasped.

"We have very flat bottoms offshore." she advised.

Terence couldn't help himself. "I'm glad you said offshore."

"Eat up." she said. "It's your last free meal."

He picked up the fish fork. "Perhaps I came at the invitation of your sister."

"She's taken." Michelle said, too quickly.

"As we speak?" he wondered.

"Probably." she said, almost under her breath.

"This fish is delicious. Was that your painting I admired?"

Michelle smiled in triumph. "Yes!"

He made the right response. "Then it's you I've come to see."

She daunted him. "I sold the painting."

"Who bought it?" Terence asked, disappointed.

She put one foot up on the bench.

"The man in the wheelchair."

He looked at her tanned legs.

"Did you give him a signal too?"

She giggled. "No. Apparently he's legally blind."

He found his humor too. "Admirable taste though."

"The extra sense." she returned.

"Was it a finger painting?" he teased.

She prompted him. "Don't forget the blue cheese."

He made a face. "I've an aversion to it."

"Good news at last!" she said. "You're beginning to look charming."

"When a woman says that she usually means that the man is not quite good looking enough for her taste."

"My taste has tender edges." she advised

He picked up another piece of plaice. "Pray you find a gentle man with soft hands."

As she went to walk away a young woman came out of the hotel and spoke to Michelle.

"Hello Sofi. What can I do for you?"

"I need some provisions Michelle. I've left a list inside. I let myself run out of basic stuff."

"I'll have it sent over right away. By the way Sofi this is Terence."

When Sofi turned and looked into his eyes he saw the exceptional beauty of the girl and would never forget the hint of sadness there too. Terence tried to stand up to greet her but had been sitting in the one position too long. Michelle put her arm on his shoulder.

"He has a sore leg Sofi."

"Thank you for trying." Sofi said, and smiled at him then leaned over the table to touch his hand. It was a smile and a look gesture that he did not realize at the time could be returned. She strode away her red hair flying in the never ending wind and disappeared around the corner.

"She's a sad beauty." Terence said, wistfully.

"That young woman lost her fiancee last year and came here to recover herself. I think she is making a good job of that."

"Where does she live?" Terence asked.

"Just over the dunes from you." Michelle readjusted her dress then rose up and began to walk away into the hotel. "See you for breakfast. Whole wheat! Café con leche!"

Chapter 5

As Terence wandered homeward he found himself drawn over to see Sofi in her cabin. She was sitting outside on a bench writing.

He was taken by the fact that she had changed her clothes as if preparing for a lover. Her red hair was tied up except for some loose strands that seemed to catch the golden light. She wore a green dress with drapery across her breast suggesting thin strips of beaten metal. Sitting there on the bench so demurely she pulled the drapery across her shoulders with delicate fingers. Terence thought she looked like a poet ; a beautiful woman worth painting for posterity, to admire as she read her work. He was sorry when he saw her sitting there that he didn't have the bouquet of dog fennel he had once brought to Frances.

As he approached she stood up to greet him and he noticed the silk scarf around her waist. Sofi fluffed up her hair as if feeling that it had still not recovered from the quick wash of the morning. She was pleased to see him.

"It's very kind of you to come over Terence."

He smiled. "You remembered my name."

Her welcome affected him.

"It's not the usual William Robert or John."

"Neither is Sofi not Christina Lise or Jane, but I don't think you need one anyway."

"Sit down." she said, in her soft voice. You're living in the red house."

"Yes," he answered, "do you know it? Have you been in it?"

Sofi sat down and picked up her empty flower basket.

"Oh yes. I had a dream in it once when I thought we could rent it for our time here."

"That turned out badly Michelle says."

Her reply was not forced but slow.

"Yes…badly. There were no stars last night." Sofi continued standing up and stretching. "It's a bleak world without them. Especially without Venus. I always look in the late night and early morning for it."

"What about the moon?" Terence asked, admiring her.

She looked down at him from the end of the table.

"I was born on a Monday. The moon disturbs me."

Terence felt comfortable despite the hard bench.

"I saw a few bees this morning."

"Sometimes," Sofi said, her lips slightly convex, "they look like we do for the first crocus. They might be having some fun before the queen wakes up or they're searching for the black rabbit."

Terence was at a disadvantage. "The black rabbit!"

Sofi enjoyed his surprise. "Yes, it's a fairy story. If you see the black rabbit then you will have a long life."

He saw her momentary smile. "But bees only last a season."

"I know," she said, "but they may have some hope for another life like we do."

He replied with mock seriousness. "Everything, all reason seems to revolve around our expectations."

Sofi had the last word. "Yes, but that's a fairy tale too. Don't you think?"

He tried to brighten her day.

"I love your early roses."

"That's all I've got at the moment. These roses always rise to the occasion no back no front just roses, and like me they are often troubled by rust and powdery mildew or leaf spot."

"No white ones." he commented.

"Those are rare here," she said, making herself comfortable on the bench, "little white roses". Supposedly in Scotland, I've read they have a *'sharp smell that touches the heart.'* Sub arctic I think the sharpness I mean. It doesn't put the bees off. There should be no bees here until May I've been told and no butterflies just lots of wind. Do you love the house?"

"It's nice," Terence replied, "but I haven't really bonded with it yet. You seem quite at home here. I'm having breakfast at the house with Michelle in the morning. Would you like to come?"

"Some other time perhaps." she said, almost absentmindedly.

Her otherworldliness affected him.

"So you've been to the house. What did you think of it?"

"Oh yes." she replied. "The first day I was here that was the first time I was in there."

"It was empty of course." he said.

"No, Terence," she said rather seriously, "that day it was haunted."

"I've seen no ghosts." Terence replied, with a smile.

"They are there." she insisted. "Even the flowers nod like ghosts.

He was still doubtful. "In what form?"

"In what might have been." she said, mysteriously.

"Sofi, you are more mystical than any ghost. I have voices sometimes." he confessed.

She brightened up. "I do too! And sometimes I think of Joan of Arc and her voices. In my case I think I was on the English side."

"I think she would have forgiven you."

Now she laughed for the first time.

"The irony is that my voices speak better French than I do. I suppose that's the kind of life I'm living through at the moment but only for the moment. At some point I'll resume my human form again and fill my clothes properly the way I did before."

He gave her a worried look.

"Have you lost weight?"

She laughed again yet was touched at his concern. "No, just energy and animation. Now I know ahead of time that they are the first to go."

"I'm sorry Sofi, but you must come soon and let me see your work. I need some inspiration too you know."

She gave him advice. "Just sit quiet Terence and let it come out. A word here and there. Who knows when the hour or the day will come when the dam will burst. I write things too and try to set them to music. I need the words first you know. Sometimes something unexpected comes out. The music attracts it if I'm lucky. But at least I get some pleasure from constructing something new to me even if old in the repertoire no doubt."

"I have no music Sofi." Terence said, not sadly.

"It's in everybody's head." she assured him.

"I do have a piano." he said. "So I have no excuse."

She surprised him with her knowledge of the house.

"That Viennese music sitting on it is easy to play and sing. But I don't feel like singing not yet anyway."

"When you do come along and entertain me."

Her bright eyes lowered. "Those songs are for Spring Terence. It hasn't come yet." She picked up a bloom. "I'll be leaving here soon."

"Why is that? Aren't you settled here?"

"In other circumstances I might be but everybody knows why I came back. You see I'm allowed to smile but not to laugh. I can't sing and even a whistle might draw a frown. I must walk but never skip. All conversations are short otherwise I may be upset by an inconsiderate word. I must be perfectly groomed or else the man in the white coat may be called in to check on my mental health. If there's an empty shell then I should crawl into it. Everybody is kind sweet and gentle with me and on their best behavior. So I stay home most of the time when I should be out there walking and talking away whatever ails me. They probably think I'm like an anemone."

"Why do you say that?"

"They imagine I don't like to be disturbed."

Terence understood. "I'm lucky Sofi. Nobody knows any of my history. I can hirple around and nobody thinks anything of it. The only curiosity is my tenancy of the red house but now that they know I'm related to my Aunt that mystery is solved. I have asked Michelle not to say that I am attempting to write a novel and I haven't been asked about the plot etc. So far anyway."

"You are so young Terence to attempt it."

"Oh no! I've lived and died three lives already. Time has no place in my life. I've made all my recollections. I'm finished with the past. I can't remember it well enough to trust it. There are four tides a day but I am not one of them. Neither sadness nor joy has a hold of me. I look along the beach and see a mirage in the sky. The real world has not fallen down so far that I cannot raise it up. I have no expectations. That would only bring back my sorrows. Whatever is to come for me must be patched up with small incidents mostly physical in nature and not of the mind as before. See! I look at cherry blossoms as they fall. I am one of them. Completely out of control except to know I will fall to earth but to where I know not."

Sofi picked up a pair of scissors and chopped at the few flowers she had in the basket and her lack of response to his heartfelt exasperation with life daunted him but he persevered.

"What do you think is important to you now?"

Sofi looked at him knowing it was a genuine question.

"Finding a language to discover what can be salvaged. Perhaps your knowledge is greater than mine yet I suspect you are on a similar quest."

"No." Terence said. "I am just learning the shape of it. As if Proteus would stand still. Evil constantly changing its contours. Perhaps not only eternal but infinite. I'm not here to convalesce. I'm not sick. I didn't come to be cured. Why did you come back?" he asked, surprising her.

"To be in a place I fell in love with and where I was when my first love was lost. I could see the conjunction. Finding and losing was the place to be until time made a connection and then the place might have less meaning. I know you've had a loss of some description Terence. Hardly anybody comes here unless they are very happy or very sad. You and I don't look happy but you're a man and people expect you to be stronger. Well, I'm over my sickness if that's what they call it nowadays and quite ready to face the world the way I did before I ran away from it some months ago. I'm leaving though I love this place. I'd rather be invisible for a while get lost be a woman and not a figment of one. This would be easier to bear if I was responsible for it but of course I am as transparent to the locals as a jelly fish. They seem to me to be a group that rarely vent their feelings and now those faces that can rarely be read register my misfortune in their very silence and care for me. I must become anonymous or go mad."

"Are you religious Sofi?

Sofi thought for a moment.

"I'm free and that's as close to divinity as I'll ever get I suppose. I lost my balance for a time but I'm gradually getting it back like my music, some harmony. This is just a temporary rest I think. It's not permanent."

"When will you go?" Terence asked.

"In the night." Sofi stretched out her hands. "I'll leave all this behind me beautiful and tranquil as it is. I should exit this place before I get within a mile of a mad midsummer."

Terence protested."There are plenty of hares around Sofi but I don't think you're going mad."

"Sometimes the sacrifice of gold can temper passion. When the sun finally getsround so far north as the front of the house I should be gone."

"You've thrown off one sadness and perhaps taken on another." he said.

"No, Terence. It has got rid of me. The horse I was riding threw me off looked round at my astonishment and wondered how long it would take me to walk home by myself in one piece. People say I have become a recluse you know but it isn't true. Getting through this time in my life has made me feel more connected to the world than ever. The poetry and the music are my spiritual connection. I don't see how we can be human without music."

He praised her. "Michelle says you've written some lovely poetry."

Sofi gave a wan smile. "I've used it all up Terence. There is no more. I've emptied myself. I'm cured and have pronounced myself fit."

"It may take me longer." he said. "A man is only half human without a woman or so my aunt says."

"Your aunt has a great belief in womanhood."

"Especially her own! he assured her.

"I'd offer you some tea Terence but I've been careless with my supplies. Hopefully Michelle will send them soon. I've got some lemonade I think. So you are writing. Is it going well?"

"It comes and goes Sofi."

She was quick to reassure him. "I have no head for prose and poetry is so moody or you have to be in the mood."

"I'd like to share that with you sometime Sofi."

"That would be fine Terence. Perhaps just before I'm ready to leave. If you can spend some time with Michelle the time won't matter. Do you feel close to her? You seemed to be enjoying each others company so much. She's a fine person."

"You're very direct Sofi."

Sofi smiled. "Michelle can't ask."

Terence looked across the dunes.

"Nor can I answer and perhaps she knows that already. I'm writing but finding it hard going."

Sofi laughed shyly. "There's enough trouble in this world Terence without taking on the perils of another."

Terence brightened up. "At least I have some control over this one the one in my imagination."

"Even our imagination can mislead us sometimes," Sofi said, "it's so flimsy and full of traps. Whoever your characters are Terence treat them well, and if they can't support your dreams let them join in."

He looked at her with a rare smile.

"You're a very profound young lady."

She was philosophical. "Terence, just as a man is only as good as the woman he is with so it is with the woman."

Terence wanted to touch her face but instead stroked one of the blooms in her basket."You have a sister at least Michelle says you have."

"Yes. Actually we are twins sisters but not really alike in more ways than one, though people sometimes have trouble telling us apart."

"Sometimes that happens." he said, sympathetically.

"Did you have siblings?" she asked.

"No." Terence said. "I'd have liked a sister."

Her face lit up. "I'll be your sister!"

Her sudden animation flattered him.

"I'd be better looking then."

"Michelle seems to like you the way you are."

"We became friends just today."

"I've seen you and heard you together. You had fun at lunch. I was afraid to come out. As I sat inside the hotel she kept up a commentary for me about you so I know more than you think. She's been in need of that for some time. Actually since I've been here, a few months.

Terence looked into the cabin. "You have a piano in the house I believe."

"You have a house Terence. I have a hauschen a place to play."

"Will you play something for me? Something I will remember you by." The wind had suddenly died in the light brown air. Terence looked at his watch. "I've taken so much of your time Sofi. What is your sister's name?"

"Sara. Sara and Sofi. She was out first."

LOVE IN AN UNEXPECTED PLACE

Terence stood up preparing to leave. "When the song comes Sofi then you must come and sing it for me."

"I will Terence. I'm working on it now."

"Then I'll take my goodbye." He bent down and kissed her brow and she touched his hand again slipping her fingers across his palm.

Sofi went inside and in a few moments the sounds of Bach played tenderly almost muted came out to him. When Sofi stopped playing she did not come back out and Terence knew to walk away and disappear over the dunes. The image of the red necklace the alabaster skin and the wistfulness of the music to carry him home and inspire him to sit down to have the courage to write.

Sofi turned over the sheet she had on the music stand and read the words she was putting to music.

"We have taken our goodbyes,
it was hard but there it lies.
But what does it matter
if we find such love again.
Lost love, love, love.
Found love, love, love.
We must look for love again."

***

No sooner was Terence home than the shutters began to shudder against the walls. The ocean had decided to welcome him with blasts of wind and vicious rain that lashed the windows. Terence took out his notebook and went upstairs in the hope that the storm would inspire some descriptive words or perhaps a situation or two. As he sat at the window seat all he found was an early darkness and the beginning of depression. He remembered a conversation with his mother in the middle of the war.

"Do you think I raised you to give away your life so cheaply as cannon fodder? All this time through the generations of us nobody cared. Now they want us to save them. Well, you're not going!"

"Everybody's going." Terence said, as stoutly as he could.

His mother was unrelenting. "We gave them your Uncle. One is enough."

Terence held his head in his hands.

"The girls are giving out feathers."

"Not your Uncle's girl! They'll soon run out of them. Look at the bread it's black! There's no flour in it. There's no food in the house. When did we last have an egg? No! You're not going!"

He tried to reason with her.

"One less mouth to feed."

"It won't be yours!"

When he was posted missing in action she took the telegram into her bedroom and never came out alive. In all the random ways of fate his survival could not save her end. He had the feeling of growing old too soon when he got the news.

Terence had not got past writing his name a hundred times a day. Yet in other more stressful times the ideas scenes dialogue had poured out. The house was full of books and he relapsed into reading the works of others. He considered using a black man in his stories. He had seen some soldiers from Africa in the war and remembered being told that it was supposed by both Christians and Muslims that Ham the son of Noah descendants were black. When he saw men not naked or drunk he was pleased.

Terence had found a dry spot on some planks and took out his notebook. A few moments later he attracted the attention of one of the African soldiers who stopped on the other side of the dry spot.

"Do you speak English?" Terence asked him.

When the man answered: "Of course." Terence realized that he was just as racist as the men who called these men rag tags.

Sahib the Indian said. "Why do you sit out here with us and not inside with your own people?"

"You know very well," Terence replied, "that sometimes you must sit with your back against the wall in a separate place."

"Yes, I know. But you are the first of your kind that I have known who might be dreaming of his own garden. We believe that if God has not granted us one that he at least allows us to imagine that we do." As he pointed across the wasteland of war beyond he continued. "Even some animals like to be alone. I see you writing down your dreams but I wonder at those ones."

"Words are not instinctive." Terence said. "We make them up."

The man readjusted his muddy turban.

"Yes, we do. But I am curious sometimes whether even with the lack of them that the animal understands more about his life than we do about ours."

"That my friend is the mystery we have been burdened with.'

"Why would God do that?" the man wondered.

"I don't know," Terence said. "Perhaps the evolution of the body is too slow and God grew impatient and let the mind change faster."

The Indian qualified."But not always forward or permanently."

Terence stood up. "Let's hope we have the time left to determine the purpose."

"Do you know there's a crazy officer who is asking his men to kick footballs as they attack the enemy trenches?"

"Yes, I know." Terence said, shaking his head.

"Will you be kicking them too?"

Terence smiled. "No. I'm a cricketer ; wicket keeper actually."

"Well, you'll be taking the field tomorrow better pad up. No sign of the sports of kings."

"No, they are all safely in stables." Terence assured him.

The soldier picked up his rifle.

"All I know my friend is that this short silence is sweet."

Terence was pleased that he had stopped calling him sahib.

He introduced himself. "My name is Terence."

"I know. I am Assad and I believe we might have met before."

With this mysterious sentence he climbed over the parapet.

In the morning they lay in a bloodied peace. Bodies at ease; minds asking no questions ; the survivors looking on dumbfounded ; wondering where to start ; like the first search of bees for honey.

Terence now regretted that he had never looked at a map of India. When he saw all this waste he wondered at the authorities allowing it. But then he remembered ; those who had made a profit from it had already been paid. The market was as limitless as the unpopulated mud he saw every day through the periscope from his observation post.

He thought he must recover now that the war was over, whatever he had lost. However he was having a hard time determining what it was he had lost. In the hospital the wounded were full of prophesies good and bad. He had decided he didn't want prophets. He would be his own and make up his own world recall conversations of bright and dark outlook. Of how the new rulers of defeated countries would be blamed for every blunder and before long they would be held responsible for the defeat and not the real culprits the warmongers the supposed men of action. One of the soldiers though wounded wanted the war to go on forever. He had no other life.

'Where else will I get pay and food?'

Terence considered now that he was well out of the political pantomime. There were so many horrors not to be forgotten but hopefully walked or run away from. He wanted to go out into the woods and shout messages to those who had died but there were no trees and he didn't think you could call into the ocean. They were all under the earth.

Terence thought about Michelle and how sharp her tongue and mind. His aunt had been right he did compare her with Frances. He'd had little time with either of them to be able to find their shades and was not so sure as he began to ponder whether or not he had really loved Frances. He had a photograph of her standing in medical white beside another woman. Now, as he looked at her he realized he might not be able to fill her loss. Yet whether his feelings had been deep enough or not he knew that she had loved him. In so many ways she had shown him her care and affection. He recalled the time when a whiff of her perfume came over him as she leaned across to make him more comfortable in the hard hospital bed. He remembered how the memory of it had sent him into an amorous dream that turned to desire in the following cold and misty mornings when she had wheeled him around the hospital grounds. Those hoary morning times when little birds look for cream and love strikes without warning.

Frances walked toward him when the sun came up that morning. She came over and sat down.

"I don't know what to do.' she said.

He held her hand and she took off her glasses before kissing him. His depression lifted. He got mentally well and fell in love with the fair haired girl who had dedicated her life twice ; once to the easing of human suffering in general and the other to Terence in particular. In the black and white image before him he could not now see the blush in her cheeks or the bluebell in her eyes nor could he forget them.

Terence sat down and tried to write an inspirational paragraph for his novel. He strugged with his feeling and aspirations

"There's a whole life of regret and forgetting. Lay it down flat and be aware if it's natural. Feel free to put it away by just a little each day. There's something magical or semi comic tragical in a way. At times in the depths of love there is no inspiration ;so complacent and happy the soul and the heart can be. God of Inspiration suspend some words in the air for me to touch. Send me...a modest gift; let me be your guest. I won't ask for much and I'll do my best. For early flowers open all the doors; welcome them home from colder shores."

Chapter 6

The first thing Terence knew about the morning was when the sun came through the white curtains just above the bedroom window sill; the pattern of the fabric elongating the width of it and as it slowly rose turning the white walls of the room to cream. As he wrote later. *The sun on your eyes as you wake up is better veiled like this. Raw nature can be overwhelming. As we first come into the world headlong so, as we awaken again we should be sheltered a little from its reality. It feels good to be caressed by the world and not pitched into it so nakedly.'*

With the weather cleared and as arranged Michelle appeared on the beach. Terence watched her walk all the way from the town entrance to the shore and then quite slowly towards him as though looking for treasures in the drift. She came closer walking so well even in her rubber boots he remembered his mother saying that you couldn't fatten a thoroughbred. She wasn't a horse but her class and grace were evident.

She came within hailing distance and raised her hand in greeting and triumph with what turned out to be a small red shell in the shape of a heart. He had wondered how she would dress for their first meeting and was quite taken when he saw the lovely pearls on her neck and the bright red lipstick that did not really look right on her pale face. She had long insubordinate hair and seemed to be constantly brushing it from her face.

Below a brown corduroy skirt she wore a pair of green wellington boots. She had been wearing a wide brimmed hat but had lost it a few times in the wind and now held it in her hand along with a lavish, very chic bag.

He greeted her with a smile.

"You look dandy in those boots."

Michelle came on to the concrete deck and dunted her feet on the side of it to get rid of the wet sand.

"Don't worry." she reassured him. "I've got proper shoes in the bag."

"What else have you got in there?" he wondered. "You might need a torch to find anything in it."

"Six pancakes!" She blurted out. "In case you can't make toast!"

He teased her a little. "Any maple syrup?"

"You must have butter and jam!" she cried out, pretending to be exasperated.

"I've got those," he said, "and marmalade."

She sat down on a wooden bench and put on her shoes

"That will do then." she announced quite calmly and happily.

He was so taken by her spirit he wanted to take her hand but contented himself with another welcome.

"Come on in. Have you been here before?"

"Oh yes." she said. "Half the town looked in here while it was being built and even later I am told before the lady moved in and I'm no stranger."

He purposely stammered over…"My dear Aunt Elizabeth." substituting p for b in Elizabeth. Terence thought he should tell her that in case she had acid poised lurking, at the tip of that quick tongue.

"Really! I only met her once as she was passing through. She seemed nice. Always courteous to the help you might say. We fed her sometimes."

"She's old style. Manners matter. You're a little wet."

"I won't melt." she guaranteed.

"No." Terence agreed. "I think you are quite substantial. How do you reckon good weather?"

"I look into the south eastern sky as the sun rises and if I see Venus then I have a good idea it will be good."

As they came into the house they were greeted with the smell of frying bacon. She looked on the stove.

"So you can cook!"

He turned down the gas. "Eggs and bacon and a little speciality I learned from a Scotsman in hospital."

"What's that?" she was curious as all good cooks are.

Terence played with the food.

"A little treacle bun he called it fried with the bacon and eggs. I brought some up with me and keep them frozen."

She sat down. "I'm starving. I usually eat breakfast at six in the morning."

"This won't take long." he told her. "I just have to grind the coffee beans. Would you like to see the house while it cooks?"

His weather beaten smile affected her. She turned away from the stove. "Yes. I know a lot of the furniture has gone."

He touched her arm softly for just a moment.

"Go and explore while I turn myself and this pan down to a slow heat."

Michelle had never heard that line before.

In the living room Terence had lit a fire and she was taken by his care and preparation; he was serious. The logs had a fresh smell and nothing more. The house was too new and unlived in. She sat down on one of the armchairs and adjusted the silk cushion resting her head on the white antimacassar and dreaming as the eastern sun forced itself through the windows. The flowers in the room had been watered and brought back to life before growing old. The older ones plucked but not before their time. Her appetite grew in more than one place and she moved back to the kitchen to satisfy one at least.

"Let's have a look and see what you think." Terence suggested "We should start at the entrance passage. Around the corner."

"I love those benches." she enthused. "I wondered if that was real stone?"

"I'm not sure." Terence said. "I think that's what they call faux marble."

Terence opened the wide door and they looked right into the interior across the dining room and out through a window that was topped by fresh looking blue and white check roller blinds. Almost directly from there they found a bedroom with an antique bed that had a camel back curved posts and was draped around in yellow then topped by a crested tester.

"This is lovely." Michelle exclaimed as if she had never seen the house before. "She walked across the bare wooden floor to the window and fingered the matching curtains. In one corner there was a lectern with some music open on it.

"I think this was meant for my Aunt's tenor friend." Terence advised. " But I'm as musical as a one armed pianist."

"That covers most of us." Michelle warned him as she trilled a few keys.

Michelle sat down on the little ottoman and the light flooding in gave her blonde hair another shade almost of cascading cream.

"Where do you sleep?" she asked, coyly.

Terence didn't notice the coyness which pleased her.

"At the top of the house overlooking the sea."

"Wasn't there a piano?"

"There's a music room too, upstairs. I had it moved." he assured her.

As they wandered through the house Michelle continued her praises. "I've always liked the way she combined the rustic with the sophisticated."

He looked around him with some pride.

"Parisians always seem to have dreams of the country." As they looked around together there was an easy quietness.

Michelle was first to break the hiatus.

"Has this house affected you yet?"

"Why do you ask that?" Terence wondered.

"Well," she explained, "it seems to have affected everybody else who has lived in it. Even Sofi who only spent a few hours in it."

"Yes, she did mention a ghostly feeling. My Aunt couldn't afford a church so she built a flying buttress and hoped the rest would follow but of course it didn't and it does look unfinished from certain angles yet sometimes the dreams of the builder can affect the future owners."

Michelle mused a little. "It's not everyone who can find a dark spot on the moon."

As they traveled through the house Michelle found nothing she could criticize.

"It's so uncluttered. She has wonderful taste. Painted surfaces and furniture. Scrubbed floors and the house is full of our wonderful light. You should do well here. Someone had a dream when they made this place this palace. I notice there are lots of clocks in the house."

"Four to be exact," Terence explained, "though none of them are exact. That one is twenty minutes slow and chimes the hour at twenty past it. The one in the hall chimes exactly one minute before the hour. The alarm goes off but once at two minutes to nine in the morning. The one on the far wall in the living room is close to being at the correct time."

"So how do you tell the time?" Michelle wondered.

"My watch is always correct."

She was puzzled. "But you love clocks?"

"No," he insisted. "like whoever set them up I prefer intervals and reminders."

She was still puzzled. "How so?"

"The bird that chimes the hour a minute ahead every hour encourages me to do something if I'm idle. The alarm asks me to get myself together. I have no place to go so that its only use."

Michelle smiled at his reasoning.

"And the one twenty minutes slow?"

"That reminds me if I hear it that I may not have started what the earlier one suggested."

"And the nearly correct?"

"Oh I never pay attention to that one because it doesn't chime which is why I have it in a place where I can see it very easily."

"And your watch?"

Ah, he said. "I only wear it because otherwise I wouldn't know the time when I'm not home."

"Don't you wear it in the house?"

He pulled up his shirt sleeve. "Never."

"Sounds like a good system." she agreed, impressed.

Terence continued. "An uninterrupted hour drives me mad. I must have some order in my life."

Michelle walked to a window and looked out at the water. "Sounds like just an approximation of disorder to me."

"It's the way I work." he said, somewhat pompously she thought. "Not an exact science."

When they finally got up to the music room there was an operetta piece on the the piano. Michelle sat down and played a few notes and spoke the words... *When the moon is shining bright, through the darkness of the night, then I wait alone, for love has flown.'*

"We'd better go down and eat," Terence suggested, "before the bacon burns away. Yes. It's a palace of dreams. Too bad they didn't come true."

"Has it set you off dreaming too?" she wondered, as they sat down to the meal.

"No, at least not until yesterday." he said, a little mysteriously.

Her interest was piqued.

"What happened yesterday?"

"Oh all sorts of things have crossed my mind since I got here. You should eat up!" he urged her. "I lie in bed or on that chaise, and everything that has passed as experience collects itself and seems ready to overwhelm me. I've begun the novel I came here to write but whatever comes out is stuttering out and quite incoherent. Hardly anything of substance has come. For a while I thought the sea was rising to drown out whatever voice I had gathered together in the years of somber existence. And then for some reason or another when I came back here after lunch with you yesterday and had my brief talk with Sofi all the fears went away as if they had never existed. I couldn't believe that the cure was simply a conversation with women I hardly knew. After all I've had many of those but somehow something blew up between us that made a difference and opened up the cloud over the world. I've the feeling now that I can get something done."

Michelle stopped eating.

He picked up the coffee pot but did not pour any coffee. "I don't have any explanation," he continued, "I hardly know how it happened. But the cynicism that seems to have depressed me was raised. For the first time in months I didn't dream myself to sleep last night. I just turned out the light and woke up at seven o' clock. I don't know what else to say or even what to do."

Michelle made to rise towards the stove.

"The rest of the bacon is burning but I do like it that way."

He attended to the bacon.

"Is that all you can say?"

Michelle reached for the brown sauce.

"Do you think I came here just for breakfast? Why don't you just turn off the heat under the food and stop talking. The sun rises in the east which is just outside that lovely patio. Why don't we sit out there for a while and hold hands in between eating the burnt bacon and see where that leads us."

Once outside Michelle poured two cups of coffee.

"Is that enough cream?" she asked.

He shaded his eyes from the watery sun and for the first time in half a year was able to praise a woman.

"There isn't a man in the world who wouldn't want extra cream from you."

Terence said this with such artlessness and meaning that Michelle found it hard to mask her pleasure.

"Sit round a bit away from the glare. You're full of words."

Terence was not so sure.

"Not usually. It seems you're bringing them out of me."

She was open. "I have no relationships with anyone right now."

He was a little flustered. "Is that another signal?"

Michelle caught his hand. "Some might call it a right of way."

He lifted the coffee. "You should be writing the novel."

"I'll stick to the watercolors. How is your leg?"

"Why! I forgot about it. I suppose you've heard all this before. Oh, the bacon is black."

"What do you mean?" Michelle wondered.

"You know." Terence said. "A man saying he admires you likes you."

"Not so often." Michelle said. "Men say lots of things and I don't always hear them if they're at the uninterested side of me."

"Attraction not working both ways." he conjectured.

She agreed. "Yes, like that. Never quite being right for both parties."

He wiped his mouth. "No conjunctions."

Michelle elaborated. "You could say that but it's a bit too formal. It's all flesh and blood and careless words in the end. When every word was so carefully chosen at the beginning."

"You've been in love I think." he said.

She made a face. "Why do you say that?"

He put his good foot up, lazily.

"I recognize it from your lack of passion. You're full of reason. So I know you might have used up your heat and not too long ago. You haven't had time to get it back. Did you lose a love?"

Michelle still had a little frown on her face.

"I might ask you the same question."

His answer cleared it away.

"She died in the epidemic."

Michelle put her coffee down.

"Oh dear. Recently?"

"I haven't counted the time." he reacted.

She took his hand and wove her fingers between his. As he raised his eyes from the gesture to her face there was a gentle rush of blood to her cheeks ; to hide it was her first move. She pretended to wipe away the hair that had blown across her face and finally turned her shoulder slightly on him. Michelle looked down the long husk of the beach. Terence moved his chair nearer to her and put his free hand around her shoulder. She was afraid to look at him.

"I know you think I may be on the rebound but I'm not." he said, quietly. "I've been going through that possibility in my mind since yesterday. But no analysis of my feeling seems to make any difference. I didn't come here to look for a woman or for love. I'm still not sure if I should be speaking to you like this but believe it or not I feel that to write a true novel what you might call making things up, I have to be honest and so my feelings have arrived."

She turned now and held his free hand.

"I'm not sorry for you. I mean for being wounded or for needing nurturing because you lost a lover. I've lost too. It was a year ago and he's still alive and was in my mind in the garden before you came there yesterday. But I've let him go now."

"Where did he go?" Terence asked. "Physically I mean."

"It seems as far away from me as he could. As a missionary to China of all places. He was the assistant pastor here. Then we fell in love and he went to hell. At least that's what he called it."

"Why do you think he chose China?" he asked.

"Probably to look for the graven image he couldn't find here."

He pushed her hair slowly, gently away from her face.

There was a curious look on his own face. "What were his last words to you?"

She smiled, slowly. "He said to try not to miss him."

Terence couldn't hide his need to know.

"What did you say to that?"

"I said I was willing." She laughed. "And he thought that was the only time I was."

Terence persisted. "What attracted you?"

Michelle thought for a moment.

"I think because he was such a gentle soul. I wanted to mother him. He needed mothering. And then suddenly I didn't feel like being such a woman. He asked me right at the beginning if I had been saved. I said I thought so but that the Devil had put up a good fight for me."

Terence entered the frank mood.

"Did you sleep with him?"

She lifted her eyes to him.

"I was never asleep. Though at times I felt like dozing off."

"There must have been more than mothering."

She continued hardly against her will, needing to get it out of her mind.

"I heard him say something I thought was wise at least for a priest."

"Do you still remember it?"

"Yes." She hesitated and then got it out. "He said that no matter how many changes of religion there had been believers considered that though there was so much to be gained by renewal they were also afraid to lose all of what had gone before."

Terence was now fully into her story.

"I suppose he might have meant the rituals."

"I think he would have been happier as a Catholic though from what I know of his lust that might not have worked for him."

Terence edged closer. "What else do you remember?"

Michelle laughed. "Are you taking this down? He was very good at being full of himself and liked large loops on his y's."

Terence couldn't restrain his own laughter.

Michelle continued. "He looked sometimes like one of those religionists who had suddenly heard of Darwinism and feared now for his living; his interest in nature now suspect; the Bishop frowning so much at his insect collections that he put them up for sale. He was always attracted to young couples in love. Interested it seemed to me in a form of love where he had no experience."

" Hiding something." Terence guessed.

" No doubt. Far too mysterious for me."

Terence decided the seriousness had gone far enough. "Well, did he ask to see your golden calf?

She responded in kind. "I don't think he got that far in his studies."

"You should have been a lawyer." Terence said.

"You're the one asking the questions and making the conclusions." she responded.

He took his hand away.

"I suppose you think I'm just a silly man."

"No. You're quite normal in my experience."

He showed his puzzled look.

"Why do women persist with men?"

She burst out laughing.

"Boredom. Lack of chocolate. The danger of cigarettes and alcohol. All the seven deadly sins but gluttony before marriage of course."

"You're fresh." he said, his admiration obvious.

She was quick. "Not off the shelf you mean?"

He took her hand again.

"You're in the front window."

She pressed his hand too. "Ah, but without a price tag! You'd have to enquire within."

"Within?"

She teased him. "Perhaps."

Terence sighed. "You said I wasn't to think you were sorry for me? Did you mean that?"

"I don't think there's a lie in me for you." she said.

Terence trusted her. "Maybe that's why the pastor went so far away."

"Oh I don't know." she said. "I think my machinery broke down. It needed fine tuning and he was the wrong mechanic. Could you put up with such a needy woman?"

Terence broke into a smile. "You smell nice."

"I am a woman." she assured him and then changed the subject. "Do you know what they are saying about you in the town?"

He made a face. "What interest could I hold for them?"

"To begin with they don't know you, and so they have to pretend to know even invent stories about you."

Terence was intrigued. "What could they invent?"

"They have seen your injured leg and so you are a hero perhaps. They were so far removed from the war that the least connection grows out of proportion. So the local storytellers are busy. Not much to tell so far but told with conviction."

"Will you add to the story?" he wondered.

She squeezed his hand again.

"I'd rather be part of it."

Terence smiled. "I'm glad I didn't bring a dog. I'm sure its pedigree would be suspect."

"Oh, we have an expert for that. It wouldn't have stayed a mystery for long."

Before he could answer a tall man came up the beach towards them.

"Who's this?" Terence wondered.

"Erik. The postman. See he has no postbag. He's one of the storytellers and a lecher."

Terence commented. "Women don't like lechers but I suppose there's a place for them."

She disagreed. "Not in my bed!" Still, she was civil to him.

"No mail delivery today Erik?" she called out.

"It came early and I've the day to myself now." He then turned to Terence. "Are you renting this place?"

"His aunt owns it." Michelle advised him.

"Oh, so you're not a tourist or a foreigner. Your Aunt is a beautiful woman."

"Lots to gossip about Erik." Michelle said.

"That's my wife's job." he warranted.

Michelle lay back in her chair enjoying herself.

"How is she these days? Still steaming open love letters?"

"Ha! Ha! Your sister is down the beach with the painters. There will be some juicy stories from there shortly. Will you be playing at church on Sunday?"

Michelle was blunt. "I will. But you won't be turning the pages any more so don't get excited."

Erik was not daunted. "Oh well. At least I've got this to pass on to the wife and she will be grateful."

"Too bad she's in a wheelchair these days." Michelle said, with little enthusiasm.

He replied tartly. "There are other compensations you know. It's not all sex."

"You can always look through the letter boxes." she responded.

"Don't listen to her." Erik said to Terence. "I'm sorry I didn't catch your name."

"Terence." he said a little tersely. Then his first impression of Erik changed when the man went on.

"She has sharp tongue but her heart is soft. Look there for the gold."

"Be off with you!" Michelle said in a quieter tone. "You've been reading the novelettes again. You're in a class by yourself."

"I'm grateful for your crumbs." Erik answered, going away.

"Watch out for the birds." she advised him.

As Erik disappeared behind the dunes Terence smiled at Michelle. "He seems to like you. He says you have a heart of gold."

"The parson couldn't find it." she replied, quietly looking him in the eye.

Terence was quick. "He didn't take it away with him either."

Michelle smoothed her skirt over her knees.

"Erik posed for me once that's when I discovered lechery. He went forty kilometers south in a train a few months ago and came home a world traveler. My sister has her knife in him too."

"Which one?" Terence wondered. "The short one she fillets the fish with or the one she uses to cut bread?"

"She's dangerous with either one." Michelle assured him.

"Do you see me in oils?" he wondered.

Her coyness returned. "No. A charcoal sketch."

"Not very flattering." he said.

She looked to the sea. "There's a storm coming. We have one every day or so this time of year."

Terence adjusted his legs.

"With all this weather how do you ever manage to get paint on canvas?"

"I don't paint much at this time. I like the summer and the autumn for that" She put her hand on him again. "But the spring has other delights."

"You are very direct," Terence said, "but I won't be running away to China."

"No," she replied, "I'm sure of that. Not after all you've been through." And then she surprised him again with her frankness. "What do you like about me?"

He didn't hesitate as if it had been in his mind had been considered. "You would do very well on the boulevards."

She was surprised. "Of Paris! You think?"

He couldn't seem to hold in his admiration.

"Even in those big boots you walk well. Your mind is no slouch and neither is your figure."

She tried to smooth her hair a little nervous now.

"I'm not the only one who speaks her mind."

"What would I have to hide?" Terence said. "I'm here to write a novel. I'd better show myself before I cover it all up in prose."

"Is that what you'll do?" she questioned. "I don't believe it."

"You're an artist," he said, "and it's hard for you to hide anything on the canvas; it's all on there. By the way I liked your self portrait in the hotel the woman walking through the cornfield looking at a world you seem to want to disconnect from."

"Really! I suppose you think that's quite perceptive of you."

"It's my version." he responded.

She stood up. "Well, it was a good breakfast but the coffee needs to be stronger."

"I'll do better next time." he assured her.

"You're not wearing the brace." she commented.

"No."

"Do you need it to walk?" she asked.

Terence got up. "I'm going to try to do without it today."

"The sand is still hard." she said. "Will you walk a little way with me?"

He pulled down his trouser leg. "It was my first intention."

"I'm distracting you," she said, not really meaning it.

"Yes." he admitted. "I didn't expect it but I'm glad of it."

"My sister is much more beautiful than I am and the painters will soon be gone. She's sure to show a lot of interest in you."

Terence was puzzled by her lack of confidence.

"What makes you say that?"

"Well, you praised my painting and she neglected to tell you that it wasn't hers. I had a feeling about that."

"You didn't show it." he said.

She continued. "You saw me twice before lunch yesterday and there was no interest from you in me."

He took her arm. "Aren't there any young men around here?"

"Yes! And she let out a yell. "But they all smell of fish!"

"They say fish food makes you smart." he said.

"There's a madhouse further south!"

"What inspires you apart from the scenery?"

Again she surprised him. "Melancholy perhaps ; I'd like to get out of here as soon as possible."

"Why the hurry?" he wondered.

"Well, I'm more or less a slave to the business. It's not hard work but there's no relief. We can't afford extra help when we want a holiday. Oh a day here and there but nothing substantial."

"You should have gone to China." he suggested.

Her reply was fast enough for Terence. "I didn't like the company I'd have to keep and I don't eat rice."

"This place once fostered great art. Did the locals realize that it was being produced amongst them?"

"Not in the least." she advised. "They have their own art their songs and dances and have no time for classical music or art that to them are just pale copies of what they see every day with their own eyes. The fiddle the song the dance ; a flagon of beer is enough for them."

"The future is dead." he suggested.

"Exactly." she agreed. "And quite right when you consider what the present has brought us. I suppose I've been too long with fishermen. They go from danger to monotony and little in between. They are not delighted by their condition. Why should they consider the future when the present life seems so unalterable? The future is dead! No, it may never exist."

"Did you lose many people in the war?" he wondered.

"No." she advised. "Getting food was more important than having our young men fight. We have so few of them anyway and armies need to eat."

"But no visitors?"

She kicked a stone. "Hardly any. Some soldiers on leave."

"None stole your heart." he ventured.

She didn't bite. "I didn't know I had one in those days. You haven't asked about my father and mother."

"You look like an orphan."

Her brow seamed. "Not too well brought up you mean?"

"No," he was quick to say, "I just didn't want to think of any other connection."

"My sister is a connection."

"Yes. But she seems…"

She put the word in his mouth. "Different?"

"I don't have a word to cover it." he responded.

"My mother is dead and my father is not much help. He goes south for a holiday this week to his sister's place. We are worried about him."

"What's wrong with him?"

"His heart is not very good since we lost our mother. It has saddened him."

"Will you continue with the hotel when he goes?"

"I don't think so. We've both been isolated too long and we've had plenty of offers for the hotel. It won't be hard to sell."

"What will you do?" he wondered.

She laughed. "Fight off the fortune hunters."

"Or pick the best looking." he suggested.

"That's my sister talking." she assured him. "I don't know what I'd do with myself."

"China is out!" he declared with some certainty.

"I'm not giving up my share to charity! Do you see that boat out there?"

He put his hand to his brow. "The sailboat?"

"Yes, the sailboat. There's a rich man on there. He grows flowers. I can get on that boat and sail away from here tomorrow if I feel like it."

"What's holding you back?"

She was loud again. "There's not enough wind in his sails!"

Terence changed the subject.

"How is your sister today?"

"She's fine. I think she's lost her virginity again."

"Really," he said, confused. "I've always though that it could only be lost once."

"Well that will be news to her." Michelle assured him.

"You're kidding!"

"No. I think she has lost it several times at least by the look on the face of her lovers."

"You've never tried that?"

"No. I don't need to use that trick. One of the Norwegians is staying behind. He seems to have fallen in love with Susannah."

"Will they get married?"

"He's a serious young man but an artist. So who knows? They're all such vagabonds ; as vagrant as cuckoos ; as jaded as horses."

"But not writers?" he ventured.

"You mean would be writers?" she reminded him.

"Time will tell on that and I have plenty of time."

"You're obviously in no hurry," she said, "but I have my own ambitions and perhaps even a timetable."

"Is that why you didn't go East?" Then Terence seemed to throw his inherent caution to the growing wind. "I'd have stayed if I'd been him."

She gave him a good look to see how serious he was seemed to be satisfied that he was pursed her lips as if preparing to kiss him but instead moved on.

She changed the subject. "Time for me to get cracking. I've work to do at the hotel."

His mood was quiet. "Will you come back later?"

"Don't you want to work?"

He was obviously disappointed. "I suppose that's your polite way of saying no. You seemed so full of exaltation earlier in the morning."

She stood up and retrieved her boots.

"Well," she said, as she pulled them on. "I was up with the larks!"

He praised her. "Do you always sing so sweetly."

"I do need some fine tuning. Let's walk on the beach and see if you can find the key. What do you know about women?"

"Only that there's nothing that a man can lose that a woman can't find for him." He was a little unsteady now. " What do you know about love?"

Her reply was quick and to the point.

"It's been a long delay and words can't cover it. We should walk just a little further down if you can manage it."

"I never felt more like it!" he said with enjoyment. "I might not stay here for long either."

"Why not?" she asked. "You probably need a quiet period."

Terence wasn't so sure. "That may pass. I need some life too."

She picked up a stone and threw it into the surf.

"I could try and make it quite interesting for you."

"You already have." he admitted. "I might have fled back to the fleshpots already if it hadn't been for you."

"What makes you think you did the finding and that this is not a fleshpot?"

They laughed together.

"I haven't seen much flesh." Terence said.

"All I ever see are pots.!" she retorted.

"Are you playing in the church on Sunday?"

"Yes." she said. "Will you come and listen?"

"Of course. What will you play?"

"*When April has come the country grows sweet here. She comes like a bride in front of the tide of emerald mist. No keen weather stays her no bird disobeys her no bud can resist.*"

Terence was impressed. "Why, that's lovely."

"A summer carol." she advised him.

He reached over to kiss her but she whisked away.

"It's not really spring yet." she called back."

***

As Michelle disappeared then Erik came back. He had taken off his peaked cap and Terence saw that his bald head had the bloom of a newly ripe plum. On his right temple there was a bump as large as a Baghdad boil which takes nine months to heal and leaves a scar.

Erik praised the garden.

"Those are lovely flowers coming."

Terence agreed and made the effort to kneel down to the flowers now suspecting there was more to the postman than met Michelle's eye.

"How far do you walk in a day?" he enquired.

"Oh, I calculate about twelve miles."

"A fair distance." Terence said, surprised.

Erik continued. "It's longer in the winter. Sometimes I have to carry a shovel the wind drifts it up so much and then the sand comes right over that wall yonder and I must walk along it to get to some of the shoreline places."

"You should try a pony." Terence suggested.

"I did once but it didn't like all the silt under its belly or the cold. Sometimes the frost in the morning stops even the wrens from singing."

Terence found his interest. "Is the wren a rare bird in this country?"

"I don't know except that in very bad weather it stays away from people and all their habitations. Some of them wear a golden crown and are not members of the common herd, to mix my metaphors."

Terence said. "You should write all your experience down."

Erik laughed. "Perhaps I know too much."

"But you must have dreams." Terence suggested.

"Oh yes, but only of oaks beeches and maples."

"You're in the wrong place then." Terence thought out loud.

"If I was in the right place," Erik replied, "then I might have no dreams."

Some birds soared past them.

Terence was interested. Are those swifts?

Erik was definite. "No. Swallows. Two more weeks for the swift."

Terence wrinkled his brow. "How do you know?

"I keep a journal. Two more weeks."

Now Terence lost his doubts. "As regular as that?"

Erik had no doubts. "Third week in April. As regular as the Goat sucker. That's a bird that only sings at exactly the close of day; that is, punctually."

Now that Terence knew of Erik's expertise with birds he continued with an experience of his own.

"I heard a cuckoo in the gorse yesterday forenoon."

Erik was doubtful. "Really. That is either early or you were mistaken. Was it your first cuckoo?"

"Yes. How did you know? When are they due?"

"Middle of April." Erik advised. "As the sun travels north then so do the birds from the southern regions."

"Which do you prefer the fauna or the flora?"

"I prefer the animals." Erik said. "They are all outdoors we see their love and hunger and plants don't talk."

Terence was finding that Erik had a sense of discretion and proportion qualities he knew were hard to find and as rare as seeing a bird feed its young on the wing. The man's vices and virtues were probably as well hidden as the correspondence in the envelopes though no doubt even some of that was no secret. When he looked year after year at the writers a change of address or name or calligraphy could have meaning over the long run and he kept a journal.

Terence kept up the questions.

"What bird sound surprises you most?

Erik put his fingers to his nose. "A snoring owl."

At that Terence switched subjects.

"You and Michelle don't get on very well."

"No. I teased her about the parson and how she departed from his amorous intentions quicker than a swallow."

Terence continued. "She wasn't too taken with your intentions either."

"She's worth a peek." he admitted, quite unruffled.

"What about your wife?" Terence asked, not smiling.

"With women as with birds. Domestication enlarges the breed and love is as erratic as your cuckoo. I have total recall and she a bad memory. We are a perfect pair." Erik made to leave. "If you want to know more about birds then I'm your man. Otherwise, I only deliver the mail."

***

Terence worked all day until darkness fell and there was no moon to lighten the sea but only its lapping sound could be heard and the rain beat down ; Terence had a feeling something was brewing. Then there was a great deal of knocking on the door and Michelle stood there, soaking wet.

As they looked at each other he said. "You're lucky I was the first man to come across you."

She shook out her coat. "Otherwise?"

"You might be wasted. We wouldn't want that would we? You're a very sexy woman."

"Am I to understand you'd like me to come in? Or is it too late in the night for you?"

"Like you," he replied, unable to hide his eagerness, "I wasn't thinking of sleep."

She came in and he helped her off with her coat.

Michelle shook the water out of her hair and tied it up. "I had the feeling that you were going to throw snowballs with rocks in them at me."

"It's not snowing." he said.

"I'm shivering." she said. "And even my goose bumps are not attractive."

"Then come where it's warm."

She pretended not to know what he meant.

"Where is that?"

He opened his arms. "Right here."

After a long hug she came into the house and as they walked upstairs hand in hand they talked.

"What do you feel like?" he asked.

Michelle looked back down the staircase and gave a shriek.

"I'm like a lobster that flies and is afraid to look down."

"Hush. The neighbors will hear you." Terence whispered.

"I am the neighbors." she said.

They sat down on the four poster bed still holding hands. Terence loosened the band holding her hair up.

"What's the difference between love and sex?" he asked.

Michelle knelt down and took off the shoe on his braced leg.

"In love you can't help yourself. With sex you are helping yourself."

"My Aunt would think you were smart."

"What about you?" she looked up at him.

"I can't help myself."he assured her.

Michelle moved to the other shoe.

"I wouldn't be here otherwise. How could I resist a man as desperate for love as a gipsy is for fresh air? Make a wish."

She stood up and walked to the window and threw open the shutters and then when she knew the rain had stopped the French window. As she undressed her pale body shone in the sudden light from the sea

As he followed her and had her in his arms he whispered what it meant to him.

"I made the wish at lunch. This is the dream."

Chapter 7

Sofi was a child of the country ; born into a village where her family had lived for generations. If you stood half a mile away your eyes would have followed a road that grew narrower as it came closer to the village its perspective served by the posts that held the telephone wires. At the end of the road you could see the spire of the church and as you got closer you soon came upon the adjacent cobbled market square ; full of people only on market Friday and holy Sunday. In this little province not quite in the country and not in the city Sofi and her twin sister Sara were born.

Their parents had been married for ten years and were on the point of despairing for children when they made a family all at once. It was that time before the world war when everything seemed golden to those who had the means and Adrien and Charlotta had the means. He was a doctor who ran a clinic in the city. Charlotta's father had been a stockbroker and when he died he left her a fair fortune. They lived well in a large house that backed on to a river and gave them complete privacy. In this environment the youth of the girls was spent in an artistic atmosphere. The mother loved to paint and the father was musical and played with a printing press in an old barn.

Here was a combination of middle class and material success. This often produces a polite vulgarity but because of the family habits and manners all social ambitions were justified by the gravity of the mother and the scientific and musical merit of the father. As she grew in years Sofi often sat in the arbor behind the house read French literature and imagined that the old mill sitting more or less marooned in the river below them was really the Ile de France. The hay piled up on the outer wall did not change the image for she was young and still had her imagination.

This morning in her northern aerie Sofi looked out from aloft her little studio in vain for a replica of the stream that flowed past her father's house. But there was no river here and none in the country. From the viewing platform Sofi took out her writing pad and the heavy black leaded pencil she always used and harked back to the last words she had written before she attempted any further headway and thereafter with each summons a line or two tumbled out ; although she knew that whatever came into her mind would most likely not come out of it in the same form she had first seen it.

Since she was alone and did not practice saying out loud what was in her mind or what could come out of it everything was seen through glass. What did it matter now that she seemed to have lost most of her connection to the world and all the people in it? Everything was being shaped inside unseen until hopefully the gift crept out. Sofi felt what all artists feel; that whatever is not creative might be futile. There was no rapture for her except in music and poetry both intuitive and feminine.

The previous night Sofi left a window open in her bedroom and a ladybird flew on to the bedside light. She handled it carefully and put it back outside where it belonged telling it as she did so that is was the best thing for it. Once, Karl had told her that this was the only insect he was not afraid of so she had a special, personal feeling from the visit and wrote some notes for a poem...

LOVE IN AN UNEXPECTED PLACE

'Love is a lady bird not afraid to stay or to do any harm. Love is a ladybird lucky if yours for a day. Full of safety and charm, love is a ladybird.'

From this vantage point she could see both lighthouses old and new, and the full stretch of the beach from one sea to the other and every vessel that passed; every figure on the beach except the man who stripped off each morning between six and seven am and swam naked in the sea. She avoided his regime. Sofi viewed winter as one who had never had to look for shelter and perhaps had only ever headed frozen flowers. The sea was there to lull her to sleep or inspire her senses.

Farther down the red house stood aloof and as sturdy as the stony shore. The intimacy of the littoral deterred fuchsias and geraniums and lilacs and lilies. There were no begonias but she had come across some old Tom Thumbs with the red still brave slumped in pots around the back door where the sun came in. It was not a poetic setting but then neither Sofi supposed is the desert yet the Arab poets managed to set their few blossoms in lush hanging gardens of the imagination. For some reason she thought of Mahler's slow section in his ninth symphony the one that made her cry when she remembered that he had composed it after the loss of his young daughter. Thus was her resolve confirmed.

In her lonely place Sofi realized that she enlarged every event no matter how trivial. Luckily she still had creative reason and was able to recognize the void before actually stepping into it. In those times the sea became quiet and as if silvered reflected the white clouds and created two worlds whose shapes might have dual images to repopulate the world with gods and demons. She was full of hope that her own demons would not chase away the sun and the moon.

In the only Autumn they ever knew together she and Karl had looked at the river flowing across the land they had walked and saw the empty fields once full of yellow corn swaying in the wind now stubble and at rest. Sofi remembered the clouds white and full of shapes they recognized together. Close in evening light they lay with love until the darkness came ; then the stars were out and they played a game of naming them for past remembrances of other people and places ; in colder regions and in warmer. Karl kissed her cheek and warmed her hands under his arms. He had quoted one of her poems.

'The smell of you is of a spring night that now seems like autumn with winter coming on.'

Now quite alone with her eyes closed and in a quiet voice she spoke to him.

"In your absence the spring has come yet my heart has not done with the seasons we have been apart. Solitary I lie out of reason in this wilderness still wild with solitude. Come, come my love, take my madness…make it fly!"

As she stood there the wind changed direction and she caught sight of the light blue smoke from her newly lit fire. She hurried downstairs to make sure it had not burned through the little logs placed on it earlier. As she came down she was reassured by the snap of the wet wood drying out in the heat.

LOVE IN AN UNEXPECTED PLACE

Sofi put on her stockings and although in no hurry she snagged the top of one leg on her nails and it ran four or five inches down her thigh. She looked down at it and remembered the day she and Karl had begun to love each other in an empty railway carriage. When her skirt rode up Karl looked at a similar run that she had thought would be hidden from the world. When he saw it he gave her the mild look of reproach that she now recalled suggesting that she had not worn her best for him. She exchanged the faulty stocking and threw it on the fire.

Sofi's mind was playing tricks. She had a dream that a large mirror had fallen from the wall down into the back of her piano when in fact there was no mirror but a painting of a sailboat in an ancient harbor. It had fallen but she was grateful to replace it for it did not represent the bad luck of the dream.

The two crows that lived in her garden, Jekyll and Hyde she called them, sounded an alert and moments later there was a loud crack at the door and so it was in this reflective mood that Susannah found Sofi. A sudden hail rattled the windows and when Sofi opened the door the wind almost blew her off her feet and Susannah's Red Riding Hood cape enveloped both of them as she squeezed inside the half open door with some groceries. The morning obsessions disappeared with Susannah's appearance. When she came in the sheer vitality of her caused an immediate surge in Sofi's spirits.

"Why are you smiling so broadly?" Susannah asked.

"I've had negative thoughts this last hour," Sofi replied, "and now that you're here I've forgotten all about them. Which just goes to show how weak they were and how strong you are."

"Oh I'm not so strong. I've got problems too." Susannah insisted.

Sofi praised her. "You always seem so carefree Susannah. It's not the hotel is it?"

"No," Susannah assured her. "That's always in the red at this time of year until the better weather comes along and we get more visitors."

Sofi took the basket from her.

"You've never been here before Susannah. Somebody else always delivers the food so I suspect you just want to talk. A willing ear might be all you need to clear your mind, just as you cleared mine with hardly any effort. So take off that wet cape and we will have some fresh tea and mebbe have a cake or two."

"I always feel shy around you Sofi." the young woman admitted.

Sofi showed her surprise. "Why is that Susannah?"

"Because you've been so loyal to the memory of the man you loved and I find that difficult, at least up until now. You must have had some good times together."

Sofi filled the kettle. "Susannah, good times can lose their savor if gone over too often and then the other times may cancel them out."

"Sofi, I've never loved a man the way you must have loved Karl. Most people are sad for your experience but I envy the happy part of it."

Sofi was touched. "Something makes you different too Susannah. You're a beautiful woman and have artistic talent. You have a lot to barter with other than your obvious attraction to men."

Susannah stood holding the wet cape.

"Sofi, do you mind if I stay here until the hail stops?"

Sofi was starting to put away all the groceries but kept out the tea and cream and some little cakes that she favored.

"I'll be glad to have you Susannah. And I must tell you that I envied your watercolors the other night."

The young woman smiled.

"Michelle's single got more praise and won the prize."

The double meaning was lost on Sofi. "We both have time to improve Susannah. I liked the color you had when the sun picked out a cloud to hide behind and your slender means with light made it softer. Sometimes there is too much light especially up here."

Susannah fixed her cape across two chairs.

"How are you Sofi?"

As she poured the tea Sofi wrinkled her brows a little.

"Keeping my head above water which seems the sensible thing to do. Something might turn up and if it does I'll keep you informed. Was there something you wanted to talk about?"

There was a shyness in Susannah that Sofi had not seen before. As she readjusted the wet cape and worried about the dripping water she got out her feelings.

"Perhaps it's because I'm not sweet tempered at all."

Sofi passed Susannah her the cup.

"Are you trying to say you're not like me?"

"Oh no! I'm not in your class Sofi," she said, earnestly. "I may be trying to be a creative person but I know instinctively that you have the sense and the intellect I may never have."

"Susannah!" Sofi admonished her. "We've only spoken half a dozen times and hardly ever on a very high level. How can you make such an image out of me for yourself."

Susannah tried to explain.

"Well, for a start here you are working things out alone. I couldn't do that without a man. I've not been privy to your work but Michelle and Albert tell me it is remarkable."

"Friends are not always good judges Susannah and I can be just as horny and can curse just as lustily as I've heard you do when I feel like it. My sheet is not completely clean. You mustn't think I'm a hothouse flower living a full life here. I am hiding, biding my time until the genie goes back into the bottle and I can start again. I like to paint but I can't paint like you do. I like sex but I'm not in the mood right now. The moon is casting a shadow. Do you understand?"

The young woman could not be gainsaid.

"I don't know Sofi, I'm in complete awe of you."

Sofi laughed. "You mean like a monster that comes out of a cave now and then and frightens you?"

Susannah sipped her tea.

"No, not quite. Michelle and I work hard but it wasn't always like that. We were quite coddled as girls. Now look at us! We have solid meat on our bones. Yet we are here in this Lutheran outpost and both of us with Catholic tastes."

"Well I suppose Luther had them too." Sofi said. "Susannah, what's on your mind that you can't talk to Michelle about?"

"I think I've finally met a man who seems to see some value in me. I've never had to take a risk with a man before; never felt like a real woman. That's it Sofi! That's what I call you and what I envy. You're a real woman! When a man says goodbye to me I know he might not be back unless he's left his overcoat behind. I can cook and I can bake. I speak three languages. I'm a fair artist. I know how to attract a man but what I don't know is how to have them look further than my breasts as I approach them and my backside as I leave. But you Sofi leave them lust less and misty eyed. But now I've met a man I like. He's a bit older than me and probably has some baggage."

LOVE IN AN UNEXPECTED PLACE

Sofi smiled as she hugged her cup with both hands.

"We all have baggage Susannah. Perhaps it's best to put it in left luggage and throw away the ticket. The more we talk the more we have to hide."

Susannah became earnest.

I can't talk to my sister without an argument about moral virtues etc.,and I know she will criticize my choice of this man. She's never trusted any of my preferences and she's completely unaware of this one as he only comes here twice a month. My sister is a feminist and tends to hide her sensual side you know. The young pastor would have been a good match for her if he'd been strong enough so I hope Terence has a whip hidden in that big house. He'll need it to tame her wild side if she falls in love with him. Do you think he's up to it Sofi?"

"I think he will be very respectful to a woman once he finds one."

"You see Sofi." Susannah proclaimed. "That's what separates you. A preface and then an opinion but no judgement."

"Susannah, I'll leave that to others. I play a passable piano and write passionate personal poems. Once I stop moping around I might go higher up the scale a stanza or two but I understand I have to go through this time first ; refill the bottle. A lot of me escaped when the top blew off the first one. I'm not a Jew or a new woman or a lesbian and so in these times I neither fascinate nor horrify. I'm not dangerous."

"You're an oasis Sofi!" Susannah exclaimed. "I can see the date palms sprouting outside your door when the weather turns."

Sofi sugared her tea. "That's the thing Susannah. We must turn. I think of myself as a woman of a secret society. An anarchist but a romantic one like they would all like to be. No, in my home town Freud doubted an objective conscience and in Paris Proust the truth of memory. That's where I am right now wondering if all this life is real. You and I Susannah are looking at life in divergent ways but in the end our womanly wisdom will in time join us together."

Susannah sighed. "Sofi, you're asking me to be patient."

"Exactly." Sofi assured her. "That's the path I'm on and the one you see so clearly as a separation between us. But later you'll find that the only difference between us was time and space. The hardest thing for a woman I think is to realize herself and still be a woman. Always remember Susannah and it has been well said, that we are born women but a man has to learn how to be a man. My life so far has been full of gestures as if there was no economic or biological necessity for any of them. I've had pain loss and death already. My last gesture has been to try and create in the face of them."

"You're a stoic." Susannah said.

"No Susannah. I wish I was. The pain is still alive in me. I've suffered so many deaths I have no room for any more. Which one would I exorcize? No, there must be no more."

That said from sadness she suddenly brightened and refilled Susannah's cup. The young woman looked at Sofi with more admiration than ever. Sofi saw it and tried to reassure her.

"Don't worry" she said. " I'm not mad." She let loose a telling laugh. "Not any more. I put away the rope long ago."

"Look at the time!" Susannah said nervously. "I must get back and help Michelle with the meals though I love talking to you and this English tea."

Sofi laughed. "It's no more English than Napoleon brandy."

As she prepared to go Susannah turned and gave Sofi her quizzical look.

"What do you mean?"

Sofi closed the package.

"They don't grow tea in England.'

"Oh, don't they? Then why call it English?"

Sofi laughed. "Why, so that the English will drink it. They don't trust foreigners."

"Oh," Susannah admitted. "I never thought of that."

"We didn't get around to your problem Susannah."

"I know. But I think I'll take a chance with my own opinion now that I've heard how you tackle yours. I feel like an ugly building today."

"Actually, Susannah I think you're just a tree like the rest of us. Renewable every year if there is enough sap left to grow new leaves."

When Susannah left Sofi picked at some photographs as she and Sara posed with their parents in winter furs and then in their summer pinafore and polkadot dresses. Even then you could tell she had a different view of the world from Sara who hated having her photograph taken compared to Sofi's wry smile and love of attention. Although she and her sister were scrupulously made equal Sofi lived another life close to her father who doted on her but was not able to show it except when they were alone together. Then he took the opportunity to point out his admiration for her poetic gifts and his high hopes for a composing career.

The death of Karl only partly shrouded the trauma of her father's passing. Sofi inherited his love of nature of birds and wild flowers. All her girlhood was an exultation of being the *chosen one* and her father's illness and sudden death prostrated her physically and mentally. In the face of Karl's death Sofi had picked up the lodestar and followed the arrow of fate that pointed to this haven. She had missed the Great Bear but the little one might still be within her grasp and even Sirius could still beckon. There was still time. When she had first entered this town with her Vienna chic still intact she had created a sensation. There was still time

Sofi remembered those walks on the hills with her father.

"You can call me Stewart up here." he suggested, as they looked over the higher hills they meant to climb. He took out his bottle of beer and she her chocolate bar. Sometimes he let her taste the beer. Sara never came on these rambles and Sofi imagined quite correctly that she had not been asked. This relationship was her first experience with a man. Because of it Sofi trusted and believed in love. When Stewart died she looked for it but always with the thought in the back of her mind of how easily it could be lost. Her father's death was natural and she could accept it. Karl had not died that way. It was a mean way to die she thought and she might never accept it or that it would ever leave her mind. Nature might abhor a vacuum she thought quite wrongly ; but who would fill this one this loss of substance?

"Life is so difficult." Susannah had said.

"Yes." Sofi replied. "But we shouldn't encourage that capacity in ourselves."

"Sofi, what about your sister? What does she do?"

"She's a soprano." From her tone Susannah enquired no further.

When Stewart died and there was no mother Sofi's Aunt attempted to coddle both girls but failed miserably with Sofi. She had been given her head and could never again be fettered by the prevailing customs towards girls.

LOVE IN AN UNEXPECTED PLACE

In the months after the funeral Sofi wandered among her childhood memories, the first serious attempts at word games as she called her poems, and the little two page plays she wrote and spoke out only to herself. She found there all the longings of a seventeen year old girl. Now she looked back at that girl and could see that today she was not much different. At that stage the good life was the hidden one. She still looked at herself carefully in the mirror ; still touched her breasts hoping they would grow faster ; still smiled at herself and placed her hands behind her head to lift her breasts higher and she still wondered how she would look with short hair. She knew she looked like Sara but she was Sofi and determined to be quite different from her sister who sang so sweetly on command though Sofi thought sometimes out of tune. They were both of the same image but one of them lacked yeast. Sofi's young ego was as strong as her will.

The secret life she had led was full of fantastic hopes and day dreams; a divided life. Now as she could sit and contemplate it she realized that she had regarded her sister sweet as she was as vulgar and mediocre for not being able to share this inner sacred life she led. The loss of her mother and father had finally shaken her out of it and her love for Karl had brought her full circle. Now, as she played her piano and wrote her poetry in solitude she had become brave enough not to slip back too far into those dreams that nobody could touch. She decided to leave everything behind and come from existence to living.

The cabin walls were bare. There were no artists to show her their view of this country. She found a photograph of herself with three dogs in the fens among her papers. It was a bare place like this one and she put it away again. As she had walked the country through Autumn Winter and now the early Spring she had not found any insight into its history its biology or its nature. She wore a mask that did not protect her face but restricted the eyes. Sofi was grateful for the original owner's foresight in planting four cherry trees, one at each corner of the small acreage. She knew now that there would not be an early frost to kill their forming buds.

Sofi wrote to her Aunt.

"It's so quiet that I can hear the crows scratching themselves awake every morning and I might as well be on the shore because I hear every wave strike it. From every book I read I expect to hear the voices of the characters. The very day the wind blows from the south west I will notice the change though still indoors."

In turn she had called upon the ghosts of her father and later Karl. She had discovered that ghosts are much more difficult to escape from than flesh and blood. It was on the last climb as they came down to the sea that her father told her that he had not always been faithful to her mother but had loved another woman. He died the next week. As she lay with his ghost she was doubly haunted by her loss and his need for confession.

Their first and only summer came to Karl and Sofi on an idle hill walk when in the afternoon the sun came out and burned their faces as they decided to have their picnic on a large flat rock where they could look across the country and the river below where they could see two waterfalls one of which was very large and strewn below with the fallen stones of a little castle house that history said had once housed a queen hiding from her enemies but not from her lover. Now it was roofless and though four walls still stood they were open to the sky and a great portion of stones lay desolate in the river below. The gardens were overgrown and the yew trees grew now in wild abandon.

"Can't you imagine her waiting there for her lover.?" Sofi asked.
"My imagination is not as great as yours." Karl replied, smiling.
"Her name was Maria you know."
Karl lay back on the grass. "Yes, I know."
She prodded him. "Have you seen her portrait in the Abbey?"
Karl held her hands to protect himself.
"Yes. She had bright red hair."
She put her head on his chest. "Do you like red hair?"
"That's all I remember."
She sat up. "Not her eyes!"
"No, just the hair. I wasn't in love with her otherwise I would have remembered more."
"Or less."
"Yes, or less." he said. "But it's early to forget who I love."
She settled back beside him. "Love makes everything beautiful." Sofi was sure of that and of Karl.

The hailstorm that at other times touched none of her memories now gained strength as she remembered one of her nights with Karl when they were supposed to visit some friends and when the weather turned bad they decided to stay where they were and forget the rest of the world. Such suddenly vivid memories when they occurred set back her decision to leave her refuge. Later, she realized that the crackle of the wood in the fireplace had triggered the memory and she had not had time to sense it until the storm completed the cycle.

Sofi looked in vain in this country for a cluster of acacia, having read of an assignation under them in a garden in a romantic novel. One day there was a sailboat in the water and as she looked at it through her glasses she saw a beautiful woman all in white wearing a lovely hat with a red ribbon tied across the brim and a red rose secured to her bosom. She was the most elegant woman she had ever seen and to her delight she stood up and embraced the helmsman. There treats were rare. Through the narrow vessel of her experience her memories flooded in until they were all around her. A smooth immovable world. The status quo! As she applied her imagination to what was now absent she wondered how long she could tolerate the present at least in one place. What she had lost was pure and her present life pinched away at it hour by hour and day by day. Sometimes she was terrified and tried hour by hour and day by day to recreate a self able to live in this new world. Subjects drifted past. Objects drifted past. She watched them come and go for none of them ever stopped long enough for her to make a choice whether to use them or to join them. They were unaware of her. They were on their way to some distant galaxy and she was fighting to stay where she was until she could untie the moorings that were her memories. She did not look outside for the weather. She heard it on the roof and against the window and when there was no sound then she ventured out or at least opened the dutch door. But soon she came to see that what came out of her had nothing to do with her experiences or memories. It had always been there and only now did she know it could feel it could record it. There, was a sunflower in full bloom and beside it another bud.

She continued her letter to her Aunt.

"It rained today. That is not so unusual here but yet it seemed to come at a bad time for me. I was looking forward to being a beachcomber. Whatever is not in the sky or the earth may come today from the sea but not to be at least for the present as the sky is so black. The birds seem to herald the rain as they were up early before it crossed the strait perhaps to enjoy the morning dryness before the downpour. I always think the animals know more about the vagaries of the earth than we do or like me they guess at what they don't know. Understanding is quite another question. The animals don't know where the weather comes from yet sometimes forecast it. We do know where it comes from and appear quite helpless. Understanding hasn't done us any good. Nonetheless, we are all in it together.

Perhaps I should do what I once saw mother do when confined by the weather which was to put on all the clothes she couldn't wear that day and flounce around the house in them. I didn't foresee the need. So I must learn to understand what the birds are trying to tell me or increase my wardrobe.

There are very few places where you can just sit and have your coffee and not think of anything in particular. Seek them out! The coffee is usually good too although in this particular place where I have ended up this morning they drink beer early straight from the bottle and the sun is only an hour old. There are lots of windows but nobody is going past them. A radio blares from the kitchen. There is a loud bell on the counter for the impatient customer yet it doesn't disturb my brain enough to make it think any serious thoughts. The odd fly is too lazy to attack me though I do hold my hand over my coffee just in case it gets thirsty.

Outside in the harbor the fish boats have been home for hours and the fishermen have gone home to their women who are well aware that they came in two hours ago and if any adjustments need to be made then there has been time. Everything is in place and the social order not disturbed.

They don't offer fish in here for any meal it is always a meat dish. There are no malt whiskies on the gantry only Cutty Sark, a grain whisky that will help you quickly forget the world if that is your choice. The short order cook is no chef de cuisine. She does fried eggs and burnt bacon without any garnish on the plate just the ever present brown sauce bottle, never cleaned, on request.

The place is not well endowed with lights except for a constant lamp over the cash register. The doors open inward so when you pull on it don't get the idea that the place is closed, it never is. Some things are right in the world. They can happen to you if you have no good reason to seek them out.

In my garden, the grass has hardly grown in the past two weeks. I watched Albert cut it and later he repainted the white tables and benches in the garden. The lilacs are trying to come out early and the faint hint of color is welcome.

Nature has a strange beauty when being reborn. The old skin going to ground the new showing its head, struggling noiseless and pervasive. Time is sometimes a winding road as if our fate did not want us to see the end of it. Spring is a time for ladybirds to try and protect the new buds. I found one on my hand this morning. I watched it flex its wings yet decide to stay with me. A poem came out of me for it.

As I sat in the sun Michelle came through the dunes to pay a visit.
"You've been writing." she said.
I told her that "it was all I had at the moment."
She saw the poem. "Can I read the poem?"

It seemed slight enough but I pushed it across the table for her.

She liked it. "What a gift Sofi!"

"The lady bird flew away Michelle."

"It came to you in the first place Sofi and that is supposed to be lucky."

I changed the subject by asking her how her romance was going with Terence.

"Oh, you heard about that."

"Erik comes by every day." I said.

"With letters?"

"Not always. He's my newspaper."

Michelle was kind enough to try and cheer me up.

"There isn't a person in this town who wouldn't like to come by Sofi. The whole town admires you and would sit around in a circle like in the old times just to look at you. Can I tell them you are on the mend?"

Her praise embarrassed me a little yet was nice to know, but I changed the subject back again.

"Do you like Terence?"

She blushed a little. "It's early Sofi."

"Are you not sure of him?" I wondered, wanting her happiness.

"Not yet. He's had a bad time too but we must go on and repair ourselves sometimes with other people sometimes alone." She gave me more advice. 'When you are well you must find love like the ladybird you are. I'd like a copy of the poem Sofi.'

I handed it over and she promised to bring it back later.

"I wish sometimes I wasn't the only one to see your work but perhaps it will foster your heart."

"You have one too." I reminded her.

'Yes, but it was my choice to break it. I'll see you later Sofi.'

"I like him Michelle ; Terence I mean."

'You were awfully good with him when he appreciated your gesture.'

"One gesture deserves another like the poem. He came by later and we talked a little."

Michelle showed no surprise. "He's very kind."

Sofi finished her letter…

It was nice to have her for a few minutes but thank goodness I have the piano. Writing is such a silent business and I can't sing at the moment. I do hope you are well…Love. Sofi.

Chapter 8

The same week she came back to the north Sofi walked around to Anna's house and got a warm welcome.

"You've come back my dear."

"Yes, Anna." Sofi said as she made herself comfortable. "Michelle says you're not feeling so good these days."

"Old age at last! What an event! But youth can have troubles too. Don't put old bodies in new clothes."

"Who knows what we will pull down Anna."

"You left so quickly those months ago Sofi. I feared we would never see you again."

"Our dreams had wandered here Anna. So I came back for my part of them."

Anna was wistful. "When I lost my husband I just pretended he was still here as usual. I looked at his work until I developed his eye again and the way he made me calm down. I was always running around being busy and getting nothing done before he came and when he left I made a promise to myself that I would behave the way I did when he was here to guide me and love me. And you know sometimes I painted for him too, at least I thought so and threw his roots over a chair though I knew he wasn't there."

"I only have poetry and music Anna. Karl was an accountant and had no art that I know of."

"Then you must invent you own art for him. Write songs you know he would like. Be the woman he loved Sofi. That's the best you can do until you get some sort of relief. First, you might imagine a world with him and gradually one without. Oh I know I make it sound easy but you are young enough and will have to do it."

"Anna, did you have any young memories that set your imagination going?"

"Oh, yes, the time we went to Copenhagen to Tivoli and boarded the frigate on the lake to see the variety show in the cabin. I was used to ships to boats but the little ride out to the ship was a magic moment full of expectancy. That's when I realized that those moments are what can make an artist. Oh there was a Moorish palace and a copy of the market at Port Said in the gardens full of jugglers and acrobats and clowns and sometimes a hot air balloon. That show had to last me all the next part of my life. We in the north love the south. We even try to paint like the French and the Italians

"How are you doing Anna?"

Anna smiled, "Ask the postman. He knows everything."

"How do you spell your name. Anna or Anne?"

"Of that depends on my mood or the person who asks. Thus one day I'll be Ann and another Anne or another Anna and if they ever meet independent of my company then they can figure it out for themselves."

"It's hard to tell from the way you sign your paintings."

"A.B. Anne Boleyn for all the public knows or cares." Then she seemed to wander off the subject. "Take that Monet poster in the railway station. You might call it a railway station but I might call it a factory."

"Monet painted a railway station." Sofi insisted.

"Yes, but was he in it when he did the work or did he just drive through it from imagination? I suppose it was a challenge for him but it tells us nothing more than that it could be painted. Anyway, to continue in what we were talking about before Monet butted in, there's one rule."

Sofi sat up straight. "What's that?"

"You can't have love on your own terms nor can you have its loss. Art labors to make whole what seems incomplete. You can mourn and forget and then you can create and remember. As time goes on that will let you move on to another life because you celebrated the one you lost. Do you think Sofi that you've said all you wanted to say about it?"

Sofi hesitated. "No."

Anna encouraged her. "Then say it now."

"Exorcise it?" Sofi wondered.

Anna was certain. "No. Use it! You're a different woman now that you're alone and I understand that and in time so will you and then you will find again whatever is missing and know how to replace it."

"Perhaps there is nothing missing just something to be missed." Sofi said, as Anna patted her hand.

"There always is." Anna assured her. "Have a look at this album I was flipping over before you came over."

As she turned the pages of the album Anna hesitated and looked sideways at Sofi to see her reaction to the image of a man and a woman walking arm in arm on the beach a little brown dog at their feet.

"They look happy enough." Sofi commented, taken by the image of love. "This beach seems to promote companionship."

"That's true." Anna replied. "But in this case it was the end of that."

"How sad." Sofi said. "Do you know their story? They look so close."

Anna explained. "By this time all was lost in his sickness. A sickness for which there is no cure; a physical impediment of the mind. And then one winter and knowing how long it would last she fled to the sun and fell in love with another. And I think this was the day she told him."

"Did she go away for good?"

Anna hesitated. "She tried, but her former love had been too deep and when she remarried and knew she was safe she came back with her new husband for the summer festival to give him some support at the end."

Sofi could not hide her interest. "How did it end for him?"

"He painted the two of them that last night at the bonfire on the beach. A brave man accepting his fate."

"That must have been difficult to do."

"Love goes on Sofi. Perhaps a poem will now come out of you for it. Some candles are never lit and some never go out. One broken heart may be enough. Turn your face to the stars."

As they held hands Sofi felt the weakness of Anna's body yet was encouraged by the strength of her mind.

***

When she came back from her visit to Anna Sofi found a letter from Sara waiting. It seemed to be full of politics and anti semitism and some of her sister's views shocked her but she decided to ignore the themes of her letter and instead substitute her own.

'I sent you some poems in the post. You haven't mentioned that so I suppose you haven't got around to them. A little sad this time. It creeps in, the loneliness. Yet sometimes I would have it no other way. It's cool here but the birds awaken me every morning. If it rained every day I would hide under the covers but in the sun my memories might inspire me. What is there to envy? I watch the tide push in and then rush out so nothing really changes. The little yellow and black bird sings to me. The owls hoot and the eagles soar above me in the zephyr. The local woodpeckers love my seeds.

I don't lack company. There are crows who listen patiently when I talk to them and try to reassure them that I mean them no harm. Thus the days and nights go on and I must speak of them too. Like one of my neighbors I am far away from the red soil of Africa exotic animals and there are no hills. I learn slowly, that there is no reason to have total recall. Perhaps it's madness to recollect reality. If I'm between heaven and earth I will be found again. I wait with my virtue intact and with patience in this certain light of slender means, and delicate touch.'

'I played the piano last night making up songs. I discovered that a song has the same mysterious origin as a poem and therefore they are united in drawing us close to the spirit in us as it wavers between strength and weakness. But who is to judge? Let us lie in the darkness and find out as the dawn breaks upon our life as we have lived it and perhaps all our conversations will construct from the delicate imagination a way to face a world that once was kind and turned cruel as our fate wound down.

A multitude of voices speak to me but I have heard only one. I am looking for a dream to heal me but none has come. As a slight mist forms outside the light turns pale and I am afraid to look at my face in it. While love is bright sadness moves, moves down the spectrum and my voice is to the west of middle c. where there is no lilt. The birds may revive me. They are never sad. As if they knew their time was short and know no regret between birth and the frost that kills them."

Sofi.

***

The morning was loud and clear as Albert walked his dog across the beach. Clear because it was cloudless; loud, from the Parisian music coming out of the red house. As he came closer he saw that the outside table was ready for breakfast and was further surprised when Michelle came out with a coffee pot in one hand and a pile of toast in the other. As he stood there Terence followed her out and seeing his surprise put down the rasher of fried bacon and stepped forward.

"Albert! Come and join us."

Albert stuttered a reply. "No, no thanks. We need some exercise first."

"It would be nice if you were to have coffee with us on your way back down." Michelle said, and Albert saw her full beauty for the first time as if it had accumulated in private and all the years of it now full of gentle swellings and leavened gossamer. Albert looked at Michelle and felt in his being the epitome that all great love is mostly silent. Just like love that always stays green and it seemed to be the end of all the dreams of apple tinted roses he had hoped to plant at her feet and the heat from her when snow was falling. For every sign that had appeared upon the moon had now disappeared so soon. Terence offered him a chair and reluctantly he did sit down with them.

Just then Erik appeared.

"By the look on his face something is up." Albert said.

Erik did not have his usual baggage with him. He flourished a yellow envelope as he approached the group on the patio. "A telegram for Terence." he announced. His use of the Christian name did surprise them since none but Terence knew that they had developed a friendship.

Terence stood up and took the telegram from him.

"I'll wait and see if you want to reply." Erik said.

Terence sat back down and opened the envelope. As he read the contents his face looked grim. He put it down on the table and told them its contents.

"My Aunt died in Paris last night. This is from her lawyer."

Erik took out an official pad.

"Any reply?"

"I'll come and see you later." Terence managed, and suddenly realized that the music should stop and before anyone could express any consoling thought for him he disappeared into the house. Albert rose and without a word he and Erik left in different directions. Not too far away there had been another death; Anna had also died in the night.

Terence drove away the same day to attend to the funeral arrangements as he was his Aunt's only relative. When the funeral was over and conducted to her exact specifications he met the hundreds of her friends who attended it but knew none of them. The executor, Stone, read him the will. Terence found himself a very rich man.

Terence said. "I had no idea she owned so much of the world."

Stone closed the books.

"Well, she did. Houses apartments horses stables, country estates, you name it, she came into them over the years and they are all yours."

"What should I do with them?" Terence asked.

"Our firm as been running them for your Aunt for many years and since you have no experience you should let our people continue. The assets can only grow. We should go through the whole estate with you.

Terence looked at the list.

"I might not want to keep all of this."

Stone reassured him.

"You can decide but you should take good advice."

"I will. In the meantime I must go back up north and clear up some business and get my manuscripts and notes."

The lawyer tried to help.

"We can hire someone to drive you up."

"No," Terence said. "I need the time to clear my head and it will take me two or three days at an easy pace."

Stone rang a bell the office door opened and he ushered Terence out.

"As you wish." were his parting words. "Take your time while we organise these affairs for your consideration."

***

According to Anna's wishes there wasn't an elaborate ceremony at her funeral and few notices outside her hometown. As they walked toward the cabin to visit Sofi after the funeral Albert broke his sad silence with Michelle.

"She'll have to wait a few years for words of praise before she's appreciated as a great artist. She was born here but bred in Delphi. When this town was a village and she walked around it brush in hand everyone knew they were under her watch were on their best behavior and tried to look their best."

Sofi didn't go to the funeral but people understood. Instead, she paid attention to the last advice she got and wrote a poem to cover the loss at least in her own mind.

She was expecting the visit from Michelle and Albert.

Michelle said: "She's dead and so far only this little village knows of it."

Sofi replied. "She had love. I don't think she needed or wanted anything else. She more or less told me that one morning as we sat up at the beacon straining our eyes to see the grey lighthouse through the mist." 'That's just like life she told me ; always straining to see what's out there when the real world the only one we can know is close at hand when you've been loved and known all the joy it.' "No, Michelle, her greatness was in the true spirit she passed down to us not just through her art. Her life is the example. I believe she gave her husband that percent of herself that most women keep in reserve. That was the piece she gave him and she knew he was aware of it."

Michelle had changed from her black dress into a grey one that seemed to make her even more demure. Albert, true to form wore a black wool shirt with an Indian style collar. The first thing Sofi noticed when they came towards her bench in the garden was how Albert seemed to be attempting but never managing to hold Michelle's hand as they walked. He did not quite have the courage to actually do it.

Michelle sat down beside Sofi whilst Albert stood dutifully and sombre beside her end of the seat. The care he had for her was obvious and he hardly spoke a word after the formal greeting. As Michelle spoke his long hair blew in the wind and elongated his very handsome face further emphasizing his dark brown eyes and feminine lips. He stood beside the Chinese lanterns which were in the shape of red hearts and a gift of his own creation to Sofi.

Michelle wore no other jewellery except a string of pink pearls that matched her natural lip color. As they had come towards Sofi she had wondered at such a strange pair who seemed a complete mismatch and yet to Sofi were clearly fitted. As Michelle sat down on the limited space on the bench she observed Albert's manners with a slight, obvious to him only, touch of the hand.

"This was not the day for a funeral," Albert finally spoke up, "but for a wedding. It's such a day out of season of spring, not the winter winds we have suffered for a month."

"Perhaps," Sofi said, "it was well. She always said she hoped to go out when she could see her perennials had survived and were about to bloom. I hope she missed those that failed yesterday. The cones on my pine were shut tight and today they have opened to catch life."

Michelle knew that Sofi was despondent.

"Is there a special place you'd rather be Sofi?"

"I don't know about rather be but Florence entered my memory once without enthusing me with a fresh desire to go there until I discovered something when my mother was arranging flowers one day and I admired the lilies. She said we must go to Florence someday you and I for it is the City of the Lilies and even its cathedral is called Our Lady of the Flowers. And so to answer your question Florence might be my next destination or at least on my itinerary. But I must get you some coffee and with that must not forget Vienna and a tale of a city refusing to be drawn down by its river to the sea. Let's put the kettle on and put out an extra cup."

Neither Michelle nor Albert questioned the addition of the extra cup. As they entered the little cabin the dying soft rays of the sun showed a spider's web on the dappled panes above the door.

Sofi noticed their attention. "I know I should put the creature out but when the sun came through that glass this morning I put up a sheet of paper and behind it found the most ingenious design reflected there. So I welcomed another artist to my home and anyway it sleeps. It's asleep now."

LOVE IN AN UNEXPECTED PLACE

When they had gone Sofi sat in the white rose garden and looked up at the gentle drift of the clouds to the north east. The previous night she had read through her poetry and decided that she had written herself out but out of what? Lately she had wondered just how deep her wounds were. As she read the poems one by one she had not shed a tear for the first time but had begun a conversation with Karl. Previously, she could hardly say his name to herself and she had never written it down.

Her feet got cold and she went inside and put on long red woolen stocking so that she could stay outside a little longer because the cabin was beginning to stifle her and because she lacked the energy to paint she rarely used the atelier on the upper floor. The doves were the earliest visitors sitting in the earth below the back fence that came ahead of the trees. Sometimes she imagined cellos playing sorrowful music yet she knew that it was only the doves waking up. But that had all stopped having any meaning now and only the blackbirds were left and they were loud enough to waken the dead yet could not for Sofi. The child in her full of innocence felt the gates of heaven had at last opened and only the child in her could explain the change. It was then that she decided to go and that was why she left all her work behind her. She was like an apple that always stays green.

'Goodbye to all that.' A phrase that came to mind; Sofi read it somewhere; it seemed appropriate. Goodbye ; no hugs, no kisses no tears no regrets ; every cliche in the book but time for them for all of them. Time to switch stars. What other way was there to go? Where would she go? She had in mind the Latin Quarter of Paris. Terence said he had lived there once before the war and described it to her with such pleasure. As he spoke about it Sofi realized there were good memories behind his recall but he revealed more than he meant to and she didn't press for more. She was reminded of her father especially his warmth when he greeted her and the pleasure they had together just with talk. Sofi was hopeful too that Michelle was capable of filling the hole in the wounded man's heart. Then Sofi saw how distracted he could be even around her…she worried about them.

When Albert came and found Sofi gone he saw on her little table by the bed what was apparently her last poem and in the peace that had been her presence he said it out loud and could hardly finish it. He knew then that she had gone for good her fears unfurled to face the world again. She had called it 'For another Day'…

Let me waken vivid Venus
on those lonely mornings
after my love is taken;
then, randomly tossed
across wailing wild winds.
Thus all the random kisses
that weave their winsome way
through each sleepless night
disappear at the speed of light.
Yet, let me then forgive
whoever stole love away
and would not let it live
or miss me for another day.

He couldn't help but remember how refined she was, how delicate all her features and her fingers as they followed a melody on the piano across the keys. Hands to be kissed and a soul to be worshiped. Albert was interrupted in his musings when Michelle came to the door. She agreed with him that she might not come back. They had lost her. He gathered all the poetry and the letters from Vienna.

"We must do something with these." he said. "I will write to Sara at this address and ask her permission."

"Sofi might not have wanted them published." Michelle said.

"I think she left them behind for at least two reasons," Albert said, " and that may be have been one of them, to have them published."

"And the other?" Michelle asked.

"Read her last poem Michelle. She had said everything she wanted and needed. I think she'll concentrate on the music now. She didn't leave any of that and I know she wrote some every day."

"Sara might know better than we do. We have not been proxy to the letters." Michelle said.

"I'd like to read them too." Albert said.

Later, when Sara came, they were privy to the last notes she left. *'It's not our dreams that bind us but what is left to remind us that all the world is ethereal, sometimes just a conversation where we speak for everyone fill every part in the cast for every idea is ours and every kiss is from the heart.*

Your words were few but I heard them all. I saw you were fair and walked on air. As you pass me by you may hear me sigh.

Hold on to my hand and try to understand it's not our dreams that bind us but what is left behind to remind us.'

Michelle held the feelings in Sofi's poem and perhaps on another level understood them. She wondered how she could deal with her own problems. Her relationship with Terence had begun on a high note for her but as time went on she realized it might be a one sided affair, a double rebound. Since she had respect for him she tried to overlook the problems he had beyond her knowledge even as a woman of her depth and sensibility who was willing to wait patiently to see her effect on Terence since she already knew that he had affected her. She found it singular how vivid her dreams had become and how sharp and quick her feelings were when she was with him. When she saw him at the far end of the promenade with fish boats on one side and warehouses on the other she always could ignore such mundane surroundings and have the urge never far away in a young woman in love of running as quickly as she could towards her lover to show him how much she cared for him and how just the sight of him in the distance could excite her feelings with nothing hidden. She always restrained herself and that to her was an omen of the lack of confidence and power she sometimes felt when around him.

"I had word from Terence." she told Albert, "he's coming back for his notes and what there is of his manuscript and some personal things of course."

"Are you one of his personal things?" Albert asked, but not without some hesitation.

"I was hoping so," she replied, with a wry smile, "but we will have to see how he feels now that he doesn't have to stay here with me. He wants me to come to Paris with him."

"Will you do that?"

"There's the hotel to think about. But we have more or less decided between the two of us to sell the place. Susannah has found a very nice man at last and he won't be able to stay around here as his business is elsewhere."

Albert packed up the poetry and the letters. Some dead leaves had blown into the cabin. Michelle picked up the broom and swept them away hoping that Spring was here to stay.

Chapter 9

It was the evening of an opening night; Helen sat in front of a large mirror. She did not look into the mirror but sat pensively with her hands on her knees. She wore a recently crocheted woolen cap of a bright auburn color. Her newly dyed hair also auburn was too copious to be entirely hidden under the cap. She had knitted it herself. It was a skill passed down to her from her mother who, depending on the amount of spare wool around could make half a dozen before lunch. It helped Helen relax.

She was in her dressing room trying to get rid of her pre performance nerves by exposing her wispy body to the air. As the star of the show she had her own dressing room. In it hung all the costumes she would need for the performance. Only one other person was allowed into the room at this time. When Marna her dresser arrived she entered with her own key. The door was always locked. Before Marna opened it there had to be a special signal rapped on the door and Helen called out her permission. Then for a final time she tried out all her costumes made up her face and arranged her hair. When that was done and never a word yet uttered the two women embraced and became human again.

These acts of detail were some of the tools Helen used to become and to stay the lead dancer in one of the premier dance companies of her time.

She was tall and lean and for all her self perceived disadvantages a very dominant young woman. All the other dancers male and female were in awe of her as a person and as an artist. But now all the steps and all the rhythms all the gestures had settled into place and her naked vulnerable period was over for the night. She was ready to dance and to that art she was dedicated.

When your talent is recognized early it's considered a good thing. If your talent is in one of the physical arts it's a very good thing. Helen's mother sent her to ballet lessons with just the hope that the child would get some strength into her frail body. Her gifts were accepted early. Helen was pleased by all the attention. She was skinny ; skin and bone actually. What else could she have done but dance? It was a good thing. Everybody said so and that it had been assumed early enough for her to have a balletic career. Of course when your talent is quickly acknowledged and you are able to spend your life developing it into an art that everyone recognizes there is always the caveat ; *'you did have the advantage of starting early.'* Hard work and admiration blessed Helen. Yet she was constantly made aware that because of her early start she had been given an advantage. It was always in the back of her mind. Did her rivals believe she'd had an unfair advantage? Only Helen knew that being a child prodigy was no guarantee of success in the dance or in life.

When she reached the top of her profession she was still lean. She would have to stay that way yet strong too with constant exercises. Despite her personal efforts Helen often felt that she was in the same situation as many a person born rich. Was all the attention she got genuine? Did she really deserve it? Fame brought many suitors for her fragile nymph like body. None of them were sensitive enough to know that every bone every muscle in her body ached. A creaking body can close down passion too quickly in what the kama sutra calls congress. Her affairs usually reached an early conclusion but not just from the creaking body; she had never been sure of her lovers. She craved a man who loved her for herself and not the art or the fame. She was a superb ballerina the critics agreed on that. Yet well into her twenties she was still an unfulfilled woman. Love was lack of doubt Helen thought. She had never known love herself but was successful hiding the lack of it.

Helen rarely spoke to anyone before she went on stage ; gave few acknowledgments. She entered graciously gave her performance and left the same way. She did not thank everyone for praise. Of course opening night was always an exception; Helen held court. One particular opening night and for the first time she lost some of her commitment to the dance. That was the night when Seamus Thomson came to her dressing room after the performance. Helen felt she was at the end of a sexually fallow period when she saw Seamus the rising star of the art world. He had just been added to the short list of artists who were calculated by the critics as the most brilliant of their generation. The room was full when she saw him enter. Helen sensed she was at a disadvantage. A handsome man who attracted her and she did not feel she looked her best. Her makeup was caked on thick and ran with the sweat of the performance. A little confidence slipped away. Seamus was with another woman. Helen noticed that she was holding on to him with the characteristic tightness of the uncertain tentative lover.

There is no woman more easily conquered by thoughts of love than the apparently strong and dominant. These traits are not as lasting as virtue which even love does not overcome. Thus, Helen had the feeling of love at first sight but unfortunately as she found out later Seamus recognized it in her look. A man can't stop looking at a shy woman because she embraces every man the same way perhaps the only constant in a woman he will ever know. Seamus of course did not see this in Helen. Quite the opposite. What he did see at least to begin with was a famous prop makeup and all. He said hello praised her performance took her photograph then indicated his card on her dressing table. He saw her pick it up before he left. Helen did not call him.

The next night Seamus came back minus the girl for a second look at Helen. He was told that she was resting after the performance and wasn't seeing anyone. Sean sent in his card anyway and waited. Shortly, Marna appeared and he was allowed into Helen's domain. He was surprised when Marna left locking the door from the outside leaving them alone. Helen lay on a chaise longue fully dressed for the street and sure enough she sat there like a blue Matisse graceful and slender her long legs tucked under her body. Seamus sat down on the dressing table chair and turned it around to face her.

"I believe I'm privileged to visit you." Seamus said, with a huge grin on his face.

Helen laughed. "I make a few exceptions to my rule. After opening night I like to walk rather than talk. I'm sure you understand."

Seamus didn't. "My work is much less physically demanding and I get visitors all the time. I usually welcome them. A little distraction doesn't seem to bother me."

Helen pulled over a book from the side table and surprised him.

You left your card so I had Marna look for your paintings."

"Ah," Seamus beamed at her, "the new book. Quite heavy."

"I like your palette,"Helen said, "but I don't have much understanding of what you are trying to do with it."

"Well, in your world you tell a story without words. In some ways my paintings try to do the same thing. I'm static you're moving. But in the end there's not that much difference."

"You have no music." she said.

"It's in there if you listen hard enough ; and the dance too."

Helen was honest as she put down the book.

"Quite a claim for geographic patterns and dots."

She moved off the chaise.

Seamus was not put off.

"I came to ask you out to dinner to make your acquaintance."

Helen powdered her nose.

"It's late for one and early for the other."

"I know a place," Seamus persisted. "Light food and music. A piano player. Love songs. Very relaxed."

He saw her weaken. "No reporters?"

Seamus moved towards the door. "Just me."

Helen smiled at him. "You paint from memory then."

"If I have anything worth remembering."

She stooped down and put on her shoes.

"Let's go then. Create some memories for you."

"I didn't realize you were so tall." Seamus commented.

"I'll try not to overshadow you." she retorted, quietly.

"You could always hide behind me." he quipped.

"I've tried that. It doesn't work for me."

"How do we get out of here quietly?" Seamus wondered.

She reassured him. "Marna will distract them. Have you a car?"

"No. We could walk. You said you preferred that."

Helen was surprised. "Is it that close?"

"So close who would suspect."

When he stood up she was taken again by his dark looks; that it wasn't some of her fame he was looking for; and then by the fact that he took down the right jacket though it didn't appear to match her green suit.

"I like your woolen caps." Seamus commented, picking one of them up instinctively knowing the praise would please her. She took it from him and fixed it on her head.

And so a sort of romance by which is meant a one sided one was born and duly represented in the pictorials of the day and night for they never sleep. As the affair continued only Marna noticed the change in her charge but said nothing. She fully understood the attraction a fellow artist could have for Helen. Watching closely she soon realized how one sided the relationship was and how it was now affecting Helen's work. It seemed she had no time for prologues but came to the theater directly from the arms of Seamus. Eventually across the facade of exuberance and excitement Marna saw a crack or two and finally a little sadness when Helen regarded herself in the mirror. Perhaps Marna thought, but still said nothing she had come to the conclusion that the affair could not last the length of the play. Marna knew how Helen hated those periods of idleness. Now to face one with a sad affair behind her might crush her confidence.

Marna was a young curvaceous woman who would have been surprised by the fact that Helen sometimes envied her. She had all the confidence of having a true lover. On the edge of such a feeling there is a substance that heightens the senses and catches every change in the wind ; steers a woman on a course that is aware of the passing sail and smells out piracy before the bones are hoisted. So, with her deep affection for Helen her view of Seamus was wrinkled. She slipped him into the shoes they threw away every week. When he smiled at Helen she saw the brush in his hand and the dollar signs in his eyes; she believed he was mercenary. When reports were made in the yellow press of evening attachments between Seamus and other women Marna made sure they appeared somewhere in the dressing room or any other convenient site for Helen's attention. Her look sometimes showed Marna that the tactic was working.

Neither of them knew that for months Seamus had stared in chagrin at the canvases that were bringing him fame and fortune. They were all in the abstract genre of art mainly geometric in origin. These last few months he had come to realize that he had nothing more to say in those forms; he knew they were derivative. In the first stages of his relationship with Helen Seamus wondered what had attracted him. When he found himself connected with Helen's star he suddenly knew she might be the beginning of the escape from his lack of inspiration.

He had been starting but never quite finishing portraits of friends. As he felt his proficiency growing his artistic excitement grew. Already there had been talk that he hadn't had a show for almost a year. There had been no thought in his mind of painting Helen until he slept with her and realized all the flaws her art kept hidden overcoming reality. He knew all the famous photographs that showed her in a soft romantic light. Then he realized how much she suffered for her art. A distress he had never felt. How could he capture that side of her? His own frames had passed through him without much angst and had emerged so noiselessly that he couldn't feel the difference between inspiration and the end product. As he began to see and to feel her effort her pain he decided to express it and perhaps sub-consciously exaggerate it to justify the new approach and conception of his own gift. He then determined that portraiture was definitely his way out of the artistic impasse he had found himself in.

Helen felt that their love affair was one where she climbed towards a window at the top of the stairs yet never quite reached the top nor could trust herself to do so. The hands she felt upon her were soft but she never sensed the gentleness she craved. Being loved by Seamus Helen often felt like calling out…'There! There! There! There!' yet never did have the courage to take or to give all that was in her. She could not open herself or release herself until she was empty; always, she held something back. Helen had made her life for the dance and now wondered what love would tell her. During her distraction with Seamus she discovered that such a love was a lonely business ; all the valentines confined to paper print and flowers. The dreams were neglected. The voices of the players who brought the words of the poets to music and dance mere vapors in her mind and apparently out of her reach. From all the strength of her life to the weakness of love was a long journey for Helen. Yet she decided to persevere. In life she was perverse. How could she change it? The answer was not far away.

In the respite when the ballet was transferred from one venue to another they went to the beach. From their bedroom window they could see the ancient beacon that had now been replaced by an automatic lighthouse further up the coast.

Helen grew nostalgic. "It must have been a wonderful sight when they lit the basket of dry wood to guide the fish boats in. I don't suppose anyone remembers now it was so long ago."

She rose from the bed and sat by the window in the moonlight. From the shadows Seamus commented. "You look like an angel in silhouette. All silver but tinged with gold."

Helen was pleased. "I'm glad you see me that way." But she couldn't resist some mockery some disbelief. "Is there a halo too?"

Seamus yawned and ignored the halo.

"I'd like to paint you that way if I had such talent as nature is showing at the moment."

Helen stretched herself like a cat and cast a shadow over her face. She wondered where this affair would go and despite his easy way with words she was still full of doubt not knowing him from one minute to the other. There was a quietness in him that she was afraid of. If their lovemaking had been a measure of their regard for each other all would still not be well in her mind. Seamus had no inhibitions and Helen entered a new world that somehow was not her place. Her life of rigid discipline had killed some of her sensuality and what was left she kept for the dance.

"Come back to bed." Seamus said. "I don't want to fall asleep by myself. Come over. You'll catch cold sitting naked like that."

"This is how I'd like to dance." she said, more to herself than to Seamus. "Naked in the moonlight on the shore."

"You don't get paid for a free performance." he said.

"When you dance for the passion of it money loses its importance. It's good to do things for love and when it's in your mind."

Seamus disagreed. "When you live by your art you have to know what it's worth. We both get paid for what we love to do. Come back to me. If I could paint you as are you are now it wouldn't tell who you really are."

"What does that mean?" Helen wondered.

"What you've suffered for your art." he said.

She turned to him. "It has been worth it. I have no regrets."

He persisted. "If I could capture it then the world would see another side of you."

Helen was doubtful. "A woman in the raw is not always a pretty picture. Have you finally decided to make a change?"

"Yes, my mind was finally made up just now. When I saw you that way. I know I need the change and to do it with any success I need more than a pretty picture. You've just inspired me."

Helen wasn't sure of his meaning. "You mean not being a pretty picture?"

Seamus tried to explain. "No not in the least but minus all the trappings. I need to show you the way I often see you as nobody else does or can. Being with you has shown me for the first time that I can reach another level."

"And I'm to be the catalyst?" she mocked.

He did not hear the scoff. "The exact word. You would have to trust me. I couldn't show you the painting until it was finished."

Helen's reply sounded her doubt in his integrity.

"Really! Why not? What is there to hide?"

"You might divert me from the truth. From what I see and want others to feel."

She continued to doubt. "I might not like it.'

"You won't!" Seamus said. "But will you risk it?"

His reply seemed honest and swayed her decision.

"For your sake I will. I have no notion of what is in your mind."

He laughed. "No pun intended but my own vision is rather sketchy too."

"When would you do it?" she asked.

He thought for a moment. "In the hours after your rehearsals."

Helen snorted. "I look like hell then!"

He begged her. "Will you do it?"

She came back to the bed. "And I will not see it until you finish it?"

"Nobody will." he assured her. " Our secret."

Seamus put his arms around her but she was not diverted.

"Yours only."

Seamus yawned again. "I could sleep on the edge of a razor."

Helen felt his thigh. "Is your skin so thick?" She brushed her hand across his brow. " But take care and beware. I am not that Helen the dame who launched a thousand ships. Yet she is still in my blood if you bring not fame."

At the new venue as promised she sat for Seamus after each rehearsal. She was so proud of how the years of discipline had shaped her body yet over the weeks she had no idea of what had unfolded from his mind. She kept her promise and did not ask to see the painting. Unknown to Helen Seamus had it photographed at every stage. In the twenty five days it took to complete he had a full portfolio of film. It was a remarkable recap of his changing view of Helen from day to day.

On the day Seamus put the painting on show without publicity and in the small gallery he sometimes used he sent the photographic portfolio to the rehearsal hall he sent a note telling Helen where the painting could be viewed. News traveled fast and by the time Helen got to the gallery it was crowded.

The photographs were bad enough but the actual painting was much worse ; the cruel twists of paint applied with the knife. Even the little wart she had below her cheekbone that she took such trouble to hide was in full view from the angle he chose to expose it. She had posed in profile but now her body was poised like a witch. Seamus had not glossed over the stretches of skin that the makeup and the hose hid each night. He represented her long plaited hair with a severe cut and did not round her sharp nose. The bones in her shoulders stood out with clear cut highlights. There was no softness in her eyes. Her breasts which were small and firm now hung like little ear pendants of a peculiar shape. The public view of her was shattered Helen was sure of that. She had no means to destroy the painting. It was if a secret letter lay in a safe not to be opened except on the death of the person who had put it there. It was too late now. The painting had been photographed extensively before she had seen it.

As she stood before it she heard a woman behind her mouth the cliche : "Warts and all! How honest." Helen was not in the mood for artistic integrity. As she looked at it she knew it was the end of their relationship. When Seamus came upon her in the gallery he knew too and watched her silently as she turned to face him and said nothing.

Helen walked past him. As she retreated he saw she was wearing the dark green suit he liked. She had come prepared to make the best of things and the blow he had dealt her the one she was least prepared for had undone her inner strength which she had built up with supreme dedication and training over the years.

Outside in the hot sun she knew the suit was wrong and the heels and even the little hat with the veil. Now the spangles on it upset her so much she took off the hat tore the veil from it and threw it to where her heart had dropped. Meanwhile the art critics were writing reviews of the painting that elevated Seamus to new heights. There were no bouquets for Helen.

***

In his studio Seamus looked around at the inventory on the walls and on the floor. There comes a time he mused when a stage in one's view of the world is over and it must be seen only as a building block to the next. He suddenly had a violent antipathy to his world of just a week ago. Seamus wondered if a change of style was possible. He tried to analyze his work so far. The major critics had hailed it and praised the honesty of it and could not find any derivative feeling in it. Probably that was why they were at a loss. How long would that last? Seamus knew the origin. He also knew that whatever they built up also had to come down sooner or later. Now he was the one at a loss. Where could he start again? His friend Albert had suggested a little fishing village where the light was pure. Perhaps this chemistry would produce the power and the patience he knew he would need.

There were letters waiting for him. Invitations to private and public functions. Guarantees his agent said of a fortune in fees and commissions. His credit was good and his bank account stuffed why was he thinking of changing all this success? He recalled the sound of her voice of Helen. For the first time in his adult life he had not been moved by just the physical beauty of a woman. She held a subtle hold over him. She had pulled off his armor without a fight. You don't need it she seemed to say. Let the wind blow through you. Where on earth he wondered did she get all her confidence and all her life force and why had she chosen him to share it with her? Yes, the sound of her soft voice her gentle voice. Now he knew for the first time the strength of gentleness. All the acid stored up in him had been neutralized in one hour. She been lying in wait for him. He could not tell what her motive was yet he was not suspicious but trusting. There was no doubt in him about her. Lack of doubt she had suggested that was love in its purest form and that is where his art should take him in whatever form it might take and no matter how long it took. Was she indicating that he had come to where he was too quickly? She was nine parts a mystery. As he sat there along with a life of work he realized if he returned the faith she had in him it would melt his doubts away. He stood up and looked over the city. From his vest pocket he pulled out the card with her phone number on it and saw for the first time the kissing cross she had made below it. He tore it up; he knew it was now unlisted.

The next day his agent appeared at the door.

"Allan it's time to make a change." Seamus pointed at his work around the studio. "I can't go on like this. I've run out of inspiration. I need to change my way of art and of life. I'm going to the north and perhaps the light there will show me another way."

Allan was shocked. "To walk away from this new success!"

"I've finally decided that's not how I should measure it. It's become meaningless."

Allan mocked him. "Has that woman set you on the road to Damascus?

Seamus sat down resigned to the argument. "I haven't found any answers. I need some quiet time to think this through."

"You're a successful artist," Allan insisted, "what do you have to think about?"

The blood rose in Seamus. "Where my life is going! Where the rest of the art is!"

Allan was not dismayed by his tone. "The public at least the buying one likes it just as it is. Why change it?"

Seamus tried to be patient. "Allan, you sell art. But have you any idea where it comes from?"

"I have a good idea where it goes," Allan assured him, "and I don't see you in a country cottage. You're living well above the poverty line which is where I found you a few years ago. I suppose you will be telling me next that you were happier on baked beans and toast with the occasional wedge of cheese to feed the rats."

Seamus turned around from the window. "What are you saying? That I'm an ungrateful bastard! How did you get that luxury car parked outside? You know it may be true what some of the better critics are saying…"

"Who cares?" Allan interrupted. "Nobody reads them! Images Seamus, and keep them simple and a little mysterious. Don't worry about light and shade. Don't you see that this is the age of abstraction of purism and all else you see around you is provincialism at its worst. And now you say you must get away to some northern province or other and I think that the further away you get the more you will sink into refinement filigree and ornamentation. You should just stay in the limelight. That's what sells or would you rather be a Van Gogh."

Seamus smiled. "I don't think you should mention that name in the same breath as that rubbish of mine."

Allan looked around at the art. "It's not on the dump yet."

"You're not Theo Allan."

Allan continued in his frustration. "So what do you want to do. The coal miners are a dying race. You're not religious. Where are your subjects?"

"Allan, I am hoping they are at the end of the brush."

"Oh well," Allan said resignedly, "I suppose no matter what you do now I'll be able to sell it providing you don't disappear for too long and

I will admit you have started your new career off with a bang. How do you want me to display the ballerina material?"

"I don't! Put the painting and the photographs in the vault. I'm not proud of them."

"Why not? It's made both of you even more famous than before."

"I don't think she needed more fame she's a great artist. I've decided it wasn't worth the hurt I've caused her." Seamus moved away to the picture window.

Allan kept on. "You've got other clients and the rich are getting richer."

Seamus turned from the window.

"Are there funds still to come in?"

"That takes time." Allan had a good look around the studio. "Do you want to sell all these now?"

Seamus was tired of the argument and his mind was made up. "Yes. The quicker the better. I won't be here much longer so perhaps you could collect all these canvases and sell them or put them in storage while I give up this space."

"What a terrible phrase. Give up!"

"I'll keep in touch Allan. You're my friend. The least you can take from this is that I trust you."

"As I look and talk to you," Allan responded, "I don't think you really care about the money anymore and I didn't think you had it in you."

"I'll still need some money."

After they had shaken hands Allan moved to the door. "I'll see to it."

"Thank you."

Seamus sat down not able to shake off his damp mood or Helen's face as she had turned her head to him at the gallery.

Chapter 10

The boat came in through the fog.

"Are we far from the shore?" Seamus shouted, not able to hide his jitters.

"We will soon see." The nonchalant reply from Captain Andersen irritated Seamus. Andersen turned to him.

"Sit you down. We've done this a thousand times."

"Have you ever been in the water?" Seamus asked, the sarcasm hardly disguised.

"No. I can't swim. I'm reluctant to have that experience and let that be a comfort to you. We will try and get you within five minutes of the shore. Any longer in the water and you would freeze," Andersen blew the horn again, "unless your name is Sinbad. Ah, there's the light."

Seamus sounded his relief. "A lighthouse then."

Andersen chuckled. "Well, a sort of lighthouse. Not quite but good enough. They have lit a fire for us and those like us. It will let us land right up in the middle of the beach if we have to."

Seamus was still nervous. "Is there a pier there?"

"No. Just a peaceful piece of sand and some grassland made to take us safely if this does not lift in time."

Seamus continued in the negative. "This won't lift now!"

The Captain explained further with patience.

"We might come under it. There's sometimes a wisp of a breeze off the heights."

"The light has gone out." Seamus warned.

"Never fear." Andersen again reassured him. "We have our bearings."

"Are you going to beach her?"

"Oh no. We will just sit offshore and bob along until we get some clearance."

Seamus gave him indirect praise. "Do you ever panic?"

Andersen responded. "Do you hear those voices behind and below you murmuring under their breath?"

"Yes, I do." Seamus replied.

"That keeps me calm. Like a psalm it is. Kind of holy. I think we can stop now and let out the small boat to see where we are. Will you see to it James?"

"I will."

Seamus did sit down when a voice called out through the mist. "We've got about thirty feet."

The anchor dropped and disturbed the peace.

Andersen turned to Seamus. "Do you want to go ashore now?"

Seamus had no hesitation. "No. I'll stay aboard."

He heard the Captain laugh softly. "You got more than you bargained for my lad. You know I wouldn't want any of your paintings but when I get used to you I perhaps will not mind your company."

The man who was a carpenter came along to them.

"I had a few nervous moments out there."

"The hammer missed your finger this time." the Captain quipped.

"My legs are wobbly."

"Sit down with Mr Thomson there. We will be around here for awhile."

Seamus had decided to come across to the peninsula by the direct route in this fish boat. Now, after a nervous hour or two he stopped regretting it.

"Is there anything on this beach?" he wondered, his tone entirely changed.

"Oh, just a few crosses for absent friends." Andersen assured him.

"It's dangerous then?"

Andersen laughed softly. "Only in bad weather."

Seamus couldn't hide his astonishment.

"And this isn't?"

"Oh no. We can't see but we can hear."

"Is there much traffic?" The carpenter asked.

"The shipping lanes are well offshore. But the bigger ships can come closer as they leave one ocean and enter another. That's the dangerous place." Andersen put his hand on Seamus' shoulder. "We left there half an hour ago."

"You could have told me that earlier."

"Well…there are a couple of rocks too at the low tide."

Seamus laughed. "You said there was just sand!"

Andersen continued, seemingly relaxed and enjoying himself. "Only at the low tide and we are just half way through it. But we are too far in to fret about them now. Perhaps some air would do you good. Mebbe you should get out of this cabin and go ashore after all. We can put you down. The town is just over the sand dunes. I'll see your stuff gets delivered to the hotel when we get in. James is still in the water. What do you say?"

"Whatever you want me to say." Seamus quipped, and when he had buttoned up his jacket quite relieved and ready to go.

Once he put him ashore James shouted directions to Seamus. "Walk to the left and turn right at the first opening in the dunes. You will soon come to some sort of habitation. Tell them you have landed from the drifter *'Demoiselle'* and good luck to you."

"What whisky do you drink James?" Seamus shouted.

"Malt!"

"What kind?" But James was already out of hearing above the lap of his oars.

***

As Seamus came further up the raised beach the mist began to lift just as Andersen forecast. As he turned the corner to go off the shore he made out a tall figure coming through the dunes. It was Albert. Seamus was surprised to see him.

"How did you know I was coming this way?"

"Andersen sent a message by ship to shore that they were putting you off opposite the old beacon. How are you?"

"Queasy. But a good breakfast will sort that. How long ago did you get the message from Andersen?"

"A good hour ago."

Seamus smiled to himself. "Where have you fixed me up?"

"It's not too far to the inn of the two sisters to begin with."

"Ah, I didn't know about them."

"Well, you soon will." Albert said, a little out of breath. "They're both very artistic types at least for this part of the world."

"I'd like to get some work done with local models."

"That's what they all say. The artists who come here are attracted by the light but very few of them seem able to reproduce it so far I know. Our houses are not full of their work." Albert added.

As they walked along Seamus began to notice the strong odor of fish and it nauseated him further." I hope I can face the food."

"The smell comes from the fish processing plants. That's the main industry around here. Let's get you to the hotel and have Michelle and Susannah look after you."

"Lead on…" Seamus called out.

Albert laughed. "I won't say it."

The sun suddenly broke through and showed the blue and white facade of the lodge looking as grand as a hotel should yet quite unexpected by Seamus in this small community.

As they came inside Michelle met them with enthusiasm.

"Ah, we have a new resident! An invasion! How long do you intend to stay?"

"A season!" Seamus said.

Michelle replied. "Let's hope you have some mellow fruitfulness."

Seamus plumped himself down. "Very poetic of you."

"So," she said, grinning "you didn't enjoy your sailing experience."

"Not in the least."

"Perhaps you should stick to those ships in a bottle.

Seamus was at ease with her. "There are some things you cannot bottle including your wit.

"What can we get you to eat?" she asked.

"I think some scrambled eggs and toast will do the trick and a strong cup of coffee. Any marmalade?"

"No marmalade the rest coming up. Sit down and relax."

"She's quite a woman." Seamus observed, as Michelle disappeared into the kitchen.

"You should see the other sister." Albert said."She is spectacular."

"This one is not bad either." Seamus observed.

"Yes, but stubborn." Albert warned.

Seamus dismissed the girls. "I'm not looking for a woman and especially not a stubborn one. Are there no other guests?"

"We don't get many visitors this time of year." Albert said, as he looked at the menu."The Norwegians haven't arrived yet."

"The Norwegians!" Seamus exclaimed.

"Yes. We get a group of them usually seven. They paint here every year in the early Spring in fair weather or foul."

"All men?" Seamus managed showing his tiredness.

"A mixture. But there's usually an extra man."

Seamus smiled. "And that's when the spectacular one comes in I suppose."

"It has been known. She's in awe of artists but her sister has beaten her to the punch with our latest visitor a writer directly from Paris. Here to write a novel, but has recently lost his Aunt in Paris and may be considering moving back and taking Michelle with him."

"What does she say about that? Seamus asked.

"She likes him and makes no secret of it." Seamus noticed that Albert's smile had drooped a little when he gave out that information.

"Not much to choose from then?" Seamus supposed.

"She was engaged once to the assistant pastor but he left for China and she stayed."

Seamus took off his jacket.

"A wise decision for all concerned no doubt."

Albert was quick to agree. "I think so. She's so practical and straight forward and he was just weird."

"What did she see in him then?"Seamus wondered.

"At least he was gentle and refined and quite a change from the rough houses around here."

Seamus moved his chair to look across at the bar.

"Hard drinkers too by the look of that spirit galley. I want a quiet time."

"Then don't stay in the hotel." Albert suggested at once. "It's rarely quiet when the fleet is in."

"Where can I go then? I only want room and board. I aim to paint while the sun shines. I've never painted outdoors before."

Albert had the solution. "Well, nature will take care of that part for you. In the meantime I know of a lonely cabin."

"Does it have a bath?" Seamus asked.

"The ocean is at the door!" Albert cracked.

"You're a great wit."

"The place is full of them." There was a slight noise from above and Albert stood up to see what had caused it. "Ah, here she is your ticket to heaven."

Susannah came down into the bar through the mezzanine entrance. She wasn't long out of bed and had obviously just washed her hair which hung long down over her breast. When she saw the two men she struggled to get herself together.

"It's too early." she said, tucking in her shirt properly at the back "but look what came in on high tide!'."

"His boat docked ahead of time." Albert said.

"In this fog! She stood back now and looked at Seamus. "You don't look like a fisherman and I can't think what I look like so early in the morning."

As she went behind the bar to make further adjustments Seamus was gallant.

"The day is young and all our senses are dulled including our sense of beauty." He gave her some privacy and turned to Albert. "After I get my eggs perhaps you could show me that cabin before my luggage arrives if they ever get that boat to the harbor."

"Why not stay here?" Susannah asked, still putting up her hair in the mirror.

"Albert says it's noisy."

She smiled over at him and teased him.

"I know a quiet place at the top of the house."

"And for that offer I thank you but a cabin by the sea sounds more rustic for my present sensibilities."

"Come back for lunch. The world always looks better then. Have you met my sister?"

"Yes, I've had that pleasure." he assured her.

"We're not twins you know."

Seamus laughed. "It's not that early in the day!" As he looked around and noticed how eclectic the decor and the furniture was including some religious prints Susannah refilled his coffee.

Albert stood up."If you really want the cabin I had better have a look inside it and get it ready. I won't be long."

Susannah settled herself down with the coffee pot.

"Take your time Albert." She turned to Seamus."I've only got the one customer. What do you think of the place so far."

Seamus smiled and openly admired her.

"It has the quietness of the world after a snowstorm. Who had this place before you and Michelle?"

"They were a very holy family. But luckily for mankind none of them were born towards the end of December."

At this unexpected wit Seamus let out one of his famous laughs prompting Albert to leave. As he went through the kitchen on his way out Michelle spoke to him as she was filling the tray for Seamus.

"Albert, you've introduced me but have not told me why he's here."

"He's an artist and well known but of course not locally at least not yet, and wants it to stay like that for a while though no doubt Susannah will get everything out of him."

"Susanna will have intentions on him. She likes artists."

Albert put his hand on her shoulder.

"Perhaps she thinks he can improve her palette. What about you?

"He's quite handsome and I'm sure witty with it. What's his full name?"

"His name is Seamus Thomson."

"Sofi was interested in such a man an artist of that name. She mentioned him and quoted from some article. Sofi was worldly in her own way."

"Your sister will have to watch out. She will have lots of competition. He's quite a ladies man or at least has that reputation now according to the magazines. We went to art school together and have always kept in touch through the years. He became a famous artist and I wound up here. I'd better go and have a look at the cabin. I'll be back to collect him. Look after him."

She called after him. "Save him you mean! I hope I'm not too late they are having a good laugh together."

When Albert came back from the cabin Seamus had finished his breakfast and was sitting alone which surprised him.

"How are you doing with Susannah?" Albert asked.

"She's tempting. I have to admit that."

"To old style Seamus?"

"And the newer edition."

"I think you will find," Albert said, "that her real worth is less evident than her sensuality."

Michelle came over to greet them.

"Is this a serious talk or can I sit on somebody's knee?"

They both drew back their chairs.

"I pick you Albert but only because I see you have brought your straw hat with you."

"That's not fair!" Seamus moaned."He probably just carries it for effect and never wears it."

"Don't fret Seamus," Michelle advised, "you will soon find the kind of girl you need with the proper prop of course."

"I've never needed a prop before." Seamus retorted.

"Seamus, that's what you think." Michelle came back.

"Your sister is beautiful." Seamus said.

"Yes, she is." Michelle agreed. "She keeps me on my toes."

Seamus continued smiling teasing her.

"She's older."

"Yes, quite a bit." Michelle whispered, making sure Susannah who had just come into the bar with some crockery could not hear her.

Seamus went on."She's very calm."

"She can get excitable." Michelle said, calmly.

Susannah came over to the table but did not sit down.

Seamus smiled at her. "You're wild."

"But lovable." she responded with glee.

"Yes very lovable."

Michelle stood up and flared her skirt. "I'm taller."

"Yes," Seamus grinned at her, "you are a little taller I see that now."

She sat down again and crossed her legs.

He complimented her. "You're funny and wild and tall."

"And lovable." Michelle said, hopefully.

Susannah tried to be calm and lovable.

"That's up to you Seamus. I must advise you that my sister is otherwise engaged at the moment. Considering your lack of response since I met you you might be too at least in spirit."

Seamus said. "You know more than I suspected."

Susannah responded. "Once upon a time I was a very honest woman because I knew no better."

He looked right into her golden eyes and saw only Germaine his first love. "I'm afraid I'm in limbo right now." he replied.

"Isn't the next step heaven?" Michelle said.

Seamus sighed. "I'm sure I'm not good enough."

Susannah had a facetious smile on her face.

"I know a closer place where you also have to be good."

Seamus frowned. "And if I'm not?"

She reassured him. "In my version of heaven there's always a second chance."

"Just two?" he asked.

Michelle stood up and adjusted her skirt again.

"Double or quits. I think that's fair."

Seamus admired Michelle's red jacket.

"Yes. I don't fancy limbo."

Albert chimed in. "I think it's time for the cabin inspection Seamus."

Seamus stood up and embraced both women then followed Albert out into the brisk air.

When they had gone the sisters sat together.

"Albert says he's famous." Susannah said.

Michelle sat down again happy with the attention she had got with her skirt. "Then you wouldn't know him."

"All I know is that he's young and good looking. A rare commodity."

"Men are not commodities." Michelle insisted.

"You know what I mean." Susannah responded. "The only excitement around here is the odd visitor."

"You make us sound like a desert island in the Pacific."

"I presume you're doing alright yourself with your castaway."

"Not quite your type." Michelle said sharply.

Susannah lit a cigarette. "I don't need to take up religion or nursing to attract men."

Michelle blew the smoke away. "I don't do back flips."

"You should wear black you're such a rude prude." Susannah puffed out.

"This Seamus has a reputation you know." Michelle said.

"I'll add to it." Susannah said, full of confidence.

"He doesn't paint nudes." Michelle informed her. "Abstraction is his game."

Susannah took a long draw from the cigarette.

"I'll distract his abstraction soon enough."

Michelle did a pirouette across the floor.

"You'd better hurry. At the rate this place is going into debt you don't have much time."

When the first customers of the day came into the hotel they were surprised to see the two sisters dancing with each other and laughing hysterically.

Chapter 11

As they made their way to the cabin Seamus questioned Albert.

"Where does the writer live?"

Albert pointed to the west.

"In a big red house on the beach."

Seamus looked for the house. "A rich man."

"No." Albert said. "It belonged to the Aunt who just died in Paris."

"How long has he been here?"

Albert thought for a moment. "A few months."

Seamus looked towards the beacon on the hill in the west.

"I'd like to meet him."

"He's fairly antisocial." Albert advised.

Seamus sympathised. "Probably struggling. I know the feeling. Albert, your voice has changed. It used to be so highly pitched you could tune a violin by it."

"It's the refreshing tone of a dilettante artist when his colors change. Any other complaints?"

"I've been advised that there are bugs in this town that only bite strangers and there was no marmalade for breakfast."

As they walked the wind blew on and the mist began to clear completely and the grey lighthouse at the point gradually came into view.

"You might have a nice day yet." Albert commented, while pulling up the zipper on his jacket.

"I need a sleep first. How much farther?"

Albert pointed out the cabin. "Look down there between the dunes. It's old but it has two rooms and an attic. You can cook if you want. There is beauty all around it."

"Who normally stays here?" he asked.

"Usually artists will rent it for a season because it's so near the beach. Come on in." Albert was enthusiastic. "The living room is quite bright and the bedroom has a bathroom attached. There's a studio upstairs and a nice balcony."

Seamus wandered into the bedroom. On the bedside table there was the previous month's edition of 'Stare' magazine with a photograph of Seamus on the cover.

Seamus fretted at Albert. "Did you put this here?"

"Actually," Albert was quick to advise. "The young woman who rented here recently left it behind. According to Michelle she borrowed it from my art class library."

As Seamus flipped through the magazine he came across the centre piece showing some of his early work and a short article on his broken relationship with Helen.

Seamus showed his displeasure.

"She must have formed a bad opinion of me after reading this stuff."

Albert reassured him. "I think she was just interested in the art. She's very sophisticated and had just been the victim of a tragedy. Her fiancee was killed on his way up here to be the manager of the bank. Would you like to see the studio?"

Seamus recovered. "Of course." He kept the magazine in his hand as they went up the wooden steps. The first thing he noticed in the studio was an easel in the corner with a painting of a young woman.

"Who is she?" he asked.

"Sofi." Albert said with some pride." The young woman."

Seamus absorbed the painting. "Where did she go?"

"Nobody knows. She left in the night." Albert said.

Seamus lifted the painting from the easel and took it to the light. "Who painted the likeness?"

"Can't you tell it's one of my masterpieces?" Albert said.

"You're so modest Albert but there is some of the beauty left."

Albert ignored the faint praise. "I couldn't improve on that."

Later, while he waited for Albert to return with food and clean sheets Seamus found a note stuck on the inside back page of the magazine where there was a full sized photograph of him collecting an award.

'Is there something in your heart that might surprise me?'

For some reason whose source was as unknown to him as it might have been also to the writer Seamus felt the words personally as if she had left them for him. And as time went on and he tried to put the phrase out of his mind Seamus would become attached to the unhappily painted likeness for even the dilettante Albert could not obscure all her character or separate her from the words he had taken to heart.

When Albert returned Seamus was full of questions about Sofi. "Tell me all about her. I feel her still in here. She's powerful."

"She's a young woman who lost her lover unexpectedly. She stayed here awhile and wrote poetry and played the piano. Her poetry is lovely.

It is written as if she is having an affair. I know she wasn't but was trying to recover from lost love."

"Where did she go? Did she get anything published?"

"We don't know where she went but Michelle and I have collected what we can of her poems and are trying to get them published in collaboration with Sofi's sister."

"I'd like to read what you have. Is that possible?"

"Of course. Will you take the cottage?"

Seamus was certain. "I wouldn't live anywhere else. Do you have another likeness of the girl?"

"I don't, but I'll ask her sister to bring one with her when she comes up next week. Oh, and Michelle has one posed with her fiancee that she left on the mantlepiece but it doesn't do her justice either. She seems to be waiting for someone to capture her spirit. "

"Who took the photograph?"

"I don't know but she valued it." Albert said.

"She did leave it behind." Seamus remarked.

"Yes. " Albert agreed. "She left in a hurry I'm afraid, but perhaps wanted to leave a memorial of what had been. Oh, it's so cold when the wind comes from the east but down here in the dunes you can have peace and quiet too. There's lots of wood for the fire and the rent will be reasonable. I brought you bedclothes etc. The furniture is comfortable. There's good light in the attic don't you think?"

Seamus was still full of curiosity about Sofi.

"How long has it been empty?"

"Since Sofi left I've kept it free in case she comes back, but I don't suppose she is coming back."

"Then why rent it to me?" Seamus asked.

"I think you will make good use of it. She would have liked an artist to follow her I think. Now she will have a man to share it with her. She has a presence."

Seamus put his hands up. "Please! No ghosts!"

"Perhaps a very pretty one to speak to you while you sleep."

"Apart from teaching what do you do around here?"

"I came to be an artist. I'm not so I just teach and live like one. Put the kettle on and make some coffee and then you can have a nap. Light the fire. You will happy here I guarantee it."

Seamus still held the painting of Sofi. "I wouldn't dream of doubting you. I'll need more than coffee."

"I'll bring some bread and cheese. You can fill up the ice box with an order from the hotel."

"I'd like cream for the coffee." Seamus insisted.

"Write me a list while I'm away and I'll have it delivered. You can pay at the end of the month. Did you bring artist's supplies with you?"

"They're in the luggage." Seamus said, absentmindedly.

"I'll fix that too."

When Albert came back and they sat drinking coffee Seamus held up the painting

He was brutally frank. "I think I can do better than this."

Albert didn't show his chagrin. "I thought you were putting women away for the season."

"I think this is one I can live with. You must tell me her story."

"I've told you all I know. But I think you should sleep. I'll bring your luggage when it arrives."

Seamus lay down on the bed. "Tell me her name again."

"Her name is Sofi. You can be comfortable here. Nobody will bother you unless you want them to come around. Look outside at the pathway. It's hardly ever used. There aren't any bugs in here."

"No matter," Seamus said, "they never come near me."

"You are unique then." Albert quipped.

"No. Just poisonous. See if you can you find me a good likeness of this woman."

"I'll ask her sister to look around for one."

"Oh yes she has a sister."

"She does and I'm in touch with her on the publishing side. She will wonder why you are so interested."

"With your permission I'd like to paint the cover for the book."

Albert was surprised and showed his delight. "That would help introduce her to a wider public if you did that."

Seamus held up his hands. "You must not advertise that I'm here. People are looking for me and I need some private time."

"The last thing I read," Albert said, "had you down as a drunkard and a womanizer. You took a woman we all considered virginal and made her look like a prostitute and here you are sober and only interested in a woman you've never met and who can't be found."

Seamus took the criticism without dismay.

"Too bad I missed her."

"She would have haunted you."

Seamus lay akimbo on the bed the painting of Sofi in his right hand. "She might yet."

"Did Sofi know we were friends?" Seamus asked.

"I never spoke to her about you. Do you think I go around telling everyone that I know Seamus the rake?"

Seamus laughed. "The rake!"

"That's what the magazine called you.

"You must be dreadfully short of reading material up here. What else did she leave?" Seamus asked.

"A wunderkammer. A cabinet of curiosities."

Seamus was curious. "Where did that word come from?

"From Albert Durer I think."

Seamus took up the painting again.

"Are you in love with her face?" Albert asked.

"No. With her sadness I think. That's what fascinates me. From what you tell me. Her struggle with the spirit."

Albert was curious. "What spirit?"

"Why, loneliness!"

"You've never been lonely." Albert said.

"No. But maybe now for awhile from choice. None of my memories are serving me well at the moment."

Albert stood by the bed. "How will you get more from seclusion?"

"I'll have to find out." Seamus said. "Perhaps I'll know when I wake up. A dream or two sometimes soothes the soul and serves us well. I haven't been doing that lately."

Albert moved to the door. "I've never looked on this place as being good for dreamers. It's a day to day storm to storm existence here. Raw life ; raw faces and raw hands; raw souls and no time for dreaming."

"I don't have wanderlust" Seamus said,"unless you deduct the prefix. With me it's 'what shall I do now?' Or…'it's what can I do now and get away with?'"

"There's nothing up here," Albert said, "to excite a traveler. No watercolors of exotic places in the barber shop and burning you boats does not go down well here. But you could be like our postman who when he briefly escapes his wife at the end of his shift can sit at the hotel bar and pretend he's sorting mail on the Orient Express."

"He sounds like me. I know what I'm doing but don't know how I do it. There's always a time to start. No sign of my luggage?"

"No sign of the boat." Albert said. "It may be still drifting in the fog bank. It was a fluke that you were able to get off it as easily as you did."

"Maybe they're still fishing." Seamus advised. "The captain said they hadn't made a good catch and he was crazy enough to fish in the fog. It took me awhile to get used to him. At the last minute actually. Art doesn't always travel well."

"Artists you mean? What does travel well?" Albert asked.

"A good question. You're full of them."

"Isolation stores them up."

Seamus was still wide awake. "Keep them coming. I need stimulation."

Albert obviously wanted to leave but hesitated. "I have a table in the hotel every morning. Why don't you make it a habit to have breakfast with me."

Seamus broke away from a recollection of Sofi. "Which sister will serve us?" he asked, facetiously.

"You choose." Albert suggested.

"Aren't you interested?" Seamus asked.

"They've known me too long." Albert said. "They don't see me anymore. A man with a limp and a mysterious artist have more appeal to them."

"You should travel." Seamus advised.

Albert now had the door open. "I'll wait for the spring when the new flock is ready to spread its wings."

"You've quite a way with words Albert."

"Thank you." Albert said. "Not much practice. All on paper."

Seamus surprised him. "I'd like to see some of that."

"Did you bring any work with you?"

"No." Seamus sighed suddenly tired. "I'm making a new start getting away from abstraction."

"You seemed to be doing alright." Albert said.

"A dead end." Seamus admitted. "I ran out of ideas."

"And customers?" Albert questioned.

"No. Plenty of those once your name is made and you might show a profit for investment."

"A commodity?" Albert stated, flatly.

Seamus agreed. "Exactly! A magazine artist."

Albert encouraged him. "You'll change that?"

"That world forgets quite easily," Seamus rejoined, "when you don't sell their product for them."

It was Albert's turn to sigh. "What a hellish life. This will be slow enough. There now the wind is freshening."

"How can you tell?"

Albert was now over the threshold. "I saw the smoke from your fire from a distance. Walk over for breakfast in the morning. Nine o clock. What made you decide against coming here by road?"

Seamus laughed. "I'd never been on a boat before."

"How did you like it?"

"I didn't. Which is why I abandoned ship as soon as I got the chance."

Albert was reassuring. "Perhaps your ship really has come in this time. If I get you some of the poems what will you do with them?"

Seamus thought for a moment. "Find out what they makes me feel and if they inspire me too."

"I thought you had given up abstract art."

"Love is not abstract Albert. When is the sister coming?"

"In the next week."

"Is she younger or older?"

"Actually," Albert finally informed him, "they are identical twins."

Seamus was roused. "Why didn't you say that in the first place! A ready made model! Hurray!" Seamus put the painting down. "The flesh will be much better. What's her name?"

"Her name is Sara."

"Sofi and Sara! Will she be agreeable to my efforts?"

"We will wait and see." Albert closed the lower half of the Dutch door. " Get some sleep. You look tired."

"I am tired." Seamus admitted. "But I think I might take a walk by myself along the beach. In which direction is the writer located?"

Seamus came to the door for directions. "Turn left over the dunes. You can't miss the house. It's the only one on shore towards where the two seas meet. See you in the morning."

"Thanks for everything Albert."

***

Seamus wandered out towards the shoreline and from the beacon height above his little cottage he could just see the meeting of the waters thrashing away past the grey lighthouse. In contrast to the early morning it was now bright with a brisk almost warm wind and the slipstreams of the fishing boats coming from the open sea filled the waters. He took time away from the sands to have a look at the lighthouse as he passed but found it no different from any other in construction and not as interesting as the old beacon that would have been lit in other days with firewood and swung around to show the seafarers the way in. As he walked back through the heather he heard but could not find his first cuckoo. Later when he told of this he found that what was unique to him was quite common to all the locals yet it left him with his own wonder intact as the same bird had left Terence earlier.

Almost to the water's edge and to his surprise he came across what looked like an old cist but instead turned out to be the resting place of a poet whose name he recollected but had not read. He would later come to that man's house still full of his memories hear his songs and browse his paintings; see, that this place had not changed much ; it was just one more hook placed in his heart. Now for a man who had lived in abstractions that seemed to need no specific detail the world suddenly was full of it engaging another part of his mind. *The shock of the new.*'

As a figure in the distance grew more distinct Seamus realized it was a man sitting in a chair with a notebook on his lap. He wasn't asleep but neither was he aware of the approach of a stranger; he was dreaming. What struck Seamus was the upright carriage yet so relaxed. He was looking at the seas as they convulsed in the wind coming so strongly from both directions until they rivaled the gale that apparently parted the Red Sea at least that was so in Seamus' imagination. But in this world where so many had died for so few yards of ground where was the promised land?

Then, the forthrightness of Terence's face gave him hope.

"I might be disturbing you." he managed over the roar.

Showing some surprise Terence turned and replied.

"Certainly not. I'm pleased to see another soul braving this chaos. Just sorry I can't offer you a seat."

"That's fine. I'm sure Canute only had one."

Terence smiled. "He might have had more hope than I have at the moment."

"Ah," Seamus agreed, "there's always the moment. I'm having one of those too."

"It might not be as long as mine." Terence said with a little too much certainty.

"We're both young." Seamus replied, sitting down on the nearest boulder.

"Were young," Terence insisted, "some cynics might say."

Seamus folded his arms across his chest feeling the cold. "Who knows what the salt wind will preserve."

"Best not to turn your face away as it may carry the food of the gods. I'm Terence."

"I suspected you were. I'm Seamus. Here for the wisdom of solitude and to find it with only a paintbrush."

"You may find solitude easily enough but the other may defy compatibility so rare is it. Unless an uncompromised mind can comprehend. What have you tried?"

"Abstraction." Seamus said, "But it seemingly led me astray. Down a divided path."

"Are you changing your style?" Terence wondered

"Just as your war killed the world of the waltz," Seamus replied, "it's possible that what we thought might replace it was a false step."

Terence smiled. "Have you fallen out of step too?"

"I had the diploma but couldn't dance." Seamus looked out at the current. "I'm part of the cultural crisis at least in my own head. My geometry was rational but suddenly I became psychological man searching for more feeling something instinctive. I've been wearing a mask to hide my anxious face."

"Which ocean will you choose?" Terence enquired, indicating both places.

Seamus stared out past the incoming tides."I've a feeling that it may have already chosen me."

Terence stroked his left thigh. "Ah, not quite a fatalist."

Seamus noticed the hand movement but still did not see the brace. "I don't see any other option."

Terence pulled down his beret tighter. "Perhaps you've been wounded more than me."

Seamus adjusted his seating arrangement. "Appearances can deceive even a born again artist."

"I don't know any zealots who can paint." Terence said.

"Though the world was once full of them."

"Let's hope it empties out." Seamus looked down the beach.

"I was looking for your house."

"Then why don't I show it to you." Terence said, yet made no move to get up. "Time I got up out of here anyway. Are you Albert's friend?"

"Yes."

The light forced Terence to squint. "He mentioned you might be coming. Have you known him long?"

"Since childhood."

Terence rubbed his thigh again and stretched out his good leg. "He's a quiet man."

Seamus grinned. "I may have made up for him. You haven't been here very long. How long will you stay?"

Terence gave nothing away. "The house is free I don't eat much and it's quiet."

Seamus now noticed his leg brace and Terence looked at him cautiously."Hopefully this is not permanent. A war wound. Of which it has been well said: *'Glorious to receive but indecent to expose.'* Especially to attract women. I was one of the lucky ones."

Seamus was embarrassed. "No Terence I was. Being too young to go. Another year and I might have the same scars as you or worse."

Terence turned wistful. "The only advice I can give you is that in order to escape the trench mind I tried to remember the oranges I ate in Spain one year and the first time I saw a lemon tree. By such simple means a man may survive."

Seamus moved again. "No apple dreams?"

Terence laughed. "I wasn't in Eden."

"Did you find any evil?"

"Yes. But never a tree of life in sight."

"Perhaps God was looking after you." Seamus suggested.

"If he was," Terence said, "he imagined me as a worm and not as a man." Then for some reason he changed the subject.

"Our dear departed poet Sofi supposed that only the unhappy come here to stay."

Seamus gave a rueful look. "I missed her but she has already affected me in just a few hours of being in her cabin. I'm sure she was very wise as well as beautiful."

Terence brightened up. "She had that kind of influence on people. She could calm them down. There she was the one with the most hurt; the youngest amongst us; and possessing the most strength."

Seamus began to fidget again. "Albert says that he and Michelle plan to publish her poetry. Perhaps they think she will be forever anonymous."

"Well," Terence agreed, "she did leave everything some would consider worthwhile behind and over time she hasn't turned up anywhere despite all our enquiries. So they thought the poetry might come to her attention and bring her back."

"I'm hoping they will let me design the cover of the book."

After Seamus blurted this out, Terence showed some interest. He leaned forward. "Oh. What did you have in mind?"

"Her portrait. I'd like to paint her."

Terence was doubtful. "In absentia?"

"Albert says her sister is an identical twin and she'll be here in a few days. She could model for it since there doesn't seem to be a reliable likeness."

Terence moved along. "Albert told me you were coming Seamus. Lots of subjects in this wild place and a lost classic group to follow upon."

Seamus was doubtful. "Sometimes that can only be done once and there's nothing much left to say. I haven't had a close look at what was going on."

Terence said. "You could do worse than take up where your predecessors on this beach left off."

Seamus gave his quizzical look. "And where was that?"

"Filling nature with the people who survive in it and with a little poetry thrown in."

As he listened to Terence Seamus had the memory of a cock crowing that January morning when he looked through his work and knew at once that he had to make a new beginning.

Terence continued. "I must let you know right away that I am well acquainted with your work Seamus and have never admired that style of art. Not for it's lack of detail but having spent four years in geometrical situations I can assure you that Charles Darwin would show more recognition to their evolution than any practitioners of the static plastic arts who have neglected to discover the patent fact…that, over time, they crumble."

"I fail to see your point." Seamus rejoined rather tartly. "I'm an artist not a biologist or a mathematician or an ex soldier."

Terence was ruthless. "Well, you certainly show some of the skills of a laboratory technician. I'm sure a multitude of small animals could fit uncomfortably into your shapes."

Of late Seamus had gone more or less to the same opinion, nevertheless he was nonplused and showed his sensitivity. "I'm sure in time I'll be grateful for your insights Terence and I might even recall them whenever you produce your own variation on the world."

Terence seemed to regret his critique at once but did not apologise. "I agree it's easy to criticize and I admire your own good grace though it strikes me from your lack of reaction that you may be paying some attention to some of your more vocal critics who seem to expect more from you than design derivatives of Miro and Picasso. The farther north you are from them may provide us with a revelation of your own genius."

Seamus was still upset. Trying hard not to show it. "I suppose you're trying to tell me that I've been out of my depth."

Terence pointed to the sea. "The longer we paddle in familiar waters the more likely that the tide will cover us. Making flesh and blood so mechanical seems a contradiction in terms."

Seamus had a sense of reconciliation "It's only natural for you to seek peace and quiet."

"That's only one part of it." Terence replied. "I suppose it may be a retreat from superstition good luck charms miracles and rumors. Barriers to terror!" Terence offered more advice. "Better to leave what you had to say behind you and see what crops up here. If the sister is anything like Sofi she may be a find an inspiration."

Seamus stood up. "I'm not looking at the moment."

Terence smiled. "She might be."

"You look well traveled." Seamus said.

Terence put that to rest. "I'm not here to write a travel book; to set out on a journey to experience the past in some time warp filled with distracting adventures and then to return in triumph to my native hearth with perhaps some physical symbol in my possession to prove that I've been here and rediscovered myself ; can hold up some sort of grail to prove it; and then be reintegrated into the society I left behind."

"So what are you here for?" Seamus asked.

"Escaping from the known world ; hoping it's healthier to make up another ; and then live in it for as long as possible."

Terence made no mention of his current dilemma; to stay here or go back to Paris. As Seamus looked more closely at Terence his artist's eye saw a mask. It would be a fine talk between them but not a conversation. Terence could never be trivial.

Seamus continued his probing. "Don't you think that Paris or Rome or Vienna are better venues for stimulation for inspiration for novel writing?"

Terence realized at once that Seamus was reconsidering his reasons for coming to this northern outpost. He tried his best to reassure him that the resting place wasn't always of consequence. "As I recall Conrad didn't write the "Heart of Darkness" in the Congo. He used a vision of Caesar invading Britain up the Thames to start him off and ready the reader for the results of the Belgian encroachment up the Congo into Africa. In your own art Delacroix had never been to Babylon yet painted the death of one of its ancient kings. No Seamus, if you are worried about inspiration I think it may have more to do with what you brought here than any fancied isolation."

"I'm not crazy you know." Seamus said.

"You look very sound and very sensible." Terence held his arm for a moment to reassure him.

Seamus, as his feeling for Terence went from one side to the other was doubly touched and said sincerely. "How kind of you."

Terence continued. "Still, from my own point of view one wonders if there's enough sense and sensibility left to fill another novel."

Seamus laughed. "I'm sure manners have changed far enough over the years to allow at least one more exposition."

Terence laughed too. "Well, I was planning fewer characters than Jane Austen. So far it's just a welter of dullness."

"There's only two of us!" Seamus exclaimed. "If I get into it please make me witty. I've been called a comedian and sometimes essentially a libertine with the occasional bout of piety."

Terence picked out the lighter of the nomenclatures.

"You don't look comical."

Seamus smiled this time sensing the irony. "I just stepped off a ship ; a bunch of pirates made me walk the plank and it was then I discovered I should have learned to swim."

"These waters are for wading no higher than the ankles." Terence advised.

Seamus threw a stone into the sea. "I'm just testing them. I've been traveling for two days but don't trust sleep yet."

Terence offered more advice. "Better get some in the daylight the sparrows here sing all night." He pointed over to the east. "I know this place looks as though it has no color but even the fog can turn blue like Monet's haystack. In the next month Michelle says the sky will be full of spider's webs and the country as dry as powder."

"I look forward to that!" Seamus said, tongue in cheek.

Terence was tolerant of the urban smugness. "I hope you can handle it and stay around awhile."

Subtle as the change of voice was Seamus picked it up. "I've a lot to learn. I've lived mainly indoors and in cities all my life."

"Let's hope you're not another bird of passage like me."

"We'll see how far I can fly," Seamus responded, "and learn to keep my mouth shut for a while."

Terence put his hand to his ear. "Even the crickets grow quiet here when the wind blows strongly enough. There's no seediness here. You'll have to travel elsewhere for squalor or grass huts or to contract malaria or be eaten alive by red ants. The light is good but it can't penetrate the rocks. We are too far north for that."

Seamus grinned. "I think all of the above is for your trade and I will stay with the dancing girls."

"It's too cold for them here." Terence insisted.

"Will you write an adventure story?" Seamus wondered.

"Only the disillusioned and the cynical write those."

"Perhaps they write them to make up for missing the war experience." Seamus suggested.

"I'm glad they did miss it. I'm done with that because I was there and don't have to invent it or imagine that I will come across anything worse.

All I can do now is perhaps to recollect what violence has created in me in tranquility. The main thing you come away with from those situations is the feeling of helplessness. You smell like a coward and only a hair away from doom. I suppose that's why I felt so close to Sofi. The day her fiancee died it was doomsday for her and I suspect there may even have been some guilt that like me she survived. That's why she and I turned to the only security left for us which was a creative instinct that promised an armistice if not a lasting peace."

Seamus was impressed. "You might have taken up politics."

"Who knows?" Terence chuckled. "Fate brought me here and it may take me there too."

"I'm hoping myself," Seamus continued, "that as I'm seated at a dinner party I may be introduced to my neighbors as having just returned from two years alone with the cannibals; just so long as they don't look for the non existent labels on my luggage. If you have an overactive imagination then a travel book may be the best place to exercise it without being found out."

"Then you came to the right place for your first journey," Terence said, "there are no touts or pimps here and certainly no inquisitors."

Seamus looked out to the dark swirling waters. He felt as lost as a tenor who has just missed a high note. "What do you see ahead?" he asked, pensively.

He got an enigmatic reply. "A soft afternoon."

Seamus smiled. "A quiet expectation."

"We are obliged to each other for it." Terence replied.

"These waters seem to me to encourage pandemonium." Seamus commented.

Terence recalled something similar that Erik had said.

'Sometimes the water is hungry and when the lost come to the surface they are as naked as the sand.'

But for Seamus he just shook his head agreeably. There was a smirr of rain and Terence made an awkward move to stand up ; managed it rather unsteadily then turned to fold up his chair. They walked together until the red house loomed up ahead of them and Terence pointed out a shortcut to the cabin between the dunes.

"Just follow that little spring from the beach and it takes you right above your place." Terence continued, "There are some nice views from there. Would you like to see inside the house?"

"I wouldn't mind," Seamus replied with returning enthusiasm," and I'd like to paint the outside."

"It has a lot of stories to tell inside too."

This is a nice funk hole." Seamus suggested using a term from the late war that implied safety before duty.

The expression cut Terence and he made a sharp reply. "Better than a mass grave!"

Seamus wondered what had brought that on but continued on a wartime basis. "What about all those gravestones?"

Terence was still in his dark mood. "Most of the lost men are not in there. Even Yorick couldn't find their bones."

"What is your conclusion?" Seamus wondered.

Terence made another terse reply. "Maybe there's nothing worth dying for."

Seamus was taken by surprise. "Maybe…nothing?"

"Who can be sure what is?" Terence replied."Sometimes things seem to lose their significance."

"How cynical." Seamus replied, his head down.

Terence realized the innocence and obvious lack of experience of the man and tried to elaborate.

"I would just call it a departure."

"What kind of departure?"

"Oh," Terence said, quite sadly, "one where you think you are never coming back from."

"Like death?" Seamus questioned.

Terence was curt. "I've seen the dead."

Seamus then got to the heart of the matter. "Did you ever consider suicide?"

Terence gave that some thought. "That's a philosophical problem. Of course the problem with being a philosopher is that you are required to have a philosophy and a further demand must be that you are not the only one who fully understands it. Hopefully my mind is stronger than any such philosophy." And then he referred to the disabled veterans of the war who congregated in Paris in government provided tricycles. "I'm not ready for a three wheeled self propelled carriage yet!"

"At the moment," Seamus said, seemingly out of context, "I can't tell the difference between a snowdrop and a snowflake."

Terence seemed suddenly grateful for the bathos and also rose to the occasion. "There isn't much difference unless you stay here in February and March. Anyway who would consider going to Brazil just to see the amaryllis apple blossoms?"

The subtlety of Terence's reference quite escaped Seamus. They came through the house which raised no interest from Seamus until they came to the main bathroom.

"Look at the bath! It's black!" he cried out.

Terence explained. "I'm told that it once belonged to an eastern potentate who insisted on bathing his women in it."

Seamus was still aghast. "But it's black!"

"Yes so were the ladies, mostly ; muscatels." Terence raised a laugh. "Though there may have been some immigrants."

"What are you planning for this evening?" Seamus asked when they came out to the patio.

Terence swept one hand across the sand that stretched for miles and showed his regard for the lack of depth in their conversation. "I suppose I should bring in the camels for the night."

As they parted they shook hands yet made no promise to meet again. Seamus was aware but had not been informed by Terence that he was back for a few days to collect his papers and to persuade Michelle to come to Paris with him to share his sudden inheritance. His mind was still in transition from imminent poverty to unlimited riches. Hardly anyone here knew of the change in circumstances. In fact he was having trouble accepting the change. Too many changes on the planet ; the chemistry not able to catch up; nothing solid; still gaseous.

Chapter 12

Albert sat outside the hotel waiting for Seamus and serving his memories at the same time. His father had planted oaks on his property and they had done well over the years of Albert's youth. He had watched the trees coming out to bud only when the predators had been eaten by their enemies. There was a place for patience and enduring with the gifts given and passed down. And why should he travel far from there except to meet his fate and perhaps a fair Rosamund. He had been born a beautiful child and perhaps a too handsome man came out of the child. Sometimes when there is such beauty then nothing more is demanded; no depth is looked for and none explored; everything taken for granted.

Albert wandered around on the farm photographing birds and riding horses his other side not realized in the practical country life until he left it. When his hidden gifts came out he posed a little and could live loud his inner life or another of them. But his teachers thought this young man had just ordinary talents and would never elevate himself to a higher sensibility in art. He had learned how to look but not how to put it down with a life.

As a boy he would lie awake for hours after being shocked awake by a cockerel having a fit of delirium and felt almost as badly when the traveling birds came crying in the night to feed at the streams behind the house. His father had humanized them by saying that they were afraid to lose their loved ones in the dark. Now, the memory of someone he had lost came back to him and he had a conversation with her.

'I'm sorry. I did love you but was not ready. Now I am but too late. It makes me cheerless. Perhaps we could have had a carefree life. Your gestures your early ways of touching that string of pearls; and if you count them they may tell you the story of how many short days passed between us. There was many a lonely pier many a secret wonderful dream that the rain now washes over. Oh, what could have been! Now we are just like apples that always stay green.'

When he saw a woman with her high cheekbones and black eyes he would take a long look and be regretful again. She was still in his memory. Some images are etched and can't be edged out. In these cases there is no ground on which to place a flower ; no favorite corner to wander into and have a conversation like the one you had sitting astride the high dyke looking down at your mother's grave and discussing the Shelley she used to read from the tan bound book that was her bible; that held the songs of her romantic life. For who knows what a woman overcomes for the love of a man? Every woman may have a secret heart hidden away from the world. Her light is what we know her shade the mystery. But his mother had pulled up her roots and laid them over a chair. He could still hear her voice though he knew she wasn't there. His dark eyed mother whose love had many shades.

He called out to her too with the echoes of a Celtic poet :

'Stand still for me let me embrace you. Where could I find your equal? Bend your head to me and say hello. Are you that bird hiding in the trees that we knew by the sweet lilt you brought us from the Hebrides? Bend your head to me ; say hello.'

Now there was Michelle. She too had been languishing in his mind ever since he had come up here as he looked at her and mentored her all through adolescence. He wandered into her almond eyes but could search no further since she seemed to have no constant interest but now and then touched him with her quiet perceptions though her reach had rarely rambled from this lonely place.

So many memories to disturb his view of the ocean and the farther world from where these memories had returned and penetrated through the northern mist. The air rattling in the wind turned on him; reality came in and all the walls came down and the memories were no longer separated. Constant in his mind he knew that there would always be someone to love. One with a kind heart and a gentle hand. It was the only faith he had. The belief that there would always be someone to love.

From an upstairs window of the hotel Michelle watched Albert as he dreamed. Such a handsome man. She wondered what had driven him to this outpost. How could she consider she was part of his dream?

As they sat studying the menu a sombre figure pale of face crossed the dining salon.

"Who's that?" Seamus asked.

"That's the doctor who is called in by the family of a patient to confirm that death is near and that the rest of the relatives should gather around."

"Sounds Proustian to me." Seamus said.

"His only connection to Paris is the French coat he is wearing." Albert advised.

Seamus then noticed that the piano at the quiet end of the room had the lid open.

"Has somebody been playing the piano?"

"I don't know." Albert said. "Michelle used to play at lunch if they were not too busy but stopped when she heard Sofi play one evening shortly before she left us. But she might have been practicing since I believe Terence has a nice baby grand in his house."

"And now a grand baby! " Seamus exclaimed. "So they're connected those two?"

"Yes." Albert agreed. "There's no secret about that. She is quite enamored of Terence but I can't speak for him."

Seamus put down the menu. "I met him yesterday on the beach."

"Oh." Albert looked up. "What did you think of him?"

"His opinions are on the raw side." Seamus assured him.

"Really." Albert said. "From my own experience I found him quite sophisticated…for a Frenchman! His knowledge of art is especially extensive and sometimes subtle."

Seamus agreed. "Yes, the first I discovered the second never surfaced. Perhaps," Seamus quipped, "he's not living by his wits like the rest of us."

"There's nothing comical about him." Albert returned.

Seamus laughed quietly. "No, there are times when he eyes you and he looks like he just rose from the dead."

Albert agreed. "He saw lots of them."

Seamus was serious himself. "No need to frighten the rest of us!"

When Seamus had arrived at the hotel Albert could see at once that he had slept well and was much stronger than the previous day. Albert continued. "I've had a call from Sara and she is excited about your offer for the book but wonders at your interest. She has agreed that you can see the poetry and read Sofi's letters to her. I passed on your suggestion that their correspondence would be a nice addition to the book as a postscript."

Seamus still had his hand on the breakfast menu but did not pick it up. "Do you have any of the letters?"

"No. Everything she left, letters and poetry I sent to Vienna to her sister. But I do have a few copies of her poems."

Seamus took off his jacket. "I'd like to read them."

Albert fiddled with the little bar of chocolate served with the coffee. "They are mostly poems of regret you know."

Michelle approached but saw she should not break the concentration of Seamus and she changed direction..."You must have a high opinion of them to get involved in their publication."

Albert wondered why Michelle had not come over but did not comment. "They are as delicate and lovely as she was."

Seamus grew anxious. "She was! You suspect a bad conclusion?"

"That girl is strong but she lost her lover so suddenly that it almost undid her. She came here to recover but she may not have managed it and gone somewhere else to get over it."

Seamus continued his questions. "Have you met Sara?"

"No I haven't. I've read some of her letters to Sofi and she is not as literate but apparently just as dedicated to her singing in Vienna as Sofi once was to her music."

"Will she come up here?" Seamus asked.

"She has promised to be here next week anxious to meet you and to get some other details fixed between us for the publisher. After we've eaten we can go back to the cabin where it's quiet and you can have a look at some of Sofi's writing."

Albert was keen to let Seamus see his trove. Neither of them ate much and went directly from the hotel to the cabin.

Albert drew out a large envelope.

"These were her first poems. According to the date it took her three weeks before she could write anything. They are beyond poignancy. This is a woman's soul but she's out of our reach now."

"I'll have to lie down here and feel her presence." Seamus said." Can I keep the poems for a few days? Are these originals?"

"No. Copies. She seemingly wrote them straight out without any doubts."

"Perhaps she had lost them." Seamus considered.

"Not in three weeks!' Albert exclaimed.

"How long did she stay here?"

"A year and one month. She left when the spring came on. It was late. Her sister and her letters say she waited for it. Do you see her now?"

"Not physically." Seamus admitted.

Albert regretted asking. "Who would expect that?"

"These things happen." Seamus said.

"You are set up here now.'

Seamus gripped the package. "I'll read this in the twilight and then I'll be ready for the morrow."

Albert smiled. "I'll see you for breakfast."

When Albert was gone Seamus went upstairs. The poems were still in the original envelopes and he removed them carefully. The sender's address was on the bottom of each envelope; a nice touch that would see that the contents were carefully preserved when the flap was opened. Before he started to read Seamus examined the handwriting. She used a little circle above the letter I.

'Shutter up the sun close my eyes let me dream. What now but care disturbs this silence desperate for love as a gipsy for air. I have waited until the first flower was ready to drop; for gentle swellings and leavened gossamer ; become as shy as the wren with

the golden crown ; shuttered from the sun with my eyes closed this care still a noun. I will make a wish and call it a dream. The gift was given to say to speak out my poems ; but the wind waited its time to blow everything away that should be sublime. Oh what has there been that we could not find? Of all the hands we touch before day breaks the spell ; in all the spaces between where all should be well ; I will make a wish and call it a dream.'

It was so delicate Seamus could almost hear Sofi speak the words and it affected him so much that he read it aloud time and again before he picked up the second poem.

'Among the flowers of the field how can we ever try to sleep without love? As kept to keep makes absence easier to bear when no stars salute with wine and daffodils fill cups with tears while we add wrinkles to the years. Then do memories remember, care for all the ruptures never healed. Of all the roads love may take to the ways a heart can break, then we must sigh for every sign that may appear upon the moon for they disappear so soon.'

Seamus was so affected by the poetry that he turned to the only letter he had, from Sara to Sofi. When he had read it he disagreed with Albert's contention that she was not very literate.

'Dear Sofi, I should not dwell on your poems in the letter today for I am not fit to judge them except to hope by their expression that you rediscover your hope in the world. I have never had the love that you had with Karl and so have only my work. Plenty of chances but not taking any of them up, at least there has not been any temptation I could not resist. My studies are so time consuming and money is short. I haunt coffee houses and it is mostly older men who frequent those places ; some of them are of interest *especially those who write for newspapers or magazines. I sometimes fall in step with one of them and learn the history of the city for free. All of them are cultured interested and knowledgeable about music and Vienna's place in its history.*

There were only two poems. Seamus began to know that his opinion of love so easily obtained in his life with women was a world Sofi had never inhabited, and was so far from his imagination that the stream of love affairs in which he had never really been deeply involved unless sexually, began to mock him. He put the poems down for the moment and took a series of deep breaths that seemed to synchronise with the sputter of the spirit lamp by the bed. He tried to improve his posture in an attempt to regain his composure. He wondered how it would be possible for him to reach into the high art of feeling he had just experienced. Seamus was in a cone of light but he was not at its center. He kissed the poems and fell asleep. He did not have her letters but they were not needed. Her hand was on his cheek.

***

Albert met Sara at the train late in the evening. After he collected her luggage they walked the few hundred yards to the hotel. The only difference he found in the beginning between the sisters was Sara's voice that was pitched higher. Otherwise until she revealed her dark hair they were identical twins.

"I've booked a room at the hotel just for the night, then you can sleep for free on my houseboat if you like. The two sisters who own the hotel Susannah and Michelle are looking forward to you coming. They were both very close to Sofi."

Susannah met them as they entered the hotel and for a moment forgot that Sara was the sister not Sofi. She quickly recovered and was wise enough to leave the personal stuff to Albert. She led them into the dining room for a meal and to let them get acquainted.

"Is Michelle in the hotel?" Albert asked Susannah.

"No. She's at the red house getting things ready for Terence. He's going back to Paris and she might be going too. She'll be here shortly." Susannah knew that this news would be hard on Albert. She was well aware of his feelings for her sister and was quite surprised when Albert didn't react.

As she looked at the dinner menu Sara got right to business. "Are you sure Seamus is the right man to be connected to Sofi? These are love poems after all. He's not a good example of the constancy that's in them so far as I know."

Although he had shown no reaction to Susannah Albert's mind had wandered from Sara and he seemed a bit slow in replying to her questioning.

Albert recovered himself. "You should meet him first before drawing any conclusions. I've known him a long time and have no problems with him. As an artist he's well regarded. He's quite a different man from that painted in the papers. I have a long talk with him over breakfast every morning and I grow impressed with how much he seems to have matured."

"Has he done any work since he came here?" Sara asked.

"That's all he does." he assured her.

Sara looked across at Susannah who was discussing an order with another couple. "What about the sisters?"

"Michelle, as you've just heard is otherwise engaged at the moment. Seamus cares about Susannah in a paternal way really but goes no further which chagrins her. She paints too and is full of admiration for Seamus. In actual fact he's been sketching Michelle."

"He's handsome then?" she asked, coyly.

"You will pick him out quite easily. He's the only pale face in this town among all the ruddy fishermen and he has the dark curly hair of the Irish and their dark Celtic eyes. Oh, you'll recognize him."

"I'm here to sit not kneel." she advised him, shortly.

The pertness of the reply chagrined him a little governed as he was by the gentle ways of Sofi.

"I think it's the idea of your sister that haunts him, her suffering her sadness and yet her strength. Not the flesh and blood. He's taking a rest from that. Not even the seductiveness of Susannah has altered his course."

"Has he painted anybody here apart from Michelle?"

"The local postman is next in line."

"A worthy subject?" Sara wondered, without looking up.

Albert didn't like her condescending tone. "He thinks so."

"And the adoring sister?"

"Not so far." Albert said. "She's been painted before, many times."

"A damoselle." Sara guessed but not convincingly.

"If you mean by that courteous discreet and companionable then you have struck the medal." Albert said, perhaps seeing that Sara had already made an error of judgement.

At that moment Michelle came into the hotel and Albert rose to greet her.

"Michelle this is Sara."

"Sara! I'm so pleased to meet you. Had you a good journey up here? We're a long way from Vienna but we hope to make you as comfortable as possible."

"Once I'm fed and get some sleep I'll be fine Michelle. It's a pleasure to meet you too. I know you did your best to help Sofi while she was here. I'm hoping that when we get her work together we can find her."

Michelle walked away and Albert said nothing as Sara pulled her coat around her shoulders. "You know I'm not really hungry but I do need some sleep. When will I meet Seamus?"

"I think breakfast would be a good time. Get some rest and I'll arrange it."

"Goodnight then and thanks for everything."

Chapter 13

Sara found a note slipped under her door the next morning.

"There are times when there is movement in the air yet the heat is oppressive. You are a young woman; you may be frustrated and bored as you open all the windows to escape from the heat and also to hide the smoke from your illegal cigarette. You explore your dreams once more. Ah, those dreams. Is the sea calm or rippled? It looks placid but then you receive a note…
'Can you meet me in the hotel for breakfast at eight?'
Best regards Seamus Thomson.

When Sara came into the dining room Seamus was already seated at a table above her on the mezzanine and she recognized him at once.

"You are so quietly spoken." Were her first words to him after they introduced themselves.

"Thank you," he said. "I've discovered that we don't have to be loud in this part of the country."

When the server came with the menus she took out her glasses to read it. He was taken by how unaffected she was. "Thank you for coming on time." he said.

"I'm just glad I was here to greet you." she said. "I suppose I'm not the first in line."

He gave her a gracious smile. "You've been reading the magazines in the beauty shop."

"I don't shop for beauty." she said, rather crisply. "With a woman Seamus it's not always first come first served. What do you say to that?"

"I say that the post has arrived. All the letters are in place stamped and sealed and at the right address."

"I suppose the trains will be on time too." she teased.

Seamus paid her a compliment.

"This place has found an edge now that you're here. The genes have improved."

She could not resist it. "A strange thing for you to say considering I just came out of a cave and you've been in the sun for quite some time."

Seamus agreed. "That may be true. I sometimes feel like a waitress who goes back to work for a meal and doesn't recognize her customers".

"She's lost her focus." Sara said.

He thought a moment. "She wants to lose it."

Seamus mused that if there was a right height for a woman she had it; about five seven. The place was full of women. He looked at none of them. He did not overhear any of their chatter the way he normally did. Sara was no fading lily and looked him straight in the eye. She had no little tricks. He'd seen all of them. Perhaps she was the second pearl in a sea of oysters. Like all connoisseurs he wondered if this one would need some polishing or was she worth more with the patina as transparent as it appeared.

"That was a Skattegat of a wind last night." he ventured.

"I've been told to wait for the Kattegat." she replied, determined not to play second fiddle. Nevertheless, her body took on the unaccustomed heat that wouldn't settle. She noticed how soft his features had become. He kept his hands in his pockets as if not tempted to touch her hand on the table. She hoped her legs were in the right position ; crossed, with one lower than the other. She leaned forward and pulled down her skirt an inch.

Sara began a conversation about Sofi.

"Albert tells me that my sister haunts you."

"Like magic her form just appeared." Seamus responded.

Sara missed the reference which was to Sofi and not her own appearance. "Not quite. I have an extra mole."

Seamus was gallant. "Unseen, so far no impediment."

She smiled. "Thank you. I admired your portrait of Helen. I wonder if she was as happy."

"It came at high cost." he replied.

"For her or for you?" she wondered.

He gave a grim smile. "She's still dancing and I'm almost a recluse."

Sara looked at the menu. "Sofi's loss was permanent."

"I've read some of her poems." Seamus observed. "She's recreating herself."

Sara wasn't so certain

"Yes, but in the old skin. She might have turned chameleon."

Seamus creased his brow at that remark but kept his own counsel.

"How long can you stay?" he asked.

Sara put down the menu. "How long do you need?"

"No matter how long it takes it won't be an exact copy." he replied, showing his very white teeth.

"Albert says that Michelle is sitting for you. Will you finish her first?"

"You're well informed in so short a time. She and her friend Terence are going to Paris tomorrow. His aunt died suddenly. That's her house they are staying in. She had good taste and Terence too. Michelle is a lovely woman."

"Yes." Sara agreed. "I met her sister too…"

"She is more of a dear sweet lost young woman." Seamus said before she could go any further. But Sara persisted.

"Albert says she is quite attracted to you. Infatuated actually."

Seamus put down his menu. "You got close to Albert so quickly."

"He's a new friend for me but he loved and protected my sister. She came to depend on him. She will be pleased he is trying to show her work."

Seamus drank some water. "Wherever she is."

"Yes. Wherever she is. We hope she will see it and her chances are better now that you will paint the cover."

He took a long draught of water and asked again.

"Will you stay here for very long?"

Sara displayed her short temper.

"I just got here and already it seems long enough."

"You miss the city so quickly?" Seamus asked, quite surprised. "This is a lovely place you know."

Sara smiled. "Perhaps I need more talk than scenery."

Seamus summoned the waiter.

"Isn't this a conversation?" he asked, his smile still in place.

She teased him. "It might be if my face gives you trouble."

They both ordered a meal and Seamus continued.

"Do you play the piano?"

"Of course. I'm a music student. Why do you ask?"

Seamus flapped his napkin into place. "I'd like to hear the piano in the cabin played. Your sister used it I believe."

"She was once a brilliant player." Sara said."Too bad she had to give it up to get married and now she has neither man nor career."

"Did you like her fiancee?" Seamus asked.

"I never met him. It was a very fast affair almost an elopement. I was in Vienna they were elsewhere and his life ended before I could know him."

"Too bad." Seamus said.

"Yes." Sara confirmed in a lower more temperate tone. "Apparently he was a very quiet young man and was to become the bank manager here. They had such plans. A house too all picked out on the beach somewhere. I must visit it. She said it was red and full of ghosts. Will you come with me? Do you know it?"

"Of course. Terence lives there. But we must make arrangements for the sitting. After all that's what you're here for."

Sara was showing some travel tiredness.

"Yes, that's what I'm here for."

"You were able to get away from Vienna so no permanent connections there." he asked.

"Practically." she replied, smiling.

"Your sister was red and you are dark." he commented.

She pulled back her hair. "Is that a problem?"

"You have other prominent features."

"I'm glad you noticed." Sara said. "Except for the hair we are identical twins. Where will you work?"

"There's a good light in the attic at the cabin."

"A good title for a story." she remarked.

"Are you looking for one?" he wondered.

"No. I'm learning to sing big. I haven't the words of my sister."

Seamus leaned forward.

"I've read one of your letters to Sofi."

As the waiter delivered the food Sara hurried past that. "Albert says you've suggested we include our letters from over the last few months in the book."

"I do. If it's as revealing as the poetry then I think it may lend a lot of resonance to the book." Then Seamus changed the subject. "You didn't have second thoughts about coming?"

"Well you do have quite a reputation you know but Albert quieted my fears."

Seamus creased his brow. "Fears!"

"That I would just be proxy for my sister. I'm young you know."

Seamus grinned. "So am I. What did he tell you?"

"He said you were genuinely interested in my sister's work and personally wanted to make sure that it got out to a larger audience." Sara then surprised him. "What will you do with the original painting?"

Seamus answered quickly. "Give it to you of course."

"That's very generous. It will be worth quite a lot."

Seamus finished his coffee. "Perhaps it will pay for your search for Sofi and Albert's painting hasn't really done her justice."

"Perhaps she didn't inspire him in that direction but I think he fell in love with her as far as he could go since I think even on a short acquaintance that he is attracted elsewhere. The thing that I admire about him is that he's not possessive. He's willing to share her with you. I wonder what your reaction would be if she walked in right now."

Seamus told a positive lie. "Probably the same as when you did."

She was still inquisitive. "What was that like for you?"

"I wondered how you would be dressed."

Sara was surprised. "Really."

"Yes. If you would carry your mood in your clothes. Yellow is a good color for you and a light blue skirt. Elegant shoes too. Suede aren't they?"

"You have a good eye for color." she admitted.

"For color, yes. The choices in my other faculties have so far been deficient."

She reached down for her bag.

"Of women you mean?"

"You could say that. I suppose Albert was fully able to reassure you not to believe all you read about me in the papers."

"I'm from Vienna where the newspapers are so full of hate mail we have to read short stories to get a handle on the world. No. I've admired your art and I don't know why you are moving away from what you've done so well."

He was flattered. "It's the signature of my life; though written a thousand times still not fully formed. Will you trust me with the painting?"

"Oh yes," she said. "I've got that far."

Seamus paid the bill and stood up. "The sun is coming out. Let me have a look at you in this light. It's a powerful stimulant especially near the water."

She complained. "I can't walk on the beach in these shoes."

"No need to walk once we get there. We can sit on the sea wall down by the rocks and look north."

As they walked Sara wanted to take his arm but didn't.

"I thought young men looked west."

"I'm not adventurous." he admitted."How about you?"

"The voice has no geography. Nothing sure all at random. Chaotic until pulled out of the air."

"I hope you'll play and sing for me? I've a feeling you will be worth listening to."

"Thank you. Yes, I will and if your faith in me is justified perhaps you will put my eyes in the right place. Will you do that?"

"Yes." he assured her.

"And my nose?"

He laughed. "Yes, and your mouth."

She continued. "And no further south ; no elongated neck ; no liberties with the shape of my face; no outlandish blue colors just boring and correct?"

"I'll just show your heat." he said.

She looked aside at him. "My heat!"

"Yes," he warranted. "Passion has heat and I must find the vividness of it in your face."

She insisted further. "No enigmatic smile no earrings?"

"I promise." he said with a smile.

She wasn't entirely convinced. "You looked for the dancer's flaws. I wonder how you will find mine. Albert said he thinks Helen must have been in love with you to let you paint her. Is that how you find them, your subjects?"

"All I am has not been laid out very faithfully over the years. As time goes on perhaps I'll correct the errors."

"Or overcome them." she interjected.

He accepted the challenge. "Yes. Who knows? I may need some help."

"That will not be hard to find." Sara assured him. "The world is full of women trying to change men to their own ideal."

"I wonder if I'll find a woman who will take me as I am?"

She made a sharp reply. "First, she has to know who that is below all that paint and the infamy."

Seamus found this unexpected. "That's a harsh word, infamy."

"You seem from what I've read and heard to have led a harsh life."

"More likely been treated harshly." he thought.

"You shouldn't balk so hard at those who celebrate or denigrate your merit. Your public life at least might be easier."

He stopped at the entrance to the seawall. "You've paid some attention to my public persona."

"Not from choice. You have rather forced it upon me. I'm not wallowing in it. But I admit I see another person now."

He walked on. "You might be famous someday."

"Not sexually!" she said, too adamantly.

"Quite a cut! he replied. "Women are cruel judges."

"I'm not the woman on the wall the one you are idealizing."

He mused a little. "I wondered where that would lead me."

She was sure of that. "To a girl of red yellow blue and suede that's all. You will have to find the rest or the other for yourself."

"We can sit here." he said. "You go from innocence to perception very quickly."

"I won't be slowing down now that I'm up to speed."

"I'll soon get out of your way." he advised.

"Back to the magazines?" she suggested.

"Perhaps in a different language." he insisted, still smiling.

Are you staying at the hotel?" Seamus asked, changing the subject.

"Only for the night." Sara replied. "I've a houseboat for a week at least."

Seamus was surprised. "A houseboat!"

"Yes. Albert has two of them and he gave me one free of charge. He knows I'm just a poor music student."

"Where are your parents?" he wondered.

"My father and mother are dead. Why don't you come down to the water and see the boat. Albert moved my stuff in there this morning. And showed me the way down before we got to the hotel."

Chapter 14

With the sudden arrival of Sara in his life Seamus temporarily lost interest in her sister. Yet all sorts of visions went through his mind. All he had of Sofi was the face in Albert's painting. Sara's appearance confirmed his poor opinion of Albert's work and yet he realized that even such a result had led him to envision a rare creature and now here was her proxy on his arm in flesh and blood matching him stride for stride in her confidence. Whatever likeness there was Seamus could not quite find the same feeling in the flesh that he had developed from the image and the poetry and the impression Sofi had left among a group hard to impress. He saw the same beauty but none of the mystery he had manufactured for himself as Sofi's words took hold of his imagination. An imagination ready for inspiration and whatever else it might bring. Sara was not a disappointment nor did she fit any of the lines of the new poem he had read that morning... *'Unknown places should be lit by candles to make them soft when we find them. New found lips should just fit gently over those full of desire to kiss them.'*

As they walked through the town every eye was upon them, but mainly on Sara; fresh from the fleshpots of Vienna and chic from head to toe. Quite a few people greeted her as if she was Sofi and Seamus had to enlighten them. The little town was soon agog with what might be the beginning of an affair or the least a scandal.

As they came towards the dock she strode ahead of him to open the gate and the full physical beauty of her struck him with her poise and grace. He smiled broadly at her as she held open the gate and then let him put his arm around her waist.

"If I didn't know Albert better I'd suspect that he set you up here for himself."

"Why do you say that?"

He pointed ahead. "It's right on the end of the pier in this little alcove. A lover's nest if ever I saw one."

She was quick to tell him. "I'm not interested in Albert."

"No, I don't suppose he's interested in you either as a lover I mean. How about you? What are your interests?"

"I'll wait until I get my sea legs." she replied

"The boat is at anchor!" he assured her, laughing.

"Yes," she said, "but you know what sailors are, though you don't look like one."

"No," he said,"I had that experience on the way here and I hope this thing doesn't sway too much."

"Don't get giddy or I might distract you too."

He agreed. "You've already done that."

A slow smile came over her face.

"You might have kissed my sister by this time."

He was a lot taller than Sara and looked down at her.

"You think so?"

"She's the one with experience." she advised.

"You're seductive enough." he assured her.

Sara took her shoes off sat down on a bench and put her feet under some cushions. "Albert has good taste." she said this as if noticing it for the first time.

Seamus got down to business.

"Have you any photographs of your sister?"

"I have if you still need them."

"I'll have a look and then decide."

"Take off your jacket and I'll make some coffee. I had a tiring journey and don't want to fall asleep on you." There was a gust of wind as she came back in from the galley. "Did you survive that?"

"Just so long as there's no smell of fish I think I'll be alright."

She lowered her eyes. "Perhaps the coffee will stimulate you."

Sara wore a red fitted sweater and a white skirt. She had just kicked off the suede shoes with the louis heels. Her hair was black and long. It wasn't tied up behind and to Seamus seemed uncontrollable."

As she gave him the coffee he had a good look at her. "You're from Vienna yet you wear no makeup."

"I can't afford such luxuries." she advised.

He praised her. "In your case they would be a luxury."

Sara was doubtful. "A compliment has such a fine line hasn't it?"

Seamus persevered. "I am an artist you know."

She put her hand up to her ear and mocked him.

"I have heard."

There was a slight sign of desperation in his voice.

"Let's not spoil the conversation."

She leaned over and took up the pot, quite confident. "Drink up the coffee then."

Seamus changed the subject.

"So how is Vienna these days?"

"You've been there I suppose."

He put sugar in his coffee.

"For a few weeks when I was a student."

She seemed interested again.

"Was that very long ago?"

"Ten years now, though I didn't graduate."

"You got impatient?"

"No," he admitted. "I fell in love."

"Really!" she feigned surprise. "Yet you didn't get married."

"No," he smiled across at her, "she took up with a broker."

"For insurance?" she suggested, wryly.

"He was the one who had the heart attack. Last year I heard."

"Wow!" Sara let the breath blow out of her. "She took a while to have any effect; she was lucky to find love twice."

"She had ambitions beyond any dreams I could offer at the time." he informed her. Sara was quite unaware that she had lost his interest at least for the moment and continued in her self confident way.

"It might be different now." she suggested.

"If you asked me to paint her face from memory I couldn't recall it."

"Skin deep love!"

"Lucky escape for both of us I would say."

Sara seemed interested. "Was she an artist?"

"No, she modeled."

"But not just her face."

Seamus put his hands around the coffee cup.

"Is your sister as witty?"

"She's rather infectious. You would remember her. She was my father's favorite."

"Oh oh! Is Sigmund working on you still?"

"No. She not only plays music she also writes it or did before she met Karl. I believe she was about to give it all up for him yet she had a brilliant career ahead of her."

"Such is love."

"With Sofi it is always all or nothing so she ended up with nothing."

Seamus wandered to Sofi. "The poems are significant you know. There's no piano on this boat you must play the one in the cabin when we get started."

"I thought we were already started."

"If you wore glasses I'd ask you to take them off."

"I've got a cat. Would that bother you?"

"Not so long as it doesn't need as much attention as you might."

"I'm not house trained." she retorted.

"This is a boat! Listen it's early yet. Come to the cabin and we can get started since it seems you want to get back to Vienna as soon as possible."

***

"This all happened so quickly," Sara said as they went up to the attic. "I don't know what to do."

Seamus looked out over the water. "There are four seasons and I think you may be Spring."

"Do you like spring?" she wondered.

As Seamus decided where in the attic she should pose, he said… "It's a good place to begin."

"I am a bit green." Sara agreed.

"It has many shades." Seamus commented.

"I may be just above the white of the onion." She suggested while opening the window.

"Perhaps choice enough to be picked early."

Sara smiled at the double meaning.

"Too early then bitter."

Seamus moved the chairs. "Depends on the cook."

Her confidence suddenly returned. "You're a broth of a boy Seamus. Are you Irish?"

"My genes may have come from that direction."

Sara sat down. "In what direction are they going?"

He sat opposite. "One of the problems I've had since I came here is to find the north and south of them."

"There's a compass on the boat." she informed him.

"First I have to find it."

She pointed it out. "It's to the east."

"Exotic?"

She was enjoying herself now. "I suppose they don't sell incense here but bring your turban next time!"

Seamus surprised her. "Did you expect me to come to see you at breakfast?"

"Why do you ask?" she asked, mystified.

"You're wearing pearls."

***

Sara's intended visit for a week expanded into two. When she wasn't sitting for him in the attic atelier she was downstairs playing the piano from memory not having brought music with her. They went for long walks on the beach and had breakfast every morning at the hotel with Albert. Sara became attached to Seamus although she worried about the presence of Sofi in their lives. Seamus read and reread the letters and the poetry on a regular basis and had Sara read some of them aloud to him. She could not help but see the effect her sister's words had on Seamus. She knew she had fallen in love and needed a lovers undivided attention. Seamus was well aware of the problems but sometimes his sensual side lapsed and he was more interested in Sofi than the girl in front of him who was strong enough not to beg for attention yet at the same time needed it.

As the painting progressed Seamus struggled to find the angle of the face ; how the eyes would look ; would they smile to show a recovery from sadness? Would the colors be bright or dark? Should he include the full neck and shoulder? When Sara came into the studio for the preliminary sketches his problems only got worse. She was excited and vivacious with her black hair and eyes so how could he convey Sofi's feelings? The feelings of a poet who had been unsparing in her passion ; in her travels between the joy of finding love and the insecurity of loss. Sara was no help. She was a blank page except when she played the piano and sang for him. He asked her to play the songs Sofi liked and it was then he found that despite their being twins they had never been close and apart from music their interests had not been similar. Sofi"s obvious gift for language had not been shared fully by Sara and she was apparently oblivious to most of the allusions in the poetry. A comparison of the letters showed Sara as a phlegmatic, pragmatic, attention to detail personality and to be quite different in temperament from the lofty language of a young woman's mind in travail. Here she sat full of doubt in the shadow of her sister yet by an effort of will, willing to subject herself to comparison.

Seamus finally decided that it was a good thing that they were so different. Yet how would he find Sofi? In looking for her he did not realize that she wasn't present and yet he never became really attracted to her proxy who tried to encourage him and played her heart out every day for the first man who had attracted her and yet always aware there was another woman hidden away. It was a difficult place for Sara to be until she thought she saw that every time Seamus smiled at her and touched her it was not her flesh and blood he was loving. What moved him was the ghostly image emerging on the canvas.

When the painting was finished Seamus asked Sara to find Albert and they could see it together for reaction. It was a bright early summer day and Seamus left the dutch door open for them when he saw them come over the dunes.

He had a huge smile on his face as he welcomed them into the cabin. "Come in."

"It's done then?" Albert asked.

"Yes, so far as I can tell." Seamus answered, as he ushered them upstairs.

"And who would tell you any different?" Sara said.

"You look tired." Albert commented and put his arm around Seamus.

"Seamus look across at Sara. "An unknown woman is hard to live with. Well, here it is"

They were both struck by the ethereal look and of the northern light blue of it.

"She looks like a ghost!" Albert said.

Sara stood back and smiled. "My sister will love it. She always wanted to be mysterious; to be a puzzle nobody could solve. Look, you even put her hair up. You didn't ask me to pose like that.?"

"I didn't want her to have a gothic look."Seamus responded.

"She looks as though she's hiding something." Albert said.

"What could she be hiding?" Sara asked.

"Perhaps only she has the words to cover it." Seamus said.

"But will it attract buyers to the poetry?" Sara asked and then regretted it.

"Who knows." Albert said. "But with this wonderful painting it will make her famous and you too Sara. Was there one special poem that inspired you Seamus?"

"Oh yes. "*Wandering girl come home.*"

"That was a memo to herself." Sara suggested.

Albert turned to Seamus. "People will look at this and say you caught her soul without knowing you had never met her or heard her speak. A painting rarely has such irony when you think about it."

"Anything objectionable?" Seamus wondered.

"She looks so formal," Sara thought, "and Sofi was always off the wall. She was crazy sometimes."

"Perhaps your formality rubbed off on me." Seamus said.

"If it did then it's the only thing that did." Sara rejoined, the note of regret palpable to both men.

Albert went down below to the front door and emerged in the attic with a bottle of champagne and four glasses.

"Why the extra glass?" Seamus asked.

"It's a local custom. One for an absent friend." he replied.

Sara stood by the painting. "It's a shame you couldn't show her full personality. She is much more beautiful than this."

"It is difficult to give sadness beauty." Seamus said.

"The more I look at it," Albert exclaimed, raising his glass, "the more I realize that I've forgotten the technical problems you faced. You've left her as plain as can be with no jewelry or makeup to enhance her or to take away. Yes, just the suggestion of a woman stripped of love almost of life yet all the vital signs are still there."

Seamus smiled. "I thought she was too young for pearls."

"She looks ready to get up out of that chair." Albert said.

Seamus turned to Sara. "It was uncomfortable wasn't it?"

Yes, Sara said, grateful for his tenderness. "After two or three hours I could have slept on a bed of nails."

"There's no black in it." Albert said.

"Merely suggested." Seamus thought. "Are you both satisfied with it?"

"It's never too early in life for a masterpiece." Albert was full of praise.

"It helps if you admire the subject." Seamus pointed out.

"Which one?" Sara asked, rather too quickly.

Seamus laughed. "Fate has treated me well so far."

"You mean you have no choice?" Albert asked.

"I mean that the choice might not be all mine." Seamus answered. "Who will write the biography on the inside cover of the book?"

"Perhaps you could do it." Sara suggested, a little half heartedly. "That would be interesting."

"I think that Albert or Michelle are much better equipped since at least they knew her." Seamus commented.

"Yes, we did," Albert said, "but I had no idea of the depth of feeling within her that I was dealing with until I read the poetry and the letters. I saw her every day and she had a different face every day like the facets of a diamond depend on the light."

"Well, now she's a blue diamond." Sara said, giving a little sigh as if to say… "let's get this over with."

Albert heard the sigh and made his exit. Sara picked up the poetry and read out the poem Seamus had picked out as his favorite.

Woman wandering alone come home ; guitars are playing here for you. See all the names on your wall ; hear the voices singing your cue. Planes and trains are at your call ; woman wandering alone come home.'

Sara stopped short putting down the poem. She looked from the painting to Seamus.

"It seems a little absurd to me to think that writing a poem serves to repair such an emotional disturbance as the death of someone you love."

"Ah, there speaks the unloved." Seamus informed her.

Sara made an immediate response. "Between losing my sister and feeling affection for you Seamus I'm afraid my heart might be broken too. I suppose one of us has to make a parting and it might as well be me. I'll spend the night at the hotel with Susannah and get back to Vienna tomorrow. Someone will collect my clothes. Don't feel bad. I knew in my heart it would end like this."

***

Sara, an intelligent woman knowledge reserved, trying to hum a German folk song without drawing the attention of the man opposite her on the train who was trying to sleep. In the early morning she could see her tired face in the window but turned away from it wondering when the attendant would deliver her breakfast. She had ordered coffee and toast and was pleased that when it did arrive there was also a miniature jar of jam. She considered her life, short as it had been, and found there was a bitter sweetness in more than the half finished preserve. Her objective had been to help Albert and Michelle organise Sofi's poetry and have it published as at least one way to attract Sofi out of whatever cave she had retreated into. But now her good intentions left her and she pushed the food tray away so noisily that she disturbed the sleeping man opposite who gave her such an evil look that she changed her seat.

Later, when she changed trains in Munich she had a compartment to herself and no further stops until Vienna. As they passed Salzburg it was dark and the lights shone on the hillsides. Sara practiced on a phantom piano and was full of Mozart all the way home. Amadeus was her only welcome committee. The city was quite oppressive that year and not just from the weather ; her political friends were busy that weekend learning the anti semitic disruption rules sent down to them from Berlin.

As she came to the chapter in her musical textbook that studied Plainchant she was mortified to learn that according to legend it originated from a dove dictating music to Pope Gregory the Great, or alternatively had its roots in the Jewish tradition. Faced with the option she chose the dove. Then she returned to thoughts of Seamus.

How was it possible for a man to fall in love with a woman he had never seen except by proxy? What was so different about Sofi? She thought about this for hours as the train trundled on. They had each inherited equal parts from the mother and father. Only the color of their hair was different; the puzzle of sexual attraction. She took out her little mirror and examined her face. Seamus had kissed her cheeks but never her lips. He had put his hands around her waist from behind as he set her up while sketching but they never went higher. Sara allowed her hair to come across her face but he never pushed it back into place. He hardly ever showed any appreciation for her appearance but instead kept wondering if he had got the look of Sofi right. Despite her own brightness all he saw was her sister's sadness or at least his presumption of it. The little mirror gave no answers.

Sara tried to put the past behind her but soon found that it had not ceased to exist. And pieces of it she thought she had forgotten disturbed her again; memories that grew sharper and took on new meanings not only remembered but in need of resolution. Yet she was not resolute enough to make out anything positive; nothing to give her any sense of her power which now in the subdued light of the carriage was low. She took out her little mirror again and thought she saw a wrinkle. She was not long through twenty years.

***

When Sara had gone and the painting finished. Seamus was at a loose end. What should he do? He sat on the marble plinth nearby the grave of the famous poet buried deep in the sand and had a conversation. The time was late evening ; the wind had dropped for once to a zephyr ; somehow or other ever since he had spent some days in the poet's house and read his poetry listened to a concert of his music and admired his landscapes Seamus was in some awe of such a creative genius and was inspired himself.

So far he had done some sketches of Erik and Michelle but now he had been faced with Sofi and how to search out the soul of a woman he had never met. His change from a flat palette to a more lively assortment of colors that he had embraced when painting Erik and Michelle had to be abandoned again for the pale light of Sofi as he imagined she veiled herself in a soft bloom of blue spurred him on and he eventually thought there should be more than one vision of white through the pink of a flower preferring partial shade to sun and which would prosper in most soils; needed nurture and could provide it; rooted in the Spring. Whatever is lost to the mind may be recovered in dreams. Earlier in the morning he had seen some children cavorting in the water. On the hot sand further up the beach stood an eight year old girl, a silhouette in a blue dress and a little rakish hat her stomach pressed out. As she watched her friends the naked boys gambol in the surf Seamus wondered what was in her mind. Was it envy of the raw sienna freedom or for desire of female power over them? When she turned around and caught him looking at her she smiled and he guessed the answer. Seamus then decided to go to Vienna and look for Sofi.

Chapter 15

In the restaurant where the food often did not live up to the four stars the owner put on the lintel above the outside door, the chef Daniel often complained of lack of cash to buy the best meat and seafood but neither had he shown any intention of shooting himself in the fine tradition of Parisian chefs who had failed to live up to expectations. Fish could swim upriver and be hard to catch at lunch cows apparently took their time to herd together in the evening. It was better to avoid the roast at dinner.

The music was playing when Sofi entered the café. Lafargue's daughter Margie played piano and could sing bright or sad chanteuse songs on request. Occasionally a friend came in and played a soft trombone and could also double up on an African drum. All the while Lafargue stood proudly behind the bar especially when the customers applauded or called out songs for Margie to play or sing. She drew students from the University which was hard to do against more glittering attractions nearby.

Sometimes Sofi played at lunch and drew another set to that profitable meal. She never ate in the café, much preferring her own cooking and coffee. Technically she was far superior to Margie but could not emulate her jazz technique. They often held sessions to compare their bases and this drew another group of afficionados.

Sofi often lay awake in bed and unconsciously rolled over to find heat that was no longer there. Her lover had gone for good. She chose now to end the sense of loss that had come on the shore with a cold wind on her face yet full of the expectancy that whatever came from the south could bear no ill, and yet as she stood there almost suspended in happiness she had been forced to dig her feet deep into the sand to anchor her courage. She had imaginary conversations with people she hardly knew. "June here is not so hot as to make you sweat as you hold on to your lover. It's a pungent dry month that tests the senses and finds exclamations of joy when we look through the early mist and find a flower."

A young girl asked her to tell her something funny in Shakespeare and she quoted a Dutchman.

"Omlet. Omlet. Dies is dein Feyder's spooke."

Someone else wanted to know her spiritual values.

"Do you believe there's a God?"

"I think it's important if it's true. That's as far as I can go."

The yelp of a dog distracted Sofi from her conversations and dreams. Later as she walked towards the bridges she made out Isabel and her bulldog. The dog was so strong that when it brushed against you there was a good chance you could fall over. It had never bitten anybody but Isabel insisted that it could and everybody believed her. She also said she needed it for protection but nobody believed that. When the dog saw Sofi through the mist it pulled Isabel so hard she had to let the dog run free. Sofi braced herself for the collision but the dog stopped short and greeted her like the lady she was. Isabel arrived a little later, breathless and relieved.

"I thought he was going to attack you." she said.

"I don't know why women are afraid of dogs," Sofi said,

"I've never known one to bite a woman."

Isabel picked up the leash and chastised the dog who sat there with infinite patience well knowing that adoration was sure to follow.

"I think he likes you." she said.

"You know Isabel your dog is like you and you are well known to like everybody."

"What about dear Franklin?"

"Franklin is a cat Isabel."

"I know but flesh and blood too. Choco doesn't like Franklin."

Before Sofi could fathom this logic Isabel was pulled away again by the dog. Luckily Franklin was a late riser.

Where Sofi ended up in Paris suited her mind the moment she arrived. The neighborhood was full of chaos prejudice and poverty that grew worse as the franc lost its value and every sou seemed to feel heavier, which was appropriate, as more were needed. In the street there was one barber a baker a butcher a man who stuffed birds; various streetwalkers who only came out at night. This was so far removed from her recent experience in the north that it was almost a relief to be lost in it. Sofi found a little hotel room that had lots of light from a picture window that faced the garden of the lonely man across the way who never seemed to be inside the house if the weather was reasonable. Sofi was soon adopted by the owners, a woman who had separated from her husband and a Greek she had picked up in Marseilles.

In the first week Sofi rented a piano in a music shop and left it in place since she had no room for it. Maurice the owner moved it into the back room then opened all the doors and windows and she played it in the afternoons. Before long she had an audience. Maurice stopped charging her the rent since she brought him so many customers. In the beginning if they didn't buy anything, sheet music for example, he wouldn't let them back into the store until Sofi insisted he did. He had lost his son in the war; his wife had died of a broken heart people said ; and he was left with his daughter in law who showed no sign of recovering from her loss. She was beautiful and had many offers but was too sad. Maurice enlisted Sofi to get her out of her silence. It was no use ; she was not to be consoled and Sofi could understand that. As she passed her each day Sofi touched her hand. Eventually when Maurice saw her react he had hope that she would recover. But Sofi had learned that loss is too personal to share and one must find a way out of it. Sofi knew that sadness might leave the mind unless you should decide it should stay.

Sofi did not go to any of the two nearby churches but the strolling priests sent musical requests. Next door, Henri the butcher and his wife Nellie also opened all the windows so that their customers could listen to Sofi playing. Although everyone was curious and they all knew each other's business private and public Sofi was never questioned or propositioned. Two rich grey old men had second thoughts but that was the extent of it.

Sofi was always an early riser. She often walked in the mist that cooled everything after hot days. The haze made her wet but she felt in her blood that the day would be brighter and had confidence her world would too, like the change in the weather. She sensed a new form of things to come when the taste of hot chocolate was still in her mouth. The bracing walk and the coolness gave her pleasure and she walked along swinging her arms a smile on her wet cheeks. In the night she had awakened and by candlelight had written down some personal thoughts into her diary. These had come from the question in her mind that anyone could have captured her so well with such insight as the artist who had formed the cover on her poetry. She could see that he had made some of her features in one stroke like a Chinese master would do when copying an ancient manuscript. Sofi felt now in her pocket to make sure the book was still there. She knew it was the work of Seamus and had gone to the library to search out a likeness of him. Now she dimly remembered the magazine that Albert had given her and the anxious face in the center page alongside Helen. She had none the less searched out his work found it and admired it, then obtained a smiling lighthearted image of Seamus.

That image was neatly folded between the covers of her poems. She had not known that Sara and Albert had published her work until Albertina found it and bought copies for all her friends in the area. When Sofi looked through the work she realized that some of the poems were just cries for help and many others she had forgotten. At first her creative instincts cried out. Sofi had great faith in the creative process and had used it to bring herself through the dark time. She had left the poems on purpose for they had served it. Then she reconciled herself to the fact that a shift had taken place. Sofi put them behind her and concentrated on Seamus. How was it possible that a man who had never met her could find her out. She guessed that Sara had been his model yet knew instinctively that Seamus had not slavishly copied her sister but had sensed the original, probably from the poetry one artist to another. The candle she lit in the night was the symbol for within its soft light she considered that fate had stopped playing evil tricks on her.

As she came to the river the old river, she felt her youth again. Already the push cart men were coming back from the central market with meat and vegetables. Those she knew called out and Marcel the fruit merchant gave her an apple before hurrying on to his stall. The spring was approaching the best time for the pushcart vendors and the first warning for the permanent shopkeepers that a lean month was coming. Sofi had come in the Autumn when the Luxembourg was filled with scarlet and vermilion flowers damask and mahogany roses. Later in the year when the river was high the cellars usually flooded, to everyone's surprise, and the barges could not pass under certain bridges and had to tie up and wait for the water to recede.

That year the Seine went up just as the Franc went down. This morning Sofi put that behind her and looked forward to seeing the food the shelter the produce and refreshment and flowers she knew would soon be on the quai in pots and as cut flowers by the time she made her way home. The goldfish the precious books and stuffed bird shops were still closed. When the candle had given out Sofi prepared herself to walk in the dark until the light should come. She stopped under a street lamp to look at her book and drew the attention of a policeman standing in a doorway near the police station waiting for the last few minutes of his shift to wear down before he could go in. He started to wander across toward Sofi to move her on ; she was breaking one of the local rules strictly enforced. A woman of the night must not stand under a street light to wait for customers. Just as Daniel was about to call out to her he recognized Sofi and retreated into the shadows. She, quite distracted had not noticed him.

There was only one house lit in the street. It was in the apartment of the woman who walked alone every day seemingly dressed for death she was so pale and fragile. Her husband had been a proud Sergeant at Arms and was now in an unknown grave deep in the mud of the Marne where he had foundered helping to deflect the initial German advance on Paris.

LOVE IN AN UNEXPECTED PLACE

The supporting cast was gone. She was a subject for Rembrandt; living her life in private hurt and public grief yet traveling with grace to the grave. Whatever depths Sofi had briefly touched were slight in comparison to the tragedies of the urban peasants which would always remain full of scars; pitted, hardly held together passed down through the generations. The knowledge of them sobered her. There had been a great war and these were the survivors; hardly alive, blooded, nearly coagulated.

Her new friends now filled her mind. There were the two young Communists Silvia and Gerald who were forever testing each other though not always seriously.

"What would you say separates the rich from the poor?" Gerald asked with tongue in cheek as the three of them sat one day in the midday sun sipping coffee.

"Bedbugs!" Silvia quipped."The rich don't have bedbugs."

Gerald disparaged her answer. "How do you know?"

"The rich never talk about bedbugs," Silvia responded, "and we have lots of them."

"Marx might have had bedbugs yet never spoke about them." Gerald quipped.

"That should tell you something." she retorted. "They have no added value. Marx would not have wished them on anyone!"

There were no bedbugs on the expectant white sheet the three of them spread on the kerb to collect money for the Spanish children being bombarded daily in Madrid by Franco.

Then there was Heidi. On her fifteenth birthday she quite candidly told Sofi she meant to love another woman just so she wouldn't be seduced too early by a man. When Sofi smiled at her the way she did Heidi knew she would have look farther afield for a partner.

There were ugly residents too. Especially a supervisor from the civil service. She soon discovered that most people rose in government offices because of their willingness to persecute those under them; Jaime was one. He was fond of sitting at the bar and pontificating as if he was still in his government office. Here, there was usually somebody to contradict him.

"The Spanish Jews caused all the trouble down there that's why they have a civil war."

Vincent was quick to oppose him. "There haven't been any Jews in Spain since the fifteenth century."

Jaime was undeterred by lack of facts. "Well, they all came up here and caused us trouble."

Henri the historian took up the opposition. "Don't cudgel your brains or go too far back in your family history. I believe you are from Clermont-Ferrand and your cunning local hero is Laval who prefers Mussolini to Spanish republicans."

"And Blum is a Jew." Jaime retorted.

"At least we can enjoy his wit." Henri said.

Jaime finished his beer. "I don't see the comic side of him."

"Old Petain is more your style." Vincent insisted.

"Yes. You got that right. I fought with him at Verdun, and saved France."

Henri exploded. "He never fought and I've yet to see you around the parade on November 11th."

Jaime ignored this cut. "He's a Marshal of France!"

Vincent kept up the attack. "From what I've heard he's more interested in mistresses."

Jaime stumped out. "Slanderous foreigner!"

Henri had the last word. "That dull ass will not mend his ways without a beating."

Henri the butcher and Charles the baker whose memories of women were fairly cold had them warmed up when Sofi appeared into the area.

"What do you like about her?" Charles asked.

"She doesn't eat much bread." Henri said, tongue in voluminous cheek.

"What difference does that make?" Charles wondered.

Henri continued on his whimsical way. "She doesn't talk too much."

Charles was doubtful. "Bread makes such a difference?"

Henri kept the twinkle in his eyes. "That's what I think."

Charles exploded. "But you're a butcher."

"I know" Henri said quite soberly. "Meat is harmless; it has only the beast and none of the yeast!"

"You liked the Madam too." Charles cautioned.

"Yes." Henri browsed for a moment or two through his memories. "She said some witty things apart from the sex."

Charles was curious. "Such as?"

"Only death can make me faithful."

Charles thought he had the last word. "That's not wit it's wisdom."

Henri had more. "I told her once that she should be happy. She wondered if she would ever be. How can I be happy she said. I asked her what more she wanted from me. She said I was just to cry a little when she died."

Lately Sofi had found a second hand bicycle for sale.

"It's for a man." the seller advised.

"I'll manage." she said. He paid lots of attention as she made her first attempt to ride it. With it she traversed Paris and as she steered her zig zag course through the streets she gained the attention of the taxi and bus drivers. That Sofi wore a skirt and rode a bike with a high bar was their focus. She was lucky that her first venture out was at the onset of May when Paris taxi drivers took a holiday. She learned more about the city in the heat of August when those who could manage it went to the country and the city slumbered.

Another time she had biked while wearing a turban because she had read in Proust that Mme. Bontemps had worn one during the war with a military jacket shorts and knee length boots. The only jewelry Sofi had was a pearl necklace which she wore wedged between her breasts. When her friend Noel asked her what that was about Sofi told him she was hoping for pleasant possibilities. Since the boy was only twelve he had no idea what she meant nor did he have the nerve to ask. She rode the bike not like a racer but as if she was on her Viennese pony. Despite the getup the fastidious Helga said she still looked delicate and had good taste. Sofi's sorrows were behind her and she struck a cheerfulness like the music she played daily.

Her Spanish friend Vincente was a tall man from Valencia. A fugitive from despots. A victim who through the loss of his arm in the Spanish civil war would not have been out of character if he had fallen into despair, considering all he had lost apart from the limb. Instead he quietly described to Sofi his previous circumstances with love and pleasure and quoted the Roman poet Martial's description of the country life he led in Spain in contrast to that of Rome.

LOVE IN AN UNEXPECTED PLACE

'The poplar grove and meadow the springs with their open conduits of water. The pot herb in January the rose trees and vine trellis the tame eel in its tank the whitewashed dovecot the tepid river in which one could bathe. Here we live lazily and work pleasantly. I enjoy a vast sleep which often lasts until ten and so make up for all I've lost these thirty years. You'll find no togas here; if you ask for one they'll give you the nearest rug off a broken chair. When I do get up I find a fire heaped with splendid logs from the oak forest which the bailiffs wife has crowned with her pots and pans. That's how I like to live and that's how I hope to die.'

At various times of day and night he sought her out, walked with her and quoted from Spanish poems depending on the time of day…cock crow…from the hour when lamps are out…for bedtime. Sometimes in the bar they pored over maps of the Ebro valley and he illuminated them with folk tales. His courage inspired her as he represented for her the triumph of spirit over brute force. He was a native of the high desert country where the bare living and life encourage frankness; where men say their thoughts without thinking; there is no reserve good or bad.

"A hungry man," he said, "sees things a well fed one might never notice."

One night he held a little book in his good hand and for the first time she realized how spiritual he was. In my village we believe in the resurrection like Prudentius, and he quoted from the book for her.

'I know that my body will rise up again in Christ. Why do you want me to despair? I shall follow on the same road by which He returned after triumphing over death. This is my belief. And I shall be just as I was; I shall have the same face and strength and color that I have today; not a tooth nor a nail will be missing when the open tomb vomits me up again.'

Sofi had not the same faith as Vincent but she was gentle with his. "If Jesus returns you may not be there to bring out the relics of the new Spanish martyrs to intercede for you."

"No." he replied with a sadness that made her draw a deep breath. "There are too many of them now. More martyrs than citizens. After a century of supposed liberty equality and fraternity France is no better off either. Republican Spain should take note.

Sofi's enthusiasm for this quarter was equalled by her new Scottish friend Ewen McTaggart who was in Paris to follow the steps of many of his Highland breed; to learn the language and take in some of the culture. Sometimes as they walked together he would regale her with scenes from his own canton above the highland line and hardly needed her questions.

"What is it like in your own country?" she asked. "Is it anything like how Sir Walter Scott described it?"

"Nobody ever knew it like he did," Ewen said ; "walking and riding through the length and breadth of it. He knew it so well he decided to reinvent it."

"A strange idea." Sofi thought.

"Yes, but his version is the one that will survive us all. His mountains are still listening in silence, emptied out. They had no knowledge of the coming industrial revolution to disturb them ; a sense beyond us where a madness can come over you that not even the golden eagles can lift. A wilderness so explicit yet so secret. And that is just one of its quarters. The others are quite differently peopled. *'A heap of wheat set about by lilies.'* Dear Sofi," Ewen continued, "I liked your water color of the Quai Saint Michel in the rain. It was a brilliant stroke to give the little girl in the foreground a pink scarf."

"That's our little Hyacinth." she told him.

"Oh. Now I understand. She will always stand out. Then of course you show the top of the thin lamp standards but not the top of of bulky Notre Dame. That puts the whole thing in perspective as you look from a low angle right across the book and poster vendors against the wall."

For once Sofi asked a personal question. "Is there any future between you and Susan? You seem so close lately."

Sofi had become friendly with Susan who was around her age. Susan had all the uncertainty of a young woman not sure of her feelings for a man who had gone away temporarily.

She confided in Sofi. "My friends are telling me that he can't be trusted while away from me."

Sofi held her hand. "Do you believe them."

Susan made a slow reply. "I know he's faithful."

"Then that's enough if you're sure. Are you sure?"

A little doubt crept in. "He's older than me." Susan said.

"Older! What age is he?" Sofi asked.

"Twenty nine."

Sofi laughed. "He might be better when he's thirty."

Susan was still serious. "That's what I thought too."

"Is he coming back?" Sofi asked.

"Yes," Susan said."He's coming back."

"What about Ewen?"

Susan fiddled with her bag. "I'm affected by his quietness and gentleness his lack of suggestion."

"You must be patient and not give your life away." Sofi insisted. "What can you tell me about the other man?"

"I think he only cares about himself sometimes."

Sofi ended her advice. "Perhaps you should reshuffle yourself and see what card you draw, dog eared or shiny new."

Ewen continued his conversation with Sofi.

"I think Susan might be too sophisticated for me. It was a culture shock when I first met her and even now…her knowledge…"

"She's a socialist Ewen and believes that the peoples of the world will eventually come together. In order for that to happen she thinks she has to understand more than one culture."

Sofi kept asking questions "What are you studying apart from the language?"

"Actually, she has got me interested in Chinese poetry. Tang dynasty. I tried their style yesterday while I was sitting out here on the river."

"Can you remember it?" she asked.

"I'll try. Hold on while I get myself in gear."

'If you sit quietly
nature accepts you.
How fast is the river?.
How slowly leaves fall.
How gentle the breeze
and the lonely birdcall.
The sun is too warm
and I prefer the moon ;
there are so many stars.
I hope you come soon,
Earthly brightness ;
My River Princess.'

"You are wishing for a lot too." Sofi said, impressed.

He agreed. "I'm halfway there."

LOVE IN AN UNEXPECTED PLACE

"I see love but no wine." Sofi said.

Ewen smiled. "I can't afford the wine. Not yet."

As she stood on the Pont Petit the half light seemed to still the water and the shadows of it turned to rust like fall leaves in the wind ; soundless. Even the hint of a blue sky was not always sufficient to lend light to lift the head to brighten the eyes. A few days earlier she had been startled by the looks of a young man crossing the Pont Double because he walked with the same stiff backed style of Karl. Sofi had put Karl away for some time. She pretended a longer time that it actually had been. To encourage this she paid little attention to current events outside her arrondissment. Then for a period of time hardly anything held any importance for her except her inner life. She did not want to relive an earlier life and so she mostly ignored her present one unaware she was now what was called an Existenialist, and quite up to date.

Sofi was involved with song birds and the smell of flowers and sought out the parks of Paris. In the process she connected herself to nature and not relationships past or present. Which is not to say she was anti social. Yet true feelings were conversations in her head perhaps to be later written down; preserved. But what of this Seamus? Here was someone different and significant. The lonely look for omens. Sofi took up Marcel Proust. She had gone to the last chapter of his novel an act that she knew was bad taste but did not regret it for long. It brought forth a determination to start at the beginning of what she suspected might take her a lifetime, more or less as it had Proust. She abandoned all other literature and entered his world with a feeling like Alice in Wonderland; the world being full of holes but one must choose what is not accidental or predestined ; create her own world from selective memories of the past. She soon learned that the more indifference one shows a memory the stronger it gets in proportion to the loss of the emotion it once had.

That time in the world young women about town at least began when influenced by fashion magazines to abandon simplicity and get up to date with each fad. The paste they wore as false as the taste. In her district there were lots of these young women. Sofi separated herself with her simplicity and was praised. And thus her quiet life went on but now with Seamus in spirit at least and new dreams. As she sat by the river the fresh day brought out the latest words written in the night, the release and the balance...'*I have been loved, I have known all the gain of love. What can other lives contain that have not seen its light? Or felt the passion that comes when all the suns still shine so softly in the night. I have known the pain it too has been mine. What might have been forever can it return again? Shall I unfold my arms let him see me whole, try to touch...hold...my untouchable soul? Should I kiss his brow hold the light in his eye? Listen to him cry and touch his face. Make his lips lift and start with desire. Should I let my breast swell and taste in his embrace?*

Chapter 16

In Paris Michelle loved the room where they slept. It had a marine motif and every sailing ship wrecked on the Atlantic shore was represented by a black and white photograph or where that was not available by a miniature of the figurehead. Downstairs there was a bar carved in the shape of a boat with masts at both ends of it and a sail spar above. Behind the bar there were two little alcove windows placed for the rising sun. Terence's Aunt had wanted to entertain in style but Terence had no such intention though he was making inroads into the vintage wine. No matter which upstairs room they were in there was a glass door to a protected balcony protected from the ever present buzz of the city.

Michelle wondered if Terence would ever say he loved her. He had used every other form of endearment except that crucial phrase. She knew he was an honest man and had not developed the nerve herself to tell him how deep her feelings were or to ask him how he felt about her. Sure of her own feelings doubtful about his it was a long trail from juvenile lust and dreams to the more mature madness that had now overtaken her. Love is a long twisting road with no end to it and a high gate at the entrance and the keys in someone else's pocket. Michelle often looked at Terence and wondered when love would break out of his skin. The missionary had blabbed all over his collar and she couldn't shut him up. He was the very Imam of love; had to call it out three times a day. Michelle decided it was the wrong religion and wondered how Buddha would affect him. In the end he was a fallen idol and she found she had no faith in him.

In all his weeks of love with Frances Terence remembered that all their lovemaking had been in hidden places stolen hours sometimes just minutes of being alone together, a furtive love without the long hours of companionship that loves breeds and needs for sustenance. Now when he and Michelle came together it was for long periods of time and Michelle's physical needs came with all her energy and tenderness. In his ignorance of women Terence suspected that her liaisons had included more men than the Chinese missionary she had admitted to. This thought infused his experience with her and the lack of prudishness faced by a woman who delighted in physical love brought out his own priggish side. Michelle saw it and scaled down her sensuality in the hope that he would love her and accept how a woman feels when in love. The emotions and desires long suppressed for propriety and respect suddenly had overtaken her. Both Terence and Frances had been virgins. A fully fledged carnal woman frightened Terence. In addition to these problems Terence was not doing very well with his novel and when he discussed it with her he had a sense of criticism when Michelle gave her guileless opinion. She sometimes lay next to him afraid to make the first move. Towards the end she quietened both her mind and her body.

It was an uneasy alliance heading for rupture when the news of his Aunt's death reached Terence and they traveled to Paris together after he learned that he had come into her fortune; her town and country houses; a considerable stock portfolio and a stable of racehorses. He was suddenly one of the richest and most eligible men in Paris. Every age has its problems but almost anyone looking at Terence's prospects of almost unlimited resources and the attention and love of a beautiful intelligent and highly artistic woman would surely have had a trace of envy.

With all the estate business to get over it was a month before Terence indicated that he would be staying in Paris. Michelle had cleaned out his Aunt's apartment for him. Her taste was good but turn of the century. Michelle gave it an art nouveau touch and wondered how long she could stay or be welcome. Terence helped make up her mind.

It finally had not worked. When he put his hands around her neck and kissed her brow there was no reaction. She did not come against him as she always had before. She stared a little fixedly at him. He took her hand but it was lifeless. There was no pressure no interlocking no kisses. All the signs were there. He chose to ignore them in the hope they would go away but they did not. Instead he found her on the couch pretending to read intently. She paid no attention when he asked her if she needed anything. She was a dead thing. Of course he did not know that there was nothing to be done with a woman in such circumstances. It was not like a woman scorned; with her you might know the cause of the problem. But could a woman out of love be understood or assuaged? What can be done?

"I once hated more than two people in a room." Terence used to say. "Now I'd have a party every night twenty four hours a day if I could. There's a lot to be said for the more the merrier and cliches in general." He discovered that a beautiful woman can look as ugly as Medusa fresh from the hairdresser. As he told one of his friends while Michelle was within earshot..."It's no use being perceptive. I know all my problems. The trouble is they took so long to materialize. The sword does not apply to women. Slow poison is their weapon. It takes a while to turn her heart to stone. One minute she was a happy blondethe next a heartless brunette."

Michelle questioned him tartly when they were alone.

"Why are you writing in such short sentences? Have you been reading Papa's stories again?"

He ignored the criticism, the implicit plagiarism. "It's raining."

"That won't change things." she said.

He was tired, "Do you want to change things?"

She was so sharp with him. "There's no alternative. If I don't do something where do you think I'll end up?" There was the sound of a train at the crossing. "I'll be on that train tomorrow."

His bitterness seeped out. "Why not today?"

"I have to get down to the bitter end and that will take another day. I'm hoping one day will do it. I'm going in the afternoon. You'll have to get over this by yourself."

There she once stood he remembered dark eyed and dressed in a brown suit. She had a lovely silk band around her neck though there was nothing to hide. Her hair was blonde but turned strawberry in the sun. She wore little boots that laced up the side. Her voice was not as sweet as her character. She had a slight drawl. These details came to him when he regretted the loss.

Terence could not focus. He thought he had lost everything during the night. Now in the clear light he tried to forget what exactly he had lost by trying to overcome that feeling of regret of all the wrong moves and ill-timed decisions. He knew that what he was trying to do now was to be grateful for the chance to be reborn. He was tearing off the old skin. The sea he was swimming in had gone from whitecap whipped to a cool calm. He felt the tide was ebbing. Thus a formerly latent gambler looked at life. He was the oversexed man who had become celibate from choice. Were his spots too deep for the world to notice? Was his heart still his own? The less you know the less you can tell. Had he said too much?

"Please tell me what I said," would be his first question. The answer might be that he had been less than kind. He felt like a dead dandelion on the wind. He remembered a few lines of a poem.

'Dandelions are not for lovers, bring out the roses.'

But then there was the woman. She had gone. She had left tired of the lean periods and the near madness.

"Gambling is an obsession." she said that last day of her.

His temper flared at first. "You're saying I'm obsessed?"

She was quiet as usual. "You are in many other ways so why not in that way too."

Her calmness cooled him. "Will I ever get better?"

She could not console him. "It's hard to say." Michelle chided him further. " I've seen you say in your writing that love never dies. Yet all the so called compulsive times in your life have ganged up on you and there's no relief no cure. It has eaten away at you and you are becoming more vulnerable to change in an attempt to escape the trials of it. You have many weaknesses yet you are still stubborn. I'm not at ease with you."

He smiled grimly. "You're saying I'm a control freak."

She picked up her coffee. "No. A controlled freak!"

His voice rose.

"You mean we can't help ourselves?"

Her coffee was cold and she put it down.

"I mean there's no help for us.".

There was a quiet desperation in his voice.

"Not even love?"

She lit a cigarette.

"Not so far."

So that was over. That he might have lost the youth to go on depressed him. Thirty eight winters he thought and had not died one yet as his mother used to say coming from a time when life was more fragile. She had often reminded him of that winter when all the cattle were found standing in a circle one morning frozen to death where they stood. The loss split the family up and some had to emigrate to let the others survive. But that was common in those days and all that remained of them was the odd letter for births marriages and deaths. Life and death would go on. He had first seen Michelle in a garden. It was the time he had decided to swear off falling in love. He pondered what had led him to such madness. He was looking for love that she could not supply and in the end did not want.

***

As Michelle prepared to leave Paris she had begun to sell off the few paintings she had managed. She met Hannah in the sports club and formed a short friendship. Unknown to her Hannah was attracted to Terence. Now Hannah was considering Michelle's work.

"I like that one." Hannah enthused.

Michelle was pleased. "The sailing ship."

"Yes. Where did you paint it?"

She squared it up in the light. "In my home town."

"How long did you get to do it?" Hannah asked.

"Luckily it was a fixture for the summer and I had the time to paint it.'

Hannah was surprised at the length of time she had taken. "A whole summer!"

"On and off. I had other work."

"Such as?" Hannah grew in enthusiasm. "Show me if you have them here."

"Some portraits of local worthies. Some beach scenes."

Hannah lost her eagerness. "The world is full of beach scenes and local worthies."

"Not with this light in them." Michelle responded.

When Hannah looked at them she marvelled.

"Yes, you're right that beach is quite different. It must be difficult to show the depth of focus for that distance. How did you mix the colors?"

"The light does it for you if you let it in." Michelle said.

"A light touch my dear. Oh I know it's not that easy. You have a superb gift Michelle. What have you done in Paris?"

There was some sadness. "Not much really. All dark."

Hannah responded. "This is the city of light!"

"I seem more in the fog here and out of my depth."

Hannah couldn't help bringing up Terence. "I've seen you with Terence. He doesn't look a happy man. I know him through his associates who of course are my political competition."

Michelle was frank with her. "I know he's unhappy but I don't know how to make him happy when he has so many other distractions and the money to carry them out."

Hannah probed further. "I heard he was writing a novel before you came down here."

"Yes," Michelle responded, "but that is shelved now. All his time is spent at the racecourse or carousing with his journalist gambling and right wing political friends. You know them."

"Parasites you mean?" Hannah said.

"I suppose so. I'm leaving anyway."

"Where are you going?"

"Back home to begin again. It seems any talent I do have is not transferable and only comes out of me there and my sister needs a break. Apparently she has met her match and might be getting married."

Hannah looked again at the paintings. "I'll take the yacht Michelle and good luck. I think you're doing the right thing to start again if this isn't what you want."

***

Albert lay in the spring garden of the cabin and suffered the loss of Michelle. He came across a short story by an author he had never read before, left there by Sofi…

"Oh to shake out the life we lose in dreams and all those proxy moments beyond our discretion where the will is lost and all the sirens we failed to wake disappear into the void yet those we do remember have never occurred or we could not avoid. When the wind stops and you look out at the silver birch that enjoy only the wet ground around the river then you wonder why you came back to find that beyond all the years there is nothing left but the image of a girl as she walked beside the water. Her white dress contained her virtue at least in your eyes but later you were to find that there was no end to it and you wonder why it mattered so much then. As you looked at her you knew there might be no other ever in your stars. She searched your face as you washed your feet in the water letting loose her hair and waited for you to make a move in any direction. You crossed the shallows that seemed so deep but for once you were brave for you knew your

life depended upon it if you were to leave even the slightest evidence of your existence and for that we are bound to gather up our courage so that the light of love should touch whichever shadow we are under."...the words seemed to sum up his feelings. He never knew that Karl had once read them too and quoted them to Sofi.

Albert existed here on the periphery of the world mainly because this little town valued the heritage that a few artists had left them half a century before. As it became prosperous it had become more aware of its history apart from fish and fishermen. There was to be a new school and the aldermen all agreed that there should be a special place for art. Some of this desire came from those who had inherited some of the artistic legacy mainly incomers aware of the growing north and the interest of the world in the paintings that had been produced in the superb light found nowhere else. So Albert was hired.

He was a fairly young man then. His own pedestrian artistic ambitions had not been apparent to anyone else and thus in the manner of many another failed. Like those creative men he had strayed into teaching and found his niche and perhaps even some of the fame he craved. So he was hired to be the artistic director of the new school and the decision was never regretted though there had been some naysayers.

"He looks so effeminate. I hope he's not queer. That would never do here."

"Well he is qualified in fact over qualified and we can't ask him his sexual preference on looks alone."

"Time will tell. Our town is full of lovely women. Perhaps he's too good looking for the safety of the girls. We can wait and see. It's a one year contract and he's the only candidate."

There was one wit amongst them. "He probably would not have come up here if the Foreign Legion at Side el Abbes had not rejected him." The school board were not the only doubters of Albert's sexuality and so he suffered in the first year from a marked examination from all concerned.

Albert sensed these doubts because he had suffered them before. To get over them he managed to find and encourage a few pupils with talent, mainly girls, of whom the most talented was the teenage Michelle and to a lesser extent her sister Susannah. Michelle knew he had picked her out but was unaware that he had done so not only for her gifts. Albert started to love her and gave her all his energy and Michelle mistook it for artistic reasons although she was herself attracted to this gentle soul but put that attraction to the back of her mind like every other woman who looked at his feminine good looks.

As the years passed it became obvious that although initially Albert's sexual preferences may have been in question his conduct never was and he was a brilliant teacher. Of course people wondered. Where there is a seed of doubt it has a habit of flowering every now and again. Where did he disappear to almost every weekend? Nobody ever asked him perhaps fearful of the answer. There were some suggestions.

"Perhaps he's taking elocution lessons. I've noticed a marked change in his voice."

"He certainly looks like one of those little birds that are able to fluff out all their feathers to get rid of a bug."

Albert soldiered on expending much of his effort to encourage Michelle to continue with her art and to get it shown every now and then. Then the local pastor hired a substitute. The town was expanding and with it his duties. To Albert's chagrin Michelle formed an attachment with the new pastor. Eventually the only hope he had was when it was announced that the man was to go to China on a mission. Michelle refused to go with him but no sooner had that encouraged Albert when Terence arrived and on the rebound she went to live with him in the big red house on the beach. Albert had a high regard for Terence and so was reconciled to the likelihood that this romance would be permanent and his weekends away got more regular.

Sofi's arrival distracted Albert for the duration of her short stay. He knew her story and admired her courage. It also gave him the chance to be with Michelle more often as the two women became close friends. He and Michelle tried hard to get Sofi through her grief including having her pose for a portrait. But she was so uncomfortable that he hurried the painting and was disappointed in the result. Sofi took it and hung it above her bed.

Albert loved the young woman and then she disappeared and not long after his friend Seamus appeared and the whole world turned upside down. Michelle and Terence left for Paris and Sofi's sister Sara appeared smitten to no avail with Seamus as he painted her likeness, a proxy for Sofi's book of poems. With the departure of all his friends depression set in for Albert.

Then all the waiting and frustration took a turn as Michelle came back from Paris full of disillusion.

***

"You came home." Albert said at their first meeting.
"Yes, I came home."

"To stay?" Albert posed the question he was almost afraid to ask or hear the answer.

"I don't know." she replied. "I'm quite unsettled right now."

"And Terence?"

Michelle gave him a frank look that he knew so well.

"I don't think I'll ever see him again. Too much money and too many cronies trying to relieve him of it. Gambling and drink. If there had been love in the mixture for me then I would have stayed with him. It's a lonely life when only one is loving and the other has lost care."

"He never got over the war." Albert said, quietly.

"I think it was the loss of the woman." she replied

Albert was unaware of Frances. "His Aunt!"

"No, his lover Frances who died of the great sickness after the war and he has not got over it. He feels guilty that he survived the war and the pandemic. He says I was too strict but all I wanted was for him to pay attention."

Albert forgot the coffee. "Did you paint?"

"Yes, and that kept me sane for a while."

"Did you bring anything back?"

"No, I sold them all off." she told him. "Now I'll start fresh like Seamus. Is he here?"

"No. He went to Vienna."

She brightened up. "You mean to find Sofi?"

"Who knows. He's a very complicated fellow." He was pleased to see a little smile.

"I wonder Terence, which sister he'll fall in love with."

"The last one standing." Albert said. "There's always the hotel business Michelle. Your sister's Norwegian painter has come back for her."

"Yes, I know. She's happy and maybe she can settle down with one man at last and he's a good artist. He sells his work and has shows all over the continent and beyond. Perhaps she can travel a bit and get some fun. I told her I would stand in for her for a month at least. But what about you Albert? Always worrying about other people."

He pointed to his bald spot. "There's always the monastery."

She smiled again at his humor. "I don't see that for you."

"No, I'm not a recluse though lonely at the moment."

"Is the money holding out?" she wondered.

"Oh yes but nothing to spend it on."

She gathered the crumbs of her biscuit into a little pile.

"Any good students?"

"One or two promising something. Not one as outstanding as you were."

She moved from that. "You went to school with Seamus."

"Yes, a private school. He was the only one who understood my predicament. He'd been around the world with his parents. They were rich you know. He protected me."

"He's not that robust himself." she asserted.

"No, but lean and mean and a tongue that would lift your skin off. He's changed now, matured."

Michelle was glad to turn to Seamus.

"What do you think was the turning point?"

"Coming here. Sensing the strength of Sofi and realizing how cruel his lack of care had been in the past especially to Helen. I'm told she almost gave up her career because of his painting. I suppose all her training came to her rescue in the end or another man. In actual fact it made her more famous though it hurt her ego at the time and some say he broke her heart.

He didn't keep his word to let her see the painting first, he just put it on display. It did him no good. The critics blasted him and his credit fell where it mattered least at that time, in his pocket. He is not suffering. All his other paintings sold at fair prices since his agent announced a genre change."

"You keep up Albert."

"We've always been close." Albert responded a little proudly. "He asks my opinion now and then so I must follow his progress."

She touched his hand. "Dear Albert I owe you a lot too."

"You've paid me back many times over. To tell you the truth I wish I had your talent."

"Oh, I don't know Albert. Your painting of Sofi moved Seamus."

"He hated it!"

Michelle encouraged him. "There was something in it that disturbed him not how you managed it technically."

"Yes." Albert responded. "He saw the subject. That's who he's searching for in Vienna. Sara might still lead him a merry dance through the woods. She has Sofi's looks but not her soul."

Michelle looked across at Susannah drying glasses and singing softly to herself.

"I wonder what he would do with Sofi. Such a gentle creature. Too bad we never did meet her fiancee?"

Albert responded. "He's in the poetry. She'll never lose him."

"Why do you think she left? Disappeared really."

Albert didn't hesitate. "She moved on and didn't want to explain how she did it. Her grief ran its course and the Spring came into her blood."

Michelle brightened again remembering her friend.

"Whoever gets her will get all of her. She covers that in one of her poems too."

"She was so young." Albert marvelled. "How on earth did she get to know so much so quickly?"

"Who knows where it comes from." Michelle commented. 'When I talk to creative people they have no idea. Everything is out there age old."

Albert picked up his courage. "I am not so old Michelle. I could look after you."

Michelle looked him right in the eye. "Albert, I'm surprised at what you just said."

He looked for her hand again. "I've wanted to say it for a long time actually since you were a teenager."

"Oh dear," Michelle said, "that long ago."

"Yes ten years of watching you with others."

"Only two Albert."

"Too many! Am I too old? I mean do I look old to you?"

"Albert you are a very handsome man so much so that I've always wondered why you didn't attract women."

"I was accused at school of preferring boys but it's not true. Ask Seamus, he's known me all my life and he knows the truth. I love you Michelle and that's the whole truth now."

"Albert, it's too soon for me after Terence, that was bad mistake."

"Your mothering instincts came out again Michelle."

"I suppose so."

"I don't need that Michelle. I have all the health and needs of a man in love and I'm healthy."

"I've never seen you with a woman Albert."

"Perhaps I've been too secretive, added to which I didn't want you to know I had female friends."

"All those weekends away you mean?" Michelle began to persuade herself. "Sara was very close to you was she not? And I once saw you embrace Sofi."

"She's the special one, quite extraordinary."

"She trusted you, perhaps making the same mistake we both made that you loved us too."

"I've been in love with you ten years Michelle ever since we came together when I was coaching you for the art project and competition. You have so much talent Michelle and along with love a creative life with you is all I look forward to. Let Susannah run the hotel and come and live with me. I wish you had brought your Paris work home with you."

"It's funny to hear you call this place home Albert."

"Why is that?" he asked.

Michelle put both hand across for him. "It never seems to have really suited either of us."

"I think it does now. Terence will sell me the red house if it doesn't have too many memories for you to live there.'

"Not so many memories to concern me Albert but certainly a place where love has not been successful."

His enthusiasm knew no bounds. "Then a new house for a new life!"

"You're very persuasive Albert. I'm sorry I never fully realized your feelings for me. I adored you when we worked together when I was sixteen but like everyone else I took your good looks and quietness with women for something else. I could have lived a different life."

"You've had these experiences Michelle and we all need them at least the most creative among us seem to invite them. Look at Sofi. I wonder where she went. I miss her."

"Wherever she is," Michelle said, "the place is the better for it and you know I have a feeling she will come back to where she wrote the poetry. She can paint too and of course there is the music."

"Quite a girl." Albert agreed.

"She came a girl and left a woman." Michelle responded."I saw her once put her hand on Terence when she discovered he couldn't stand up to acknowledge her. I won't forget the look he managed for her in spite of his pain."

Albert responded. "Terence came here as one person too and left to become another. This seems to be a place for transformations. Perhaps as time goes on they will work out for the better. I'm asking you to marry me Michelle. What do you say?"

She teased him. "You won't want me to go to China?"

"No, my mission is here across this table full of more spirit than any church contains."

She continued the tease but happily. "Or Paris!"

"No." he said. "We have better light here."

She laughed out loud drawing Susannah's attention.

"Paris is the city of light!"

"Yes, I know," Albert agreed, "but it was raining the week I was there."

"Is a week to make the judgement of Paris?"

Albert caught the inference and replied with certainty.

"It was for me. Could you just adore me again Michelle?"

"I can try Albert. It won't be hard. Do you remember the lines Sofi wrote about first love?" Michelle without hesitation spoke them out...

'Unknown places should be lit by candles to make them soft when we find them. New found lips should just fit gently, over those full of desire to kiss them. Outstretched hands may touch the kindled yet trembling face; leading the other to love and grace."

"You read so well Michelle and your memory is perfect."

"I would rather have written it myself Albert. Let's just see whether our lips can fit gently."

His face lit up. "If my dreams were right then they will."

"Let's hope you have many more Albert. Let's walk on the beach and see how far along it we can reach."

Chapter 17

The first time Terence saw Hannah she wore a tan suit which he didn't think went with her coloring. It had been her twenty first birthday and she sat at a table with her friends full of gifts and good wishes. From across the room he tried to attract her attention. One of the other young women, Alicia, mistook his attention for herself.

"He's older than he looks." Alicia commented to Hannah

"I like his looks." Hannah replied.

"He's quite pleasant has money of course," Alicia continued, "but his eyes are sleepy. He's only half awake."

Hannah tilted her head to look across at Terence.

"I'll take that half you take the other."

Alicia kept on negatively. "I don't think he likes the company of women because no woman would put up with his bluster."

"His bluster?" Hannah asked.

"Yes. He criticizes everything. Nothing is exempt. How could a woman suffer it? If you pull down a building he likes he will publish your name and address in the paper and your phone number. He's impossible!"

"Well then," Hannah said, rather wholeheartedly, "I'd like to meet him and test his bluster!"

When he was later introduced to Hannah Terence was disappointed over her reluctance to give him any encouragement but she did set up a lunch date so that she could interview him for her magazine and this kept his hopes up.

He admired her even more in the green suit she wore the second time but thought she might look better in a little black dress she was so petite. This was Paris and men noticed what women wore. She had ankle high boots that matched her suit. She had such dark eyes almost black. Her sensuality was not hidden in her slow self confident walk. The interview took place in a popular café around the corner from the Madeleine. Hannah ordered Vichy water and a Nicoise salad. It was soon plain to him that she had taste and intelligence and was not the hard bitten journalist he had grown used to in Paris.

"Journalists usually come in twos." he said, as they sat down."

"I think one woman will keep you going."

"More than enough." he agreed.

"Weren't you wearing glasses the last time I saw you?

"Perhaps." he agreed. "But today I only have to be able to tell the difference between a blonde and redhead."

" I'm neither." she reminded him.

Terence laughed. "Maybe I do need glasses but who can tell the colour of good luck?"

She gave him a double edged compliment.

"Your wit is sharper than your sight."

Terence looked her over as she sat down fixing the green skirt of her suit."In that case the most attractive will be the first to laugh." He teased her, though nervously. "You look as though you don't eat much. Are you a model earning money as a journalist?"

"I just got into this suit." Hannah insisted, acting it out.

Terence chuckled. "Many might have preferred to see you get out of it."

"I'm flattered but I might not accommodate you."

He liked the pun yet disagreed. "You're not so green. When I was a younger man I'd have pitched my tent over you."

Hannah finally made herself comfortable. "I'm not a girl guide. I'm supposed to be interviewing you. I'm a limited company and I need the money."

He praised her again. "Your assets are quite visible."

"Terence, are you putting off the inevitable?"

"Ah, you mean the interview. I'm not a fatalist if that's what you mean. Hannah, you're much more slippery than I expected."

She fingered her jacket. "This is a tweed suit!"

"You mean you're a lady with no loose ends?"

She put her hands together in front of her breast. "That would be a sin in Paris."

Terence coughed into his hand. "That too in some quarters."

"Your reference is Latin to me." she said, her frustration present.

He explained the reference. "Nobody coughs in the bible you know so it may be counted a sin."

Hannah couldn't suppress a smile. "How about a sneeze?"

He considered that. "I believe it's alright."

"Let's get down to business Terence."

He smiled faintly. "For a limited time?"

She crossed her legs in the tight skirt and he looked the other way.

"I'm free all day." she said, noticing his good manners.

"A bargain!" he exclaimed and then changed the subject on her again. "I believe you met my friend Michelle recently."

This change of direction aroused Hannah's suspicion that she wouldn't get much out of him yet she went along."Yes. She's an exceptional lady in these parts."

"How is that?" he wondered.

Hannah looked for somewhere to hang her bag. "Walking away from money."

He grinned and showed all his teeth. "Actually she ran away."

Hannah put her bag on the floor."You didn't chase her."

"Didn't chase from beginning to end." he assured her."So I suppose that tells you something."

The waiter brought the Vichy and a glass of the house wine for Terence.

Hannah clinked his glass."I think I covered it with her. She's a frank woman."

"Yes," he said. "not French."

Hannah laughed. "You'll be quoting Caesar's Commentaries next."

"Veni, vidi, vici was over the Channel."

Her reply was sharp. "I've heard you're a stranger to water."

He lifted his wine glass. "They spend a long time making good alcohol and water runs out of a tap."

She twirled her glass of water. "You're drinking wine today. Are you slumming?"

Terence took his jacket off. "Now milady. You've got me cornered. You must have a list somewhere though I can't imagine where you could hide it."

Hannah shrugged her shoulders. "There's no list Terence. I've done my homework."

"Then put your glasses on," he advised her, "let's get started and see what needs correction in your archives."

Her frustration grew a little showing in the pursing of her lips. "Why did you agree to this interview in the first place?"

He didn't care for the pursing of the lips but remained gallant. "You are quite charming you know."

"Oh Terence! This is Paris! How can I quote such nonsense. Help me out or I'll have to invent something or send you a cheque in the mail."

He took a swig of the wine. "Alright. A very charming lady asked me for an interview and in a weak moment having come across her and admired her I accepted."

She beamed at him as if to encourage him further. "I might just might be able to do something with that."

"Such as?" he enquired. "Speak up!"

She played her part. "Mr Terence Townsend fancies himself as a womanizer but is unsure if it's his money or himself that women find attractive."

"Well that just about sums me up. We're done! It's obvious you've come straight out of Vienna the home of the short speculative piece with hardly any facts. You see I've done my homework too."

She was calm but deadly. "Was that your ego or your id?"

He was just as quick. "Perhaps stream of conscience."

"You're thirty years too late with that crack."

"I did read the first chapter of Ulysses much earlier."

"I'm not..." she started to say.

Terence completed the sentence. "Molly! No, you'd prefer Penelope."

She tried to get him back on track. "Can we safely assume that you have at least adopted a style for the novel you're supposed to be writing."

He put the empty glass down. "Michelle was candid."

"She says you have a fair amount finished. I'd like to read it."

He indicated his need for more wine to the waiter. "So would I but it hasn't reached that critical stage."

She was blunt. "Perhaps you have. You've had two bumpers of wine on an empty stomach and I'm not looking for the dregs."

He again tried humor. "You'll never scratch my bottom."

It didn't work. "I never scratch!" she retorted.

Terence took both her hands and examined her nails. "You must wear gloves! Go on paraphrase that. Sexual perversion perhaps."

Hannah's eyes yielded. "Terence, I've got the feeling that whatever vices you have are soft and don't need polishing."

He agreed. "An innocent in Paris."

She put aside her papers. "I don't think the city makes any difference nor its cliches. I'll put you down as a learned rustic."

He pleaded with her sarcastically. "Could you change that to witty?"

Her head made an annoyed movement he didn't notice. "Why don't you just write up a phony interview." she suggested.

"I thought you could manage that." he replied.

She took on her relentless can't be shaken off attitude.

"Look! We've been here a while. We've emptied the place. What's your game?"

He nonplused her. "Dinner for two at the Ritz!"

She was slow to reply. "Really? I've never been to the Ritz."

"You do know where it is." he asked, innocently.

She burst out laughing. "On the way to the tumbrils I believe. You'll be putting your life in my hands Terence."

"Well, I'm hoping you're not Charlotte Corday."

She put her bag on the table. "I presumed we would eat together, I usually bathe before I leave the house."

He thought now that he was losing the battle. "I always bathe before I eat. How about you?"

"I wash my hands at least." He was sure she was about to leave but she didn't. Instead, she took him down another peg. "Which is probably what I should be doing with you now."

Quite relieved he made the arrangements with her. "I'll meet you there at seven and we can do a real interview this is far too early for me. Will that suit you?"

"What should I wear?" she asked as he picked up his jacket

"A suit that fits you!" he said, smiling.

"I will if you don't wear your Legion of Honour."

Terence knew he was well matched. "I don't have one. It doesn't go with my other medals."

"With your money it soon will." she said, upset at allowing him to decide when the interview was over and hardly a note even in her head.

He saw her angst and made up for his bad manners. "A dinner with you is a suitable substitute. If you can't find me interesting in the Ritz what chance has your editor got."

Hannah was relieved that they might part on good terms.

"Did you mother ever have a good word for you?"

"Yes." he said, quite seriously. "She once called me a louse."

"Only once! She was a good judge. There's an old saying that if you want to survive you shouldn't frighten your mother."

He gave her the biggest smile he could muster.

"I discovered early that one must never argue with a judge."

Hannah wanted to say something else, something more encouraging but could only get out the obvious. "I bet you did."

He stood up. "I'm walking. Do you need my company to get you safely home or wherever you are going?"

"Terence, I know where you live and it's not even close to where I'm going but thanks for the offer."

"Hannah. Are you looking forward to the Ritz even with me in it?"

"Strangely enough Terence I have a little white dress that needs airing. What do you say to that?"

"I say Hannah that I hope you have delicate little white boots to go with it."

"So, no glass slipper at midnight?" she asked, then surprised him with some personal information. "I am an only child and was adopted had no sisters but I'm not claiming to be the belle of the ball."

"I'll be the judge of that." he said.

"Then I'll take your advice and not argue with a judge."

"You said you were an only child and I'm no Prince. Hannah, I think I just went on the wagon."

"Oh dear," she quipped, "and here I am looking for a golden coach!"

"Hannah, my mother told me never to tell a woman she was beautiful because if I took her for a fool despite my inventions she wouldn't have to guess my intentions."

"What are you trying to say Terence?"

"You're not one of the ugly sisters. If you hadn't put on your gloves I'd have kissed your hand to make up for the scratching crack I made earlier."

"Terence." she assured him, her face so soft and lovely he could have kissed her then and there, "the gesture is enough. I'll be sure to remember it next time. Au revoir."

As they parted he watched her and couldn't remember a woman he admired so much looking back at him but she did, making a gesture waving her right hand with the glove removed. The slight shake in his hands that he'd had lately was gone when he put them out in front of his chest palms up. For all the world like happenstance Terence thought he'd found a girl who wanted to dance. She was elegant and sweet and as he touched the little book of Shakespearean poems in his jacket thought that not even fourteen lines of one of his sonnets could do justice to this time when love finally took off her bonnet. In other intervals when there was no love Terence knew that he must just dream alone of all he once had known. Now all the tambourines and chanting Byzantines that he had heard in the night when he awoke from dreadful dreams and waited for the morning light to explain just what it means when you cannot open the door or swim to the safety of the shore, were silenced.

The waiter cleaning up an outside table smiled at him and Terence sensed it was not just the big tip he had left that caused it. Terence had a memory of the red house during a storm. Outside the lack of trees and birds, a desert except for an island or two of pines and lost creatures. What Alicia and others had mistaken for bluster was lack of confidence. He looked at the half empty glass but decided that his new courage would not come from what was left in it.

Hannah wondered if the desire she felt of that cold misted morning when little birds look for cream was love striking without warning. But then as she sat at her desk with no credible notes she wrote out with passion a scene from an opera... *'Oh, if love has made any sense then off and away with pretense! 'Tis better to die in the seeking than to suffer without its keeping.'*

Her thoughts turned to her childhood. Hannah's adoptive father Anton was a well known Bohemian man about Vienna and a pacifist. He had a monocle and a flamboyant manner which he wore without arrogance and that made him attractive. When the world war came he escaped the army because of his inability to control a nervous facial tic and having had a slight heart attack in 1913. The only job he ever held for any period of time was as a journalist but even that bored him. His heart took umbrage after a second attack and he died a fairly young man.

On the evening before the funeral Hannah and her adoptive mother Christina sat at the fireside discussing Anton. Christina had been long suffering during her marriage.

"There was never any regular money coming in and when Anton did sell a story he just switched from coffee with cream to coffee with rum."

"I've heard him called the last of the Bohemians." Hannah said.

"I suppose he'd have given up that lifestyle if he'd had the energy but he never had it. He was waiting for a windfall. It never came to rescue him from that life. In his ethic you mustn't try to escape it has to come to you without effort and it never came. Please promise me you won't marry a poor man no matter how handsome."

"Don't worry Mama. I want a man who has all the time in the world to love me. But if I say no to poverty then who knows where I'll end up considering how paradoxical life is."

"Do you love your work in the newspaper? Anton said you were born to write."

"I suppose I have to thank him for that," Hannah said,

"for getting me started for his inspiration. That was the hardest thing getting my foot in the door."

"Why did you adopt me?" Hannah asked Christina for the first time since she had found out.

"After a few years of trying and having no success I wanted a baby and we agreed on a girl."

"Simple as that." Hannah exclaimed. "Have you no idea where I came from? I mean my mother and father."

"That was hidden from us and of course from you. You just take the chance that you'll be lucky and we were. Look how lovely you are and how smart. I don't remember Anton ever having such feelings as he did for you Hannah."

"Not even for you Mama?"

"Well, of a different kind of course. When I skipped past the coffee house one morning he was waiting on the patio for me the next."

"Did you like him right away?"

"He looked very nice and was tall and lean not like the others who had to sit two feet from the table to get their bellies in. No, he was tall and handsome. He wore a white shirt with a white bow tie and he had a white handkerchief in his top pocket. He was clean shaven too. Don't you just hate those big moustaches and straggly beards? Of course I had to get over the monocle but he took it out when he kissed me, at least the first few times. And he could talk; there was never a dull moment those first few months. He began at law school but gave that up. He was on the wild side politically and opposed the war from the beginning. He couldn't resist a literary battle and fought many of them in the newspaper and won a few. He was quite famous once you know for his storytelling for his honesty and ethical conduct. There was talk once of collecting his stories but I don't suppose that will happen now."

"I think you may be wrong there Mama. One publisher has already been collecting articles and essays at least that's what my editor has told me. You had a better education didn't you?"

"Yes, I did get my degree. Anton often called me an overeducated woman. You know he was a writer yet there isn't a scrap of paper or a pen or a pencil of his in this house. All his work was done elsewhere."

"In the coffee house." Hannah supposed.

"In the coffee house yes. In his other home where he spent most of his time."

"Did he go with other women?"

Christina thought for a moment too long. "I don't know or want to know. Just so long as he took his monocle out to kiss me then I was quite sure I was the only one. But those places are full of women looking for famous men."

"Have you had a sad life Mama?"

"No, not really. I've lost my husband and there's no money in the bank. I don't know which is worse at the moment."

Hannah encouraged her. "I have a good job Mama. We will manage and if they publish his collected work that may keep you going for a while."

"I have the feeling my dear that I might not be needing that."

Hannah recalled more than once that her mother had said that winter was a better time to die than the spring and God met her wish a few months later as the first frost came in the night. Christina died never knowing all that Hannah knew about Anton but like her mother it didn't diminish her love for him nor did it excite her desire to find her real parents. One set was enough.

***

Anton usually tried to meet Madeleine just before midnight; after that she became busy with clients. As they sat having coffee sheltered from the smirry rain Madeleine commented on their relationship.

"I'm not used to luxury you know. It must cost you a lot to surprise me with such nice things. But what I like is that you never buy me material things useful things you just lead me into new experiences new culture at least for me. Except for that lovely dress you picked out so that I could easily stand in the vestibule near you and watch the beautiful people during the intermission. It's too bad we have to sit separately at the opera and the theater. I'd never ridden in a carriage before. I liked it when the footman opened the door at the Opera house. Of course I've had other nice experiences. One man took me into his library. He had more books and photographs in there than the Albertina and he said a lovely thing to me when I asked him if he'd ever loved a woman.

'Why should I tamper with the human heart.' he said.

He was different. He chewed tobacco and spat under the table but then I meet all kinds of people. Why don't you have sex with me Anton?"

"I'm a married man Madeleine."

She chuckled. "Anton all the men who come to me are married."

Anton touched her arm. "Not really."

"No." she said, "not really." not smiling.

"In a guilty world you're so innocent Madeleine."

"You're the only one who ever touched it Anton."

Anton, when he was at a loss for a story in other words the times in the café and during his midnight walks the city had not brought forth an incident that Vienna waited for every morning, would turn to nature. Like all writers who cannot find a story he wondered if he would dry up and therefore sometimes his piece would have a little sadness, even pessimism in it.

'It's August and the earth is on the turn into the valley between the seasons. The oak trees, the last to form their leaves to avoid predators are also the first to shed. I noticed this morning that they have turned brownish in the crown. The oak is a wise tree; it doesn't ask for too much and therefore lives a long time ; is much admired ; and also cut down by a weaker species from whom it cannot hide its strength and who after attaching canvas to its trunks ventured to the ends of the earth.

The chestnut trees have fruit on them about ready to fall on us earlier than usual this August. In a last gasp for survival they are making more fruit than ever before. But there is no need to feed the nuts now to horses to prevent or cure sickness. Little boys afraid to climb don't throw sticks at them to bring the nuts down so that they can mount them on string and play the game of striking another nut to see who is 'bully'…an ancient game. The fire is out for the man who used to sell roast chestnuts in the street. The trees are still with us. But for how long? And the birds; perhaps they watch us from the phantom trees those winged ghosts who while still able to seize with wild swoop and cry cannot know they too are on their way to die? It does not grieve us now even though young and true we might not miss their voice. It will not grieve us then if at first we could not feel the loss. But it will come to us too; that we may not live again.'

The previous night he had missed the young woman whose life in the city had not reached the place where sometimes bitterness sets in and a cynical view of humanity too. Instead, she was unfailing in her joy of life when time was her own and not paid for. He knew a duchess or two and a few other highfaluting admirers; none of them fitted his soul like this one, this waif. He had tried to keep her inside away from the cold nights in the winter. In the summer Anton took her to the Prater where she flounced and traipsed for fun and for pleasure totally free with Anton who of course had a wife and a daughter. He consoled himself with the thought that they were not threatened by this relationship. Just this one had ever supplied all his non physical needs. Then she disappeared. All sense in the world went with her. Never again would he see her walk down the street with another man while she worked yet turn her head when she could to smile at him. Once, she wore a fur hat that he bought her.

She said her name was Nadia but he liked to call her Madeleine. It gave him pleasure to know that on some nights no matter who lusted after her there was not enough money in the world to buy her favor or could replace the days they spent together or the steady look of her brown eyes and her full lips as she bit them. To him at first she was a flashing hawk but later he found that her heart was centered on the dove.

He offered to take her to a popular revue but she refused.

"Are the boys naked?" she asked.

"I doubt it." he replied.

"Then why would I want to look at naked girls? There's no nourishment for me in that."

He smiled and looked at her wonderful figure.

"I didn't know you were counting calories."

"I'm not. Nor am I a prudish vegetarian."

He decided the revue idea had no nutritional value.

"Your innocence is touching."

She was so full of innocence. "I was hoping you would touch it tonight."

She always asked the same question. "Where will we go tomorrow Anton?"

"My dear we are not going anywhere we've arrived. Where else in the world could we go better than this. If I were a King and you my Queen what else could I offer you but this view of the world? What would you want from me tomorrow?"

"I want you to pamper me with golden poppies, tell me I'm elegant and sweet like the apple tinted rose you may place at my feet."

"You've been reading poetry again."
"I only read yours Anton."
Her memory stunned him and then she went further.
"I want to go to the mountains someday Anton and sled on the snow where everything is clean and perhaps you can feel what freedom is like. When I look at our river all I see are the dregs of the world go by."

To Anton her depth felt like a slight breeze coming across a hot windless day picking up bouquets of flowers along the way.

"I see you around St. Stephens sometimes." he said. "Do you ever go inside?"

"No. I stay in its shadow. I can attract the host but I am always the one entered." She had a sad wit.

Anton never told her of Christina or Hannah; ever asked her how she got into the life she led; did not know her friends and so had no resources to trace her when she disappeared.

"Hannah, did you love Anton?" Christina had asked.
"Yes, Mamma, I loved Anton. Why is that so important to you?"
"I don't know Hannah. It's just that his life seemed such a waste and if he knew you loved him then he would have been happy. He had no worries about me for that was always certain from the first kiss to the last."

Hannah, well informed of Anton's innocent liaison with Nadia was pleased that her mother had remained ignorant and later wondered whether it would have made any difference to her anyway she had loved him so long and so much and without question or questions. Love has so many ways and being without doubt is just one of them.

***

Hannah looked around the luxurious dining room of the Ritz as she entered but in the end saw none of the famous or infamous faces she had expected; just Terence, standing for her at a discreet corner table.

For Terence Hannah represented at last one of the many dreams he'd had in the mud of Flanders ; that one day a woman might bring him heat when snow was falling. In one swish of her white dress she swept all the debris away.

As she sat down Terence could not hold back his admiration. "You caused quite a stir when you walked in here."

Hannah settled ; a trio struck up.

"False teeth clicking!" she said, a smile on her face that would have melted the glazed icing on the millefeuille that she ordered later.

"Even the waiter might think you were quite a wit," Terence responded further charmed, "and I suppose he's heard nearly everything not worth hearing."

She couldn't help herself. "I see you had water served with the brandy. Sobering perhaps."

He shook his head and picked up the menu. "We'll see."

The occasion and the luxury could not deter her.

"Terence you were writing. Have you stopped?"

He was surprised at the question. "I'm not sure. I don't see anything significant in what I've written so far."

"Perhaps only the reader can find it. So you must just get on with it get it out of your system. Perhaps others will finally create the meaning not the author."

Terence thought this over. "The problem I see with that is the restriction in my time line ; my own experience. How can I expect so much from the reader?"

Hannah brushed her jet hair away from her face and looked across at the man she knew by instinct should stay in her life beyond this tete e tete.

"Terence. Write a novel not an autobiography. Forget having any substantial meaning."

He brushed a crumb from the table. "You should be writing this novel."

"No Terence," she assured him, "I'll be like everybody else and just put the finishing touches to it as I read it."

He saw she was serious and despite her confidence in him a confidence he had not expected he still had doubts.

"Everything in the world seems so meaningless at least anything coming out of me in comparison to the state of the world."

Hannah pushed her menu away.

"And what is the state of the world?"

"Like me." Terence admitted. "Quite confused."

She tried to reassure him. "It doesn't have to be like that you know. There are ways to figure it out. But in your case I think that first you must separate yourself from the gang you run with."

He had mixed feelings about her advice but nonetheless reached across and took her hands. "I'm glad that you've adopted me but why do you call my friends a gang?"

"Actually," Hannah continued, "there are two gangs. The political and the opportunists although both are related. You know Michel is a closet fascist yet you keep his company."

He was defensive. "Hannah, I don't admire his politics only his language."

The waiter full of experience looked at them from a distance but did not approach.

"Ah, so French," she said, "to be hypnotized by a learned liar."

Terence tried to hide behind the menu again.

"You're a socialist aren't you?"

"Hardly." she proferred.

"I'm afraid to ask you where you do belong."

Her eyes darkened. "Why? In case it will worry your friends. The racist course and the race course are not places for you Terence but I bet Michelle told you that too."

"How did you get to know her?"

"I bought one of her paintings. She's better off in the north with her art. This place at this time is not for such a tender heart."

Terence repeated something he had said to Michelle. "Perhaps she should take Ruskin's advice *'and this coming Spring paint nothing but opening flowers and in the Autumn nothing but apricots and peaches.'* You see, my heart is not so hard."

"No, but it doesn't appear tender to her at the moment, just weak. Terence, a woman never expects a bargain from a man ; she contracts to pay in one form or another for what she gets." Seeing how unsettled he was by this statement she held her peace for a moment or two and then brought back the melting smile. "Now you're wondering why you asked me out for dinner aren't you?"

Terence was wondering. "I didn't know whether you had done the asking. Did you take pity on me like the other two?"

"I'm not counting and I know you don't need charity."

"You're a beautiful woman…" he began.

"Oh cut that out! I'm just a German woman who can speak French and I've got big feet you know."

He managed a retort. "That's a feature at the bottom of my list."

"Terence, earlier if you'd been sober I might not be on your list."

"I did remember to come." he reminded her.

"I'm told that you come here every night!"

"I don't see the gang." he responded, looking around.

"They won't be seen with me on your arm." she assured him.

"Why not?"

"I'm the wrong color Terence. I'm the lady in red!"

"You look white to me and more like a femme fatale."

He was still on her hook. "I'm not as fatal as that brandy bottle hidden in the corner in case this doesn't turn out as well as you'd hoped."

He pointed to the label. "Napoleon."

"Look at the small print Terence… 'bottled in Waterloo!' "

He had to laugh. "Your eyesight is good."

She brushed aside her long hair from her cheek. "If only my foresight was to match."

He changed the subject. "Would you like to eat? I've decided on oysters."

"Things are looking up. Have you any money left? My spies tell me that you went to the races today."

He was surprised. "You're keeping a close watch. I don't lose all the time."

"I'm on a diet so I won't cost you much."

"You look thin enough." he said.

"Good tailoring suggests substance but also hides it. Say Terence what do you like about me?"

He reached in for the first line of Sofi's poem. "*You have all the juices of Babylon.* Everybody has a political religion these days ; even beautiful women but you seem agnostic."

"Not beautiful enough?" she suggested.

"Sobering perhaps."

She looked again at the brandy bottle. "Doubtful. Have they asked you to work for them?"

He was genuinely doubtful. "Who?"

She had lost her smile. "The patriots of vitriol!"

She still hadn't solved his problem. "Who are they?"

"Enemies of the people." she exclaimed.

He went along with her. "You've decided that?"

"I think I'm in the majority."

He looked for a waiter but they were all busy. "I don't always like majorities."

"What do you like?" she asked.

Now he was certain. "Not another war."

She was cynical. "At any price?"

He touched his sore leg. "I'm hoping Hitler's plans are to the east."

"Terence, if you read the French version of Mein Kampf you will find that the section where he defines France as his main enemy has been omitted. There is a welcome committee here. He's coming. He had a bad experience his first time. What do you think?"

His laugh was thin. "That's a good question."

"Are you searching for answers Terence or should the fascists solve our problems?"

"Hannah, there are other choices."

"You think so. I don't think there's much choice left though the politicians seem to want us to believe in their brand of certainty."

"I get lots of that at the races." he assured her.

"Terence, picking the right color is difficult."

"There's always popular demand." he argued.

"Don't bet against it if it picks the Swastika."

Hannah had a pale face and dark hair with cupid lips of bright red lipstick. She wore a white dress with a red sash around her waist and shoes to match. It crossed his mind that she was very chic for a communist but later discovered that there was no hair shirt next to the skin. He imagined she was so different from Frances and Michelle. Cool, he thought, almost to indifference. When he discovered how wrong he was it was too late. Once over the onset her effect on him was contagious nor was there any antidote in alcohol or gambling. She led him down the road to political satire and there he had finally found his metier and all the contained spirit squeezed by the trenches of Verdun burst out in volleys of grape to cover a multitude of the shades of French opinion.

"I know your address." she continued. "But where do you live?"

She saw the agonising need to lift a glass but he resisted. He put his hand on the glass of water. "I'm surprised you don't know."

Her eyes followed the water but she was firm. "That's not an answer."

"I could take you there if you're patient." he said.

Her face turned soft again. "Perhaps you're the patient."

Terence had recovered himself. "I'm not so far gone as I once was so you don't have to patronize me."

"What happened to you in the north Terence?"

He took a long moment to answer. "I thought I had found love ; then the sadness of a shipwreck. I looked for a place to hide in then somersaulted mindlessly and at random."

Hannah saw the emotion drain out of him.

"What would you have me do?" she asked stretching out her hands across the table.

He tried his luck. "Embrace me. I think I need that."

"I'm willing," she responded, "but across a table would not be much inspiration for either of us."

He stretched the subject. "Have you no appetite?"

She patted her stomach. "I've had an apple."

He had enough strength left for wit. "Now the worm!"

Hannah spoke very softly. "Terence, there might not be one if I'm not at the bottom of the barrel." She kept the conversation warm. "I have no politics at least none that I'm too serious about though I do lean left of center when I do have opinions of my own and not one hammered down my throat by the popular press."

"Take a look at the menu Hannah."

She couldn't stop looking around. "I'm not really hungry."

"Then have an appetiser. I recommend the beetroot tart with black truffle."

Hannah laughed. "Terence, I'm neither beetroot nor black and certainly not tart. I might settle for the lobster bisque."

"Any writers you admire?" Terence wondered, hoping to keep up with her.

"Not one in particular but one or two I don't have much time for after reading their vituperative stuff full of hate and antisemitism."

"You're not Jewish are you?" he asked.

Hannah smiled at him. "Not that I know of but who knows who they are in the mixed up world of Vienna and I am a woman so that rules out one possibility you could check?"

"You know your own family surely." Terence said.

"Not really." she advised. "I found out not so long ago that I was an adopted child given to a childless couple who raised me."

Terence was curious. "Were you happy with them?"

"I was but they really were too old for a young girl. But at least they got me a good education and when my adopted mother died last year I decided it was time to strike out on my own. I speak French so this was a natural move for me."

Terence took out a cigarette but when she gave him a look he did not light it. "Among all the other surprises you've piled upon me in fifteen minutes I'm surprised you're still on your own."

Hannah responded. "Who says I am?"

"Oh…"

She took a deep breath at the hint of disappointment and then put her hand on his arm and was completely forthright with him. "I'm very attracted to you Terence. I'm not thinking of anyone else within ten thousand miles."

His heart hesitated for a moment with the evident truth she spoke. "One moment you're an open book and the next at little mysterious."

Hannah smiled enigmatically. "Should a woman not be mysterious and especially an adopted one?"

Terence managed a smile. "It seems that every woman I meet has to be."

"Have you solved any of them?" she asked.

"I was close to the first one but she died of the flu and then there was Michelle and I failed miserably with her as you know. I'm not sure if I could manage another heartbreak at this time."

Hannah absolved him. "Perhaps they demanded too much."

Terence turned pensive again. "I might not have much to give. I want to write a novel but I can't seem to find the energy to get it done."

Then Hannah surprised him again. She moved around the table to the chair next to him and put it as close to him as she could manage. She put her hand on his arm. "You could leave Paris for a month or two." she suggested. "It's getting hot anyway. Pick a place and I'll go with you and help you get started again. I've written for a few magazines you know. I might be able to support your needs. So far as I can see your writing will be your salvation."

Through the pleasure of this offer there was still sadness in him. "When Michelle left I wasn't too sure if there was anything left worth saving."

"I think there is." she said, full of confidence.

Terence gave her a serious look. "But you don't know me!"

"Really." she said, and then continued. "You came out of the war with a serious leg wound. You fell in love with your nurse but she died on you. You went north to your Aunt's house to write and met Michelle and she fell in love with you but you were not over the nurse. Then you got all this money you didn't deserve and you're well on your way to dissipate your life and your good fortune away. You have bad company. You drink and gamble from boredom. You have lost Michelle, a fine woman. Your erstwhile friends impose their political views on you since you have none of your own. What did I miss?"

"It's not much of a resume is it?" he admitted.

She stayed positive. "I need a change too, Terence. Let's go for a working holiday."

He was quizzical. "Why do you want to do this?"

"Perhaps I like horses." she answered.

"But not sure things." he retorted.

She leaned back and laughed at him. "If there's a war you wouldn't have to go."

He pulled back his jacket and patted his stomach.

"I am getting on."

"Terence, if age is your only advantage then I'm in trouble."

He made a sudden observation as he picked up the brandy. "I haven't had a drink since we sat down. It must have been the click of your heels on the tiles the sexiest sound I've ever heard."

"There's more," she quipped. "when I've taken them off." She watched him closely and was pleased to see his shoulders relax. "All you need now is to get on a horse and enjoy the ride." she said

"Do you know a place?" he asked.

She knew she had convinced him. "I do."

He was still tentative. "It's not too quiet."

"It has a nice place to eat among the grapes. They make good wine and grow wheat. It's warm at this time of the year but not hot. I counted twenty three species of birds. The river is full of trout. Lots of atmosphere."

"You don't look like a girl who goes for atmosphere." The meal was delivered.

She waited until the waiter had gone. "It might be for a month or two or longer. I can arrange it in two days."

Terence smiled at her not able to hide his pleasure. "You're such a schemer."

"All woman are when they see what they want."

"I've never been led before." he admitted.

"Don't worry Terence I don't believe in altars."

"Two days!" he pondered.

She hit him low. "Long enough to pay off your gambling debts."

"I pay cash." he responded.

At the mention of money she made sure he knew she was quite independent. "It may interest you to know that I have two commissions for articles and all the royalties on my stepfather's estate which have turned out to be substantial. Maybe you could help me too with my essays."

"Are they political?" he asked.

"More historical." she replied.

He pushed the empty oyster shells away. "You're an intriguing woman. You know Hannah when you walked in here the whole of the harem came in with you but you will always be first choice; most called upon; eventually separate and unforgettable."

Hannah lowered her eyes but did not retreat from the praise. "If you think so then make it worthwhile for both of us."

"I may have some trouble keeping up." he advised her.

She kept her wit going. "My kind of trouble is debt free but lots of interest."

"Keep it simple." he replied, I'm not that complicated.

Hannah made sure he had better be serious. "It's up to you if you need to compound it just so long as I'm the principal."

"I like your shoes." Terence said.

"Apparently they're only good for riding a horse or at least that's what the soldier who gave them to me said." Hannah pulled up her skirt. "Only a day old."

"A soldier." Terence repeated.

"Yes. I like soldiers even older ones." Her face lit up hardly hiding the facetiousness in her eyes. "You don't mind do you?"

As the waiter edged closer with the bill Terence flinched a little ; his leg felt sore and he regretted throwing away his medals.

He sat back in his chair. "When does the interview begin?"

"What colour was your mother's hair?"

"Black, like yours."

"And her eyes?"

"Dark brown like yours."

"Was she as tall as I am?"

"Yes, as tall."

"Did you love her?"

"Yes I loved her."

"If I see a twinkle in your eye after digesting a dozen oysters perhaps we can continue the questioning and take your life a step further from the cradle."

"After just one interview?"

"Terence you didn't touch the brandy. That was the test."

He turned the bottle around to face the wall. "I think it was the Waterloo crack that did it."

"I'll give you more than a hundred days Terence but first to Elba!"

From afar the waiter smiled at his colleague as Hannah kissed Terence so quickly that only the sharp eyed Hannah and Terence knew how slight the whisper and the delicate promise.

Chapter 18

The ferry ploughed its way up the calm river and Seamus sat with a coffee on his knee. He considered his new circumstances. The music coming over the loudspeakers did not help him parse all the promises he had made to himself just to find and love Sofi. He was on the water and at a watershed. At this point before all the dams had been burst and drowned his relationships and he had just floated until he could find another island he knew he would eventually abandon if he found himself shipwrecked. He could never seem to find the lagoon with the secret caves. The coffee grew cold but he drank it anyway and discovered that the sugar had sunk to the bottom of the cup. He had never struggled to believe the women who said they loved him. There was never enough risk and less care he supposed.Now he began to think that a woman who could make him employ such self examination must have touched a hidden core and found the caves. He thought too of his art and the effect that Sofi would have on it. His paintings like his loves had hardly touched him. It was all too easy. When would he be found wanting? Could she be the one to do it? He crept farther into the corner. The hard seat squeezed his bones. The chemistry in his body changed. He knew that as he sat lonely and afraid. All the nerves raw every muscle tensed to take the leap of the tiger whose breath he could still smell and whose claws he had not seen but he recognized the markings. The hunt was on but the game not yet over.

As Seamus looked at the vineyards the heurigers and imagined that the cliched concertinas could be changed to oboes for everything seemed so robust and full of flourish when what he needed was the sensitive smile of Sofi and her gentle hand upon him. The wind sent another chill through his bones. From the shore was that a whiff of her perfume? Life!

"More coffee?"

"Yes, thank you."

"Cream and sugar?"

"Cream only."

Many castles and churches were being passed by the river. Nature ignoring the past and depending on the present. The dark clouds as murky as the history the rain was sure to fail to clear from the air. Seamus wished he could be as sure of himself as the young man twenty feet away sitting with the unruly hair dark glasses and a weak beard on his chin. Opposite him a glorious young woman waiting on his attention desperate for a kiss while he supped his glass of chocolate. She wore a black dress modestly cut around the neck with a golden locket nicely poised between her breasts. Yet the young man did not lean forward and kiss her cheek. Seamus wondered what held him back. Where did his poise come from? He was obviously outclassed and seemingly had no knowledge of his treasure. Seamus turned away quite annoyed with the lack of passion. Somewhere from the back of the ship a solo musical instrument played. He tried to recognize it but it was beyond him being so delicate. He looked back at the lovers and wanted to pretend to the girl that he was writing a novel and that she would be on page 294 or so. The man stood up and limped away to the bar. The eyes of the woman followed him all the way there and back. So recently devoid of such attention Seamus moved outside into the rain. Just the other day he had found some words from Sofi that seemed to cover his predicament. *Whatever holds the heart together sometimes fails. Yet, how are we to know? For time never warns us that life is a ship that sails without lights into the dark.'*

Later, as he came around the ring the city appeared like a studded bracelet of eclectic stones; the entrance to a baroque cathedral. The central nave was approached through an avenue of lime trees surrounded by the perfume of lilacs. 'Can Mozart be far away?' he thought. Poor man. He at least was unaware of a broken culture. Some said the city was doomed by its decadence yet there was still some gold between the strata. As he walked around he wondered how he could get to the river but discovered that it only inspired waltzes and was perhaps blue in a certain light from the heights of the Kahlenberg looking upstream towards Klosterneuburg. The Fohn, the wind, was as enervating as any Sirocco. His guide book spoke of Roman remains but he knew they were the same no matter where you found them. Once the Romans had established a formula they stuck to it and whatever they built seems to have fallen down everywhere at the same rate. This was the case in Vienna where the form if not the spirit of every architecture known to western man and others was still preserved.

When he came into the house on the way to the apartment he had rented for a month it seemed to have no ventilation, no air. What little there was swamped by the smell of paprika stew or goulash ; he never could tell the difference especially when it was confused by the odor of the usual cheap Egyptian cigarettes the landlady smoked.

It can be painful to see young people in love. Especially if only one of them is truly smitten and the other just quietly amused at the effect the lust they are having. As Seamus entered the house a young man moved away from the landlady's daughter a little embarrassed yet she was quite calm and in full control of herself. The young man had come to give her a violin lesson. He came three times a week. The instrument was still in its case. The youth pulled it over towards him and opened it up. Later, as Seamus drank some coffee on the verandah the pupil had taken up the instrument but played it badly. She had no talent. She had the sullen beauty that some young girls have after puberty but never again. When her mother came in the music stopped. Apparently the neighbors were complaining. It was Vienna after all; they were used to good music. The woman looked at her daughter. She could see her beauty but seemed to take no enjoyment in it. She had seen it before in a thousand mirrors that she now avoided until at least midday or when she had found some fresh air outside this hothouse. There was a picture of her on the wall. She wore a lovely hat with a broad feather in front. It had been her wedding day. Her hair was naturally black under the hat that day. Seamus decided to go out into Vienna. It was his birthday.

'How pleasant to have one's birthday in midsummer when all the young girls can be enjoyed and the older ones celebrated. If it's too hot have a reason to pray for rain or a cool breeze or the late evening walking and talking and solving all the problems of the world. It's your birthday and everybody listens to you with curiosity and looks at you as your memories flood through you and you mood varies like a rocking horse. You try not to feel giddy with your own importance. And that was the one day when you walked around the town to all the places you had followed whenever you could the regular routine of a lovely woman far above you in status and with whom perhaps because of that you fell hopelessly in love. She went to church and you followed her there. When she took lunch so did you. Now you have lost sight of her but you had loved her. With years behind us perhaps I could talk to her; have the courage.'

When Seamus reached Vienna he was not welcomed by a waltz or a warm day or a young woman running towards him not able to contain herself until she was in his arms. Not by an invitation to her favorite coffee house or for hot chocolate at the café tables. There were no bright skirts no high heeled parades or a flash of silk stockings. No red kiss seeking lips. No hand to hold or waist to cinch among the trees. No offer to climb the hill at the palace or visit the zoo. No cruise on the Danube or a search for bargains at the Saturday flea market. No talk of tickets for the opera or the musical theater and no artistic introductions arranged. No coach rides early in the morning when the dew was still fresh in the gardens and the city was refreshed. Instead, a welcome to riots and political demonstrations; to ugly symbols; to bullies ; to a vicious anti semite press dedicated to the overthrow of socialism. The newspapers toadied to the patrons of the hateful side of mankind and those prey to the social evils of lost causes and unemployment. It was not a pleasant introduction to the world for a sensitive constitution who had felt for love and found frenzy. There was no Mozart or sign of the cross in St. Stephens only a denunciation of Mahler and his ilk who were very anxious over their coffee and told him stories of how their work was no longer being commissioned ; that they did not stay out late anymore for fear of the thugs who were prone to lie in wait for them.

The poet Gustav became friendly. "We sometimes adjourn our chess game rather than go home in the dark. You should have been here in the balmy days. Then we all made some money from our stories as far away as Prague and Paris they asked for them. We were famous then."

"Your Emperor Josef moustache was more famous." Seamus joked.

Gustav continued, growing more intense.

"They wrote books about us you know and people bought them. They were literate then the people, but now they burn books with any of our names on them. I shouldn't take it personally these people don't know how to discriminate. Mein Kampf is their bible. It's hard to think that all the hate that's in it came from here from Vienna. Not our Vienna of course, another one we don't know or want to know but now it has come across us and it doesn't like us. I suppose that's been twenty years in the making or longer. I was in the war you know the Italian front. They gave me a medal too but now I'm just a Jew that sold them out lost them the war stabbed them in the back. I lost some friends over there."

Seamus was compassionate. "Most of these people didn't fight, they're looking for scapegoats. Cowards always do that. When a war comes they'll be hard to find until success is guaranteed."

"Have you heard of the camps?" Gustav asked, quietly.

"No." Seamus was surprised. "What camps?"

"They opened them in 1933 and there are thousands of them now full of people who object to fascist policies but mostly German Jews and gipsies. Nobody is talking to us. They are stealing our property. Who can be trusted? Have you seen the signs on the shops? Jews not welcome. Jewish children are not in school. I have heard that some families are sending their children to Great Britain."

"That's a long way." Seamus agreed.

"They are the only country that will take them. We are outcasts. What will happen next?"

"I don't know," Seamus said, "but I was reminded last night of an old

Spanish monk who prayed night and day that the people should have bread peace truth moderate rain showers love and charity."

"What about a glass of good wine?" Gustav wondered.

"He was from Rioja so that goes without saying."

"I feel better. Where did you say he came from?"

"Spain."

"He prayed in vain for his own people," Gustav said, "but let's hope they've still got some wine."

A man passed outside the window of the coffee house.

Gustav told his story. "The first time we saw him we thought he had just been shot from a cannon."

"Really?" Seamus was amused.

"Yes. His head was shaped like a beehive. Then he rose to our bait pretending to be a friendly pike and we swallowed the man's character whole. That man knows everything except what's good for him. If you look outside you'll see his opinions nailed to every fence."

"You mean he's stupid?" Seamus asked.

"Yes of course, but of the sort to be approached with caution."

"Why is that?"

"The poor fellow is still alive so we know he has a heart but we can only agree with him on the fact that he has misplaced his mind and until we find it then we will take nothing for granted."

"You must have a hundred anecdotes on him."

"Oh yes." Gustav laughed. "One evening in here he sneezed twice.

"I think I have an allergy." he told the waiter. "Could you move those flowers?"

"Certainly sir. Would you like some fresh ones? These are artificial."

"He does look as if he has come down a bit in life."

"Yes," Gustav continued, "but too many rungs at a time. And this little story will tell you why we are a bit apprehensive about him."

"Go on." Seamus urged.

"He was at the opera one night and somebody asked him in the foyer where he was sitting."

"In the front row."

"Do you really need those opera glasses?"

"Matter of habit I suppose."

"Ah yes. First time at the front."

"Actually, I was at the battle of Limanouva."

"No need for glasses there."

"No, nor conscientious objectors either!"

"Why on earth do people come here when they are satirized so much?" Seamus asked.

"To be anonymous ; to be known ; but only to these residents. To speak ; but only here. To listen; and they consider this place to be the only one with people worth listening to. To be alone ; but in good company and so never lonely. To have the best of the only world they care about where they know everything about everybody. If they come here for any length of time then their life becomes everybody's life and nothing is hidden."

Seamus looked around at the customers. "I think you have to be brave to come in here on a regular basis."

"Oh no!" Gustav said, "the brave are outside these walls and have no need for this life."

Seamus kept him going. "So you all talk about each other."

Gustav continued, happy to have a new ear.

"Oh no! There are silent types who only want to be talked about. They are borrowing the use of another voice for an hour or two and gradually sometimes find their own. Being here that's the thing. Lack of purpose. Look at that fellow over there. He's so shortsighted and sometimes his moustache changes position. You have to look him in the eye or he gets suspicious."

"There must be times when you hate these people."

Gustav was not so sure. "It follows then that there are times when we love them too. Ah, you see a good example. A dictionary just walked in. Unfortunately he got stuck at bee."

"In his bonnet I suppose?" Seamus quipped

"He's very welcome here. He's been called a poet at least in this dive. He rhymes limericks with chopsticks. A clever fellow from green to yellow but don't look over or he'll say hello. I can make you a rhyme anytime is his mantra."

"I suppose he coupled that with Sumatra?" Seamus suggested, enjoying himself.

Gustav agreed. "I think you're right he looks in form tonight."

"You're a poet yourself." Seamus said.

"Yes," the poet agreed, "but I keep mine on the shelf and that bore behind the door. Come on let's go I feel a feuilleton coming on."

As they walked along the dark streets Gustav could not stop talking. "We are so far behind the times here that Louis Xiv would not be out of place riding down this street."

"He was French?" Seamus reminded him.

"Of course, so was Napoleon. I don't like the French. I went to the Arc de Triomphe once."

"For Remembrance day?"

"No. It was the fifth of May and I wanted to see the sun set behind it."

"How about the Tsar?"

"Of Russia? I didn't like him either."

"The Kaiser then."

"I preferred Queen Victoria."

"She's dead and gone."

"Well, so is Vienna."

"Coffee house logic."

"Of course! What else?"

As they walked then Gustav suggested a shortcut down a lane. As they reached halfway he pointed out a small sign to Seamus that was once fixed above a door but was now hanging awry over the lintel.

It said: *'Desire. Art and the Dream.'*

Gustav stopped and addressed the sign.

'Wollen macht frei.' As if Seamus had not been there or was another person to whom he was explaining that *'desiring liberates'*

Seamus questioned the slogan. "Is that a Jewish thing?"

"Yes, that's right." Gustav replied, wearily.

"Were you involved?" Seamus asked, trying to make the sign straighten up.

"Yes, but not to join just to get away from traditions."

As they walked on Seamus questioned him again.

"Jewish traditions?"

"That's right." Gustav replied."Lost identities. It was a dandy who made up the slogan but he couldn't wear it. It was too big for him though they finally buried him in it." The poet rambled on and Seamus realized he was reliving a personal drama and the failure of it or that his failure in it had brought him down. Seamus also knew that the shortcut had been carefully chosen so that he could unburden something still left in his soul.

"They were so proud of their Secession but we had one too." he continued, recovering himself.

"Really. Where?"

"Why of course it was to Zion; to Palestine; to Israel."

"Not quite yet." Seamus cautioned.

Gustav was more certain. "Coming earlier than we expected."

"Perhaps not welcome everywhere." Seamus suggested.

Gustav continued, full of emotion. "Or anywhere! No heaven? We have one but not on earth. We had to make one up. You must come and join us. The only strong ones among us have faith in Zionism. Our own country. Think of it! I'm not just a Jew, I'm an Austrian Jew. My family have been here for a hundred years or more. Find a gun you'll need it.

"You have a gun?" Seamus asked of this mild man.

"Yes of course! Now look down the avenue. Do you see those young men with the shorts and white stockings? Those are juvenile thugs. They wear white stockings because the swastika is banned here."

Seamus grew nervous. "What are they doing?"

"They are roaming the streets and attacking anyone who looks like a Jew."

"You look very Jewish." Seamus said.

"I am a Jew."

"Will they attack you?"

"No they won't."

"Why not?"

"Why not? I have a gun."

"But they don't know that."

"Oh yes they do. I meet them here every night and after the first night I let them see my gun."

"Is it loaded?" Seamus asked, a little apprehensively.

"Not yet." Gustav replied.

"They are saying Hitler won't last long." Seamus said.

"If he does then the bullets will have to come out of the bedside drawer."

Seamus felt lucky to have made the writer Gustav's acquaintance on his first few days in the city. He had walked through the streets with a him and he was recognized and seemingly respected by every one they met including policemen, flower sellers, ladies of the night and fellow habitues of coffee houses. It was a lesson on how to be among your characters. When they went to his hotel room there was a bottle of slivovitch outside the door with a note from a lady. Inside the room was a breath of fresh air since all the windows were open. The room was cold.

"I believe in a cool room." he said. "It's the only healthy thing I can afford."

The walls were covered in photographs and postcards. "You can read them if you like." he said.

"I'm sorry." Seamus apologised. "I don't know the language that well."

They had ended up drinking tea though they were both coffee addicts.

"It's good first thing in the morning." Gustav said.

"What inspires you?" Seamus wondered.

"The length of time it takes me to have the courage to pick up the pen."

"And when it takes a while?" Seamus wondered.

"Then I can be sure the piece will be short but in great detail and hardly any passion. That is the short breath the beginning of boredom and like the end of love.

Seamus admired the man. He had read the short pieces and the long ones. They were all so personal they couldn't be separated from the artist or his poetry.

Gustav continued. "I don't know where it comes from or what it's worth." he said. "All those people we met tonight know. You should ask them. No. I can speak for them. It's not literature, it's life!"

On that passionate note Seamus prepared to leave.

There was a large table by the open window. The writer took his shirt off and lay on it as Seamus left.

Chapter 19

As they had agreed, Terence and Hannah met again two days after their dinner at the Ritz. Hannah said she would arrange the transport and that all Terence needed to bring was enough to last a few days until he was sure he would want to stay. She showed up in a sports car and jumped out of it in blue figure tight pants and a revealing top. He couldn't help goggling at her and she was a great attraction to passers by. She drove him away at top speed into the country.

Terence looked at her in admiration.

"Were you so sure I'd come?"

"No. But I aim to make sure you stay. It's a lovely day isn't it?"

"I'm glad of that at the speed you're driving this jalopy. Is it yours?"

"It is mine," she said, "and the last thing it is, is a jalopy, whatever that slang means."

"I don't think it's too unkind and I didn't mean it to be."

"I'm just teasing you Terence. This car can take it. It's English!"

Two fast hours later down a driveway lined with trees they came to a small house overlooking the river."

Hannah was full of enthusiasm.

"Here we are. This is not the main house. That would be too large for us. It's another mile or so in the bush. Isn't this lovely?"

"How did you find it?" he wondered.

"It belongs to a friend of mine who's on a sabbatical at the moment and I'm not sure when he'll be back but a month or two at the least."

Terence got curious. "Where is he?"

"Spain!"

"He might never come back from there."

"No," she agreed, "but he had to go."

"Good luck to him. I've seen a war and hope we never have another one like it. I certainly wouldn't volunteer myself for that one."

Her reply was mild but definite. "I don't think the world needed that last one but this one has to be fought. It will be dark soon and you must be hungry so let's see what there is to eat."

"Have you been here before?"

"Yes, Terence I've been here before and lots of other places too."

In the morning there was warmth outside among the cherry trees. Two blackbirds were having a wake up conversation. Terence sat in the morning sun with his notebooks on his knee. All the last year he had written hundreds of pages for his novel but had never seemed to find any continuity or an overriding theme. He had imagined that his war experiences would enhance the stories he wanted to tell but he soon discovered that being at witness to death and indiscriminate mass murder did not make art any easier. He came across some lines he had written in the sadness and shock of the death of Frances. Terence wondered at his inability to find enough love to keep Michelle who seemed to have everything a man could possibly want in a woman. Then he realized that from their relationship nothing creative had come out of him.

Then there was this girl fast asleep inside. She was brave with her feelings and he envied her. She had found him and was making sure she would not miss the experience. It seemed typical of her adventurous spirit that in a few days she had infused with hope a world dulled by alcohol and nihilism with care attention and love. The figures of his past danced before him; love won and love lost. Frances and Michelle were intelligent women but for some reason or another had not wanted to challenge him or at least he thought they had not. He could not realize that both of them sensed his insecurity and hoped that loving him would be enough to get him through it.

Hannah was a different creature. She was making him face his weakness not in a miserable judging way but through her joy of living, her company and a complete trust in his virtues. She dug down every day into his soul and she wouldn't let it go. She was funny too.

"You have a musical snore you know." she advised him.

"Really."

"You're a brass band."

"What instrument?" he wondered, grinning.

"Mostly the tuba but sometimes when I tire you out you become the base drum."

"How do you silence me?" Terence asked.

"I wave the baton."

"The baton?"

"The one that wore you out!"

He heard the shower going and shortly she appeared in a thin white shift. Her wet nipples showing through it bobbing up and down as she picked her way towards him in her bare feet. Terence put his papers down. When he discovered that was all she wore he put his hand between her legs where it was still wet."

"Have you eaten?" she asked, holding his hand.

"No."

"Then let's go back inside for a while and let you have your fill."

In the evening Hannah cooked the trout they had caught in the day. They preceded that feast by an innovative soup made by Terence.

"This is good," Hannah admitted, "but needs some salt and pepper. It's a good idea you have of steaming the vegetables first."

Terence was enjoying himself. "I used the water that was left for stock. I learned that in the trenches where nothing was wasted."

"It's delicious," she said, "but I'd better not eat any more bread with it. We have two fat trout each to come and those little potatoes that grow in the sandy soil. I've been peeling them for hours."

"I helped you a little."

"Terence, you're not here for domestic chores."

He was grateful that she never asked him the progress on the book. It was better when he found his own speed and enthusiasm and felt her excitement as he read something he had discovered from the past or managed new in the day or even the night. When she found him missing from the bed she came to the couch and lay before the fire he had stoked up. Hannah made coffee to keep herself awake with him. She seemed to know there was a time to be left alone and in the night he needed her physical presence. She brought her blanket out and when he ran out of words he crawled under it with her and then they lay awake with the call of the birds just before the sun came up.

In a month Terence was a different man mentally and physically and did not hide his feelings for her. Somehow Hannah had freed his emotions and the tense nervousness that alcohol had helped him with before fell away. In the meantime the Paris papers and magazines came every day and they were both fully aware of the state of the world. Gradually he learned where her thoughts on life and liberty came from. She was the antidote to all the poisons and her soft opinions gave him a chance to renew not only his life but the way he looked at the world. Now the experiences among his wartime comrades stood out to him and he spoke them out to Hannah day after day. He did not speak of death but sent for his copy of Barbusse's 'Under Fire' and read a chapter to Hannah every night. She was taken by his passion as he identified with Volpatte and the rest of the squad in the horror of the war. As time went on he rediscovered his youthful strength. They fished and walked and talked and loved each other without a heed some days for the outside world but gradually he knew he could face it again.

Hannah had finished her assignments and the novel was taking shape as were his political views sometimes from her gentle persuasion. If it's true there's a part of the brain that can be taken over by love and by another person then she owned that part. If she knew it she never took advantage but exchanged her own for it. Their feelings were mutual. As he read her articles and found them so rich in historical anecdote he wondered out loud where that lovely little head had learned to much so soon. He found that she had read most of the books in her friend's library, a considerable literature. She came down hard on the elite right wing writers who were full of vicious attacks on personalities whose policies they disagreed with. Her methods were full of logic and gentle reminders of the past history of such ideology. She was full of hope and seemed to Terence at least to have a happy knack for the right phrase to expose misplaced patriotism and the jangle of jingoism. She refused to write for either wing in politics but few could fail to realize that she was a champion of moderation. It was sometimes lonely on her island.

"I thought you had no politics!" he said.

Hannah thought for a moment. "The art is in appearing to be in the middle of hostility and yet the only one to be approached by those still making up their minds whether to live with one side or to die with the other."

"Well put." Terence said. "France is still free!"

"Yes, but for how long?"

"You see the philistines at the gates?"

Hannah became more serious. "There's a new phrase for that coined in Madrid. A fifth column! An enemy within!" Then she changed the subject. "I've read your work and there's an edge to some of it that would be useful if you put it in the right place."

"One of your magazines."

"For a start. What do you say? You are well versed now in what is happening. A few satirical pieces would not be out of place. I believe you have the gift for it."

Terence responded. "You're full of encouragement but I'm not so sure I have your courage."

She gave him another boost. "I've never been in a war! It would help if you could prevent another. It will take many honest voices."

"There's the novel." he said.

"You can do an article a month. Two thousand words. You'll feel better. You're not doing it for the money or fame. You're free so say your piece. A man of means speaking out."

In the next week Hannah went back to Paris with her articles. When she came back he could see the change in her."

"What's wrong? Are we being evicted? Is your friend coming back?"

"He's not coming back Terence."

In the next few days it was his turn to give his strength to Hannah and the depth of their love reached a new level.

"Will we have to leave here?" he asked.

"It will come up for sale. Robert has a sister. I spoke to her. She will let you have it if you want it."

He took her in his arms. "I want more than these four walls! It's the memories within them that I can't do without, can't live without the woman I found inside them."

"I'm glad you said that."

"What else could I say? You are my life and blood. The only strength in me. My veritable Venus."

Even now her humor would not go away.

"I would like to know if you will still love me if I paint my toenails red?"

Terence laughed out loud. "What is life or love without some color?"

"But red!" Hannah looked him in the eye. "Do you find it so difficult to say you love me and watch me grow fat?

"Thoroughbreds never grow fat." he assured her.

Terence changed the subject. He had decided to explains the source of the novel to Hannah.

"In my mind I saw two people standing together on a beach. He had red hair and she was a blonde. They had a little brown dog with them. They had obviously been walking for a while because they looked tired or perhaps they had argued longer than was good for them. Whatever it was it looked like the end of things between them. Later, I imagined that their relationship had begun well but over time the man had lost his way."

"You mean his mind?" Hannah wondered.

"Yes along those lines. She had suffered with him but had recently spent a month in Italy where she met another man and now wanted another life."

"What kind of people did you think they were?" Hannah asked. "I mean, what kind of lifestyle did they have?"

"They were both artists but he was famous and she was not although very good. That might have been another problem for a long time."

"And that's all you had at the beginning?"

"Yes. And now 300 pages on they are not the same people. They've changed and evolved as they went around in my head as they developed into other characters."

"But you have a novel?"

"Mostly, but they are not in it exactly the way I first saw them."

"Did they talk to each other?"

"Oh yes. When I first started the red headed man tried to evoke memories. As he looked out to sea he took her hands and spoke quietly and sadly to her and quoted a poem he knew by heart... *Flowers fade and smiles too. Out in the springing garden there was once a flowering cherry winding down on the wind my hand around your waist is what rests in my memory, or what's left of it. But flowers fade and smiles too.*' "When he was finished speaking he kissed her hands. Not like a greeting on the back but on the palms as a symbol of farewell."

"You have lots of poetry in you Terence. I hope you never kiss me that way. I'd like to stick around and see how it comes out."

"What brought you here Hannah? Into this world with me. What did you see?"

"I heard you laugh."

"You heard me laugh."

"You have an attractive laugh a substantial laugh. I heard it across a room. I had to have it."

As he sat behind her with his arms round her waist she turned her head to him.

"Can you put your hands higher up."

"Now," she said, when he did so, "you're closer to the right place."

"And where is that?" Terence asked.

"My heart."

"Have you any regular habits." she asked.

"Yes. I look at the same rose every day as long as it lasts."

"What does that accomplish?" she wondered.

"A life cycle outside my own." he replied.

"All through this novel," Terence said, "there are women of my imagination but you are not in my imagination."

Hannah put her bare legs on his lap.

"I'm real enough."

"Yes you are." Terence said, as he stroked her leg.

" is there nothing left to imagine?" Hannah asked while pulling down her short skirt.

Terence smiled. Hannah knew she had roused him; that he was full of expectation the way he replied.

"All the notes are there; limitless possibilities; and sometimes I don't know where to begin."

"You could start at middle C!" she proposed, with a slightly suggestive readjustment.

***

On one of her sorties to Paris Hannah tried to get her magazine editor to hire Terence for occasional essays.

Arthur was doubtful. "Has he published anything?"

"He's writing a novel."

"What's it about?" Arthur asked.

"I don't know the whole story." Hannah admitted.

"He writes novels!" Arthur snorted. "Who has time for novels? It's like taking Zionism to Rome the samba to Riyad the diaspora to Berlin; capitalism to Moscow socialism to New York porridge to London or forbidding the cook to lick his fingers. Well, you get my meaning. Who has time? No, our short accommodating witty and transient wordiness suits the masses who can't think for themselves. Let the intellectuals read the Prousts."

She stopped him short. "So far as I know there was only one Proust. I thought you'd be proud of Proust, at least." she managed to keep her temper.

Arthur shook his head. "I am, but I don't want to be cooped up in bed with him. Will there be sex in this novel?"

"I'll see what I can do." she attested.

"Then I'll buy it." he promised.

"You're such a hypocrite."

Arthur doodled on his pad. "Is that what they call it nowadays? I must get up to date."

Hannah teased him. "You're so successful. You must seem avant garde to your readers."

"Oh no that might mean being honest." he replied. "So that would never do! He was in the war wasn't he?"

"Yes. Wounded too."

Arthur moaned. "I hope it's not another war story. We're up to here in those. Everybody who got mud on their boots has written one or is writing one."

She sat on the desk. "Arthur, it's a love story."

He stared at the telephone as if hoping it would ring. "Funny?"

"It might be sad too." she thought.

He looked at her legs. "Have you read any of it?"

"Yes. I've read the first two chapters."

"Why not more Hannah? Couldn't you go on!"

"He crossing his t's but what I have read is wonderful."

Arthur crossed his arms over his head. "And you think he would bring himself down to be a yellow journalist?"

"He's neither yellow nor a journalist but I think he is worth a try if just for the integrity factor. He's honest."

Arthur appeared aghast. "You mean he won't lie! "

"Exactly."

He twiddled his pencil. "So if I give him an assignment I can't depend on him to represent our attested policies?"

"I don't think so but you need an independent and open mind among the caterwaulers. That would be a nice reputation to have."

He opened the window. "What about his politics."

She fluttered her lashes. "He's learning."

"And when he makes his mind up where will he come down?"

She closed the window. "He's working on it and when he's through what he does in print should be interesting."

Arthur grew more doubtful. "Flights of fancy?"

"To put it mildly." she said.

"What do you see in him Hannah. He's been well known as a rich sop."

She frowned. "He's still rich but not a drunk."

"On the wagon eh? Will you quit if I say no?"

Hannah put her feet on the ground. "Will you say no?"

"I value your opinion Hannah. We all do and we did talk this over quite seriously."

"If I didn't know you better Arthur I'd say you're on the verge of saying something. Out with it!"

He hesitated… "We agreed a five article contract."

Hannah was jubilant. "You won't regret it. Have you any ideas for him?"

"We have about ten suggestions and you can pick five."

"You know," Hannah said, "I just thought that he should pick his own stories. One a month and each a surprise."

"What about overlap?"

Hannah reassured him. "He's not likely to duplicate any of your…people."

It was his turn to frown and put the pencil down.

"You almost said hacks didn't you?"

"Some class won't hurt sales." she insisted.

He rejected that. "It never does but sometimes the little rat pickers get things done and find the hole where the smell comes from while the class acts just hold their noses."

"They've all eaten too much poison." she said.

His face was grim. "We must chase those who put it down."

She smiled in triumph. "An artist doesn't have to stoop so low."

"Why does he want to do this when he's in the middle of a novel? Is this your idea?"

"I thought you liked my ideas."

He leant toward her. "I like your legs."

She moved away. "Your taste is improving."

"It hasn't done me any good with you so far…"

She gave him advice. "A girl with better legs will come along."

Arthur was resigned to failure. "She'd better be quick while I can still afford her."

Hannah was remorseless. "Class is priceless my friend. You will discover that when you hire Terence and he delivers some."

Hannah was only one day and night away from Terence yet not able to call him she wrote him a letter…

My Dear Terence…I might as well be writing left handed so slowly is my brain working tonight. We have a honeymoon couple in the hotel. I am a little envious yet I know we love each other just as much. The older one gets the more settled the heart. Do you agree? I don't know what you are doing right now and that is a little frustrating. A woman likes to sense her love. I am sitting at my work desk supping a good brandy. This is the time when I used to smoke a cigarette to calm my nerves of the day and lessen them in the night. Now I just open my drawer and put out your photograph. If I have a secret life then I am glad it is with you. Of course we have nothing to hide but our version of ourselves and how and where the world will take and make of us. Why is that? What are we afraid of I wonder? Why is a letter so often a cry from the heart?

Chapter 20

Somewhere below the falling moon in the frost early birds were chattering in the pine trees in the park and Sofi was still full of dreams as if never ending she held on to them until as the sky lit she lost Venus and yet the bliss was still on her face and her blood flowed fast like the river that was excited to reach the shore not in the same way as before but restless for some resolution in the eddys and feeling it nearby drawing her taking her hand catching her eyes touching her cheek nudging her wild hair behind her ears and touching her lips. Temptation has many forms.

After breakfast she stood waiting for Charlotte on the winter bridge across the Seine but saw only the cherry trees of her childhood with the blossoms falling into the dark river as the wind touched them off; and in all the moments the sound of the bells. She stood just outside the full light of the sun yet not quite in the shade ; she felt the attraction of falling from a great height ; the fear from the light coming under a door while in a dark room alone ; news of an unforeseen fortune that never materialized.

Sofi stared at the water. Last night she had looked at her map to find out where it began. She knew it ended in the English Channel ; but where? Why did they call it the English Channel? Who gave it that name? Certainly not Caesar or the Conqueror. Then there was the river. She laughed to herself ; thoroughly confused. This early in the morning after a night of rain there was still the smell of cooking oil from silent kitchens and the slung beer and the gin slings from the empty bars filled the air and in fact combined with the cigarette smoke to form a signature well known to the locals. It was the time of the first light when the garlic presses were stilled and chefs dreamed of chicken breasts filled with chili peppers and livers and how the Greek would compete against the Turk and the Frenchman was so proud he never slept except on Monday to keep his advantage. From the waiters had come another awareness of politics when one of them went to deliver food parcels to the young men at the Gare de Est Austerliz as they boarded trains for Perpignan on their way to fight in the Spanish Civil War.

The enigmatic Charlus came towards her. Sofi knew she was in for a curious conversation from a man whose life was apparently built on his limitations. Many people tried to discover how he made his living; where he went each morning; none were successful. She recalled that his wife had such an innocent quality towards him that Sofi could see how she used it to inflame his lust, especially between Christmas and the feast of Epiphany considering that all three of their children had been born in late September early October.

"Where are you going?" he began, full of enthusiasm.

Sofi responded carefully."I have an appointment with a friend."

He looked her up and down."You look and sound mysterious."

"It's no mystery to me." Sofi said, wondering what was on his mind.

"Ah!" he seemed sure. "Then there might be a mystery."

Sofi didn't encourage him. "There's never any escape from it." By which she meant Charlus.

"You do look different today." he went on.

"That's because I have the weight of yesterday on me."

He agreed, which was good because then she knew he would soon run out of words. "You are correct. I too am not the same person today and will be another tomorrow."

"So there is no mystery?" Sofi ventured.

He partly agreed. "No. Unless the future stops giving us days."

"Freezes us out." you mean.

"Yes." he shook his head in mock sadness."Obituary time."

"Oh dear. " Sofi was hopeful that the conversation was concluded when she saw Charlotte approach, and Charlus did have the sense to move on.

Charlotte was in her own happy mood skipping towards Sofi the minute she saw her standing there waiting. Sofi had realized at once that although not as chic as other women in the quarter this woman had once been lovely and she still had class. They had first met her over lunch and become instant friends. Plainly dressed yet full of pride she eyed every newcomer yet said nothing or was ever inconsiderate. She was as vagrant as a cuckoo and had the knack of saying something you would remember; one of the shining morning faces; shy as a flower that hides from the rain. For the bullies of the world her look could wither an oak tree. No matter what prejudice you had she could address it, not with an argument but with a story or an example, or she might suggest a book that would better inform you. In these parts she said… "People hide what they can't eat, like hawks." She preferred the Madeleine to her local church though it was famous too and traveled there by bus. On other days she sat along the benches at the Champ de Mars and watched her favorite military Officers ride past.

As they walked along they met the public school children wearing their black aprons with fresh white collars wrapped around their necks. They wore high wooden soled boots bought second hand from the corner cobbler and made to fit either foot. Later they would create a loose clatter as they hurried home for their afternoon snack; a piece of bread and a square of chocolate.

"I love your rose painting." Charlotte said.

"I took Proust's advice." Sofi replied.

"Which was."

Sofi hesitated, like the advice. "To wait until the flower was ready to drop."

It was to be a warm day so they decided to take a bateaux mouches, a small excursion boat that boarded close to the Louvre and went out as far as St Cloud. They were seated on the hard benches but hardly noticed the discomfort. As they went down the river the terraces were empty but later would be filled with women sipping lemonade while the men drank beer. In the evening these couples might go dancing in the Luxembourg district where there were many bals musettes and they could learn to fox trot. In the evening, almost home, on the opposite side of the Seine to Notre Dame as the sun set they looked at Paris from one of her bridges.

"What is the world coming to?" Charlotte asked from whatever historical context had entered her mind.

"Yes." Sofi remarked with a grin on her face and following up with her own tangent. "That's what I heard some American tourists say yesterday when they heard that the dollar had slipped to thirty nine francs to the dollar."

Sofi thought Paris was bright then full of life and with a soft heart. Earlier, as they walked outside Le Theatre des Champs Elysee with its stark facade she stopped Charlotte and they listened to the music of the ballet. She had been there the night before and had been inspired by it. Sofi felt the book of poems in her pocket and the little art booklet full of the work of Seamus with a close up of his face on the back cover and took a deep breath that she felt all through her body. She made the mistake of moving the work of Seamus from one pocket to the other.

"Where did you buy that book?" Charlotte asked.

"Down by the shop where the Englishman buys his boots."

"He's no Englishman! Charlotte declared. "He's just pretending to be one. He's a victim of Anglomania."

"But he speaks very bad French!" Sofi insisted.

"That's because he knows no English," Charlotte reminded her, "otherwise he'd be telling us how to arrange our houses like William Morris and our minds like Ruskin."

"That seems a bit out of date even for a pseudo Englishman."

Charlotte was caught up in the moment. "Oh, I think the war made them nostalgic and he caught their religion."

Sofi wondered about that. "Nostalgia. A religion!"

"Well," Charlotte was not plussed out, "perhaps not that far but as a temporary replacement until they get over the loss."

"The loss!" Sofi laughed. "I thought they were on the winning side!"

Charlotte punctured the thought. "That idea soon wore off as they counted the dead on their monuments. Here too."

Then she wandered to the edge of the Channel and no further. "What have the English done for us?"

Sofi offered up a plea. "I read they licenced the brothels."

Charlotte was shocked. "Here?"

Sofi brought a smile to her face again. "No, in Egypt!"

"My religion is against that." Charlotte was sure.

"Well," Sofi advised her, "I suppose you haven't been reading Saint Augustine or Saint Thomas Aquinas recently because they saw it as a necessary evil. Still, I don't see any signs; no scarlet threads or lamps; no spy for Joshua; none worth a pyramid; no Solon astride the street."

Charlotte was not lost. "All you do Sofi is add to your mystery."

"The mystery stays with the beholder should they pay enough attention." Sofi said, putting her arm around Charlotte.

"You have a lot of that Sofi. You're like a bee that never stings."

Sofi was pleased. "I move more like a butterfly visiting the flowers yet making no honey."

"My dear," said Charlotte, "you're the butterfly the bee and the Queen. We'd like to subdivide you so that we could all have a patch of your pollen before you fly away."

"I had my wings clipped some time ago." Sofi assured her.

It was Charlottes turn to smile, remembering the booklet with Seamus on the back cover. "I have a feeling they're growing back again."

Once back in her own room Sofi looked at the first poem and remembered the joyous day and night that inspired it and especially the last line *'that all great love is silent'* because Karl was so happy and yet so quiet, just looking at her sometimes taking her in and she became so confident with the power of it.

Even in the short period of time she and Karl made love Sofi sometimes did what all women will do for a man which is to pretend satisfaction when in fact she doesn't need it. Such was her morning passion that those few occasions of simulation came back to her mind and curiously enough crossed it when she saw photographs of Seamus in the library. Not only did she find her sex rising but it was her first desire in almost two years.

LOVE IN AN UNEXPECTED PLACE

The next day Sofi came across a newspaper article written by Terence. The name sounded familiar but at the top of the piece they featured his photograph and so she was sure of him. She was surprised he had left the north since he seemed such a fixture there with her only confidant Michelle. She did not seek him out but central Paris is not so dense and now that she knew he was there she kept looking for him for no good reason that she could think of or rationalise in her mind. But she knew he was a kind man and had been given his own share of sadness. So it was no accident that they met as they both came out of a concert at the Madeleine.

Terence had Hannah on his arm so Sofi hesitated but he did not and spoke to her at once, though still not sure whether he had Sofi or Sara because she wore a beret that hid her red hair and he knew that Sara had darker hair. However he also knew that Sara had gone to Vienna and this was Paris after all."

"Sofi. Is that you Sofi?"

Her first instinct was to run but the lovely smile on Hannah's face stopped her flight.

"Terence! I'm so surprised to see you. I thought you would still be in the north writing."

"Sofi, this is Hannah." The women shook hands."

"I've read your poetry Sofi." Hannah said. "It is so wonderful."

"I didn't expect it to come out." Sofi said, biting her lip.

"Your signature is all over it," Terence said, "the world is looking for you. You're the missing celebrity. Come and have a drink with us. We live nearby."

Sofi hesitated, but it seemed obvious to Terence and Hannah that she not only wanted to come with them but needed to.

"Have you no need for your relatives?" Terence wondered when they had settled down in their flat the luxury of which took Sofi by surprise.

"I really only have Sara and I see her each time I look in the mirror. There is an Aunt too but she seems remote at this time of my life."

"Are you upset that Sara helped to publish your work?" Hannah asked, softly.

"I've got over worse."

Terence now anticipated her question.

"Michelle has gone back home."

Instead of finding a negative comment Sofi came from a place Terence did not expect.

"Albert will be happy about that. He has a true love for her. Perhaps she'll see it this time."

Hannah picked up Terence's copy of the poetry.

"Do you know the artist who painted your portrait?"

"No, I don't."

"He's made your face famous. The Mona Lisa of poetry."

"I hardly recognized myself. I presume he used my sister."

Terence interrupted them with the clatter of coffee cups on the occasional table. "I think he had a vision of you quite unlike your sister."

"Where is he now? Still in the north?"

"Michelle thought he went to Vienna."

A little shadow came over Sofi's face.

"With Sara?"

"Probably more without." Terence said. "Those two are no match. Michelle always said that."

"Michelle says so? I miss her." Sofi said.

Terence poured the coffee. "She would be pleased to know you are alright."

"I should have left her a note but I needed to go out of the darkness by myself I thought it would be part of the cure. It was a sudden emotional decision not to be shared."

"Has it turned out that way?" Hannah wondered, coming down beside Sofi on the couch.

Sofi found instant comfort with Hannah who was not much older. "I suspected now, know that love lost can only be replaced by love found."

Terence came down on the other side of her. "You should go to Vienna with us Sofi. I have a feeling you might find it there."

"The artist you mean?"

Neither Terence nor Hannah seemed surprised at her reaction it was so innocent.

"His name is Seamus. Yes. Look at how he painted you. It's timeless. Albert says Seamus may have fallen in love with you while he painted Sara."

Sofi was doubtful. "Sight unseen! Hard to believe."

"When love is in the air, " Hannah said, "who can see?"

Sofi thought there was some hope that... '*Of all the ends that meet nothing is quite as sweet as a vision walking by, your star not in the sky but there in the street.*'

Chapter 21

It only took Seamus two days to find Sara. He went to the music academies and in the second one he found that this was where she studied. He left a note for her to meet him at the *'Central'* coffee house.

Apart from being hardly pleased to see him she began with her normal aggressiveness.

"Why do you prefer the coffee houses to respectable restaurants?"

"There's a better class of people in them."

"Lots of ne'er do wells." she said, and not nicely.

"That's what I mean." he responded. "Antifascists."

"Jews you mean!" she retorted, looking around.

Seamus tried patience. "If you like. Take your pick."

She was in no mood for it. "My friends call them leeches."

Seamus swallowed hard. "I thought I was your friend."

"Even with you I wouldn't go near them."

He tried again. "What have you got against Jews?"

"It's a long story. You're not from here how can I explain it to you."

His temper was going. "Perhaps a fairy tale with a moral? How does your sister feel?"

She fidgeted now with her bag. "Oh she loves everybody, or did. There's no meaning to that for then nothing is special."

"I've read her poetry," Seamus said, "and it's all special to her. A rare sensibility at work holding on to life and love."

"All lost now." she declared.

"Never lost Sara, never lost."

She confronted him. "What have you learned from it?"

"You'd better hold on to love if you find it and even if you lose it. There's a place in all of us that young woman touches. Love won and love lost."

Sara looked around as if ready to run. "Even the bums in your coffee houses?"

"Especially them. They will celebrate her view when all these strutting fools around here have run out of ideas except to kill."

She protested. "My professor is not a killer. He believes in the new world coming."

"Perhaps he's just the finger on the trigger Sara. One of those who buy the bullets. Only the white gloves he wears separate him from the butchers."

"Rubbish! He's the gentlest man I ever met. You should see him with children."

"Even dogs can be good with children but get no credit for it when they bite."

She laughed at him. "You didn't come this distance to tell me that."

Now he asked what he had come for. "Still no sign of life of Sofi?"

She lowered her eyes. "Only in the painting."

"You're in there too." he said, trying to calm her.

She wouldn't have it. "I don't think so."

"Why do you say that Sara? You sat for it."

Even the sound of his voice saying her name could not divert her opinion. "Yes, but was I really there in your mind? I don't think so. I should not have done it."

"I thought we were doing it for Sofi."

"Sofi! Sofi! You're so obsessed with her."

He tried to reassure her again. "I've not met her and you're here flesh and blood. Sara you are in there. Take another look."

"Seamus I can't focus. I can't even find the notes on the piano I'm so unbalanced, so flat."

"It will pass." he tried to reassure her. "There are too many emotions going through you. Look at your face! It' so pale. Yet you came to me tanned and lovely. Something here has taken you down. Tell me what it is? It can't be just me that has disturbed your world?"

She was near tears now. "Seamus, why do you support those people?" she looked around again. "When did you ever think of social accountability? When were you ever political? No, you talk about my friends influencing me but look what your coffee house politicians demand of you that you get involved to protect them. You are like a man who has suddenly found religion and is not ready for the consequences. Is your faith blind?"

"I don't need faith. Look around you city. They helped make this place and gave it its culture."

"With other people's money." she retorted.

"We are all enjoying it, you included. Better than having it locked up in a palace where we dare not trespass."

"Seamus we can't be together, even friends."

"That's hard to understand. That our opinions should separate us so easily."

She stood up. "There was a time up there Seamus when I thought I loved you. I was wrong. I was acting as proxy for my sister. It's not just our opinions it's how I feel now, now that I'm in this city among my own people."

"Geography made such a difference?"

"I'm not usually impetuous. I left that trait to Sofi. She could go off…I never could. Then I met you and I'd never been in love before had not even considered it. As I sat for you and you spoke to me I thought it was love. I wanted it to be love. I wanted to think that it was me you would love in the end but I was wrong. I know from her poetry what loss of love is and I don't want it to happen to me. If we go on the way we are going then I don't see a life for us in it. I don't. I'm sorry it's not right. I really am. If we find Sofi…oh I'm so afraid of that too. I know deep down that it's her travail you want to put your arms around. I'm beginning to think we should not have put your painting as it stands in the book. I'd like you to go back to the genre I know, an abstraction, not the real thing. I know it's not my face that should be on there. Do something else! I'm so confused. I'm so lost! Do this for me. Help me a little if you can but don't say you love me. The stars in my eyes have fallen off. I've lost my identity. I didn't know it was so fragile."

She walked away quickly and left him stunned by her passion. He looked at the photograph he'd made of the painting. She was right. It did not in the least represent her nor did it Sofi. She wasn't the only one who had lost the way. Seamus looked around him at the busy tables. He looked down the avenue of trees and the bustling waiters from the sidewalk cafes; at the couples perambulating in the evening air escaping hot apartments. As far as he could see he now began to wonder if he had seen far enough.

One of the customers from the coffee house walked past him. Seamus paid his bill and caught up with him. Sara had gone and he did not miss her. The change brought on by Sofi had been permanent. He needed her flesh and blood and her voice and her gestures and her eyes and her hand on him. He had no idea what to do next or where to look. The man ahead of him had more purpose than he and yet he was probably only looking forward to a cup of coffee. A leopard hoping to lose its spots must first realize that they are skin deep. He had lost the chance to ask Sara if she knew where Sofi might be found if she had come to Vienna.

As he rambled around he passed the opera house and was startled to see Helen's name on the show banner. The ticket touts dressed in eighteenth century costumes and wigs were giving out programs among the other commercial offers they were paid a pittance to sell. The ballet company was in rehearsal. Seamus bought a tour ticket and came into the building. He left the tour at the earliest opportunity and was able to enter one of the upper boxes and look down on the stage. Practice was in full swing but there was no sign of the principal dancers. He made his way down to the front of the apron stage and engaged one of the musicians in conversation.

"Is madam Helen working today?"

"No. Apparently she's sick and won't come in until tomorrow."

"Is there a place I can leave her a message?"

"Do you know her?"

"I'm a personal friend but haven't seen her for a number of years."

"You're in luck then. This is her last season. She's leaving the ballet company to get married."

"Who's the lucky man?"

"He's standing over there. He's the director of this production."

Seamus took a good look at the bulky dark haired man. He stood at the edge of the stage in his shirt sleeves with a grim face on him as the tour group finally reached the heart of the theater. He beckoned to the tour guide and advised him in a loud voice not to stay too long.

"We're in the final day of rehearsal you know."

He spoke in German and as the tour group was being conducted in English all they saw was his stern face and heard his aggravated voice. Behind him a lovely young ingenue practiced and he turned to give her his attention. All this time he had not smiled but now he fawned over the girl took her hand and led her to the back of the stage. Seamus wondered what Helen had seen in that personality unless it was safety, in which case he thought she might have been mistaken.

Just as the director and the dancer were embracing Seamus noticed Marna in the shadows. At the same moment as the couple disappeared Marna looked up and met the smile of Seamus. She stood up moved to the light and looked again hardly believing it could be Seamus. Then the sight she had just witnessed on the stage and the shock of Seamus seemed to wither her face. Seamus identified with her horror. She put her hands up to her face. He thought she would fly but instead she sat back down, loyal to Helen to the last. Helen could never enter the theater and not find her waiting; the kettle on the boil and the tea pot warm on the pipes. All the flowers arranged, the cards unopened. Everything brought to hand for Helen, except love. Not for the first time Seamus felt Marna's chagrin. He thought, at least, there had not been another woman between Helen and himself. He forgot the painting. Offstage a woman was singing. In his pocket Seamus had the photograph of Sofi that Michelle had taken. He left it there, chastened by guilt and deciding not to risk even her image to leak into this partial reconstruction of a former life. There are elements in the world that spur only the evolution of each life as it is being lived and perhaps, both never end.

As he left the theater he tipped his hat to the bronze bust of Mahler. Coming out he saw a vision in a wide brimmed hat walk along under the arches of the building as if to go through the main entrance. Seamus was immediately persuaded that it was Helen and he rushed to catch up with her. As he came closer he thought he recognised the yellow dress and was certain that only she could step out that way with such grace; her jet black hair fell over her shoulders in the style he remembered. Seamus called out but she did not turn around as the doorman held the door open for her and saluted in the same motion. This man looked at Seamus as if he was an intruder and could not be admitted to the hallowed halls and barred his way.

"Is that madam…" Seamus enquired, hoping that would be the sesame.

"Not at all sir. It is the Princess Royal."

Seamus turned away slightly crestfallen and feeling foolish enough to have put himself in the hands of this arrogant man. Still, it was lucky he thought that he had not overtaken the woman. As he stood there a bevy of young women approached him all smiles yet but he hardly noticed they're attraction. The failure of fantasy sometimes blinds us to reality.

***

On the train to Vienna Sofi questioned Hannah.

"What attracted you to Terence?"

"I thought he might be a gentle soul and I needed that."

Sofi sighed like a southern belle. "A woman's dream."

Hannah was undaunted. "I suppose so but mine came true."

Sofi showed her admiration for Hannah.

"You took the risk."

Hannah responded. "I've learned to be patient with my desires and I had a feeling it might take me some time to find out. I found out in the first hour that perhaps I had made a good choice."

"Definitely your choice?" Sofi wondered.

There was just a nod of the head.

"You were willing to be fooled." Sofi said.

"Only if I wanted to be." Hannah responded with a smile. "Like every other woman. You might meet Seamus soon."

"Of course but I must prepare my heart first."

Hannah and Sofi almost the same age and from the same city yet from quite different backgrounds became fast with each other and Hannah decided from what she heard from Terence that Seamus had come to Vienna for Sofi and not for Sara.

"Do you think Sara knows that?" Hannah asked Terence.

"I suspect she does." Terence thought.

When they were together in Vienna, Hannah commented on how innocent Sofi looked, and Terence felt it could be true, yet knew another Sofi.

"Her beauty will blind him," Hannah said, "and she's come from Paris. She didn't have many clothes in her closet when I went over there with her to help her pack but she has all the usual elan. A combination of Vienna and Paris. Unbeatable!"

Terence gave Hannah some history. "Seamus was full of guilt for his past behavior when he realized or had it confirmed through Sofi's work that he had been living a very shallow life. He fell in love with her courage and she inspired him." Terence closed his book as if preparing for something else. "He's not so easy to know. He's an artist and must show his soul in paint and hide everything else."

Hannah changed the subject. "Will you finish the novel in Vienna?"

"We've never really talked about it." he responded.

"I wasn't sure you knew yourself. You can tell me now."

"I wonder how you will take it." Terence said.

Hannah placed her hand on his. "I will take it the way I took to you."

You are more of a mystery to me Hannah than any novel. What are you about?"

"A wandering woman coming home." she said.

"By request?" he wondered.

"Willingly!" she said, emphatically.

Terence took her hand. "Love is one thing being in love another. The first can be managed and the other can't. Do you feel like that?"

"Yes, I do." she said.

"Then there are two of us."

She stopped him. "And where will we go?"

"I think I'd like us to go up to the north again and live among the fishermen and see how successful the big Dane Hans will be with his restaurant down at the harbor. Just sit in there and write and watch the tourists and love you."

"I thought we might go back to our lovely place in the country." Hannah said. "With all the trouble in the world there might not be any tourists in the north."

"Not right now but you will be there." he responded.

"Would you really like that? I mean so many coming to spoil your paradise."

"My dear Hannah that's why they call it paradise. You can't spoil it."
"Sofi wants to know the title of your novel."
"Tell her I have it now."
Hannah couldn't hide her excitement. "What is it?"
"Love in an Unexpected Place."

***

Sofi had excused herself after breakfast in the pension.

"I must go to my old house. My Aunt lives there now and I expect she would be unhappy if I stayed elsewhere while in the city. And I'd like to walk through the city again. I need that atmosphere, the warmth and the wine in my soul. I want to see the horses and watch the pizza man make pasta in the shop window. The style here is different from Paris."

"In what way?" Terence wondered.

"In Paris it's chic and sometimes cruel and here it's sleek and smiling. I see lots of brown this year."

"To go with the brown shirts perhaps." Hannah said.

"I haven't seen any of the hoodlums yet." Sofi said.

"The dew is still on the ground," Hannah said, "wait until it warms up and they take off the leather jackets."

"I might not wait that long." Sofi said, quietly.

"Is the beach drawing you back?" Terence asked.

"It might be I'm too old for this."

"You're just past twenty!" Hannah said.

"I'm not a girl anymore I've crossed the line." Sofi said, a little sadness in her voice.

"Me too." Hannah said. "How about you Terence?"

"I don't remember ever being young." he replied.

Hannah picked up the pot. "Well at least the coffee is."

They all laughed together and Sofi went away for her stroll through memory lane.

"She's not in the best of moods for meeting Seamus even if we can find him." Hannah said.

"She's nervous." Terence thought.

"The way you were when you met me for the first time." she laughed as she said this.

"I was too drunk to be nervous."

"You've been sober since. Any regrets?"

He leaned over and gave her a good kiss on the lips. "Not about being sober!"

***

Somewhere below the falling moon in the frost early birds were chattering in the trees and Sofi was still full of dreams as if never ending she held on to them until as the sky lit she lost Venus and yet the bliss was still on her face and her blood flowed fast like the river that was excited to reach the shore but not in the same way as before but restless for some resolution in the eddys and feeling it nearby drawing her taking her hand catching her eyes touching her cheek nudging her wild hair behind her ears and touching her lips.

As Sofi found her way street by street through familiar landmarks and places of memory she wondered where all this was leading. She had left Paris where she was comfortable and as solitary as she wanted to come back to Vienna to perhaps meet a man she had never met and knew as little about. She was still a young woman with all her fears intact. The way he had envisaged her through the proxy of her sister intrigued her.

In a secluded courtyard she had especially sought out, Sofi sat brooding over the fact that a lemon tree that once had flourished was now fruitless. And the fair walls of the garden seemed farther apart and less friendly than before. When she'd been a girl her father had brought her here and she knew, though young, that he had a romantic attachment to this place and later he showed her a heart carved into a beech tree with his initials and one other inside it. She had been too young to wonder why they were alone but as she had come in here quite often to look at the heart and sometimes seek out her own memories she wondered who the other person had been. At this deep moment of loneliness she craved a voice from those she had loved and lost. Here, where at least one of her loved ones had been and had perhaps loved another. Today she wore a yellow dress and a small spring hat feathered across the front and one side. She wore her hair long and it shone like copper in the sun. The walls were red brick except for a frivolous row of corinthian columns on either side of the gate which had been of bronzed cast iron. They were missing.

When Sofi had looked around Paris just walking by herself, talking to herself, she felt a little like Joan of Arc there were so many conversations going on in her head at the same time. The internal cradle of all her memories and not just Paris but Vienna and the northern time with its brief joy. Much of her talk was with Karl not what they had said to each other but what she wanted so badly to say now. As time went on she realized that their short passionate time together had not touched all the places she had dreamed of since. There was still much to find and perhaps to forget and she knew it now. It was time. She had realized it and written it down earlier in the day... *If the sun picks out a cloud for you to hide behind don't turn your eyes away. Sadness never leaves the mind once you decide it should stay.* Next door she heard a young woman laugh and the sound restored some of her confidence. Regret is always a part of revelation. Whoever takes the confession should remain anonymous.

As she met her Aunt Marianne at the door the woman could not stop talking in her joy and enthusiasm.

"Where have you been? Why didn't you write to us. We thought you were dead or something terrible had happened to you. Have you seen the poetry? It's so wonderful and sad at the same time. And that painting. I could hardly recognize you but now suddenly, that you are here, I see you in it. I called Sara the very minute you said you were coming over. She is attending a political meeting and wants you to meet her there."

"Where is it?"

Her aunt fumbled among her papers. "Here's the address. It's close to the Café Central."

Sofi was in no mood to go. "I wish she had come here."

"I don't like the company she keeps." Marianne confided. "And she won't stay here. I suppose I ask her too many questions. I don't know who she is with but I have reliable knowledge that it is the new order people. Oh how I hate them. There are rumors too that Hitler is about to come into Austria. These Anchluss people want to give the country away to him and his thugs."

Sofi tried to calm her down. "It hasn't happened yet. Perhaps the government will stay firm against him."

"I thought when Sara went to find you she would come back with some change in her but now she is worse than ever. She hates the Jewish people so much. Why is that Sofi?"

"It seems the popular thing in Vienna beginning with an anti semitic

Mayor before the war and when it was lost then somebody had to take the blame. The Jews have been easy targets for Catholics and fellow travelers since the Crucifiction."

"But these people coming in are not Christians not even Catholics."

"It really doesn't matter what they call themselves. In the beginning was the word as they say, and they have been altering its meaning ever since it was printed."

As the time went on Sofi realized that the woman was well past her best in the manner of her memory and how closely she now clung to the Imperial clutter she had brought to what had been a modern house.

"I love my little vases." she crooned. "Just look at those lovely ceramic flowers."

Sofi tried to be enthusiastic but failed. "Yes, they are lovely but of course they have never existed in nature. They are not real."

Marianne felt the slap on her taste from across the room.

"That's a plum!" she countered.

"Perhaps." Sofi answered. "But not the blossom. The artist made that up."

"How do you know?" Marianne demanded.

"I had one in my garden and it doesn't look like that."

Marianne was not pleased. "You gave me an ugly vase once."

"Have you still got it?" Sofi wondered, smiling broadly so that her Aunt would know that she was just having fun with her as in the old days.

Marianne relaxed and put her china back into the case.

As she did so Sofi laughed again and hugged her as hard as she could then turned to the cabinet. "You know. I think that's an Australian plum."

"Sofi I never thought I could love anyone who made fun of my ceramics."

Sofi went into her old bedroom where she found that the shirt she had laid out seemingly a lifetime ago still sat on her dressing table alongside her Chinese rectangular plate with a red rose motif in the bottom left hand corner and her perfume and two shades of lipstick. To the left a small white candle in a shallow bowl matching the plate, never lit. All her girlhood passions and dreams came back to her as she moved to the window and looked out into the garden.

Marianne came into the room.

"I hate to disturb you but I suppose you had better go and see Sara. After all she did try her best for you."

Chapter 22

As if to have moved from a brightly lit place Sofi found the meeting rooms between a movie house and a police station. Sofi's apprehension was heightened by the sudden appearance of a little man with a face like a cat. She discovered soon enough that ironically he was guarding a cache of rats. In her vivid imagination the air was already flecked with blood and alarms of cankered hearts sounded in her head. Sofi did not trust the safety of the little bag she carried for her papers and held her poetry and the likeness of Seamus in the hidden pocket of her jacket; next to her heart to sustain her.

From the quiet efficiency of the doorkeeper who carefully checked that she was visiting Sara she came into a room where everybody except the man at the head of the table seemed to be shouting at once. Sara rose from her seat and the sisters embraced. To her horror the quiet man stood up and came towards them to shake her hand. Sara introduced Sofi to him. He kissed her sister on the lips and then went back to his seat. Sofi was at least grateful that he made no attempt to kiss her.

As they sat down the leader called for silence and went directly into a vicious monologue accompanied by the loud chimes of a clock from within an alcove. It was an omen that stayed with Sofi through the hour as the man's words promised a new beginning yet an old end; no progress;

a lineage of cowards cloaked in putrid skin. When his diatribe seemed to be over or perhaps the orator was just taking a breath or wiping the sweat from his brow; Sofi thought of her little atelier in the north. Of its lustre and the comfort of the drifting smoke from the red house. The knowledge that the gentle Terence was there if ever she needed him. Now she only had these soulless Boschian creatures. The smell of cigarettes and beer was pervasive. She looked at her sister who was apparently transfixed by the orator and the first to applaud his speech.

People were now encouraged to report the progress of the party in the country.

"Jews aren't allowed in my town anymore."

"About time too. I've just come up from the country and the signs are everywhere that we will soon be rid of them. More and more people are joining the party in the wine country."

"I'm from the west close to the fatherland and the rumors are flying that troops are on the border and ready to cross."

"What about you Sara? What have you to report?"

"I've just come back from another country where all they talk about is fish and dairy products. They have no idea of our politics and even if they did would hardly care but at least they are still homogeneous."

"It's our job to make them understand that we're trying to clean up the continent and save them trouble later. Did you take the chance to ask questions or find out our likely reception?" Sara pointed out Sofi. "I was searching for my sister. I wasn't there long enough. It's a bare existence in that country for most of them."

"So you didn't come across any Jews?"

"Not that I know of."

"Maybe not enough money to be made."

LOVE IN AN UNEXPECTED PLACE

Sofi looked around her and felt a great trepidation about where she had got herself. She had previously just been listening to students and academics but now her sister had brought her to this beer parlor where she was finding out that there were some very nasty people with the same ideas that she now knew Sara had been playing with for months. These men and women were older and from a different social class than her usual friends. Both men and women drank too much and the leader began making suggestive remarks to Sara and she soon found out that the women were supposed to sleep with the men. As she looked around her a flap of nausea went through her and she indicated to Sara that she wanted out of there.

Sara took her aside. "I can't leave. I've joined the party. It's too late Sofi they're not all like this, please stay. We are making a new world."

Another man reported on a beating.

"What do you remember about him?"

"He was humming a lieder so we questioned him."

"Which one was it?"

"I asked him that. He said Mahler and we both hit him at once."

"He stopped then?"

"We thought he would because he had lost his front teeth but he continued strumming with his fingers."

"He was brave!" Sofi could not help herself.

"No. He was just a Jew who forgave Mahler for becoming a Catholic."

***

Whatever minarets might have been reflected on the water, whatever foreign flags flew on flagpoles, whatever Canaletto forgot to paint, whatever light you see on the hill, there are no Arab dhows no Gondolas on this river. Whatever light would never flash again, whatever music floated down to the whirlpool of the world it was a place and a delight never forgotten. There's a symphony for every pleasure dome, a song for every love affair and every calamity. Whatever belonged to the north south east or west of it stopped here to be sampled and if found palatable and pleasurable was considered to have found its birthplace in this city or environs. For Seamus it came too soon after the vision of the little girl on the beach in the north watching a crowd of naked boys. Innocence had no place here and later, much later Seamus knew why and wondered: "why not?" In every dry deserted place you ever went you would remember your lover. Whatever memories you had perhaps they would lead you back here to remember every fallen star. And whatever mountains you fell asleep on to this city you might dedicate your dreams. And wherever you found the madness of love here you could also make it fly. And if you stood in the night waiting for showers perhaps you might find your lost dreams while you waited. And if the truth came upon you too late perhaps you could find another while standing there. Even at a distance her spirit will work on you although you will be lost, and renew the will you lost. From here nostalgia needs no future to give up its pleasures. And although you are young and have no thought of dying this city will be the death of your innocence, so soon. Though you are tired and living on the last of your dreams still you will wait like Tristan waited for Isolde's white sail full well knowing her presence will not calm your blood.

In Vienna the coffee houses were packed. It wasn't the hint of the sun that brought people out, there was something in the air. They all felt it and almost but not quite could touch it. No use looking at the sky for it was still blue and not a cloud. There are times when there is no explanation for what is about to happen. Take a ticket, your number will be called sometime but you must wait your turn, it's in the rules. If you want to avoid them then you must go to a lonely place where there are no rules but you must learn to survive there too, because that world doesn't wake up, it never sleeps.

Suddenly there was a small demonstration of marching people. As they passed with hoisted placards and crying socialist slogans Seamus was surprised at some of the people who passed by; neighbors and casual friends from near his apartment and the most unlikely people. He felt the older ones should be out in the sun enjoying their last years. But no, there they were, a mob.

The coffee grew cold and he couldn't think to renew it, there seemed to be more important things to worry about. He had not seen Sara again and made no progress in finding Sofi. He looked for Sara in the crowd half expecting her to be among the marchers. But were they rioters or were they expressing their opinions? He supposed the answer to that lay in the fact that the crowd passing by were not members of a faction so far as he knew, that tried to repress any other opinion they could. Still, he considered it a riot and was further alarmed when horse police rode by and there were shots soon afterwards in the distance probably at the front of the crowd as they met opposition. A few minutes later people were running in the opposite direction.

Gustav, the coffee house poet joined him.

"That didn't last long. I don't think a few policemen on horses can stop what it stands for. This plague is spreading across Europe now but the rats have sent their fleas ahead of them, and if we wait a few minutes more they are sure to follow. He picked up a newspaper. "Look at this headline! And this is not the gutter press but a paper usually perfectly respectable. You can relax Seamus I'm the one with the dangerous name. I must get out soon."

"Where will you go?" Seamus wondered.

"I have a sister in Switzerland and she will hide me away."

"I won't stay here much longer either." Seamus said.

Gustav was curious. "Where will you go?"

"Probably Paris if I can't find the person I am looking for. The French will not stand for this. They will fight it."

Gustav stood away to order. "What are you drinking?"

"I'll have a Neuman." Terence answered.

Gustav pretended shock. "With the cream on the bottom! How can you drink such a concoction?"

"It's whipped cream you know." Seamus informed him.

"There's more than the cream needs to be whipped!"

"And you." Seamus asked. "What will you have?"

"The Capuchin of course! I like some coffee with my milk."

Seamus enjoyed Gustav's company. "Didn't I see you order a Mazagran the other morning?"

"The season is over my friend. I don't need the ice cube."

Seamus kept on. "What about the rum?"

"Later, when I need some inspiration. Look out," Gustav called out."Here comes the real riot! The fascisti."

***

Within minutes of Sofi's arrival at the meeting there had been an uproar outside the building. The leader rose up and shouted… "The time is near! Let's get on with it!" Everybody in the room stood back and let him go out first into the courtyard. A large crowd had gathered all herded together by young men in various uniforms. These were all shouting the same slogans over and over. The noise was deafening and not even the leader seemed to have control of the situation. Instead, he walked to the front of the crowd with his escort of thugs and began to march towards the city centre. In the police station yard a posse of policemen stood, either undecided what to do or having decided it was too dangerous to interfere. Sara and Sofi were swept along through the streets as part of the leader's entourage. Sara held Sofi's hand and dragged her at the marching pace and all the time repeating the slogans. Completely surrounded Sofi kept looking for an opportunity to get away from the mob but Sara's grip could not be broken. At first there was no opposition to the march. Selected shops along the way were being vandalised and seemed to have been marked out beforehand. Windows were broken and glass and merchandise scattered everywhere. As they came closer to the center of the city they were faced by an opposing mob flying socialist banners and war was declared between the factions. Now Sara had lost her nerve and Sofi was able to pull her away from the leader's side only for those behind them to throw them to the ground. Both women were in light dresses and as they scratched around to get back to their feet they became sexual targets for the drunken rabble.

As the two women were swept to the street they came into the view of Seamus and Gustav. Seamus saw their peril but was too far away to recognise Sara. Nevertheless both men leapt the street barrier and ran towards the women. As the crowd closed upon them Sofi had recovered her feet and was standing protectively over the fallen Sara. It was then that Seamus saw Sofi for the first time. Her dress was torn and she was spattered with the mud and the debris of mad drunken vultures some of whom were gathered around the two beautiful women. Seamus and Gustav thrust their way into the chaos. As he got beside them Seamus recognised Sara on the ground and at the same time knew that the other was Sofi despite her tattered condition. The men pulled them from the crowd to the safety of the café tables. Seamus was struck by the courage of Sofi as she dared the brown shirts to touch her sister. Gustav cared for Sara who was in worse shape having been trampled on. At the same time Seamus lifted Sofi over the barrier and put her down on a wicker lounge chair. He took some water from the pitcher on the table and bathed her bloodied face to which she gratefully submitted as she was struck by his care and his gentleness. As the trauma subsided Seamus decided to speak through her trauma.

"Sofi. My name is Seamus Thomson." At the other end of the patio Sara heard him say it and she relapsed back into the lap of Gustav and watched as her sister who had been clasped in his arms now sat back from Seamus and regarded him. There were no words at first. Sofi just let her deeply held emotions run through her slender body and Seamus smiled as he saw the brightness in her eyes come back. From somewhere in his mother's poetry book the wind was from the south west just as Shelley had promised but it failed to blow her vision out of his sight. He took her back into his arms. Seamus knew he couldn't kiss her today yet the softness of her eyes would never go away.

"This is not the way I imagined I would meet you Sofi." It seemed quite natural to have her in his arms and she made no resistance except to bring together both sides of her torn skirt. In the distance the sound of battle came down to them. Gustav had taken Sara into the coffee shop; his heaven in peace and his haven in war.

"I never thought I would meet you this way either." Sofi said.

"I'm so pleased even in these circumstances." He parted her red hair away from the forehead and behind her ears.

"How did you know me?" she asked, still making no move to remove herself from his grasp.

Seamus reached into his pocket and took out his copy of her poetry. "I've had you here for a long time and dreamed about you even longer."

"It seems that two dreamers have met at last." she said. Then she turned and looked towards the coffee shop. "Is my sister alright?"

"She's in good hands now." Seamus said. It was then that he saw her first show of coyness.

"She might rather be with another." Sofi offered.

"Surely," Seamus said, "she couldn't cling to any of those brutes!"

Sofi was not so certain. "I think the leading man might have been her second choice." The irony was lost on Seamus.

"She has too many choices to be so limited and my friend Gustav is surely one of them." was all he could say.

"Who is Gustav?" Sofi asked.

"He's a doctor and a poet fresh out of the synagogue they are probably burning to the ground at this moment."

Sofi slipped out of his arms. "Seamus! She's an anti semite! She hates Jews!"

Seamus was calm. "I don't think that's in her mind right now. Apart from anything else he's a very handsome man and totally capable of attending to her injuries."

"We should go in there," Sofi said, "and see how she is. I think she was badly hurt. Oh, I feel so selfish."

"You were very brave protecting her. Why were you marching with them in the first place?"

"Sara invited me to meet her. I had no idea what I was getting into. This all happened within an hour. I've only been back in Vienna for one day. I came with Terence and Hannah."

"What! Terence in Vienna! What about Michelle? Who is Hannah?"

"Terence and Michelle are not together now and he has a wonderful woman, from Vienna of course. Her name is Hannah."

"Michelle is a fine person too. Where is she?"

"She went back to the north."

Seamus held her hands. "How is Terence?"

"He will never be better. His novel is about done and he has Hannah's support. What are you doing in Vienna?"

Seamus could not hide his feelings. "Looking for you of course."

Sofi sat back again and looked at him. "But you don't know me."

"Where have you been all this time?" Seamus asked her, trying to twine their fingers. "And why did you come back?"

"I've been in Paris but found no one to hold me there and when I saw your painting on the poetry I had a feeling I might find it here. All I needed was some encouragement from Terence and Hannah."

"Two dreamers." Seamus said, with great feeling.

"Yes." Sofi allowed him to hold her again. "It only takes two."

In those first moments they searched each others eyes for recognition as if they had been lovers apart for a long period of time and were curious to know if the parting had dulled their sense of each other. When he looked at Sofi he was reminded of the little girl in the blue dress and rakish hat on the northern beach and realized at once that here she was. For her part Sofi tasted again the bite from the green apple she had found and discarded on the same shore and was sure that the eternal tide of the world had washed it back up and the spirit of her youth came back into everything; mind and blood were cleansed away; all past images were cut; there was a brightness in her eyes and in his. The recognition was complete. Sofi bit her lips until the blood flowed back into them. Another woman had once told Seamus in a fit of pique that he had not had any luck with women. Now he knew that the woman in his arms was the first and the last.

Seamus was excited and couldn't hide it from Sofi.

"I never intended my painting to hang in an attic but to go out into the world and perhaps haunt you too."

"I'm glad you gave Sara the original." Sofi said

"It was never mine. The gift came from you." It was as if a pledge had taken place but of course it hadn't ; it wasn't necessary; dreams don't fall from heaven but might surely end there."

It started to drizzle and they went inside to see Sara and Gustav. There was a crowd around Sara who lay cosily covered by a blanket on a couch dwarfed under a huge mirror.

"She's fine." Gustav assured them. "She just needs to rest now. I'll look after her." Sofi looked at him with such tenderness that he almost kissed her brow. "*I'll look after her.*" the words had a soft human sound and she forgot the hounds outside and turned to Seamus again.

"What will we do now Seamus?"

"Let's go and see Terence and…Hannah. After that I would like to get out of Vienna. I am sure bad things are about to happen here and I don't want to be part of them."

"Where will you want to go?"

Seamus was full of certainty now. "I'll go back to the beach if you will come with me."

Sofi was also sure. "I can't think of a better place."

"Perhaps we will both have better luck this time." As the color came back into her face she smiled at him but Seamus knew that it was not to deceive.

As they passed the Opera house and made towards the pension they had to shelter from a sudden rain shower in its portals. Sofi recognized the bridge between the Scherzo of Das Lied von der Erde to the final movement…The Farewell. Sofi realized that now it represented not just a premonition of personal death but the funereal death of a culture. From tender cycles to terrifying they held on to each other as the oboe and then the horns led to poignant violins and then gave way to

sighs as if from a Beethoven Sonata…'Lebenwohl' farewell. Then pointing towards a climax of disturbance of sadness and regret. When the music turned to tenderness Sofi pulled Seamus away into the darkness unable to bear the sadness well knowing that in its last few minutes she could never bear it.

Chapter 23

As Terence sat in the hotel room editing his manuscript Seamus called up from reception asking to join him.

"You're late on the road." Terence said

"I've been packing a bag." Seamus told him.

"So you're going now?"

"Not much else can be done here right now. It's too far gone," Seamus said, "and I found what I came for."

Terence asked a rhetorical question. "Where will you go?"

"I'm going north to look after Sofi and hopefully have a life with her. She's at the little cabin by this time. Will you stay in Vienna for much longer?"

"Just so long as Hannah wants me here. I thought at first to go north but our plan now is to go either to Paris or to our place in the country as soon as she has finished her work with the children.

"You're not a political man Terence."

"No, not political." he agreed.

"How is the novel going?" Seamus wondered.

Terence shuffled his papers. "This is the last page."

"Sofi will be pleased for you."

"I'd like you to take this copy up. It's something I'd like to share. The last pages are missing in the copies I gave to her before she left" Terence produced a large envelope. "I won't seal this Seamus so that you can share it with Sofi."

"Where is Hannah?" Seamus asked.

"I think she's arranging a way out of the country for those most in danger especially the Jewish children. There's a group of them getting out to England. That's the only country that will take them."

Seamus scowled. "The whole of Europe is in thrall to the fascists."

"It's usually the weak who suffer," Terence said, "but against these people it's the weak looking for scapegoats. Their ignorance not helped by their inborn prejudices. Go to Sofi Seamus and perhaps we will see you soon enough. By the way what happened to Sara?"

"It seems she is quite disillusioned with the fascists and has gone to Switzerland with my poetical friend Gustav."

Terence was astonished. "The Jewish poet Gustav?"

"The same."

"There is still some hope."

***

Terence looked down on a city that was hardly awake on an early midsummer morning and floated like a zephyr. He was hoping the last month had been a mirage, and remembered a few lines… *What if there should be no love. Nobody to love. One with a kind heart and a gentle hand.'* In his mind he knew that the city the country the continent was as beyond hope as Lot's wife who looked back despite all the warnings. No matter his somber sense of the proposed new world of the master race he knew that somewhere down among the chaos Hannah was busily raising all the free flags in the world as high as she dared. As he had walked early through the city there was a brief shower and to shelter from it he stood inside the arch of a church entrance. It hadn't rained for two weeks and Terence enjoyed watching the few people he met fiddling with their umbrellas. He preferred the rain when he saw the Juden sign on the church notice board; though he had seen it scrawled all over the shop windows on streets throughout the city. He thought then of the last time he had seen his Jewish friend Ivan, *'The Terrible'* his comrades in arms had nicknamed him, crushed flat against the framing of the fire trench by a shell blast. When they pulled him away his face was black with Verdun mud but his toothy smile was still in place; his death mask. He doubted that the thugs who daubed the whitewash stars on shop windows would die with a smile on their faces. Such grace was not likely for them. He tried to clean off the Juden sign with his handkerchief but it proved, like an omen, to be permanent. *'What if there should be no love, nobody to love?'* As he stood in the vestibule of the church he thought Sofi's poem appropriate...*'even if it's the only faith you have, then believe...there will always be someone to love.'*

Up here in the mildness the birds still sang ; and in the rain his nerves grew calmer. Sometimes a smile escaped as he felt he had lost some pain and harbored hope of happiness with Hannah. Otherwise he felt like the stuttering springs of almost nothings ; broken into a thousand dreams and scattered across the sky. As he sat there above the city he felt like Tristan waiting for Isolde's lonely sail white across the horizon. Last night as Hannah slept Terence worked on the final chapter of his novel and now as the sun wore down the clouds he looked at the last page in the bitter light and wondered how relevant it would be.

***

Sometimes a memory wears off the years. Sofi had not reached the time of apprehension which she suspected could come as she traced her third journey north. Leaving the train Sofi had expected to go anonymously to the red house. Coming around the front of the station she looked for the taxi that normally sat outside in the forecourt. Everything was quiet and empty. Usually there was only one taxi so somebody had beaten her to it. Sofi decided to walk all the way. The case was not that full. Walking past the old red bricked water tower and across the cobbles to pay her respects at the lost fisherman's monument she was surprised to be hailed from across the street by Erik who was probably on his way home his postbag still slung over his shoulder.

"Sofi!" he called.

"Why, it's you Erik. Any letters for me." she quipped.

He came across to her and she saw that he had aged a little.

"Everything is at the bookstore waiting for our poet our lovely poet to return. Oh I can't believe my eyes. Is it really you?"

Before she could reply another greeting came from a fresh faced man as always smartly dressed in a starched blue shirt that sported a bar of authority on the shoulder. This was Simon the parking policeman who was needed when the tourist season was in full swing.

"Oh dear Sofi." he cooed, softly like a dove.

"I've no car today." she joked.

"You can park in the middle of the street if you like."

Erik supported the case and Simon knew that he was taking charge of her. He took the hint, saluted and walked away straight backed mumbling happily to himself.

"Where are you headed my pretty lady?" Erik asked.

"To the red house. I've a feeling Albert and Michelle are waiting there for me. It took me longer to get here than I anticipated. It's been so long Erik. I never did expect to be recognised."

"My dear there isn't a man woman or child of your time who will ever forget the most graceful woman they have ever seen." When he saw that he had disconcerted her a little he changed the subject. "Do Albert and Michelle know you are coming?"

"There's a letter in the mail. I thought to have a day or two to myself but I doubt that now."

"Ah, well. I'll just get you down there, keep the silence and look for Simon if it's not too late." Then Erik couldn't help himself. "Will you be staying by yourself as usual?"

Sofi smiled at him. "If my luck doesn't run out I may have company this time."

He towered over her protectively. "Second time lucky?"

"Yes." Sofi knew he was bursting to know more but she decided to keep his wife in suspense."

They had to pass the cabin on the way down to the red house and before she could ask Erik advised her.

"It's empty now my dear and has been since the artist left. I know Albert and Michelle mean to keep it up. They never rent it out now. Look at the garden! It's just as you left it."

She was full of pleasure. "The cherries are taller."

"You may be back from Paris but they will never be cut."

"I don't need a museum Erik." she reminded him.

"My dear this is our cabin in the sky!"

The reply brought a tear to her eye and now Sofi's thoughts flew past from month to month before she turned away and up the path to the top of the dune where she knew she would have a full view of the house. But all the past images of it were surpassed as the noon midsummer light lit up the red ochre. As they advanced along the beach towards it two figures emerged.

Erik said. "I suppose your secret is out. That's Albert and Michelle on the patio they have one too, a secret. Why don't you take the bag the rest of the way. They haven't seen you for a while."

Sofi was so touched by his delicacy that she kissed his cheek and squeezed his free hand. He took off his post office hat and saluted her.

Albert came towards Sofi while Michelle stayed on the patio probably not trusting her emotions.

"Albert! How did you know I was coming?"

"The post came early. Erik is very diligent. How are you?"

"I am as well as the first day I was ever here. It seems so very long ago now."

"I don't see any grey hairs among the amber."

"Not for want of trying." she replied.

He took her case. "Look at Michelle she is a nervous wreck."

Michelle stood on the patio barefooted.

"It's too hot to walk on the sand." she said as they embraced, "and we weren't sure if you would come today. Let me look at you. You are not dressed for the beach Sofi."

"I have come a long way but I will change and relax now."

"Your sadness has lifted." Michelle enthused.

"Yes. It shouldn't last forever."

"Terence gave you the house. He sent me a note."

"My goodness. He has been very kind to me since the first hour I met him in your garden."

"Will you stay this time?" Albert asked.

She looked out at the sea. "I can't imagine any other place I could be."

"And Seamus will he come back too?"

"He's involved right now with the chaos overtaking Vienna, but hopefully he will get out of it alive."

"And Terence and Hannah."

"They are bound up too but I don't see any success for their side of politics. Things have gone too far."

"Has he finished his novel?"

"Nearly. I have the first draft here with me all except the last chapter. He's still working on that."

"Have you read it?" Michelle asked.

"No, not yet. I wanted to do that here in this house on this shore. He was thoughtful enough to give me two copies. Not a very subtle hint that he wants you to read it too."

Albert came back out of the house.

"Are you hungry Sofi?"

"Actually, I'm starving."

"Then let's go to the hotel where Susannah and her husband are waiting for us."

"She got married!"

"She got married," Michelle said, "and lived happily ever after and we are planning to do the same."

Sofi smiled at them as they stood holding hands.

"I only wish the Lady Anne could have seen the two of you so happy together. She loved both of you so much."

"You came in good time Sofi for the midsummer festival on the beach tomorrow night."

"Sofi," Albert asked. "Why did you leave here in the first place? Michelle says you were doing so well."

"I may have given that appearance because I really did want to be left alone at first, especially when everything seemed so quiet. Then I found the wilderness was full of screams in the night and I was filled with fear and fright. I discovered soon enough that though I wanted to be alone I didn't like being lonely. The blush of spring was soon over and I had reached the end of November's dreams."

Albert continued. "Did you think dreaming of past pleasure and love would bring you out of the sadness?"

"You know Albert sadness is not a straight line nor is it a circle that starts and ends fused together. There's a piece of energy missing. The sun is due but it doesn't come up quickly enough or if it does sometimes you don't notice it and suddenly you're looking at what the horizon does to it. You know it's there but you don't recognise it. It's like seeing two rainbows. Which is the lucky one?"

"I wish I had your gift for words Sofi." Albert enthused.

"You have enough gifts to be going on with Albert don't overcrowd your brain. Michelle would like to be the only one in there." Sofi looked to the sky. "I often wonder what birds of different species think of each other when they pass by on their journeys. Especially crows and gulls. They seem to travel a lot in the morning and in the evening. They look small to us but we are just midgets to them."

Michelle was touched. "Do you believe in God Sofi?"

"I think it's helpful to some people and harmful to others. As for myself the jury is still out and I don't have the verdict. Whoever or whatever put the world together is still trying to fix it."

LOVE IN AN UNEXPECTED PLACE

Sofi went inside to change and left Albert and Michelle to talk to embrace each other.

"I think I'll wait with you Albert." Michelle said. "Wherever you are going that's where I want to go. I'll watch the lilies ripple and sniff the flowers in your walled garden and I won't worry where we've left our clothes if we can't touch the bottom of the river or if we swallow some of the water. I would rather remember when my excitement over you flushed the coolness from your cheeks ; closed your eyes, and opened your lips."

"My dear Michelle. I've been tired for a long time, living on the last of my dreams boasting to myself of faithfulness when there was no temptation. So come fast and love me. Stem the traces of my tide on this summer flood."

***

As the midsummer fire burned away and the small boats were forced further off shore Sofi stood on a rustic fence and held on to Albert's shoulder while trying to take photographs of the scene.

"Are you alright up there?" Albert asked.

"The fire won't last much longer." Michelle said.

The crowd had begun to sing traditional songs but the only song in Sofi's head was one she had written for Seamus in a wine cellar in Vienna…

Come back and love me.
Don't stay away.

Or all my world will fall apart
and all I've known will die.

Come back and love me.
Don't stay away.

How can I think of living life
alone, and then without you.

Come back and love me.
Don't stay away.

Or all the love that's in my heart
will bid the world goodbye.

Come back and love me.
Don't stay away.

There was a sudden flare up as they piled more dry wood on the blaze and Sofi stepped down as the sparks began to rise and then fall among them. At this time she felt as though she was being manipulated by Michelle to a point across the indicator that showed the face of the west all the way to the grey lighthouse. The tip of the red house was just visible and the cabin huddled in the second row of the dunes.

"There's more than one fire on the beach." Michelle said to Sofi, who wondered what she meant and then she saw the smoke coming from the cabin's chimney. She turned to Michelle and Albert who could see at once the emotions charge up into her eyes though she did not speak but stood stiffly, not able to move or take her eyes away from the west. Michelle moved closer and clasped her waist.

"I think you could go down there now."

Sofi came down to the cabin. She knew Seamus waited for her. When she came into the garden they embraced and she whispered three lines of poetry into his ear. *"Shutter up the sun; close my eyes; let me dream."* He led her to the garden seat, handed her the envelope with the last pages of the novel and they read it together just as Terence had intended.

***

'As they sat together they admired the flowers.
Clara began the conversation.
"I wish I had spent more time learning the latin names of flowers."
"That's a full time job you know," Charles said, "but I prefer recognizing birds."
Clara sighed and wiped the mud from her shoes.
"There's so much in the world."
"Yes, I know," Charles agreed, "but it's easier when there are two who want to learn together."
"I'm glad you said that," Clara said, "because I was thinking the same thing."
"I suppose it's another way of saying I love you."
She teased him. "That you prefer birds?"
Charles chuckled. "No, just beginning to feel one of the many ways to show it."
"I'm glad you know there is more than one way."
He poked at a dead rose. "I didn't know that before I loved you. How has that affected you?"
She leaned forward from the waist turned her head and looked at him, searching

for the deepest smile she could find.

"I expect it will take a lifetime to find out myself. Because I think that a slow leakage of love will be worthwhile for both of us."

He took the hand she stretched out to him.

"You know so much. I suppose only a woman knows so much."

Clara smiled with pleasure. "A garden teaches patience, and that it takes time to get flowers every year from the same plant."

"I can see we might have lots of time for latin."

"It has its conjugations too." she said.

"What kind of man were you dreaming of spending your life with?"

She had a firm answer. "A troubador!"

"I always thought you had that fine aristocratic look about you. Languid."

"Like Languedoc?" she asked.

He drew in a breath. "And lavender."

"Looking for a peacock my shuttle came over the net and landed in your court."

He laughed. "Birds of a feather."

It was a delicate moment as they sat in the ruined garden where the walls were breached and all the glass broken. At the far end the surviving part of an apple tree bereft of fruit leaned over, almost uprooted. They stood up and walked slowly hand in hand towards it. When they reached it she held it straight while he shunted soil on the exposed roots and tamped them down until it could support itself. In its new shadow they embraced. The hirundo rustica swallows chased the mayflies and the malus domestica apple blossoms might now bear fruit. They had found...' Love in an Unexpected Place.'